genres, she found her love of romance established when she stumbled across her first Mills & Boon book at the age of twelve. She's been reading them—and writing them—ever since. Michelle lives in Northamptonshire, England, with her husband and two young Smarties.

USA TODAY bestselling author **Natalie Anderson** writes emotional contemporary romance full of sparkling banter, sizzling heat and uplifting endings—perfect for readers who love to escape with empowered heroines and arrogant alphas who are too sexy for their own good. When not writing you'll find her wrangling her four children, three cats, two goldish and one dog…and snuggled in a heap on the sofa with her husband at the end of the day. Follow her at natalie-anderson.com.

HER SICILIAN BABY REVELATION

MICHELLE SMART

THE GREEK'S ONE-NIGHT HEIR

NATALIE ANDERSON

MILLS & BOON

First Published in Great Britain 2020
by Mills & Boon, an imprint of HarperCollins*Publishers*
1 London Bridge Street, London, SE1 9GF

Her Sicilian Baby Revelation © 2020 by Michelle Smart

The Greek's One-Night Heir © 2020 by Natalie Anderson

ISBN: 978-0-263-27803-3

Printed and bound in Spain
by CPI, Barcelona

HER SICILIAN
BABY REVELATION

MICHELLE SMART

This book is dedicated to my munchkin, Zak xxx

PROLOGUE

Orla O'Reilly blew her nose and swallowed back a breath, trying her hardest to stop fresh tears falling down her sodden cheeks. She didn't want people to see her like this.

She'd flown to Sicily ten days ago on a mission to meet the man her mother had always unkindly referred to as 'Orla's sperm donor'. Only now did she understand her mother had actually been diplomatic.

Her father, who'd returned from his travels that morning, had refused to see her. He had no curiosity about his twenty-three-year-old daughter. No curiosity at all.

She hadn't expected a grand reunion or anything but his outright rejection…

It hurt. Really, really hurt. Now all she wanted was Tonino's strong arms holding her tightly and his breath whispering into her hair that everything would be okay.

At least something good had come from her time in Sicily. She'd met the man of her dreams.

Ten days ago she'd taken one look at her room in the budget hotel she'd checked into and gone back to the reception. Orla was not one for complaining but the state of it would have driven a saint to boiling point. The bed sheets were stained and crumpled, the carpet sticky under her feet and the bathroom…well, the less said about that, the better.

She'd stood at that reception desk for exactly six minutes before a tall, imposing figure had appeared from a door marked *Privato* and Orla had found herself face-to-face with the sexiest man she'd ever set eyes on.

Until that first sight of Tonino, she'd never understood what it meant to meet someone and feel as if you'd been struck by lightning.

When she'd returned to the hotel much later that day, her first attempt to meet her father scuppered due to him being abroad, she'd found her room hadn't just been cleaned but sanitised. New furniture and furnishings had been installed, including a brand-new carpet. Her melancholy mood had lifted when the gorgeous hotel manager had knocked on the door and asked if she would like to meet for coffee in the morning.

What had followed had been the most wonderful week and a half of her life, right until two hours ago when she'd returned to her father's home for her second attempt. All those glorious hours with Tonino had infused her with a sense of optimism. She had become certain that her first meeting with her father would be the stuff of Hollywood; all tight embraces and schmaltzy words.

It had taken her father exactly eight minutes to break her heart, the length of time his housekeeper had made Orla wait alone on the doorstep before she'd returned with the 'regretful' news that he didn't want to meet her.

She must try not to think about her father. Keep her focus on Tonino.

That was what she needed to keep the tears at bay. To think of the man who'd brought her to life and stolen her heart.

She wished she'd told him about her father. She wished she'd had the courage to be upfront about her real reason for being in Sicily but it was such a shameful thing to admit, that she was the secret love child of one of Sicily's most notorious playboys; a child created through infidelity.

All her life she'd shied away from meaningful friendships and relationships. The only people she'd ever trusted were her sister, Aislin, and her grandparents. Her grandparents had both since died so that left Aislin.

And then she'd met Tonino.

She was ready to tell him now. He would understand. He would comfort her. He would be the rock she'd always dreamed of having but had never believed could exist.

Tonino had left her in bed that morning with a lingering kiss. He'd stroked her cheek and promised that that night they would talk. The expression in his eyes and the tone of his voice had told her this would be of a serious nature. As hard as she tried to temper the wild emotions raging through her veins, not even her father's rejection could completely stamp them out. A future was dangling before her. For the first time in her life, Orla felt that her future could mean more than a career. It could involve…love…

The taxi driver pulled up outside her hotel behind a sparkling stretch limousine that stuck out like a sore thumb in this run-down area. Orla wearily slipped out, intent only on getting to her room and soaking in the bath while she waited for Tonino to return from his business trip in Tuscany. This was the first time they'd been apart for more than a few hours. How lucky was she to have found the man of her dreams just as he was due to take his annual leave, giving them all that time together!

'Permesso.'

A ravishing stick-thin blonde with eyes like a cat's blocked Orla's path to the hotel's elevator.

Orla held her hands up and tried to move around her, but the woman mimicked her moves, blocking her efforts.

'Can I help you?' The richness of the woman's clothes and the expert precision of her hair and make-up made Orla think she must be the possessor of the limousine.

The woman raised an immaculately plucked eyebrow. 'English?'

'Irish.'

'You give me two minutes.'

'Err…' Annoyed, Orla was about to push her way around the woman when the four fatal words were uttered.

'Is about Tonino Valente.'

Prickles raced up Orla's spine. Her abdomen clenched. 'What about him?'

The woman raised her left hand and pointed at her wedding finger. A huge diamond ring lay snugly on it. 'I am Sophia. Tonino's fiancée.'

Twenty minutes later and the two women were in Orla's hotel room. Sophia perched delicately on the small armchair while Orla sat on the floor feeling as if she'd been punched by a heavyweight with lead in his gloves. Spread on the carpet around her were photographs of Tonino and Sophia. Many photos. There were also press clippings and glossy magazines. Orla didn't understand Sicilian but some of the words in the article needed no translation. Tonino and Sophia's engagement party two months ago had been deemed newsworthy.

'I sorry to tell you this,' Sophia said in a tone that suggested she was loving every minute of it. 'Tonino has made fool of you. He has lied to you. You are fun to him. *Sì?*'

'I've been a bit of fun?' Orla whispered. 'Is that what you're saying?'

'*Sì.* That why I here. I warn you. Tonino loves me. We are to marry.'

Orla was unaware that tears were leaking down her face, and too numb to care that there was a warning in the Sicilian woman's tone as well as in her actual words.

This must be what he'd wanted to talk to her about that night.

Fool that she was, she'd believed he wanted to discuss a future for them.

Her hand shook as she picked up the glossy magazine containing a twenty-page spread of their engagement party.

How could an ordinary hotel manager attract such a wealthy, high-maintenance woman like this? And why would an ordinary hotel manager be the recipient of the kind of press attention usually reserved for the rich and famous?

Fearing she could be sick, she groped for her phone and keyed Tonino Valente's name into the search engine.

Ten minutes later she was still reading and searching but it was as if someone had taken possession of her body and was reading the damning evidence for her.

She felt light-headed. Boneless.

Tonino had lied about more than his marital status.

He wasn't the manager of the hotel as he'd led her to believe. He was the owner. This hotel was just a small cog in a vast empire.

Tonino Valente was the sole owner of Valente Holdings, a chain of mostly hugely expensive hotels across Europe that catered for the filthy rich. Tonino, who was also an enthusiastic investor in start-up businesses, was filthy rich in his own right.

The man she'd opened her heart for, who she'd dared believe she could have a future with, was a cheat and a liar. The worst kind of liar. A rich, powerful liar. His grandfather was one of Sicily's top judges. His mother was one of Sicily's leading criminal lawyers. His father was a leading Sicilian politician.

Her Internet search revealed that the immaculately beautiful woman in the obscenely expensive outfit sitting on Orla's hotel-room armchair was Sophia Messina. The Messinas were a Sicilian family as wealthy and powerful as the Valentes.

'I'm sorry,' she whispered, meeting Sophia's cold, unflinching eyes. 'I knew nothing about you.'

'Now you know…you go?' It was framed as a question, but the underlying threat hung between them.

Orla didn't need the threat.

'Yes.' Breathing heavily to quell the rising nausea, she stumbled over to the wardrobe. 'Yes. I go.'

CHAPTER ONE

Four years later

'WILL YOU KEEP still a minute?' Orla rebuked with a shake of her head. How was she supposed to fasten her sister's wedding dress if she didn't stop jigging on the spot?

'I'm *trying*,' Aislin protested.

'Try harder. These clasps are fiddly. Breathe in.'

Aislin gave a theatrical intake of breath.

Using all her limited strength, Orla hooked the second tiny clasp. Excellent. Only another fifteen of the blasted things to go. 'Are you sure you don't want to wear a bra?'

'It's a strapless dress.'

'Then wear a strapless bra. What will you do if the dress falls down and your boobs start wobbling for all of Sicily's high society to admire?' If there was one thing Orla was envious of, it was her sister's magnificent bosom. Orla barely had a handful to waste.

'It's a bespoke dress. It's not going to fall down.'

She hooked the third clasp. 'I don't get why you won't let the designer hoist you into it.'

'She's around if we need her.'

'But she's used to doing this. Her fingers work. My fingers are *useless*.' Fourth hook clasped, Orla blew out a puff of air from the exertion.

'Untwist your knickers and chill. Anyone would think you were the one getting married.'

'Aren't you the slightest bit nervous?'

'Nope.' Through the reflection of the full-length mirror, Orla saw the beaming smile spread over her sister's face. And well she should smile. Not only was Aislin marrying the love of her life, but she'd discovered a month ago that she was pregnant.

That the man Orla's sister was marrying happened to be Orla's half-brother—Orla and Aislin had different fathers—was, to her mind, only further cause for celebration.

She just wished they were marrying in Ireland, not here in Sicily. She was certain the deterioration in her coordination was down to the knots of dread in her stomach. Or were they knots of excitement?

All she knew for certain was that the beats of her heart had steadily increased in tempo and density in the weeks leading up to the wedding and now that she was finally in Sicily, there was an anticipation…or dread…that something was going to happen.

It was close to four years since Orla had been in Sicily on her futile mission to meet her father. A serious car accident six months after her return to Ireland had left her with major memory problems. Time had healed most of the holes in her memory but the period from Sicily to the accident itself remained stubbornly locked away.

She knew her wish to meet her father had gone unfulfilled only because Aislin had told her so and because every time Orla thought of Salvatore Moncada she wanted to cry. She'd shed a bucket of tears when she'd learned he'd died a year ago but even during that mammoth crying session was the feeling that she was crying for more than the father she'd never met.

She comforted herself that she'd gained a brother, Salvatore's son, Dante. He was technically a half-brother, as

Aislin was technically her half-sister, but Orla had never been able to see it like that. You didn't love someone in halves. You either loved them or you didn't. Aislin was only three years younger than her so she had no memories of life without her. Aislin was her sister and they would fight to the death to protect each other.

Dante, who Aislin had found for Orla and fallen in love with for herself, had only been in their lives for four months but it felt as if he'd been a part of it for ever.

Aislin's phone buzzed. 'Can you get that?'

'Okay, but don't move. If the clasps pop open I'm not redoing them.' She still had a dozen of the ruddy things left to hook together.

She strode to the suite's dressing table, grabbed the phone, handed it to Aislin and then got back to work on the dress.

'It's a message from our dear mother.' Aislin spoke in an unnaturally high voice.

A shiver ran up Orla's spine and her fingers fumbled on the delicate clasp she'd only just gripped hold of. 'What does she want?'

'To wish me luck.'

She snorted. 'How big of her.'

'Now, now, don't be like that. You know it isn't easy to jump on a plane to be there for your youngest daughter's wedding.'

'True. It's not as if her daughter's fiancé is a billionaire who'd offered to pay for a private jet to fly her over or anything.'

'And it's not as if she hasn't seen her daughters in, what? Seven years?'

'Or never met her only grandchild.' Finn, Orla's precious three-year-old son, her miracle of life, currently napping in one of the suite's bedrooms under the watchful gaze of a nurse, had never set eyes on his grandmother.

She met Aislin's stare through the reflection of the mirror and they burst into peals of laughter.

The sisters had long ago learned that the best way to keep the anger and pain of their mother's actions at bay was to laugh and treat it all as one big joke. If they didn't laugh there was a good chance they would never stop crying.

'I suppose you should be grateful she remembered,' Orla pointed out dryly.

'I'm brimming with gratitude.'

She sniggered before confiding, 'I'm dreading meeting Dante's mother.' Orla's conception had been the catalyst for Dante's parents' divorce twenty-seven years ago.

'Don't be. I told you, she has no animosity towards you.'

'But she sounds terrifying.'

'She's hilarious. When Dante told her she was going to be a grandmother the first thing she said was that she didn't want to be known as Nonna.'

'What will she be called?' Another two clasps were hooked in quick succession.

Aislin cackled wickedly. 'Nonna!'

'Is she here yet?' 'Here' being the magnificent luxury hotel nestled on a cliff overlooking the Tyrrhenian Sea that Dante had hired the entirety of for the weekend.

'She's going straight to the cathedral with Giuseppe.' Giuseppe was Dante's latest stepfather, Immacolata's sixth husband. 'Now stop whittling.'

Before Orla could make a cutting retort, there was a knock on the door. A moment later a member of the hotel's staff walked into the suite carrying a huge bouquet of flowers in a vase.

'Compliments of the owner,' he said in careful English.

'How lovely.' Aislin clapped her hands in delight. 'Please, put them on the windowsill and, please, thank Mr Valente for me.'

Valente?

For no reason she could imagine, the hairs on the nape of Orla's neck lifted and her gaze flew to the door that concealed her napping child.

When they were alone again, Aislin met Orla's eyes again in the reflection of the mirror. 'Have you met the owner of the hotel yet?'

Now the hairs on her arms lifted too.

'Should I have?' she asked nonchalantly, even as she ground her bare feet into the soft, thick carpet and ice raced up her spine.

Orla had arrived the day before but Finn had been exhausted from the journey, so they'd dined in the suite together rather than join the other early arrivals for the evening meal. By the time Aislin had joined them, both she and Finn had been fast asleep. Her sister had crawled into the bed with her, just as she'd done throughout their childhood. It had been a bittersweet moment for Orla, waking to find her sister asleep beside her. Her baby sister would never share her bed again.

Aislin shrugged but there was a shrewdness in the reflecting stare that sent the ice already in Orla's spine spreading through her limbs. 'Tonino's one of Dante's ushers—they're old friends. Their fathers were friends too.'

Orla's fingers tightened reflexively. Her chest tightened. The room began to swim around her...

'Ouch!'

Aislin's squeal pulled her sharply back into focus and Orla suddenly became aware that her nails were digging into her sister's back. She whipped her hand away...and pulled the clasp she'd had hold of away with it.

Tonino Valente stood by the huge entrance doors and waited for the last guests to file into the baroque cathedral.

The groom, Dante, was at the altar mopping his brow with a handkerchief.

He could laugh to see his old friend acting like this, but propriety forced him to bite his cheeks and smother it.

Who would have thought Dante Moncada, the biggest player of them all, would be standing at the altar sweating with nerves as he awaited his bride? Out of their gang, which decades before had ridden round Palermo on scooters desperately trying to look cool and impress the girls, Dante had always been the one who'd vowed never to settle down. Tonino had been the only one to assume he would one day marry and yet here he was, the last bachelor of their gang left on the shelf.

He'd almost married once. He'd even gone as far as to book this same cathedral before fate had stepped in in the form of an Irish temptress and turned his life inside out with one locking of eyes.

Strangely, Dante was himself marrying an Irishwoman. Tonino had only met her the once, fleetingly, a stunning redhead who had transformed his old friend into a smitten lovesick fool.

What was it with Irishwomen, he ruminated, that they could turn a Sicilian man's head so completely?

His own Irishwoman… Well, that had been an extremely short romance. But intense. Incredibly intense. And then she'd left without saying goodbye. Not a word. Just packed her bags and left. When he'd called, he'd found himself unable to get through—she'd blocked his number.

Her cruelty in the manner she'd ended things had been breathtaking.

He could hardly believe that four years on he still thought about her.

A commotion outside the entrance had him striding outside to help a young couple struggling to manoeuvre a wheelchair-cum-pushchair that had a small child in it up the cathedral steps.

'You're with the bride?' he asked in Sicilian then repeated in English once they were inside and out of the late-afternoon heat. The ushers had all been warned the bride's nephew had mobility issues. A special place at the front of the cathedral had been set aside for him so he could have an unrestricted view of the ceremony. An usher would be required to wait with the child until the bridal party arrived and his mother, the chief bridesmaid, could take over. Tonino guessed the job had become his.

'We are,' the young woman confirmed proudly, her Irish accent strong. 'I'm Aislin's cousin Carmel, and this is my husband Danny. This young man here is Finn.'

'He's Aislin's nephew?' he clarified, just in case there was another wheelchair-bound small boy coming.

'Yes. Aislin and the others left the hotel right behind us so will be here any minute.'

Figuring he should introduce himself so as not to scare the child, he got down on his haunches and looked at him.

Dressed in a miniature suit that matched the groom's, the boy couldn't be much older than a toddler. He had a shock of thick black hair and equally dark eyes...

There was something about his eyes that made the words Tonino was about to say stick in his throat.

After a drawn-out beat, he conjured a smile. 'Hello, Finn. I'm Tonino. I'm going to take you to the front of the cathedral to wait for your mummy.'

He was rewarded with a wide smile that displayed a row of tiny white teeth.

Straightening, Tonino took the handles of what was clearly a specially made wheelchair and pushed the child down the wide aisle to his designated space. Finn immediately spotted Dante at the altar and flung his arms out as if reaching for him.

Dante grinned and hurried over to crouch on his haunches before him just as Tonino had done. Finn's skinny arms wrapped around his uncle's neck. 'Carry,' Finn demanded in a strong Irish accent.

'Soon,' Dante promised. 'I need to marry Aunty Aislin first.'

'Then carry?'

'You bet. Now be a good boy and wait for your mummy. Tonino will look after you until she gets here.' Dante kissed his nephew's cheek and ruffled his hair then made his way back to his place at the altar.

Tonino was used to small children. His brother had two, his sister had just given birth to her third. Mobility issues aside, there was nothing about this child that should capture his attention and yet… There was something about him…something familiar. Something that made his skin prickle and his heart pound.

'How old are you, Finn?' he asked through a throat that had run dry.

The little brow creased before he held three fingers up.

'You're three?' he clarified sceptically. The boy was tiny.

A nod.

'You're almost a man.'

The tiny white teeth flashed at him again.

An audible change amongst the congregation caught their attention. The little boy craned to look around him. 'Mummy!'

The bridal party had arrived.

The beautiful bride made her way down the aisle arm in arm with her proud father, identical beams on their faces. Behind them, holding the long train of the bride's dress, were two adorable little girls walking either side of a slender brunette in a long, ancient-Greek-style dusky rose bridesmaid dress. Her face was turned to the child on her left and so hidden from Tonino's sight.

'Mummy!' Finn called out again, this time loud enough for the whole congregation to hear.

The pounding in Tonino's chest ramped up in speed.

And then he caught full view of the brunette's face and his heart stopped beating altogether.

Orla held on to the train of Aislin's dress as if it were life support. She could do nothing to stop her legs trembling.

Tonino Valente. The name she'd spent three years desperately trying to remember. Aislin had uttered his name and in that instant a light had switched on in Orla's brain. If she hadn't ripped the tiny clasp from Aislin's dress she might very well have fainted, but the panic over ruining the hundred-thousand-euro dress had been equal to the shock of recognition at Tonino's name.

The flurry of activity that had followed, the hunt for the designer, who'd eventually been found in the hotel bar and who'd given Orla more evil eyes during the fixing of the clasp than she'd previously received in her lifetime, the arrival of Sabine's daughters—Orla's fellow bridesmaids—and the arrival of Aislin's father... Suddenly the suite had been crammed with people and she'd been forced to get a grip of herself.

This was the biggest day of her sister's life. Aislin had put her life on hold for three years for Orla and Finn. Orla would never have been able to bear the scars that marked her body inside and out without her sister's steadfast support. More than support. Aislin had raised Finn for the first eighteen months of his life, been the first to realise he wasn't developing as he should, the one there every single day of Orla's rehabilitation.

And now it was Orla's turn to support her sister; her

protector, her best friend, her guardian angel made flesh. This was Aislin's day.

Sick dread continued its steady drum as they moved closer to the altar and she had to use all her concentration to keep the train of Aislin's dress stretched out and keep control of the little bridesmaids by her side, both of whom were merrily waving at the packed congregation as if they were royalty. She hardly dared look away from them in case she found the dark brown stare that had haunted her dreams.

Could it really be him?

It had been almost four years. All they'd shared was one night. Or was it two? Or three? Or more? She wished she could remember but her memory had as many holes in it as a lump of Swiss cheese. Many of the holes had closed with time and the lost memories had returned but everything to do with Tonino and her time in Sicily remained blurry snapshots. She knew they'd met at the hotel she'd checked into during her fruitless attempt to meet her father, but that had been her only concrete remembrance... apart from his face. She remembered that handsome face vividly. Every time she'd pictured it, she'd had to suck in a breath of air to counteract the lance of pain that had accompanied it and blink away tears she'd had no clue from whence they had come.

'Mummy!'

Her son's voice broke through the fog of fear in her head.

Stretching her cheeks into a smile, she finally had a clear view past her sister to the spot at the left of the altar where she'd been promised she and Finn would sit.

The smile froze, half formed.

A tall, dark, utterly gorgeous man sat beside Finn. His black stare was fixed directly on her.

Her stomach plummeted. Thick heat pulsed and swirled through her head, dizzying her.

She had no recollection of Aislin's father handing the bride to the groom, no recollection of the two small bridesmaids leaving her side, no recollection of her feet taking her to her son. All she remembered from taking those steps was the blazing heat that suffused her entire body and the feeling that she could fall into a dead faint from the shock.

The man watching over her son until she could take her place beside him was Tonino. Finn's father.

CHAPTER TWO

THE WEDDING CEREMONY passed Tonino by. He rose and sat when directed, joined in with the hymns, recited the prayers at the appropriate times but it was all noise. He could not switch his attention away from Orla. Or her child.

The child who looked the image of his own childhood photographs.

His eyes flew from mother to child, child to mother, his gaze unable to settle any more than his ragged heart-beats could.

The pounding in his head was too strong for coherent thoughts. He couldn't breathe properly. He'd only been capable of snatching drags of air into his lungs since he'd seen Orla's face.

He'd risen from the seat he'd been saving for her and they'd stepped around each other, eyes locked, like two moons orbiting an invisible sun. For the first time in his thirty-four years he'd been struck speechless.

Her green eyes had been wide. Frightened. Her face had been white.

That was the last time their gazes connected.

Not once throughout the ceremony did Orla look at him. While his stare remained resolutely upon her and her child, her attention, when not taken by her son, stayed on the bride and groom.

Gradually, anger and incredulity rose inside him and

pushed out the shock. Coherent thinking returned. His wits sharpened.

He began to see more clearly too. And what he saw proved that, despite having had a child, Orla hadn't changed at all.

She was still beautiful. Slender and elegant. The long, thick dark hair he'd last seen spread over his pillow when he'd kissed her goodbye was coiled into a chic knot on the nape of her neck. The elfin features he'd once thought belonged on the pages of a fairy-tale book had been expertly made-up, smoky eye shadow emphasising the stunning large green eyes he'd once gazed into while buried deep inside her. The long-sleeved dress she wore was far less revealing than usual bridesmaid dresses, the dusky pink silk wrapping around her body to kiss her gentle curves but displaying minimal flesh.

Her beauty had captivated him from the first look.

That first look had been pure chance. A member of his public relations team had found a litany of complaints about one of his Palermo hotels online. Tonino had rearranged his itinerary and headed straight there. The Palermo hotel in question had been part of his uncle's struggling chain until Tonino had stepped in to save it and save his uncle's reputation from the shame of bankruptcy. Where Tonino specialised in converting old castles, monasteries, chateaux and the like into luxury spa and golf resorts for the wealthy, his uncle's hotel chain had been aimed firmly at holidaymakers on a budget.

Tonino had been raised in a wealthy family but his core group of childhood friends had come from diverse economic backgrounds. Gio, the friend Dante had chosen as his best man, came from an exceptionally poor background. In their school days, holidays for Gio's family had been the result of months of overtime, scrimping and saving. The cost of their holiday had been pocket change compared to the sums spent by visitors to Tonino's own hotels but in comparison had cost them far more and had meant a hell of a lot more as a result. He always thought of Gio when inspecting his lower-ranked hotels. Why should guests be forced to accept shoddy service, cold food and an unclean swimming pool just because they were poor? It was this exact same argument he'd had with his hotel manager right before he'd fired him. He'd left the meeting room, furious at the fired manager and furious with himself for allowing the situation to get this far. A solitary woman had been waiting at the unattended reception desk.

That woman had been Orla.

His reaction to her had been like a knockout punch to his guts. He'd never had such an immediate reaction to a woman before and it had been the final clarion call needed to know he couldn't marry Sophia. That reaction had been the unwitting trigger for the rift that still existed between Tonino and his parents. That knockout initial reaction had changed the course of his life.

Orla was thankful for the bossy photographer. He clearly saw himself as an *artiste* and spent ages framing each shot in the cathedral's picturesque grounds. This allowed her to hide in plain sight with her family, safe amid their huge numbers. That she had barely spoken to any of them in the last three years was neither here nor there. She felt no animosity towards them. They simply picked up where they'd left off, catching up on their lives in snatches of conversation.

Snatches of conversation were all she could manage. Everything inside her had become so tight it was a struggle to get any words out.

One of the small bridesmaids had taken a shine to Finn and stuck to his side, gabbling away to him in her own language. Finn didn't have much in the way of a vocabu but the rapture on his face only proved that language was inconsequential.

Too scared to look at Tonino, Orla kept her gaze far from him but still felt the heat of his stare upon her. It had been hard enough feeling it every second of the wedding ceremony but outside, his solid form a good head taller than most of the other guests, she felt his attention like a malevolent spectre haunting her. She sensed his loathing, which only added to the cold needles digging into her skin.

What had she done to provoke such animosity?

Deep in her bones she knew the moment opportunity presented itself, he would pounce. She had to be ready for it. She *had* to remember.

Frustration at her Swiss cheese memory made her want to scream.

She'd been waiting for her baby to be born before telling the father. That was something she knew only because Aislin had told her so. Aislin had been unable to tell her the father's name or Orla's reasons for waiting until after the birth to tell him because Orla had never disclosed it to her.

Why was that? Orla never kept secrets from her sister so why would she have kept something of such importance to herself?

There were so many things she'd spent three years trying to understand about her own thoughts and actions during the pregnancy, desperately trying to remember, even undergoing hypnosis to unlock the crucial hidden memories.

The most crucial memory of all, the identity of Finn's father, had now been unlocked but there was still a heap of others to bring to light.

As soon as the photos were done and the bride and groom had ridden off to the hotel on their horse-drawn carriage, Orla latched onto Aislin's friend Sabine and used her as a shield while she wheeled Finn to their waiting car.

She unstrapped him and carefully lifted him into her arms. He was small for his age and light in weight but it wouldn't be long before her still-weak muscles would struggle to carry him any distance. She would carry him for as long as she could physically manage. She'd missed out on so much of his short life, days and nights spent aching to hold her baby, days and nights spent hating the body that had entrapped her in a living hell, fighting with every breath to get herself well enough that she could at least live under the same roof as her child.

Once Finn was secured in his car seat, she hurried to the other side and slid in beside him.

Only when the driver pulled away did she turn her head to look out of the window.

Tonino was staring straight at her, not a flicker of emotion on his handsome face.

Mercifully sat at the top table, Orla watched the seven-course wedding meal unfold around her in the hotel's enormous ballroom decoratively adorned with balloons and glitter. She had been seated on the top table beside Aislin's father, the man who'd been Orla's stepfather from the age of three for the grand total of two years. Aislin had so many of Dennis O'Reilly's characteristics that being in his company was usually a joy. A humble man who'd been treated atrociously by their mother, he'd always treated Orla with great kindness on the occasions she'd seen him after the divorce.

Today though, she couldn't relax long enough to find the usual enjoyment she would have found being next to him

This was hands down the most luxuriant and glamorou wedding she'd ever attended. The food was the most del cious she'd ever eaten, the wine in her glass the nicest she ever sipped; even the water had a purity to it she'd nev tasted before. She could take no pleasure from any of i

To her misfortune, Tonino had been placed to the left of the top table, facing her. Every time she glanced in his direction, she found his cold stare on her. It never failed to send a shiver up her spine.

Something different raced up her spine whenever she caught sight of the stunningly beautiful blonde woman with eyes like a cat seated to the right of the top table. Orla was certain she wasn't imagining the death stares being thrown by her, which were far more potent than the daggers she'd received from Aislin's wedding-dress designer.

She *knew* this woman. But from where? And why did she want to hide under the table to escape her?

Her torrid thoughts were interrupted when Dennis got to his feet, tapped his glass for attention, and pulled out a sheet of paper.

Much merriment ensued. Even Orla found her lips pulling into an unforced smile to see the Sicilian guests' bemusement. Dennis's accent was so thick and he spoke so quickly they probably struggled to understand him. The Irish contingent understood him perfectly and heckled liberally. Only one brave strapping teenager dared heckle Dante when it was his turn to speak, though, and was rewarded with a slap from his pint-sized mother, which had Sicilians and Irish alike laughing.

After the speeches were done and copious toasts had been made, there was an hour of free time. Many of the guests disappeared to their rooms to change for the evening party. Most of Tonino's table stood too, but the tiny easing in Orla's chest at the fact that he might leave the ballroom tightened again when, eyes locked, he strode towards her.

Fear scratched at her throat. She wasn't ready for this. She needed to make sense of the unfolding memories before the confrontation that had to happen occurred.

Fate stepped in in the form of Dante's glamorous mother, Immacolata, who Aislin had been right in saying held no animosity towards Orla. Immacolata pounced on Tonino when he was barely three feet from the table.

Snatching the opportunity to escape, Orla hurried to her feet and took hold of Finn's wheelchair. *I'm taking him to the suite*, she mouthed to Aislin.

Are you okay? Aislin mouthed back.

She nodded vigorously. 'I need to get his walker.'

Luck shone on her again when a handful of her cousins' small children bounded over and loudly insisted on accompanying them.

Guarded by an army of children barely out of nappies—the bridesmaids tagged along too—Orla took Finn to their suite.

Leaving Finn's nurse to keep order over the sugar-loaded kids, she stepped out onto the balcony alone. Familiar scents filled her airwaves and, slowly, the vertigo-like feeling that had cloaked her since she'd heard Tonino's name that morning lifted.

She gazed out at the Tyrrhenian Sea darkening under the setting sun. The Sicilian aromas weren't the only things stabbing at her memories.

She craned to her left and squinted, trying to spot the run-down beachside hotel she'd stayed in when she'd met Tonino…

Whether it was seeing Tonino again or being back in Sicily she couldn't say, but the locked-away memories that had eluded her since she'd woken in hospital were slowly taking substance in her mind, but it was all still a jumble.

Sophia!

That was the cat's-eyed, dangerous-looking woman's name. Sophia. She'd confronted Orla…but about what?

Stupid brain, *work*!

A squeal of laughter from the suite shook her from the reforming jumble of memories. The evening reception was about to start. She had to be there.

She got her army of children together and, the nurse carrying Finn's walker, they trooped out of the suite and down the corridor.

Into the lift they all piled. Seconds later they reached the ground floor, the doors opened and the excitable kids burst out like a spray of rubber bullets.

Orla's brief amusement died when she noticed the imposing figure propped against the wall.

Tonino pulled himself away from the wall he'd stood against while waiting for Orla to reappear. All the hotel's stairs and elevators exited at this corridor. She could not escape without him seeing her.

Or her seeing him.

When she appeared, the little colour she had on her milky-white complexion drained away.

Let her feel fearful. Let her take in her surroundings and know there was no escape from him, not here in his own hotel where he had staff posted on every exit into the grounds, ready to notify him should she decide to escape further than her suite.

He stood right in front of her, but it was not his deceitful ex-lover he addressed.

Crouching down, he held out a hand to the child he strongly suspected was his own, and not only because of the uncanny resemblance between them.

Orla had been a virgin. He remembered the flame of colour that had stained her cheeks when she'd told him that and had to fight back the memory snaking through his blood of the first time he'd made love to her.

'Hello, Finn. Are you having a good time?'

Finn nodded vigorously. He strained forwards but the straps of his wheelchair stopped him leaning too far.

'And do you like your suite?'

He was rewarded with a blank stare.

'Your room,' Tonino clarified. 'Do you like your room?'

Another vigorous nod.

'You're sharing it with your mummy?'

A less vigorous nod.

'What about your daddy? Is he sharing it too?' Having checked the room and suite allocation, he already knew the answer to this, but he wanted to see Finn's reaction to the word 'daddy'. Dante had been uncharacteristically evasive on the subject of Finn's parentage when he'd tried to quiz him a short while ago. Tonino understood. Orla was Dante's newfound sister. He had a sister himself. Blood protected blood. It had been Aislin's reaction to his questions that had been the biggest giveaway. She'd reminded him of a cornered rabbit.

The blank stare returned.

A little voice piped up, the Irish brogue strong. 'Finn doesn't have a daddy.'

Tonino raised his head to look at Orla. She was clasping the handles of the wheelchair so tightly her knuckles had whitened.

The expression on her face along with the child's unwitting answer was all the confirmation he needed.

Her green eyes held his, wide and pleading, before she gave a slight shake of her head and mouthed, *Later. Please,* and expertly pushed the wheelchair around him and aimed it towards the ballroom at a speed that would suggest she was being chased by a pack of rabid dogs.

Suddenly feeling in need of a large drink, he let her go.

The ballroom had been transformed into an even glitzier spectacle by the time Orla hurried through its doors. The main lights had dimmed so the only illumination came from the glittering chandeliers. The DJ had started playing music but the dance floor was empty.

The fear gripping her heart tightened when she saw her sister's face.

'Tonino Valente was asking questions about Finn's father,' Aislin whispered when she reached her.

Terrified she was going to cry, Orla blinked frantically.

Sympathy and understanding washed over her sister's face. 'It's him, isn't it?'

All she could do was nod.

'He knows?'

Pulling her lips in tightly, she nodded again. Tonino had taken one look at Finn and recognised him as his own.

'What are you going to do?'

'I don't know.' For three years she'd waited for the memories to return, assuming that, once she had them back, she would enlist her sister's help and set off to find Finn's father. She would have had time to prepare herself.

Never in her wildest dreams had she imagined a scenario like this.

Behind Aislin, Dante approached them.

His presence brought some much-needed sanity to Orla's frazzled nerves.

Whatever happened, she mustn't lose sight that this was their big day. If Aislin so much as suspected the fear in Orla's heart then everything would be ruined. She wouldn't hesitate to cancel the party or the honeymoon.

Flinging her arms around her, Orla held her sister tightly. 'I need to settle my nerves but I'm going to be fine. I promise. Now stop worrying about me and enjoy your party.'

On cue, the DJ called for the bride and groom to take to the dance floor.

'Go,' Orla urged, kissing Aislin's cheek. She was rewarded with a kiss in return.

While Dante led Aislin onto the dance floor, Orla took Finn out of his wheelchair and put him in his walker, a wonderful device Dante had bought for him that kept him secure and allowed him to use his legs to get himself about.

She had to be careful with the amount of time he used it as he tired easily, but she knew he would want to get on the dance floor with the other children.

As soon as he was in it he started bouncing with glee. His 'girlfriend' the bridesmaid shot over to admire him in it.

Orla went with them to the edge of the dance floor with the other guests.

Tears she'd been holding back filled her eyes again to see the love shining between the two people she loved so much. She didn't need to pray for their love to be eternal. Aislin and Dante were made for each other.

As the dance came to an end an arm brushed against hers. Her skin tingled.

A spicy scent filled her nostrils. Her pulses surged. Her lungs tightened. A memory of pressing her nose into a strong neck and inhaling this scent flashed through her.

'I give them six months.'

She didn't dare look at him. Somehow she managed to croak, 'What?'

'Their marriage. If Aislin has your blood in her veins then it won't be long before her mask slips and Dante realises that beneath the pretty surface lies a black, deceitful heart.' A huge hand closed on her wrist. 'Dance with me.'

She thought her knees were about to collapse beneath her.

'Dance with me or I make a scene. Do you want to be responsible for ruining your brother and sister's special day?'

He gave her no further chance to answer. Before she knew it, Orla was being smoothly manhandled onto the dance floor and pulled against the hulking body of the only man she'd ever been intimate with.

CHAPTER THREE

DANCING WITH ORLA was like dancing with a lump of aged clay. Her arms hung limply by her sides; her movements stiff and resistant.

Taking her hands firmly and placing them on his waist, Tonino dipped his head to whisper into her ear. 'Were you ever going to tell me?'

Somehow she managed to stiffen even further.

A loose strand of her hair brushed against his nose and suddenly he became aware of his sinews tightening and his veins thickening as her scent worked its magic in his senses.

Her magic had once thrilled him. Initially shy, she'd soon revealed herself to be sweet and funny, a woman who wore her intelligence lightly, unaware of her inherent sensual nature until he'd brought it out of her. That was what had made her abrupt disappearance so hard to comprehend. He could have understood if she'd been prickly and had the bitchy streak so many of the women in his world wore like a badge of honour, but she'd been nothing like them.

He could never have imagined she would turn out to be worse than all of them put together.

Disgust that he could still feel such a visceral response to her had him stepping back so their bodies no longer touched.

'Orla, you have hidden my son from me for three years,'

he said tightly, loathing that he could feel anything other *than* loathing for this treacherous woman. 'If you want me to keep hold of my temper and not make a scene, I suggest you answer my question. Were you ever going to tell me I have a child?'

A contortion of emotions crashed over her face. Frightened green eyes flickered. Soft, plump lips tightened.

Tonino's self-loathing increased at the vivid remembrance of how good it had felt to have those soft lips crushed against his.

Never had he hated anyone as much as he hated Orla right then. That he could still desire her after everything she'd done stretched credulity to a whole new dimension.

He spun her round in his arms so she faced the socialising guests rather than the DJ. Ignoring the malevolent stares being thrown his way by Sophia and the rest of the Messinas, he said, 'You see the table I was on?'

She gave a tiny nod.

'That is my family. They have spent the day celebrating your brother and sister's marriage. My parents are here, my brother and his family, my brother-in-law and my sister's children... They have all seen Finn, unaware he is their blood.'

Tonino might still feel the residue of anger over the furious arguments that had erupted between him and his parents when he'd ended his engagement to Sophia, but his parents adored their grandchildren. Nothing made them happier than news of another family pregnancy. Babies were celebrated as gifts from God.

'You have deprived them of a grandson, nephew and cousin. You have deprived Finn of his Sicilian family and heritage.'

The anger in Tonino's carefully delivered words chilled Orla's heart. Her brain kept alternating between hot and cold, a vapid mess of confusion, fear and guilt. Being held so close to him only made matters worse. Her heart pounded so hard there was danger it could beat itself out of her constricted chest. Every time she managed to take a breath his spicy scent dived into her airwaves. It shocked and terrified her that her nose seemed to want to bury itself into his neck and breathe his scent in properly, just as it had done all those years ago. It terrified her even more that her hands wanted to wrap fully around his waist and her body strained to press closer against his hard torso.

Being held in his arms had flooded her with more memories.

She remembered taking one look at him and her insides and brain melting into hot goo.

She remembered lying naked in his arms, half awake as the morning sun filtered into the bedroom, and thinking she had never been so happy.

And she remembered learning that everything he'd told her about himself had been a lie.

Orla stared at Tonino's family, her stomach churning violently. These impossibly glamorous, impossibly wealthy, impossibly powerful people were her baby's family. How would they react when they learned of Finn? She knew it was her broken brain's fault that they were not a part of Finn's life but, even as she breathed relief to remember her intentions *had* always been to tell Tonino about their child, she still felt wretched for them. All she'd wanted was to get through the pregnancy, have her baby on Irish soil and then seek legal help before telling him…

Suddenly finding herself meeting Sophia's coldly furious stare, she hastily looked away, straight into Tonino's equally cold and furious stare.

The churning in her stomach increased as she found herself gazing at the handsome face she remembered sighing with pleasure to wake beside.

He was just so…*masculine*. Thick, dark stubble was

already breaking out over his chiselled jawline and perfectly complemented the thick, dark hair he wore short at the sides and longer at the top. But, for all his sculptural perfection, it was his eyes she'd always found the most arresting. They were like the darkest melted chocolate. They had made *her* melt.

Their son had his eyes.

Wrenching her stare from Tonino, she found her son bouncing happily in his walker and took a deep breath.

From the moment the pregnancy had been confirmed, her child's welfare had been the focus of her life. When she'd woken from the coma with all memories of the previous six months lost, she'd known, even while everything else had been a blank, that she'd been carrying a child. She would fight to the last breath to keep him safe.

Suddenly desperate to hold Finn in her arms, she dropped her light touch against Tonino's waist and took a step back. 'Please, I don't want a scene but this is not the time or place for this conversation.'

His features darkened. He snatched at her wrist before she could take another step away from him. 'Then let's go somewhere private—this is a conversation we should have had four years ago. You have kept my son in the dark about me for long enough. *Finn doesn't have a daddy?* He damn well does and he deserves to know it.'

'I agree but take a look at him. *Look,*' she insisted when his now blazing eyes stayed locked on hers. 'You must see he's not a well boy. He's looked forward to this day for ages and looked forward to dancing and playing with other children. Let him enjoy the party for another hour and then I'll put him to bed. Give him time to fall asleep and then come to my suite. Please? We can talk then.'

He turned his head to the direction of their son. His chest rose and fell heavily.

Eventually he inclined his head sharply, dropped his

loose hold on her wrist and faced her again. 'Two hours, Orla, and then I come to your suite.' He bowed his head to whisper in her ear, 'And if you have thoughts of running away, know I have put measures in place to prevent it. You will never escape from me again.'

The nurse helped Orla get Finn into his pyjamas and put him to bed before Orla told her to go and join the party for a few hours.

Alone, she stripped off her bridesmaid dress, avoiding the reflection of her bare figure in the mirror. Her scars were itching but she didn't dare apply the topical lotion her doctor had prescribed for it, not when the knock on the suite door could come at any moment. Instead, she dressed hastily, donning a pair of checked trousers and a long-sleeved black top.

When Tonino came she wanted to be ready.

Could she ever be ready for this?

She'd spent three years trying desperately to remember who Finn's father was and unearth the memories of their time together. Now that many of them had popped out of the box they'd been contained in, part of her wished she could shove them back in and nail the lid back down while, contrarily, her search for the still-hidden memories became more frantic.

Much of the time they'd shared together had come back to her, but she still didn't remember what had happened with her father. Her return to Ireland was still a blur too.

When the loud rap on her suite's door finally came, it took more effort than she could believe to drag her legs to it.

Tonino loomed at the threshold looking exactly as she imagined a vampire would in the moments before it swooped to strike its helpless victim.

A vampire should not send her pulses soaring with

just one look. That was dangerous by any stretch of the imagination.

Without a word being exchanged, he stepped into the suite and closed the door. Folding his arms across his broad chest, he slowly looked her up and down.

The intensity of his scrutiny sent something thick and warm trickling through her feverish veins. Shaken, Orla hastily sat herself on one of the suite's plush sofas.

She didn't want to look at him but found herself helpless to do anything else. Tonino had such presence, a magnetic energy he carried with him. All the words she'd prepared stuck on her tongue as she gazed into the dark brown eyes of the man who'd swept her off her feet and then broken her heart in the space of ten days. That same broken heart thundered in her chest. Its thuds pounded in her head. Her thoughts, like her words and memories, were a messed-up jumble.

She had no idea how to play this. The man she'd had the time of her life with had been a lie, but he was still Finn's father. He might have all the wealth and power, but he was still Finn's father. When all was said and done, that was the one inescapable fact. Finn deserved to know his father and Tonino deserved to know his son.

After a long period of charged silence, he dragged his fingers through his hair and headed to the minibar. 'I don't know about you but I need a drink. Do you still drink gin?'

Startled that he remembered something so innocuous, she shook her head.

He arched an eyebrow then opened the bar door and pulled out a bottle of red wine.

He took a corkscrew from a drawer and opened the bottle effortlessly. 'Will you have one?'

This time she managed to croak, 'No, thank you.'

Since the accident, Orla had lost all tolerance for alcohol, which was a great shame. Before the pregnancy, she'd loved nothing more than going out with her friends, drinking way too much and dancing until the sun came up. She'd been free. No responsibilities, no pain, no dependency on anyone else. No one dependent on her.

Those days belonged to another woman.

He poured himself a hefty glass, swirled the red liquid, put the rim under his nose then took a sip. It must have pleased his palate for he then took a much larger sip.

Tonino, she suddenly remembered, loved good wine.

When his eyes locked on to hers, a shiver ran down her spine. He looked murderously cold.

'Why don't you sit down?' she suggested quietly.

Tonino, propped against the bar, took another drink as he looked at Orla, dwarfed by the sofa she'd sat herself on, fingers twisting together. She reminded him of a newborn deer that had come face-to-face with its first predator.

'I'm fine where I am,' he answered.

She raised a shoulder and breathed in through her nose. 'Then would you mind not glowering at me?'

That *voice*…

Orla was the only woman who'd turned him on with nothing but her voice. The husky timbre and lyrical brogue were pure alchemy to the senses. It coiled through his veins like the finest of wines and came dangerously close to muffling out her actual words.

'Glowering?' It was an unfamiliar word.

Her lips curled into a brief smile. 'You know—looking like you want to rip my head from my neck. It's making me feel all itchy.'

'You're safe,' he answered sardonically. 'If I rip your head off I'll never get any answers from you. Enough stalling. Tell me what's wrong with my son and tell me why you have kept him a secret from me for all these years.'

She dipped her head forwards and put her face in her hands. Her fingers dragged through her thick mane of wavy dark hair, which she'd released from its knot. It was every bit as luscious as he remembered and he suddenly experienced the deepest urge to kneel before her and cradle her face in his hands, stroke the soft skin and run his fingers through the thick mane as he'd done so many times before.

When she looked back up to meet his stare, everything inside him clenched.

'Are you sure you won't sit down?' she said softly. 'This could take a while.'

Gritting his teeth tightly, he stared at her. Or glowered, as she called it. He would not allow her soft femininity to weaken him. His height was one of the natural advantages nature had given him, his strength accomplished by his own hard work. If him remaining standing made Orla feel disadvantaged, then great. He saw no reason to put her at ease. On the contrary.

She chewed her bottom lip then sighed. 'I always wanted to tell you.'

He snorted.

'Please, just listen. Finn's condition and the reason I never told you about him are related. I had a car accident when I was six months pregnant that left my memory shot to pieces. I couldn't tell you about Finn because I'd forgotten who you were.'

Her excuse was so outrageous he tightened his grip on the wine glass to stop himself throwing it against the wall. '*Dio mio*, you have got some nerve, lady. You're claiming you had *amnesia*?'

'Yes. But it's not a claim. It's the truth.'

'And when did your memories return?'

'The ones about you returned today... Well, some of them have...'

'Very convenient,' he mocked, topping up his glass with more wine. 'You've had hours to come up with a convincing excuse and this is the best you can do? Amnesia?'

'I understand it sounds far-fetched but it's the truth. I've spent over three years trying to remember you. All I remembered with any clarity until today was your face. Everything else was hazy images. I knew we'd met here in Sicily but that was a deep-rooted knowledge, like knowing my own name—'

'You expect me to believe this?' he interrupted impatiently.

'It's the truth and it's a provable truth.'

'Really?' he sneered. 'The only thing provable is that you're a liar.'

'I am *not*.'

'You booked into my hotel under a false name.'

Confusion creased her beautiful face. 'What are you talking about?'

'Four years ago you booked into my hotel under the name of Orla McCarthy. Here, you are booked in under the name of Orla O'Reilly.'

Around a month after she'd done her disappearing act, Tonino had drunk too much wine and decided to search her name on the Internet. The few articles he'd found with the name Orla McCarthy in them had not been about her.

Now he understood why Orla had bucked the trend and left no digital footprint. She'd given him a false name.

The woman he'd experienced the deepest connection of his life with, the woman who'd been the unwitting catalyst of the ongoing rift with his family, the woman who'd had no idea of who he was yet had still treated him like a prince...

That woman had lied about her name. She'd kept his child a secret from him.

He couldn't understand why he wasn't fighting an urge

to throw her out of the suite window into the sea below but was instead fighting the powerful urge to drag her into his arms and kiss her until he'd drawn all the breath from her lungs.

He couldn't understand how he could look at her deceitful face and feel all his internal organs swelling and compressing his lungs. These were reactions her cruel duplicity should have killed stone dead.

'When I booked into your hotel four years ago I had to hand my passport over so I used my legal name, which is McCarthy,' she explained wearily.

'Then why are you here now as O'Reilly? Was it to throw me off the scent? Did you think I wouldn't recognise you?'

She rubbed her eyes with the palms of her hands. 'I genuinely do not know what you're implying.'

'There is nothing genuine about you,' he said roughly. 'You knew you would see me today. Your brother and I are old friends. You're staying in my hotel. The wedding reception's in my hotel.' He squeezed the back of his neck. 'You took a huge risk in coming here and an even bigger risk bringing Finn with you.'

'I wasn't going to come without him,' she protested hotly. 'Dante never mentioned your name. If he had I would have remembered you sooner, but he didn't. Aislin organised the wedding—she made the booking and checked me in. Aislin has her father's surname because our mother married him. Our mum registered me as Orla O'Reilly when I started school, so I had the same surname as them. Most people know me as Orla O'Reilly.'

'Why didn't you change it legally?'

'That would have been up to my mother and she couldn't be bothered.'

He grimaced and took another large drink of his wine, angry with himself for diverting from the only subject that should matter to him. His son. 'What name have you given Finn?'

'My legal name. McCarthy.'

'Why doesn't he have *my* name?'

'Because I'd forgotten it,' she answered through gritted teeth.

Anger swelled like a cobra poising to strike. 'Then who the hell is named as his father?'

'No one.'

'Now I *know* you're lying,' he snarled. He'd interrupted his lawyer's evening meal to demand he look into the legalities of Irish paternity for him. 'It is illegal not to name the father on an Irish birth certificate.'

She rubbed her eyes again then fixed them on him with a sigh that sounded more exasperated than defeated. 'It isn't if there's a compelling reason.'

'And what compelling reason did you give?' he demanded. 'Your amnesia?'

'Keep your voice down or you'll wake Finn.' For the first time since he'd entered her suite, a fierceness entered her tone.

He hadn't realised he was shouting.

But, *Dio*, it was taking all his strength not to grab her by the shoulders and shake all the lies out of her until only the truth remained. What kind of a fool did she take him for? Did she seriously think she could play the amnesia line and that he would fall for it? What did she think? That they were players in one of those over-acted soap operas his grandmother watched?

Green eyes, wide and wary but unflinching, stayed on him. 'Aislin registered Finn's birth. I'd never told her who the father was so she couldn't name you—'

'You denied my existence?' he roared.

'Keep your voice *down*,' she snapped. 'I'm trying to be sympathetic but you're not making it easy when you keep interrupting me with all your stupid assumptions. Everything I am telling you is provable—you do not have to take my word for it.'

'Good because I will never take you at your word for anything.'

'Good because now you know how I feel about you.'

'What do you mean by that?'

'That you are in no position to act all holier than thou when you consider all the lies you told me.'

Her assertion was almost as outrageous as her lies about having amnesia. 'You dare try to deflect?'

'Deflection? Okay, then, explain this to me, buster. Why did you tell me you were the hotel manager and not the owner?'

'I never told you anything. You assumed it.' He would not feel guilty about this. He'd intended to tell her the truth about who he was the day she'd run away from Sicily.

Tired eyes blazed with the same anger as coursed through his veins. 'You *let* me assume. I only found out who you really were the day I left Sicily when your fiancée paid me a little visit.'

'What the hell are you talking about?'

'Sophia,' she spat. 'The fiancée you forgot to tell me about. She tracked me down when you were in Tuscany.'

Tonino swirled the wine in his glass and stared hard at her, a rancid feeling forming in his guts. Sophia had taken the ending of their engagement as badly as his parents had taken it. He'd shielded Orla from the fallout. Shielding her had been bliss; the pair of them cocooned in his smallest and plainest apartment, just the two of them, the rest of the world locked out. 'What did she want?'

Orla's skin chilled and a throb pounded in her head to remember the encounter that had broken her heart. 'To tell me you belonged to her and warn me off you. What else?'

He nodded in a thoughtful way, but the blackness of his

eyes revealed something very different. 'Let me be clear on this—you are telling me that Sophia Messina, the daughter of one of Sicily's oldest families, tracked you down and warned you off me?'

'That's exactly what happened.'

'She threatened you?'

'Not in words but her meaning was very clear. She knew you'd been cheating on her with me. I can't say I liked the threats she made but I understood where her anger came from. No one likes to be made a fool of.'

He'd made a fool of her and Sophia both. The other woman's threats had been almost as sickening as the proof she'd put before her. So sickening had Orla found it that the minute Sophia had left her room, she'd vomited.

She half feared she could vomit now, from both the memories and the growing ache in her head.

'I ended my engagement with Sophia the day I met you,' he stated flatly. 'If you had stuck around and asked, I would have set you straight. Sophia was playing games with you.'

'You expect me to believe that when all the evidence points otherwise and when we both know you're loose with what truth means?'

He let out a Sicilian word she instinctively knew was a curse but, on a roll, she ignored it.

'You let me believe you were a hotel manager. That was a *lie*. Everything you told me about yourself was a stinking fat lie. Can you blame me for being scared when I learned I was pregnant? All I knew for sure was that you were a liar and a powerful one at that. I refused to tell anyone about you because I was frightened and ashamed and an emotional wreck, and all I could focus on was delivering my baby safely into the world. I was going to tell you about him after he was born but then I had the accident and it changed everything. I couldn't amend Finn's birth certificate after I left hospital because I *couldn't remember your name.*'

When Orla had finished her venomously delivered rebuke, the only sounds in the suite were their ragged breaths. The poison swirling between them was thick enough to taste.

Something else swirled between them too in that small stretch of silence, something that glittered behind Tonino's dark, furious eyes. His jaw was clenched so tightly she could see the angry pulse throbbing on it.

When he finally spoke, every word was elucidated with deliberate slowness. 'Do you know what I think? I think you have backed yourself into a corner and that every word coming from your pretty little mouth is an excuse to justify what you *know* is inexcusable. You hoped to get through the day without me noticing or recognising you and hoped you could get through it without me seeing Finn and recognising my own son. You have cruelly and maliciously kept him from me and, for that, you will pay, and pay by having him cruelly and maliciously kept from *you*.'

CHAPTER FOUR

TONINO'S THREAT RANG loudly in Orla's ears then became a siren when he slammed his glass on the bar and strolled towards the bedroom door.

'What are you doing?' she beseeched, trying her hardest not to panic.

'I'm going to see my son.'

He can't take him from you, she reminded herself. *At this moment, he has no legal rights. Don't panic. Keep calm.*

She took a long breath. 'You're going to storm into a three-year-old boy's room and wake him from his sleep?'

The hateful expression he threw at her wounded as deeply as his threats. He placed his hand on the door knob. 'Do not make me out to be the bad guy in this. I want to see my son.'

'If you go in there you will wake him and you will frighten him.'

His jaw clenched. Seizing this brief moment of indecision, Orla pointed at her phone, which she'd placed on the coffee table. 'You can see him through my phone—look, I'm monitoring him as we speak.'

Now his expression became cynical. 'You watch him sleep?'

'I am tonight. He has epilepsy.'

Lines creased his forehead. A beat passed before he said, *'Epilessia...?* Fits?'

She nodded. She *must* keep calm. Placing a hand to her chest in an attempt to temper her clattering heartbeat, she fought to keep her tone even. 'He has seizures—fits. He's on medication for it, which has helped a lot, but he's had an exciting day and I don't want to risk leaving him unmonitored. Normally the nurse would monitor him but I told her to join the party so we could have some privacy.'

She did not drop her gaze from his cynical, suspicious one and allowed herself only a small breath of relief when he abandoned the door. Then she found she had no breath left to exhale for Tonino had walked over and sat his powerful body beside her.

Her poor clattering heart accelerated into overdrive.

He picked the phone up and studied the live feed on it. After a long pause, he said, 'His…*epilessia*…is it linked to his mobility problems?'

'Yes.' Orla suddenly found her attention distracted by the fingers holding her phone. Those same fingers had once caressed her naked skin…

Heat pumped dizzyingly through her head and she quickly dropped her gaze to the floor only to find Tonino's buffed shoes in her eyeline. He had the biggest feet of any man she'd ever met, and tingles laced her spine and spread to a far more intimate area to suddenly remember another part of his anatomy in proportion to those feet…

'He has cerebral palsy,' she hastily added, keeping her eyes fixed on the carpet so he wouldn't see the flame of colour radiating from her cheeks. How could she feel such things for a man who'd just threatened her with her own child? What was *wrong* with her? 'Lots of children with it have epilepsy.'

A long time passed where all he did was stare at the screen of the phone. Orla used that time to concentrate on breathing. She was exhausted. The day had been long and emotionally draining. Her feelings for Tonino were bound to be all over the place. His emotions were bound to be all over the place too. She must remember that threats made in anger were rarely carried out once tempers had cooled.

'What is cerebral…?'

'Palsy,' she finished for him when he struggled to say it. 'It's a condition caused by brain damage that basically affects the muscles.'

He turned his head to look at her. 'My son has brain damage?'

The flash of distress she witnessed in the dark eyes sent a pang through her heart. Her voice softened. 'Think of it as a brain development issue. Thankfully it doesn't seem that his mental faculties have been affected; I mean, he can speak and make himself understood, but time will tell on that part.' Learning difficulties were common for children with cerebral palsy and something Orla was prepared for. If it turned out that Finn did indeed have them then he would have all the help and support he needed.

'What caused it?'

'The trauma of his birth. He was born three months early—'

A loud incessant knocking on the door interrupted their talk.

'I'd better get that,' she muttered. She hauled herself to her feet and forced her aching legs to take her to the door. She would not let Tonino see how badly she was struggling right then; would not give him any further ammunition to use against her.

She was not in the least surprised to find Aislin there.

Her sister didn't even attempt to make an excuse for abandoning her own wedding reception, looking straight over Orla's shoulder into the suite, her nose wrinkling when she caught sight of Tonino. 'Everything okay in here?'

'Everything's fine,' Orla assured her.

Aislin's eyes narrowed as she eyeballed Tonino again before turning her attention back to her sister and saying loudly, 'You look upset.'

Orla gave a rueful shrug. 'This isn't the easiest conversation I've ever had.'

'I'll bet. Shall I stay?'

The temptation to drag Aislin inside was strong. 'Don't be silly. Go back to your party.'

'I saw Finn's nurse on the dance floor. Are you not coming back down?'

'I'm sorry, Ash, but I'm shattered.' And that was the truth. Orla felt wiped out, physically and emotionally.

'Okay. I'll leave you to it, then.' Her voice rose again. 'I'll keep my phone on me. Call if you need me.'

'I will,' Orla lied. She would rather call their mother for help than ruin Aislin's big day more than she already had.

'I'll see you at breakfast?'

'Definitely.'

'Good.' Then, looking over Orla's shoulder to stare at Tonino one more time, Aislin smiled brightly and said, 'If you harm a hair on my sister's head, I'll kill you. Got it?'

Orla found herself biting back a laugh of hysteria at the shock on Tonino's face.

'Did your sister just threaten me?' he asked when Orla sat back down, this time on an armchair away from him. She was finding it hard enough to concentrate properly without Tonino's scent and body heat addling her brain further.

'Yep.' The only downside with the armchair was that she was forced to look at him. Looking at him definitely addled her brain because it quickly became a struggle to stop herself from looking at him. To stop herself staring at him.

Her eyes yearned to stare. They wanted to soak in every

perfect feature on the face she had come so close to believing she could trust with her heart.

'Why would she do that?'

'She's very protective of me. She didn't mean it. She wouldn't actually kill you. Probably just castrate you or something.'

She couldn't hold back the burst of laughter when Tonino reflexively crossed his legs and nor could she stop the laughter turning into tears.

This was all too much. Seeing Tonino again, remembering what they'd shared, how it had ended, his loathing of her, his refusal to listen, his threats… It had been a long, emotional roller coaster of a day and now her body was telling her enough was enough.

Tonino watched the tears fall down Orla's beautiful face with a healthy dose of cynicism. When they'd been lovers he would never have imagined her capable of using feminine wiles to save her own skin. He'd believed her to be too genuine for those kinds of games—for *any* kind of game.

What would she do if he pulled her into his arms for fake comfort? Would she cling to him and produce a few more crocodile tears to soak into his shirt? Would she tilt her head and stare at him with those beguiling eyes, silently pleading with him to kiss her?

And what would *he* do if that course of action became reality?

The burn in his loins gave him the answer.

Every breath he'd taken in this suite had filled his lungs with Orla's scent. He was literally breathing her in, and every atom of his body responded to it.

Furious that his attraction for this duplicitous woman still blazed with such luminescence, he jumped back to his feet and helped himself to more wine.

'I'm sorry,' she whispered. 'I'm not usually a cry-baby.

I'm just finding it difficult to get my head around everything.'

'*You're* finding it difficult?' he sneered. 'How the hell do you think I feel?'

'I can guess.'

'I don't need your fake empathy.' He took a large swallow of wine with a grimace. 'I have discovered that I'm a father and that the mother of my child kept him a secret from me for three years and now I have to deal with threats from my oldest friend's new wife who is also my son's aunt. I didn't even know you *had* a sister.' And neither had he known she was Salvatore Moncada's secret daughter. Until that day, he'd had no idea Dante's recently discovered sister was the lover who'd run away from him.

While outwardly open about who she was, Orla had actually kept her cards very close to her chest. He'd known she'd studied for a degree in zoology—he'd never met anyone who'd studied that subject before so it had stuck in his mind—and that she'd travelled to Sicily in the downtime between ending her graduate job as a veterinary technician and starting her dream job on an Irish conservation project, but it wasn't until she'd disappeared that he'd realised he knew nothing of importance about her.

'Well, I didn't know you had a fiancée so that makes us even,' she fired back.

'I didn't have a fiancée. I ended it with Sophia the day I met you.'

'You *would* say that.' Orla squeezed her eyes shut and rubbed her temples. Her head was now pounding. 'Even if I accepted that you're telling me the truth on this…'

A memory flashed in her mind of sitting on her bed at home, palm flat against her still-flat belly, masochistically searching Tonino's name for the hundredth time and seeing the press report that his engagement to Sophia was over.

How long after she'd returned to Ireland had she read

that report? A couple of weeks? The report had made clear that Tonino had ended the engagement.

She could scream. Even if he were speaking the truth about when he ended it, he'd still lied about everything else.

Rubbing her temples even harder, trying not to wince at the pain shooting through her head every time she spoke, she said, 'Whose apartment did you take me to?' She remembered more than waking in his bed now. She remembered the apartment itself.

'Mine.'

'Codswallop. Don't forget my brother is a billionaire like yourself—that was not a billionaire's apartment.'

'It was the first apartment I bought with my own money when I was twenty. I use it when I want privacy...'

His words rang loud in her head, adding to the growing agony, but pushing at her mind were flashes of what he'd wanted privacy with her for. Those particular memories were still nothing but shimmers yet powerful enough to send a bolt of heat down low in her abdomen.

Once she had craved this man's touch. She'd craved everything about him.

She'd made love to him and created a life with him.

'And as for your brother,' he continued, 'you never told me you were Dante's sister and Salvatore Moncada's daughter. You accuse me of hiding things...' He downed his wine and blew out a long puff of air. 'We are losing focus. We are here, now, for one reason only and that is for my son. He is the only thing that matters.'

If he referred to Finn as 'his son' again she would swing for him. Well, she would if she had the energy, but she could feel it draining from her body. Since the accident Orla had suffered from frequent, often debilitating headaches and this one was turning into a whopper. No doubt stress and exhaustion had conspired together and she wanted Tonino gone before he witnessed it go into full bloom.

When she answered, it took all her remaining strength not to let the pain in her head infect her voice. 'At least we can agree on that. Look, Tonino, can we call it a night? Finn's an early riser and I really need to get some sleep before he wakes up. Hopefully a good night's sleep will put us both in a better frame of mind and we can talk again in the morning about where we go from here.'

For a long time he didn't speak, just stared at her, his jaw clenched, firm lips tightly pursed, a pulse throbbing in his temple. 'Where we go is simple. We tell Finn I am his father and that from now on I am a permanent part of his life.'

'Fine.' At that point she would have agreed to anything to be rid of him. It felt as if she had a big bass drum bashing in her head.

The smile he gave chilled her to the bone. 'And, *dolcezza*, to be clear, if you attempt to leave my hotel with my son before the morning, I will have no hesitation in launching a full custody battle—and it's a battle I will win.'

He let himself out of the suite without a backwards glance.

Tonino took a long breath, arranged his features into what he hoped was a non-threatening expression and then knocked on Orla's door.

He'd done much thinking since leaving her suite, and as the hours had passed the rage inside him had subsided. His behaviour, he recognised, had not been much better than the behaviour he'd accused Orla of, albeit a different kind of abhorrence. For his son's sake, he needed to build bridges.

The door opened just as he raised his knuckles to knock on it a second time.

Orla looked at him as if he were something a stray cat had dragged in. 'What time do you call this?'

He took a beat to soak in the thick dark hair, all tousled and spilling over the thin pink robe wrapped around her slender form, and felt a thickening in his loins as he was taken back four years to their first morning together. They'd taken a shower and afterwards he'd expected her to lock herself in the bathroom to paint her face on as all his previous lovers had done. That she hadn't, that she'd been so comfortable in her skin and so comfortable with him not to feel the need to cover it, had evoked the strangest of feelings in him. Even today he couldn't explain what that feeling was, but he felt it again now as he stared at the pink, plump lips that had fascinated him as much as everything else about her had.

He'd wanted Orla with a needy desperation he'd never felt before or since. He could hardly believe those feelings were still alive in his veins.

Breathing through his mouth to protect his lungs from filling with her scent, Tonino stepped past her into the suite. 'You said Finn's an early riser. He must take after me.' Not that Tonino had had any sleep that night. How could he when he was still trying to comprehend what he'd discovered yesterday?

Forget that every component of his body was heightened for Orla, he was here for one reason only. His son.

'Tonino, it's six thirty.'

'I know.' He looked around the living area of the suite. 'Where is he?'

'His nurse has taken him for a walk around the gardens.'

'This early?'

'He's been awake for over an hour.'

If he'd known that he would have come earlier instead of pacing his own suite impatiently. 'When will he be back?'

'I don't know. It depends if there's anything out there that captures his interest.'

'He likes being outside?' There was so much to discover about his son. A whole three years' worth of living to be discovered, including his birth date.

'He loves it.' Orla padded over to the window and perched herself on the ledge. She cast a quick glance at Tonino before tucking a lock of hair behind her ear and looking out at the early-morning view. 'Unfortunately Ireland's reputation for rain is based on fact—we're not known as the Emerald Isle for nothing—so sunny days are to be cherished.'

'Marry me and he can have sunshine every day.'

She turned her gaze back to him sharply. 'What?'

Tonino sat himself down on an armchair and looked straight at her. 'I have been doing much thinking. I want Finn in my life permanently and the best way I can see to facilitate this is for you to marry me.'

CHAPTER FIVE

ORLA WAS GLAD she was sitting down. There was a good chance she would have fallen over in shock if she'd still been on her feet. 'Are you drunk?'

He didn't look drunk. His hair was damp and even sitting far from him on the windowsill she could smell the heady scent of freshly showered Tonino. She was certain that if she'd been placed in a room blindfolded and made to smell his scent, that alone would have been enough to unlock her memories of him.

He hadn't shaved but still looked razor-sharp, dark eyes clear and focused intently on her. The wedding suit he'd worn the day before had been replaced with charcoal chinos and a crisp navy shirt that fitted and enhanced his tall, muscular frame perfectly.

God help her but the man was a bigger sex bomb than her broken brain had remembered.

The four years that had passed since they'd conceived Finn had not been kind to Orla. The youthful body she'd taken for granted was now marked and scarred, unrecognisable from the body Tonino must remember. She'd never considered herself vain until she'd stood naked before a mirror for the first time after the accident and burst into tears at what had reflected back at her.

Where the time that had passed since Finn's conception had been cruel to her, for Tonino it had been kind. Incredibly kind. Adonis himself would look at Tonino and weep at the unfairness.

It had been Orla's suggestion that the nurse take Finn for a walk. She'd guessed Tonino would turn up early—although not this early—and had wanted to be ready for him. She'd wanted to be showered and dressed and armoured behind make-up. Instead he'd arrived at the same moment she'd been about to step into the bathroom for her shower and found her looking like a scruffy cat lady. She hadn't even brushed her hair. She'd bet good money that he'd done it deliberately to catch her off guard.

She knew she shouldn't care what she looked like in front of him but she did. Right then, her pride was all she had left.

Her shoddy appearance was just one more disadvantage she had against him and she could feel the heat of colour splash her face under the weight of his blatant scrutiny. At least her headache had gone so that was one small mercy.

'Marriage makes excellent sense,' he said with all the confidence of a man used to his words being heeded as if he really were Adonis.

Her stomach twisted violently. She empathised with him, she really did, but did he have to be so entitled and overbearing? And did her heart have to beat so hard and her skin thrum just to share the same air as him?

Speaking through gritted teeth, she said, 'You've known about Finn's existence for five minutes and you've spent most of that time threatening me and calling me a liar and now you want to marry me? Are you sure you're not drunk?'

His eyes didn't so much as flicker. 'I want my son to have my name and to be recognised as his father.'

'You can have that without marriage.'

'My son deserves…'

The turmoil that had been with her all the previous day

and had still been there the moment she'd opened her eyes that morning reached its peak. 'Will you stop with all this "my son" malarkey?' she suddenly exploded. 'You know nothing about Finn and for you to keep referring to him as *yours* is doing my head in!'

He straightened, his face twisting with contempt. 'If you hadn't selfishly kept him to yourself, I would already know everything about him. I *am* his father, Orla, and I will damned well be a part of his life and take on all the responsibility being his father entails.'

Her temper evaporated to be replaced by shame at her outburst. Bowing her head, she covered her face with her hands and breathed deeply, in and out, in and out, trying desperately to hold back the threatening tears. Only when she was certain that she could speak without opening the floodgates did she look at him again.

'I'm sorry,' she said quietly. 'I know you're his father. I know you have every right to be a part of his life but it's really hard to listen to all your threats and demands when you have no idea what our lives have been like and the struggles we've had to deal with. You can't just snap your fingers and expect me to roll over and go with it. You need to earn your right to be Finn's father.'

Just as she'd had to earn the right to be Finn's mother.

When Orla had finally been allowed home from the rehabilitation centre, Finn had been eighteen months old and, although too young to understand the concept of parenthood, he'd regarded Aislin as his mother. She would never admit it to Aislin or anyone but seeing her own child naturally gravitate to her sister had been unbearable. It had taken a good year before Finn had turned to Orla when he needed help or comfort.

Tonino's eyes narrowed. The weight of his scrutiny increased but she detected a softening in his stance. 'Then stop fighting me and do what's best for Finn.'

'That's all I've ever done.'

'Then *marry* me.'

Her heart beating fast, Orla found herself scrutinising Tonino with the same intensity he scrutinised her, trying hard to look past the breathtakingly gorgeous features for what was going on in his head. Unfortunately, the mind-reading powers she'd always hoped to one day achieve were as elusive as ever. 'Marriage is not the answer. An unhappy marriage does nothing but produce unhappy children. Finn's a happy child who's suffered enough disruption in his life.'

'There is no reason we could not be happy.' Eyes remaining fixed on her, he reclined back in his seat. 'We were good together once.'

'We were together for barely ten days.' She would not cause another argument by pointing out that in that time he'd actively let her believe a lie. 'We don't know each other.'

'We know the most important thing.'

'Which is?'

'Our compatibility.'

'Sorry?'

'You and me…' He hooked an ankle on a muscular thigh. Something glimmered in his eyes that sent Orla's pulses surging. His voice lowered to an appreciative murmur. 'I remember us as being extremely compatible.'

Something deep inside her heated and throbbed with such force that whatever she'd been about to say stuck on her tongue. Gazing into his eyes was like looking into a chocolate pool swirling with brilliance, and the tight pulsations heating her core spread through her veins and danced onto her skin, every nerve ending in her body stirring, every atom screaming loudly its agreement at his words.

Suddenly fearful of being hypnotised by the whirling

depths, Orla wrenched her gaze from him and stared back out of the window, trying her hardest to breathe normally.

She'd prepared herself for more threats and arguments. She had not been prepared for a proposal or caressing words. Given the sticky turmoil raging through her, she thought she preferred the threats and arguments.

Even with her back turned from him, she could feel the heat of his stare penetrating her skin.

Folding her arms across her chest, she rubbed her feeble biceps and closed her eyes.

She remembered waking in Tonino's arms the morning after their first night together, dazed but replete. She remembered the sensation that had flooded her veins and heated her skin at his touch.

But the actual memories of them being intimate together remained locked away. She hoped they never returned. She didn't think she could bear to remember how she had given herself to a man who'd only been using her for his own fun.

Dragging more air into her lungs, she cleared her throat. 'I don't want to marry you, period. It would be a disaster.'

Tonino had known getting Orla's agreement for marriage would be a long shot but once the idea had come to him, he'd recognised it as the answer to all their problems. Marriage would solve everything in a neat, orderly fashion. How could he be an effective father if he lived in a different country from his child?

He would have to work on her and make her see that it would be in Finn's best interest for them all to live under the same roof. Given a little time to dismantle the barriers between them, Orla would come around to his way of thinking. The chemistry that had drawn them together four years ago still burned. He felt its scorch with every word and look exchanged between them. And she felt it too.

Every time she tucked a strand of her hair behind her ears he was reminded of all the times she'd done that before and all the other little gestures he recognised as uniquely Orla.

She'd been a breath of fresh air in a world he'd never recognised as cynical until she'd entered it and liberated him. For ten magnificent days he had lived for the moment with the first woman he'd been intimate with who had no idea who he really was. Her every response had been organic. She'd been a virgin but making love to her for the first time…it had felt as if it were his first time too.

Their chemistry was the one thing he didn't need a lie detector for. The urge to touch her breathed through his skin and it took all his strength to keep his focus on the job at hand.

'If you won't marry me then I will come to Ireland with you and have my name added to Finn's birth certificate.' He would not accept anything less than being a true father to his son.

Her body immediately struck a defensive pose. 'That can wait.'

'No, *dolcezza*, it cannot.' Getting to his feet, he joined her at the window. She must have sensed his closeness for her back stiffened and she tucked a loose strand of hair behind her ear.

How many nights had he dreamt of that simple non-seductive gesture?

Orla was the only lover whose scent he could remember simply by closing his eyes. Close his eyes and he could remember the feel of her skin beneath his fingers.

Close his eyes and he could remember the bewilderment to find her gone.

He would close his eyes no more. With Orla, he needed to keep his eyes open and his wits sharpened. Whatever happened from this moment, he would never let her disappear again.

'I understand why I've not been named on it but it has to be done.' He couldn't force her to marry him—more was the pity—but he would do whatever was necessary to close off her options to flee.

Her head turned sharply to face him again. Tonino hadn't realised quite how close to her he'd positioned himself until he saw the sprinkling of freckles across her pretty nose.

'You understand…?' She swallowed. 'You believe me?'

'I spoke to Dante after I left you last night,' he admitted. 'He confirmed your story about the accident and your memory problems.'

Dante's confirmation had left him with a myriad emotions. There had been definite relief—Tonino's instincts all those years ago that Orla was of a different mould from the unscrupulous, duplicitous bitches who lived in his world had not been as off the mark as he'd come to believe—but there had been something else there too, something that had made him feel as if acid had been poured into his guts.

Orla's chest rose sharply then loosened slowly. She pressed her head against the window with a sigh. 'I suppose it's understandable you wouldn't take my word on it.'

'It doesn't change how I feel about you not telling me about the pregnancy,' he warned roughly. He doubted he would ever forgive her for that. 'However, I feel it is in Finn's best interest that I put that issue behind me.'

She gave a short bark of shaky laughter. 'Your magnanimity does you much justice.'

Eyeing her carefully, he rested his hands on the windowsill either side of her thighs, effectively trapping her. 'Are you being funny?'

Fresh colour heightened her cheeks. 'I'm wondering where the proof is that you ended your engagement to Sophia before you took me to bed.'

'I am not a cheat. I have never been unfaithful.'

'I'm supposed to take your word on this?'

'*Sì*. In my world, honour is everything. A man who cannot be taken at his word is no man at all.'

'Now you're being the funny one. Seriously? A man of your word? When you let me believe you were a humble hotel manager rather than a gazillionaire hotel owner?'

'I never lied to you, Orla. Not in words.'

'Well, that makes everything all right, then!' She smiled brightly but her breaths had shallowed. He moved his face closer to hear her next words. 'You didn't lie to me with words. Grand. You're only prepared to believe me about my amnesia because Dante's backed me up, but I'm supposed to take you at your word on everything simply because you say so. Can you not see why that makes me uncomfortable having you named as Finn's father on his birth certificate?'

A man could drown in the emerald-green pool swirling before him. Orla's robe had parted at her waist, exposing her smooth legs. His blood thickened to see her thighs covered only by a pair of pyjama shorts.

'All I want is to be a father to him.' *Dio*, his voice was hardly above a whisper either. 'Having legal recognition is important to me. I don't want to be forced into taking legal action to get it.'

She swallowed a number of times then croaked, 'That sounds like a threat.'

He clenched his tingling fingers into fists. If he extended either thumb he would be touching those delectable thighs. They were as close as they'd been on the dance floor and yet not a single part of their bodies touched.

Now he was the one to swallow, ridding himself of the moisture that had filled his mouth. 'A threat I have no wish to act on.'

Last night, when he'd been full of anger, all he could

think about were his rights and the fact that she had so cruelly kept him from his son. While his anger was still there—her insistence that she'd intended to tell him about the birth after the fact was something he doubted he'd ever believe—he could not escape the conclusion that she was correct that he didn't know his son. And his son didn't know him. Tonino and his mother's relationship might be strained these days but as a child he'd worshipped the ground she'd walked on. To have been ripped from her arms would have destroyed him.

'What do you intend to do with the legal recognition?' she whispered.

His face inched closer to hers. 'Be his father. Orla... I'm not going to launch a custody battle for him. All I want is to be involved.'

Her breaths quickened. 'You're not going to fight me?'

'Our trust issues are a two-way thing we both need to work on but I give you my word that, provided you play fair with me, I will not take Finn away from you.'

'That's still a threat. What does play fair even mean?'

Their faces had got so close he could smell the faint mintiness of her toothpaste.

'That you accept me as his father.'

A glazed quality washed over her eyes. Her face tilted, her voice dropping to a murmur. 'I do accept you as his father.'

'Then let us start again.' His lips buzzed and the tingles on his skin deepened as their mouths drew closer still. 'Put the past behind us for Finn's sake and look to the future...'

Right at the moment their lips brushed together, the door to Orla's suite opened and the nurse pushed Finn in.

'Have you not had your shower...? Oh!'

A bullet ricocheting through the suite could not have parted them more effectively.

Cheeks the colour of beetroot, Orla jumped off the windowsill and hurried to Finn, frantically tucking strands of hair behind both ears. 'Could you do me a favour, please, Rachel, and leave us alone for ten minutes?'

The nurse looked knowingly at Tonino. 'Sure.'

The two Irishwomen's conversation followed by the nurse's abrupt departure from the suite were mere noise in Tonino's head. The desire that had come so close to taking control of him had reversed as he stared at the tiny boy strapped in his wheelchair. Unlike the curious nurse, his innocence meant he had no idea his arrival had interrupted anything.

Orla knelt in front of him and carefully lifted him out. She carried him over to the sofa and placed him on her lap. 'Finn, do you remember me telling you that you had a daddy but that mummy lost him?'

Tonino gave her credit for infusing strength into her voice.

The little head nodded.

'And do you remember me telling you that one day we would find him?'

She'd told him *that*...?

Finn nodded again.

'Well... I've found him.'

The dark brown eyes that were so like his own found his. Tonino held his breath.

'Finn,' Orla continued. 'This man... Tonino...is your daddy.'

There was a long moment of silence where father and son did nothing but stare at each other. Finn's expression was one of frank curiosity.

Tonino waited with bated breath for his son to speak, waited for the little arms to open up and demand a carry as he'd done for his uncle in the cathedral.

He should have known better. Instead of the grand re-union he'd spent the night imagining, his son looked back at his mother and said, 'Play blocks now?'

CHAPTER SIX

ORLA HAD NO idea how she'd allowed herself to be steam-rollered into flying back to Ireland with Tonino on his private jet. The only fleeting satisfaction she'd found that day had been when she'd entered the jet's opulent cabin and stared into his eyes to airily say, 'Oh, it's just like Dante's plane.'

Saying that had been a sharp but welcome reminder that Tonino might come from an immensely powerful and wealthy family, but that her brother was also immensely rich and powerful. It was a reminder to herself as well as Tonino.

Having a brother was such a new aspect of her life that all too often she forgot that she had him in her corner as much as she had Aislin.

Four years ago, when she'd learned she was pregnant, Dante hadn't known of Orla's existence. She could never have turned to him for help back then. Now, if Tonino did try to pull a fast one and launch a custody battle, she wouldn't have to face it alone or without the means to fight back legally and financially.

Even if she didn't have Dante, she felt differently now than she had four years ago. Back then, she'd been a frightened wreck. If the accident had done nothing else, it had toughened her up.

She had a feeling she would need every ounce of her newfound strength to keep Tonino at arm's length.

They had been moments from kissing.

Kissing!

Her lips still tingled in anticipation of the kiss that had never come. Tonino had caught her in a moment of weakness, she told herself stubbornly. It had been early. Her headache had gone but she hadn't had nearly as much sleep as she needed, leaving her tired, which in itself had weakened her.

That her insides still felt like melted goo could also be explained. She didn't know how to explain it but there must be a rational reason for it somewhere.

As Finn and his nurse were flying home with them, conversation between Orla and Tonino was mercifully limited to pleasantries. Conversation between Tonino and the nurse was a different matter. While Orla read Finn a story, Tonino quietly peppered Rachel with questions about Finn's condition. There was no godly reason why this should irk Orla so much, but it did. Watching the nurse flick her hair as she answered him irked her even more. When Rachel giggled at a comment Tonino made, Orla tightened her grip on the book to prevent herself from throwing it at the pair of them.

Her silent irritation continued for the duration of the flight. Only when they were back on Irish soil and she breathed the familiar air did she manage to regain some of her usual calm.

She was on home territory now. This was her turf and the drive to her home in Dublin was short.

'Thanks for the lift,' she said with as much politeness as she could muster when his driver pulled up. 'What time shall I expect you in the morning?'

He arched a brow. 'Are you not going to invite me in?'

Oh, how badly she wanted to give him a blunt, 'No,'

but knew how ungracious that would seem. She tried to put herself in his shoes. She would want to see the home her child lived in if she were wearing them.

'If I must,' she answered, immediately feeling horrible for her churlish response. The horrible feeling lasted less than a second for Rachel visibly brightened.

'You can stay for a coffee,' Orla added, then immediately panicked as she thought of the jar of instant that had moved to Dublin with her from Kerry and had to be at least a year old.

'This is a nice house,' Tonino commented when he walked into the spacious entrance room. Set in a pretty, quiet, tree-lined street, Orla's home was airy and open-plan, cluttered with toys and books but nonetheless clean. It had a homely feeling he warmed to immediately.

'Thank you,' she muttered.

Crouching down to Finn's level, he touched the tiny hand lightly. 'How would you like to show me your room?'

Finn immediately looked to his mother for guidance. She gave a short but reassuring nod. 'You'll have to carry him—he can't do stairs, I'm afraid. His room's the first on the left.'

'I'll come with you,' the nurse offered.

'I'm sure Finn and I can manage,' he rebuffed pleasantly. His curiosity about the specifics of his son's condition had driven him to ask the nurse in detail about it, which he felt certain had annoyed Orla and contributed to the foul mood she'd fallen into on the flight over. For his part, Tonino felt liberated. Leaving Sicily with his child and future wife—he had no doubt that Orla would come round to his way of thinking on marriage—had lifted his spirits immeasurably.

Tonino unstrapped his son and gently lifted him into his arms. He didn't think he had ever held anything so precious and fragile and his heart bloomed to feel the tiny beating heart pressed against his chest. It bloomed even more when a skinny arm hooked around his neck.

Dark brown eyes that were a replica of his own stared at him solemnly. Tonino stared back, suddenly finding himself dumbstruck at the powerful emotions crashing through him.

Before he took the first stair, he looked at Orla and felt another crash of emotion punch through him.

Taking a deep breath, he carried his son upstairs and entered his bedroom.

It took a few moments before he could take another breath. Finn's bedroom was everything a child's room should be, with its dinosaur curtains, walls covered in dinosaur stickers and ceiling covered in glow-in-the-dark stars. A vast array of stuffed toys was crammed on shelves and in boxes, along with boxes of puzzles and games, boxes of building blocks, books…

But there was no escaping the bed with its bars, there to prevent Finn from rolling out, and no escaping the unobtrusive but recognisable cameras there to monitor him while he slept and no escaping the medical equipment Tonino would have to become familiar with.

There was no escaping that this was a room for a child with disabilities. His child. And, as Tonino took stock of it all, he made a vow to himself that he would do everything in his power to make his son's life as comfortable and as happy as he could.

For the second time in a day Orla had no idea how she'd come to allow Tonino to steamroller her into something, this time finishing the day together eating a Chinese takeaway. Indeed, at one point she'd thought she'd got rid of him—he'd taken one sip of his coffee, wrinkled his nose and then excused himself, saying he would be back. When he hadn't returned an hour later, she'd thought he'd checked into wherever he was staying and decided to stay put.

He'd returned while she was clearing up the mess made while feeding Finn his dinner, carrying a large box, which was revealed to be a coffee machine.

'Where did you get that from?' she'd asked in astonishment. 'It's Sunday. All the shops are closed.'

He'd had the audacity to wink at her before disappearing again, returning an hour later with the takeaway and a bottle of wine. 'I thought you must be hungry too,' he'd explained while making himself at home turning the oven on. 'I saw you only cooked for Finn.'

'I've not had a chance to go shopping,' she'd replied defensively while turning off the grill and switching the actual oven on.

A memory of the two of them sharing a Chinese takeaway in his Palermo apartment had hit her. For some unfathomable reason, tears had blurred her vision.

While their food had kept warm in the oven, he'd helped her give Finn a bath and put him to bed. Having him there in the close confinement of the bathroom then the confinement of Finn's bedroom had put her on edge. As hard as she'd tried only to concentrate on her son, she was acutely aware of every movement Tonino made.

It was only the shock of being in his orbit again and the shock of how close they'd come to kissing making her feel so edgy around him. That would lessen as she became accustomed to his presence in their lives. Sooner or later the tightness in her chest would lessen too and her heartbeat would find its natural rhythm when with him, rather than the erratic tempo it adopted every time she caught his eye or captured a whiff of his spicy cologne. He'd clearly meant what he'd said early that morning about them starting over. He'd spoken to her with only courtesy since. If he still felt anger towards her, he hid it well.

And now they were sitting at her dining table, Tonino clearly so ravenous he didn't care that their food had lost much of its moisture, comfortably drinking his way through the wine while she stuck to water. Orla ate as much as she could manage but it was hard to swallow when her insides were so cramped, hard to work her fork from her hand to her mouth while fighting her gaze from staring at the hunk of a man devouring his food opposite her.

It was the first time they'd been alone since Finn had returned from his walk nearly thirteen hours ago. Since they'd nearly kissed. Without Finn or his nurse's physical presence to distract her, Orla found her awareness of Tonino becoming more than a distraction, throwing her back four years when she'd spent ten days with her entire being consumed by this one man.

'Do you feel better now?' he asked after he'd demolished the leftovers.

'What do you mean?'

He shrugged nonchalantly. 'Only that if looks could kill, the looks you were giving me on the plane over would have struck me dead.'

She had the grace to blush. Not looking at him, she muttered, 'I just wanted to get home.'

He nodded musingly. 'Of course. You were missing your home.'

'Exactly.'

'Have you lived here long?'

'Four months.' Orla, mortified that he'd picked up on her earlier bad mood, mustered something she hoped resembled a smile.

'Dante bought it for you?'

'Aislin bought it.' She wasn't about to explain that the money to purchase it had come via Dante paying her sister a million euros to pretend to be his fiancée for a weekend. Of course, Aislin and Dante had fallen in love over that weekend for real, but the lead-up to their falling in love was a private matter between the two of them. Having been the subject of gossip for the entirety of her life, it was not something Orla ever indulged in. 'Dante paid for it to be made Finn-friendly.'

She finished her water and tried not to stare longingly at the remaining wine in the bottle. Alcohol, she was sure, would help her relax. Or, as was more likely, send her to sleep.

Relaxing in Tonino's company was something that was going to take time. A lot of time.

Now that most of the memories of their time together had returned, she found herself replaying it. Much of it felt as vivid as if it had happened only days ago. She'd been relaxed with him then. She'd found an ease in his company she had never felt with anyone other than Aislin before. It had been as if a stranger she'd known for ever had walked into her life. A stranger who'd made her bones melt with nothing but a look.

It horrified her to find her bones still melted for him. Every time he reached for his glass and his muscles flexed beneath his shirt the baser part of her melted too. Every time she caught his eye her erratically thrumming heart would jolt. Her lips still tingled for the kiss that had never come.

'You and Dante have only got to know each other recently, is that correct?' he asked.

Lord help her but his voice melted her too.

She nodded. 'I always knew about him, but he knew nothing of me. He had no idea he had a sister.'

'Why didn't you find him four years ago?'

'I couldn't go up to a stranger and say, *Hello, I'm your long-lost sister*, could I? It wouldn't have been fair.'

He pulled a rueful face. 'I suppose. So, tell me, was your real reason for being in Sicily to find your father?'

She gave another nod.

'You'd never met him before?'

'I wasn't allowed.'

'Why not?'

She shrugged. 'I was his dirty little secret.'

He winced at her descriptor. 'What changed? What spurred you into seeking him?'

'I became an adult.' She smiled wryly. 'For the first time ever, I had a couple of weeks ahead of me with nothing to do. I woke up one morning and thought to myself that it's now or never.'

'Did you meet him?'

'No. He was abroad when I visited on my first day there. I tried again when you went to Tuscany but I don't remember what happened.'

'So you might have met him?'

She shook her head. 'Aislin always told me I didn't.' She took a deep breath. 'I know it in my heart too. Every time I've thought of him since I've wanted to cry.'

Tonino stared at the downcast face with the lips pulled tightly together and his heart twisted. 'Why didn't you share this with me at the time? I could have helped you. My father and your father were old friends.'

'How was I supposed to know that? You never told me who you really were.' Her rebuke, although politely delivered, hit the mark.

'We were lovers, Orla. You should have told me your real reason for being in my country.'

His mention of them having been lovers sent colour careering over her neck and cheeks. 'Yes, well, you should have told me you actually owned the hotel rather than just managing it but there you are.'

'There we are.' He winced and mock saluted his agreement, admiring her quick, tart retort. The Orla sitting in front of him had a much sharper tongue than the Orla he remembered. 'Two people who kept things close to their chests while still getting naked together.'

'Don't go there,' she warned. The colour now flamed so brightly he could warm his hands on her face.

'If we hadn't gone there we would never have created Finn together.' He downed the last of his wine and grinned.

She smiled sweetly, then, in a perfectly pitched saccharine voice, said, 'And on that happy note, it's time for you to leave.'

'Are you kicking me out?'

'There's no food left and it's late.'

'Are you not worried I won't have anywhere to stay?'

'No. And you're not staying here, if that's what you're trying to wrangle.'

'I wouldn't dream of it. But, please, let your mind rest easy—I have a place to stay.'

'Good. Best you get going to it.'

'Without an after-dinner coffee?'

'Caffeine is the last thing I need.'

'In that case I shall return early in the morning for it.'

'If you turn up as early as you did this morning, the only thing you'll get is a long wait on the doorstep.'

He got to his feet and gave another mock salute. 'Until the morning.'

'Are you still here?'

Grinning, Tonino let himself out. He'd reached his car when he heard the front door lock behind him.

'You are possibly the most infuriating man in the world,' Orla snapped when she opened the front door the next morning.

Tonino looked at his watch and gave an expression of such innocence that she had to bite her cheeks not to laugh out loud. 'You told me not to come as early as I did yesterday.'

'So you come half an hour later? Seriously? It's seven o'clock.'

'And you're up and dressed and looking beautiful.' She looked as fresh and as beautiful as the clear blue skies covering Dublin that morning. Dressed in a knee-length leaf-green jersey dress, her hair loose around her shoulders, her pretty green eyes enhanced with a touch of mascara, a brush of colour over the high cheekbones. Fresh, beautiful and damned irresistible.

One day soon, he vowed, Orla would open a door to him with a smile and greet him with a kiss rather than a scolding.

Late into the night he'd lain in his bed thinking back over their time together. The more he'd remembered, the more he'd come to understand why the few affairs he'd had since she'd disappeared had fizzled out with barely a whimper. Their affair had hung over him. It had shadowed him doggedly. Seducing Orla into marrying him would allow him to put the shadows to bed in more ways than one. He would have her in his bed and his child permanently in his life. The fact he would never be able to trust her was irrelevant. He didn't need to trust her. He just needed to marry her, the final step that would prevent her ever disappearing from his life with his son again.

Finn was in his high chair at the dining table. He greeted Tonino with a smile and a wave.

'I was just feeding Finn his breakfast. Why don't you make yourself a coffee while we finish up?' Orla strove to keep her tone polite but she could have cheerfully strangled Tonino. She wished she could say it was some sixth sense that he would turn up stupidly early again that had had her awake before Finn but it hadn't been. It had been the dream of them, in bed together, that she'd wrenched herself out of that had accomplished that feat. She'd sat straight upright, heart pounding, burning and throbbing on the inside, not knowing if the dream had been a replay of something real or just her subconscious imagination, and dived straight into the shower to wash the burning feeling away.

She'd cleaned her skin, but her insides…

Mush. Her insides had been a hot, sticky mush the water couldn't touch. They were still mush.

Her hands were shaking. She could barely hold the spoon to feed Finn.

'Coffee?' Tonino's deep voice reverberated in her ear.

'No. Thank you. Did you want something to eat?' She ground her toes into the floor in a futile effort to stop her right knee shaking too. 'There's bread and cereal in the cupboard.'

Dark brown eyes met hers. 'I had something before I left the hotel.'

'Where are you staying?'

'At Bally House.'

'The hotel?'

'*Sì.*'

'You lucky thing.'

'You have been there?'

'I wish,' she said reverently. Bally House Hotel was once a medieval village with its own church and flour mill. A huge renovation undertaken a few years ago had transformed it into Ireland's premier hotel, the destination of choice for A-list stars to marry in. 'I tried to talk Aislin into getting married there but she wasn't having any of it—she was set on marrying in Sicily.'

'We can marry there.'

'We're not getting married.'

'I am confident that one day soon you will come around to my way of thinking, *dolcezza.*'

'And I am confident that you are full of misplaced ego. I will not marry you, end of subject.'

Mercifully, the nurse descended the stairs, cutting the conversation short.

Less mercifully, the look in Tonino's eyes told her this was a subject he had no intention of dropping.

CHAPTER SEVEN

'ARE YOU OKAY?'

Ever since they'd left the government offices where they'd officially added Tonino's name as father on Finn's birth certificate, Orla had lapsed into silence. Her head was turned from him, her body pressed against the door as if she were preparing to make an escape the moment the car came to a stop.

'I'm fine.' Her tone suggested she was far from fine.

'You do know this is for the best?'

She twisted her head to meet his stare and sighed. 'Yes. I do know that. Whether you believe me or not, I always intended to tell you about Finn. Always.'

Tonino looked at his son—now his *legal* son—fast asleep in his car seat.

He wanted to believe her. For their son's sake. But he couldn't escape the one verifiable fact that she'd made the deliberate choice to keep him in the dark about the pregnancy before the accident. Blaming Sophia's deliberate sabotage was too easy—and he did believe that Sophia had confronted her; it was exactly the kind of thing the poisonous bitch would do—Orla should have told him about the pregnancy whether she believed he was engaged or not. Instead she had chosen to swallow Sophia's lies and deprive him of the wonder of experiencing the pregnancy with her, which in turn had led to depriving him of over the first three years of his son's life. Tonino, as his parents would testify, had never been one for forgiving or forgetting.

'Can I ask you something?' she said after a long period of time had passed when he'd left her assertion unacknowledged.

He loosened his tense shoulders and inclined his head. 'Anything.'

'Last night you said our fathers were old friends. Did you know Salvatore well?'

'Well enough. Why do you ask?'

'I know so little about him. I don't like to ask Dante because I can see it makes him uncomfortable. I think he feels guilty that they had such a great relationship while I was this dirty little secret.'

He could understand why she felt like that. No one had known of Salvatore Moncada's secret love child, not even Tonino's own father, who had been Salvatore's closest friend.

He wondered how his father would react when he learned Salvatore's illegitimate daughter was the mother of his grandchild. Probably with open arms. His mother too. There hadn't been a single conversation between Tonino and his parents in recent years where the subject of him settling down and having babies hadn't come up, the implication being he needed to find a suitable replacement for the fiancée he'd so callously thrown away. In his parents' eyes, Sophia had been perfect. Beautiful and rich and from a good Sicilian family. Their engagement had been celebrated in the same way the British celebrated a royal engagement. Their fury at him ending it had been off the charts. They'd taken it personally. They'd accused him of disrespecting the family name and destroying the decades-long friendship with the Messinas. There had been threats. At one point he'd thought his mother was going to slap his face.

That marriage to Sophia would have seen Tonino spend his life in misery hadn't concerned either of them.

With a sigh, he tried to think positively of his parents. He'd had the security of their unconditional love for the first thirty years of his life whereas Orla had never met her father and as for her mother…where was she? She'd missed Aislin's wedding. Orla rarely spoke of her. She might as well not exist.

'Your father was a man of many contradictions,' he told her heavily.

'In what way?'

He thought of the best way to put it before saying, 'He was a womaniser and a gambler. But he was also a great raconteur. He could tell the most boring story and make it funny. He was not a man anyone would trust to lend money to if they wanted to get it back and definitely not someone any man could trust to leave his wife alone in a room with.'

Her eyes widened with alarm. 'He was a sex pest?'

'No. Women loved him. Some loved him a little too much. He broke many hearts.'

Her lips tightened as she considered this before giving a decisive nod. 'He didn't break my mother's heart.'

'Then she was clever enough not to involve her heart.'

'But not clever enough not to get herself pregnant by a married man.' She closed her eyes and rested her head against the leather upholstery. 'Still, who am I to judge her for it? I did exactly the same thing.'

'I wasn't married, and neither was I engaged,' he told her firmly. 'And I shouldn't have to tell you that you didn't get pregnant on your own. We were both there.'

She twisted her head again to look back at him. The faintest trace of colour flared on her cheeks as she asked, 'Didn't we use protection?'

'Of course we did.'

'Then how did I end up pregnant?'

'We weren't always as careful as we should have been…' He thought of the few times they'd come together in their sleep, Tonino already deep inside her before waking fully and realising he hadn't put a condom on. He'd withdrawn to sheath himself, knowing even then what a huge risk they'd taken. It was a risk he had never taken before or since, half asleep or otherwise.

Gazing into her confused green eyes, he felt the burn in his loins that had been such a huge part of him in their time together afresh and found himself leaning closer to her, close enough that the soft scent of her perfume coiled into his aroused senses. 'Do you not remember?'

The colour on her cheeks became a burn to match what was happening in his loins. 'No.'

'But you remember us?'

'I remember most of it, but I don't remember…' she swallowed '…the actual act.'

He leaned a little closer still and lowered his voice. 'There was more than one act.'

Her jaw clenched while her eyes darkened and her voice lowered to match his. 'I don't remember anything we did in bed.'

'It wasn't always in a bed.'

Now her face inched closer to him, her voice dropping to a whisper. 'I don't need to know the details.'

'But I can help you remember.'

Her lips parted. Their faces were so close that he could feel the heat of her breath brushing like the lightest petal against his mouth. And then she closed her eyes tightly, reared away from him and snapped her eyes back open with a glare. 'I don't want to remember, thank you very much.'

He laughed at this blatant lie. The constriction in his trousers burned but he welcomed it. He would bet his favourite house that Orla was suffering the feminine version of his burn. 'Scared you'll remember how good it was?'

'More like I'm afraid to remember how awful it was,' Orla retorted as airily as she could, resisting the urge to cross her legs tightly for fear that he would know *why* she was crossing them.

She'd been about to kiss him. Her mouth had practically salivated in anticipation. The most intimate part of her had throbbed then flooded with a warmth that still tingled acutely.

'The brain is a funny thing, but it does try to protect the body it's encased in,' she added.

Her attempt to stab at the heart of his ego ended in failure. His voice became a sensuous purr that sent fresh tingles careering over her already sensitised skin. 'I can help you remember, *dolcezza*. All you have to do is say the word.'

'And what word would that be? Do I wave my hand in the air, yell out "sex" and you whisk me to bed?' She regretted her flippant remark the moment it left her mouth.

Tonino leaned in even closer, eyes gleaming. 'That sounds good to me. Or you can do what you did on our third night together.'

Orla knew she was taking the bait of the trap he'd laid but was unable to stop herself from whispering, 'What did I do?'

The gleam deepened, the strong nostrils flaring as he stared at her appreciatively and put his mouth to her ear. 'You performed a seductive striptease for me then lay on my bed naked and touched yourself—'

'I did no such thing,' she cut in angrily, rearing away from him. She would *never* do such a thing. Hadn't her grandmother always told her that anything but straight penetrative sex within the confines of marriage was for harlots, the inference being harlots like Orla's mother? For sure, Tonino was the sexiest man she'd ever set eyes on and for sure her body reacted in wanton ways she'd never dreamed of, but to touch herself for his titillation...?

Never.

Please, God, let it not be true.

Now Tonino was the one to rear back. The look he cast her only made her feel more mortified. '*Dio*, you really don't remember, do you?'

The car came to a stop.

Right on cue, Finn woke up.

Cheeks flaming with humiliation, Orla removed Finn from his car seat. She was halfway up the steps of the medical centre for his physiotherapy appointment when she realised she'd failed to put him in his wheelchair and still had him in her arms.

Tonino, Orla decided, was some kind of mind guru. For the third time in two days he'd steamrollered her into doing something she'd thought she would never agree to, in this case, leaving Finn with the duty nurse and letting him take her out to dinner.

He'd had those powers over her from the beginning. When he'd knocked on her hotel door four years ago and asked if he could take her out for coffee the next morning, the automatic refusal that had formed on her tongue had turned into a beaming, 'I would like that.'

She hated that the same excitement thrummed through her veins as it had then. She hated that she'd found herself trying over and over to capture the memories of them making love. And she hated that whenever she caught Tonino's gaze, his knowing glimmer suggested he knew exactly what she was thinking.

She especially hated that she'd spent an age getting ready. This was not a date. This was dinner. A chance for them to talk with privacy about how they were going to manage the future. She'd still spent an inordinate amount of time dithering over what to wear. In the end she'd settled on a pretty long-sleeved rust-coloured blouse and smart, fitted navy trousers, the two items separated by a chunky belt. She'd forgone her usual flat shoes for a pair of black heels. Outfit decided on, she'd then spent an even longer amount of time dithering over how to wear her hair and how much make-up to apply. She'd ended up leaving her hair loose and applying a little eyeliner and mascara, a touch of blusher and a nude lipstick. Dressed up but not overdone. There was no way Tonino could look at her and think she was dressing to attract him.

And yet, the appreciation in his eyes when she'd greeted him at the front door had almost had her running back up the stairs to change into a nun's habit. Only the fact that she didn't actually possess a nun's habit had stopped her.

'Where are we going?' she asked when she realised they'd left the city and were driving through Ireland's beautiful countryside. That was one thing she missed about her old home in Kerry—the scenery. The home she'd spent her life in had backed onto forest. They had awoken every morning to the sound of birds chirruping. Now she awoke to the sounds of cars hooting impatiently at each other.

'You will see.'

Soon they'd turned up a narrow road lined with woodland. A mile later, the trees thinned and somehow curved into an arch to reveal a sprawling stone structure and immaculately kept sweeping gardens artfully filled with stone and marble benches and ornaments, a vast beautiful pond filled with waterlilies and with a wooden bridge traversing it. Dotted around the main structure were small cottages…

Her heart fluttered with excitement as she asked the question she already knew the answer to. 'Is this Bally House?' The pictures she had seen did not do it justice. It was like driving into a magical fairy tale.

His answering smile was definitely smug. *'Sì.'*

The driver pulled up in the large courtyard. As she climbed out, Orla noticed with a pang the young couple holding hands as they walked slowly over a meandering path, oblivious to anyone but each other under the setting sun.

Her fingers felt as if they'd had magnets inserted into the tips, pulling them towards Tonino's hands. She folded her arms across her chest and rammed her hands between her sides and her arms.

They stepped into a large reception area. Three people working at the desk clocked their entrance and, in unison, straightened. The shortest of them, a middle-aged woman, hurried over to greet them.

'Would you like a drink in the bar or to go straight to your table?' she asked.

'We'll go straight to our table,' Tonino replied. 'Thank you, Lorna.'

He'd been there one night. How could he be on first-name terms with the hotel staff already? Orla wondered in amazement. And, as she followed him over polished-oak flooring through a warren of further reception rooms filled with artful antique furniture and dark leather sofas, she wondered how he knew his way around so well. Did he have an inbuilt satnav?

When they reached the huge dining room, the maître d' greeted Tonino by name and bowed his head respectfully to Orla before leading them to a corner table.

Exposed stone walls, giant fireplaces and thick carpet all drove the feeling of the finest of luxury and yet the restaurant managed to contain the rustic appeal of its setting within it. Each table was set with its own candelabra and she counted six chandeliers hanging from the beamed ceiling.

'Your casement of wine arrived this afternoon,' the maître d' said as he placed leather-bound menus before them. 'Shall I bring you a bottle of it?'

'Yes, and anything Miss O'Reilly wants.'

'Just still water for me, please,' she said.

'Very good.' With another bow, the maître d' turned on his heel and vanished.

Immediately, Orla stopped pretending to read her menu and leaned forward to ask conspiratorially, 'You had your own wine delivered here?'

He looked at her thoughtfully. 'Do you remember that business trip to Tuscany I took four years ago?'

'On my last day in Sicily?' An image flashed in her head of her sitting on the steps of her father's villa. She'd been waiting...

Waiting for what?

Tonino nodded. 'I went to see a run-down monastery ripe for conversion.'

The image disappeared. Orla swallowed moisture into her dry throat. 'Oh?'

'I bought it. I converted it into a hotel and spa and turned the land into a vineyard. Our first wine bottles have just been produced.'

'That's what you've had delivered here?'

'Yes.'

'Wow. I'd heard the management here tried to cater to all their guests' whims but allowing you to have a crate of your own wine...'

'*I'm* the management, Orla.'

Confusion creased her brow.

'I bought Bally House three years ago.' Tonino had no idea why he held his breath after this confession.

A long time passed where all Orla did was stare at him with open-mouthed shock. Then she leaned forward. '*You* own Bally House? But how? Why? When we met you'd never been to Ireland.'

'The way you described your country intrigued me. When Bally House came up for sale, the details were sent to me—I have scouts who look worldwide for investment opportunities—I visited, saw its potential and put an offer in.'

The maître d' returned to the table with the wine bottle in hand. A waiter followed with a bottle of still water.

'Try some of the wine,' Tonino urged. 'Please. I would like to hear your thoughts.'

She pulled a forlorn face. 'Alcohol doesn't agree with me any more.'

'In what way?'

'The first glass of wine I had after the accident went straight to my head. I passed out. I've not dared drink more than a sip of it since.'

'Then try only a sip of this.'

She rolled her slim shoulders then relaxed with a small laugh. 'Okay, but if I don't like it, don't blame me.'

'You will like it.'

The laugh she gave this time was louder and huskier. When he filled a third of the glass with the burgundy liquid, she shook her head and chided, 'Are you trying to get me drunk?'

'It is up to you how much of it you drink.'

Eyes locked on his, she picked the glass up and delicately sniffed the contents. Tonino found himself holding his breath as she put it to her delectable lips and took a sip. Long seconds passed before she swallowed.

'Well?' he asked. Orla was the first person unconnected to his business or the world of wine to try it.

'It's rank.'

'Rank?' The unfamiliar word did not strike him as complimentary.

'Gross. Disgusting. So disgusting that I think I should

try a bit more to reinforce just how gross it is.' She put the glass back to her lips.

'You're playing with me,' he accused.

The smile she bestowed him with was the most genuine she'd given him since their eyes had met in the cathedral. It dived straight into his chest and pierced it. She took another small drink, put the glass on the table and tilted her head to say softly, 'It's beautiful.'

'So are you.'

Their eyes held. Something passed between them that sent his pulses soaring.

Only the arrival of the waiter at their table broke it. 'Are you ready to order?'

CHAPTER EIGHT

WHEN ORLA TASTED her starter of cured salmon, crab and smoked roe all wrapped in the most delicate pancake, she thought she'd died and gone to heaven. When she took her first bite of her main course of aged fillet of Irish beef and the shiitake tart accompanying it, she decided that if this was heaven, she wanted to stay. If reaching heaven would allow her to drink Tonino's wine without conking out, then even better. She hadn't been joking when she called it beautiful. It was easily the most delicious wine she'd ever tasted, and she wished with all her heart that she could have more of it.

'Were you not tempted to make the menu more Sicilian?' she asked.

'This hotel could not be more Irish,' he said dryly. 'I don't think a Sicilian theme would work, do you?'

She shrugged. 'I know nothing of hotels and restaurants. I was just curious. How many hotels do you own?'

'Eighteen. I'm in the process of buying another on the Greek island of Agon. I'm flying there tomorrow to deal with some paperwork.'

'You're leaving tomorrow?' That was *not* disappointment she felt.

'First thing in the morning.' He grinned. 'Are you going to miss me?'

'Like a migraine.'

His laughter filled her ears and sent a warm feeling trickling through her veins. 'I was going to discuss this with you. I will be away for two days. That will give my staff enough time to set up a bedroom for Finn—when I return to Sicily I want Finn to come—'

'That's not possible,' she interrupted. In less than a second, all the warmth in her veins had solidified into ice.

'Why not?' He asked it pleasantly enough, but she detected the underlying warning in his tone.

'It's too soon. He has medication and…'

'There is nothing he has here that he cannot have in Sicily provided we prepare well for it. It will only be for a week.'

'Only a week?' she echoed faintly. Was it her imagination or were the restaurant's stone walls starting to blur and spin? As much as she was enjoying this meal, being apart from Finn for an evening felt as if she'd had a limb removed. How was she supposed to cope for a whole week without him?

'*Sì*. I can clear my schedule for a week so Finn and I can get to know each other but then my schedule is packed with appointments that cannot be rearranged,' he continued as if she hadn't spoken. 'The weekend after that my parents are hosting a party for all the family to meet my sister's new baby—'

'Giulia had another baby?' Orla interrupted again, startled, remembering that four years ago Tonino had been excited for the forthcoming birth of Giulia's first child.

'She had a baby girl last week.'

'You never said.'

He shrugged. 'We have had other things to talk about, *dolcezza*.'

'I know, but a new baby is something to celebrate.' Orla had nearly hit the roof in excitement when Aislin told her she was pregnant.

'And it will be. The party is a good opportunity to introduce Finn to everyone. There will be lots of small children for him to play with including my other nieces and nephews.'

'How many do you have now?' she asked faintly. He'd spun her on the dance floor to face his family while he rebuked her for keeping Finn from them, but that had been the only time since their lives had collided back together that he'd mentioned them.

'Five in total.'

Feeling another headache starting to form, Orla rubbed her temples. 'I don't know if the nurses will be able to travel at such short notice.'

'There are private nurses in Sicily. It will be easy to arrange. Which brings me to my next point—the funding of Finn's medical care.'

'Dante pays for anything not covered by our healthcare system.'

'I thought as much.' His eyes narrowed. 'How did you fund it before you found him?'

'We didn't. It's what made us seek Dante out in the first place.' She took a deep breath and tried to get the panic under control. How could she let Tonino take Finn to Sicily? It was too soon. She wasn't ready to let him go. 'When his father—my father—died, Aislin and I were skint. The insurance company was fighting over any pay-out from the accident. Aislin convinced me I was entitled to some of my father's estate. Neither of us knew he'd gambled most of his wealth away. Once Dante learned about me and Finn he became our knight in shining armour. Before he stepped in, Aislin and I were basically on our own.'

Thinking about the large number of Irish guests at Aislin and Dante's wedding, Tonino found this hard to believe. 'What about the rest of your family?'

'Spectacularly useless.' She rolled her eyes and shook

her head but there was no malice in the gestures. 'Most of them live miles away and have their own worries.' To his surprise, she reached for her wine glass and drank a tiny bit more before inhaling deeply and seeming to brace herself. 'Tonino. Please. I'm not trying to be awkward but it's too soon for you to be taking Finn to Sicily.'

'I would say it's too late. I have been incredibly patient, *dolcezza*...'

She snorted inelegantly.

'But Finn has been deprived of half his heritage. It is time for him to learn the Valente half of himself.'

She dropped her stare. When she looked back at him he couldn't tell if it was anguish or anger that was the most prevalent emotion in her eyes. 'Is that what this evening is all about?' she accused. 'A nice meal together to lull me into a false sense of security before you snatch my son from me?'

'You need to get some perspective,' he said coolly.

'Perspective?' She clutched at her hair and looked as if she was preparing to shout at him. Thankfully the waiter arrived at their table to clear their plates away, giving her a few moments to calm herself.

'Tonino, please, just listen to me,' she beseeched. 'Tonight is the first time in two years that I've left Finn for longer than half an hour. I've spent the evening stopping myself from phoning home to check on him every five minutes. I know I must sound selfish, but I can't...' To his shock, tears filled her eyes. She closed them and took another long breath. 'I don't know how I'll cope without him for a whole week. And then to do it all again a week later?'

Cope without him?

Suddenly everything became clear.

Leaning forward, Tonino stared at her until her damp eyes met his. 'Orla, I never said I would take him to Sicily without you.'

Confusion creased her brow. 'Didn't you? But you only spoke about Finn and getting to know him and introducing him to your family and the party and everything.'

He muttered a curse under his breath. 'I want all these things but I cannot believe you would think me cruel enough to take him without you. He hardly knows me. It would terrify him.' And, he could see, destroy Orla. 'You seem to have a habit of assuming the worst about me.'

'I'm sorry…in fairness, you did threaten a custody battle,' she reminded him. 'It's not an easy thing to forget.'

He drummed his fingers against his wine glass. 'I accept that, but those threats were made in anger and I've assured you since that I don't want to put Finn through that. Stop thinking the worst and accept that, where our son is concerned, you and I are of the same mind—we only want what's best for him.'

She slumped in her chair and pressed her palm to her forehead. 'I can be such an eejit.'

'Sì,' he agreed.

A smile unexpectedly formed on his lips as he recalled the first time he'd heard that particular Irish insult from her. They'd been driving in his car—well, not *his* car but one of the staff cars he'd bought for his hotel staff to do their errands in—with the roof down when he'd made a comment about something, he didn't remember what. He did, however, remember Orla lightly punching him on his biceps and calling him an eejit.

That had been one hell of a good day. The sun had blazed as hot as their passion and through it all had been the knowledge that this sweet, funny, beautiful woman had wanted him only for himself. She had wanted Tonino the man, not Tonino Valente the billionaire hotelier. She hadn't wanted to be in his bed to join the Valente dynasty, she hadn't been playing the role of a chess piece taking a strategic move with the ultimate hope of becoming his queen.

She'd just wanted him.

The memories filled him with a warmth that had him reaching out to cover her hand. 'You and Finn come as a package. I accept that. Now you need to accept that I'm part of that package too and that means telling Dante his money isn't needed any more. I'll be paying for everything now.' Before she could protest, he added, 'I'm Finn's father. You two are my responsibility.'

She tugged her hand from his and wrapped her fingers around her glass of water. 'If you want to pay for Finn's care then I won't argue, but I'm not your responsibility.'

'You're the mother of my child.'

'Exactly. I'm not *your* child. I'm an adult. Dante gave me my share of what was left of our father's estate and got his lawyers to make the insurance company pay out. I have money of my own right now.'

'How much?'

'Enough to keep me going for a few years.'

'Marry me and you need never worry about money again.'

She gave a splutter that could have been laughter or exasperation. 'How many times are we going to have this conversation before you get it in your thick head that I'm not going to marry you?'

'My mother assured me throughout my childhood that it's a woman's prerogative to change her mind. I have every intention of changing yours.'

'Good luck with that. I'm a stubborn mule.'

'And I've never been able to resist a challenge.' He poured himself some more wine and contemplated her lazily. Now that he'd put her mind at ease about her travelling to Sicily with Finn, she'd visibly relaxed.

She had the peaceful air about her that he remembered from before and for a moment he could almost imagine they were the same two people they'd been then.

But of course they weren't. He wasn't the same man. And she wasn't the same woman. Her memory was mostly repaired and she looked the same as she'd done four years ago but her movements had lost much of their old grace. She tired easily. Even the way she ate, holding her knife and fork so tightly, cutting her food with such concentration…

'You were six months pregnant when the accident happened?' he asked carefully.

She nodded. A sad smile curved her cheeks. 'Finn was born by emergency Caesarean. He spent eight weeks in Intensive Care. They didn't think he was going to make it.' A spark flashed in her eyes. 'But our son's a fighter. He proved them all wrong.'

Feeling his stomach clench then churn, he took a moment to ask, 'And you? Was there a danger you wouldn't have made it?'

She hesitated before giving the tiniest of nods. 'I was in a coma for three weeks and then under sedation for another month. But I'm fine now,' she hastened to add. 'And things are massively better with Finn too. We know what we're dealing with and I always think that's half the battle.'

'Who looked after him while you were in hospital? Aislin?' She'd already said Aislin had been the one to register Finn's birth.

She gave another nod. 'She quit her degree—quit her life—to look after us both. When I finally came home, she taught me how to care for him. Finn is my miracle. Aislin is my angel.'

She'd already described Dante as her knight in shining armour. So what did that make Tonino?

He thought it better not to ask.

'Where was your mother in all this?'

An emotion he couldn't determine flittered over her face. 'I haven't seen my mother in seven years. As far as I know she's in San Francisco.'

'She wasn't there for you?'

She picked up her wine glass and stared at the burgundy liquid. 'I don't think she's ever been there for me. Aislin and I spent more time with our grandparents next door than we ever did with her. Two weeks after Aislin finished high school our mother scarpered to Asia and never came back.'

Even the edge to her voice, never mind her words, struck Tonino like a blow. It was a tone he'd never heard before and he peered closely at her. 'Never?'

The misery he witnessed on her face struck him like a second blow.

She swallowed before answering. 'Put it this way, she's never met Finn.'

A grandmother who'd never met her only grandchild? Surely not? 'What about when you were in the coma and he was in Intensive Care?'

'She texted Aislin for updates.'

That struck him even harder than Orla's other revelations.

He imagined her hooked to machines, locked in her own head, unable to communicate, unable to respond to anything and his heart swelled so greatly it became an effort to breathe. To think her own mother had abandoned her to that fate without one single visit defied all humanity.

Little wonder Orla struggled to trust and open up to people. Of the two people whose job had been to love her and raise her, one had rejected her in the womb, the other doing the bare essentials until she could leave for good.

His throat moved before he asked hoarsely, 'How did the accident happen?'

'I don't remember.' She shook her head as if clearing her ears. 'That period is still a blur. I don't even remember where I was going. I know it must have been somewhere important because there was a bad storm and I'm not comfortable driving in bad weather. I know I had a collision with a Transit van but I don't remember anything of the accident itself.' Suddenly she grinned. It made her whole face light up. 'Probably just as well. I'm terrible around blood.'

He returned the grin, glad of the lightening of mood.

But he couldn't escape the feeling in his guts that there was more to Orla's injuries than she was sharing with him.

As they left the cosy warmth of the Bally House Hotel restaurant, the breezy chill in the air outside came as something of a shock, especially as Orla had neglected to bring a jacket with her. She looked up at the sky and was disappointed to find all the stars hidden under thick cloud. Summer was practically over, she thought wistfully.

Yawning as the long day finally caught up with her, she rubbed her arms for warmth. Eagle-eyed Tonino noticed and removed his charcoal suit jacket and placed it on her shoulders.

'You don't have to do that,' she protested.

'I'm not cold,' he answered smugly.

And now, neither was she. Tonino's jacket was so big and contained so much warmth that it enveloped her body like a giant hug.

Its warmth came from his body heat.

The driver noticed their approach and opened the back door for her.

She climbed inside and was about to reluctantly give Tonino his jacket back when he slid in beside her.

'You don't need to escort me back,' she chided, smothering another yawn.

'I want to see you home safely.'

The driver pulled away.

'Don't be silly.' She smothered yet another yawn. She was utterly exhausted and yet...

Alone with Tonino in the confines of the back seat of his car, the partition between them and the driver raised...

Suddenly she was aware of the beats of her heart and the thickening of her blood.

Suddenly she was aware of Tonino's cologne dancing through her airwaves. The urge to rub her cheek into his jacket still draped over her shoulders became almost irresistible.

And suddenly she was aware of his thigh pressed against hers.

She should move away from him. Edge herself to the door. Create a distance.

She knew what she *should* do. Her body had other thoughts and was refusing to take orders from her brain. She cleared her throat. 'You've only got to come all the way back and it's not like you'll see Finn—he'll be asleep.' The car's interior darkened as they drove through the thick woodland. 'You should get some sleep too before all that travelling you've got to do...'

His hand closed over hers, stifling her words. It felt very different from the way he'd covered her hand in the restaurant. That had been for reassurance during what had proved to be a difficult yet ultimately necessary conversation. Since then, they'd spoken only of light, forgettable things and yet, instinctively, she knew she would remember every word exchanged.

If only she could remember those last missing pieces. What had happened with her father was becoming clearer. She'd waited on his doorstep for his housekeeper to find him. She didn't need the actual memory to know the housekeeper had returned with the message that he didn't want to see her. Orla knew it in her heart.

The memory she most wanted back was the accident. Where had she been going? She'd been two hours from home on the main road to Dublin...

Her desperate thoughts, barriers to help her pretend that the electricity bouncing over skin wasn't really happening, dissolved. The weight and warmth of Tonino's skin against hers made coherent thought impossible.

'I would sleep much better if I was in your bed,' he murmured.

A loose breath escaped her throat, barely audible above the humming in her ears.

She should move her hand from his and move her body away too. Instead she found her fingers lacing through his. When his thigh pressed tighter against hers and his shoulder leaned against hers, she smothered a gasp at the throb that pulsed through her abdomen and sent an ache rippling through the rest of her.

She didn't dare utter another word. She didn't dare look at him.

There was an excitement in her belly that was both new and yet familiar. She didn't remember the feelings but knew, in the same instinctive way she'd known she was pregnant and that Finn's father was Sicilian before the memories came back, that she'd felt them before.

His fingers squeezed then unlaced from hers to rest lightly on her thigh. The heat from his touch fizzed right into her veins.

Her fingers spread themselves over *his* thigh before her brain could compute what they were doing.

Slowly, slowly, his fingers crept upwards, gently caressing until they reached the apex of her thighs. She squeezed reflexively and gasped when his thumb brushed over the material covering her femininity.

She found herself helpless to stop her fingers slowly dragging themselves up the muscular thighs, closer and closer to...

Orla swallowed hard when the tip of her finger brushed something solid.

Dimly she was aware that Tonino's breaths had become

heavy. In the echoes of her mind she heard her own breaths too, ragged bursts as erratic as her heartbeats.

She pressed her pelvis against his hand.

He shifted so his chest pressed against her breast. His mouth pressed against the top of her head. Hot breaths permeated through her skin, darts of need careering through her veins and down to her liquid core.

Feeling drugged, she turned her face up to his. The heat swirling in his dark hooded eyes only heightened the sensations that had taken control of her body. The whispers of his breaths danced over her lips.

He covered her hand and gently slid it to cover the bulge between his legs. A thrill so powerful shot through her that her breath hitched, and it took a moment for her to register his hand no longer covered hers but had moved to her shoulder. Slowly it brushed down, over her breasts and stomach to the part of her body now aching with torment.

And then the warmth against her lips changed. It solidified, flesh forming from the air…

Tonino's mouth was grazing against hers…

This time she could not hold back the gasp that flew from her throat. The firm pressure of Tonino's lips against hers muffled the sound but did nothing to muffle the shaking of her right knee.

When his mouth moved she found her own mouth moving in time. She found her chest straining to him…*all* the cells in her body were straining to him. She barely noticed he'd undone the button of her trousers until he slipped his hand into the loosened space and burrowed into her knickers. Her gasp was muffled again by the delicious pressure of his mouth. Her mouth flooding with moisture, Orla cupped his cheek and tried to hold on to herself but it was a battle she'd lost before she'd started. A thick finger slid over her swollen nub, making her gasp again and turning her breaths into shallow pants that echoed around her.

Wantonly, she pressed against the finger, heightening the sensation, and moaned into his mouth.

Her fingers moved from his cheek to cradle his head and she closed her eyes, letting her body and Tonino's clever manipulations guide her responses.

Clinging tightly to him, their breaths merged together, she bucked against him with increasing urgency until the pleasure consumed her in its entirety and she was whimpering against him, her face burrowed in his neck, sensation that felt as if it had been dipped in nectar flooding her throbbing pelvis.

She had no idea how long it took for reality to snake its way into her delirious consciousness.

She opened her eyes.

That was Tonino's neck her face was pressed against.

That was Tonino's strong arm holding her so tightly and protectively against him.

That was his heartbeat thudding through his chest and reverberating in her ear.

That was his hand…

That was *her* hand…

Suddenly awash with mortification, Orla snatched her hand away from his crotch and yanked his hand away from hers and turned from him to fasten and straighten her clothes.

Tonino didn't make a sound or a movement until, moments later, the car came to a stop and he shifted beside her.

She swallowed and kept her gaze fixed forward, afraid to look at him.

How could she ever look at him again?

'We have arrived, *dolcezza*,' he said huskily. His breath danced against her cheek. She closed her eyes.

A finger touched her chin.

Her heart jumped.

The air around her shifted again. Tonino had moved even closer.

There was not an inch of her skin that didn't reawaken. Anticipation bubbled but still she kept her eyes closed.

The finger on her chin skimmed lightly over her cheek, reaching her ear. A hand plunged into her hair. Fresh tingles capered joyously on her sensitised skin.

'Are you going to invite me in?' he whispered into her ear.

'What?' Dazed, she opened her eyes, her stare immediately captured in the swirling depths of Tonino's hungry gaze.

He captured her chin again and kissed her. Kissed her properly. Kissed her so hard and so thoroughly that the heat rebuilding deep inside her liquefied her bones as it bubbled to the surface.

The hand in her hair drifted down her back. 'Invite me in,' he whispered against her lips before crushing her mouth again. His hand reached her bottom and squeezed then ran over her thigh, squeezing and massaging, his mouth devouring her, sensation running amok through her.

It would be so easy to invite him into her home and lead him up to her room rather than Finn's…

And just like that, sanity reared its gloriously ugly head.

Fixing their son's image in her head and focusing only on that, she placed her hands on his chest and pushed him off. 'No.'

He sat back, breathing heavily. 'No, what?'

'No, I am not going to invite you in.' Heart hammering furiously, she groped for the door handle but found herself all fingers and thumbs.

A large, warm, hard body lightly covered hers. 'Let me,' he murmured. And then he opened the door.

Before she could escape, he palmed her cheek and

brushed his lips against hers one last time. 'I will see you in a few days,' he murmured.

'Grand,' she answered in what she intended to be a tart fashion, but which came out all breathless.

She felt breathless. Tonino was the only man she had ever desired and it made her want to weep that the old feelings were still there inside her but impossible to fulfil.

Eyes glittering, he brought her hand to his mouth and grazed a kiss against her knuckles. 'I will count the hours.'

CHAPTER NINE

ORLA LOOKED OUT of the car window, eyes straining for the first view of Tonino's home.

Finn was beside himself with excitement. If her little trouper could have packed his own case, he would have done it within seconds of her telling him about their trip. Finn hadn't immediately embraced Tonino as he'd done with Dante and she wondered if it was because Finn detected the threat Tonino posed to their family life. Whatever the reason behind it—and she wouldn't ask unless it became a problem, as she didn't want to feed ideas to him that might not already be there—she was glad he was excited to be back in Sicily and excited to be seeing his father.

There was no point denying the butterflies rampaging in her belly were testament to her own excitement. The leaping of her heart at every alert from her phone these past three days was testament too. The few times the alerts had come from Tonino...quite frankly she was surprised to find her heart still secure behind her ribs.

Hearing his voice down the line had had the effect of turning the thousands of miles between them into nothing. The deep tones would dive through her ears and heat her veins, sensitising her skin as acutely as if she were in the back of his car with him again, a recent memory that had had her clutching her cheeks in mortification so many times these past three days it was a wonder she hadn't worn her cheekbones down.

This was how it had been for her four years ago, Orla turning into a walking tinderbox of feverish heat and heightened emotions. Her emotions were far more yo-yo-like than they had been then. Nothing could come of these feelings. She wanted to trust him but how could she after all the lies? And even if she found a way to trusting him, Tonino didn't want *her*. He wanted their son. He might still desire her, but one look at her naked body would extinguish it. If she could hardly bring herself to look at her own reflection how could she expect him to react to it with anything but horror?

The winding, narrow road that they'd been driving on for the past five minutes, through fields of crops ready to be harvested, peaked. In the distance rose a salmon-coloured stone chateau.

Orla cleared her throat and pointed. 'Look, Finn. That's your daddy's house.' She could not say where this certainty came from, but she would bet her own house that it belonged to Tonino.

Finn strained against the restraints of his car seat, trying to get a decent view.

The closer they got, the more the chateau—at least, that was what she called it in her head—emerged, but it wasn't until they drove through a high stone arch into an enormous courtyard that she fully appreciated its vast magnificence. The chateau surrounded the courtyard, which could double as a car park if the need arose, in a square. In the centre of the courtyard stood a fountain with a trio of cherubs in it, the water squirting from a certain part of the cherubs' anatomy that had Finn squealing with laughter when he spotted it.

Baskets of flowers hung on the chateau's walls, random palm trees adding additional colour, and Tonino…

Orla blinked and looked again.

Her heart soared and caught in her throat.

Tonino had emerged from nowhere, as if he'd slithered out of the chateau's walls or, as was more likely, become flesh from a marble statue, Adonis brought to life. Unlike the marble statue of the naughty cherubs, Tonino was dressed, insofar as a pair of black shorts and a lazy grin could be considered as dressed.

The driver opened the door and, as Orla carried Finn out, Tonino walked over to them. The late afternoon sun beamed down and cast his bare chest in a hazy glow.

She remembered pressing her lips to that chest and inhaling the musky scent of his skin. She remembered rubbing her cheeks against the thick hair spread across it and marvelling at the contrasts between them, his masculinity and her femininity, as different as night from day yet the two of them coming together...

Their coming together was still a blank.

His dreamy chocolate eyes caught hers. His lazy grin widened before he planted a kiss right on her lips. Immediately her senses were assailed with the scents of salt, muskiness and the faint remnants of Tonino's cologne. The stubble of his unshaved face rubbed against her cheek and when he broke the kiss as abruptly as he'd formed it, she had to stop her fingers from pressing against her tender, stubble-assaulted skin. She had to stop herself from swaying into him and pulling him back for another.

Before she had the chance to compose a greeting that didn't make her sound like a brain-dead eejit, Tonino had lifted Finn from her arms.

'How was the journey?' He rubbed his nose against Finn's in an affectionate gesture that sent her heart soaring all over again.

Only the good Lord knew how she untied her tongue to answer. 'Fine.'

He looked back at her and shifted Finn on his hip. 'My apologies for not sending my plane to you.'

She forced her vocal cords to cooperate. 'I cannot believe you're apologising for making us travel first class.'

'It is an inconvenience for you.'

The serious way in which he declared this made her snort with laughter. 'Seriously? First class an inconvenience? And you say *I* need to get some perspective?'

For a long moment Tonino stared at her, enjoying the way the sunlight bounced on her thick dark hair and injected it with strands of gold and red. 'You look beautiful.'

As beautiful and as fresh as any flower his gardener coaxed into bloom on his estate.

Tonino had arrived back in Sicily a few hours earlier than expected. He would have flown to Ireland to collect them, but they'd already left for the airport. Finding himself pacing the chateau's corridors and getting in the way of his live-in staff, he'd gone for a swim but quickly found himself bored so had resorted to playing tennis with his ball-launcher machine as an opponent. That had used up much of his latent energy but not all of it, not with the promise of Orla and his son arriving at any moment feeding him energy as quickly as he wore it out.

Gazing at her now, he felt as if he'd done no exercise at all. His veins still thrummed. His skin and loins still buzzed with anticipation.

The memory of what had taken place in the back of his car had shadowed his every waking moment since.

The three days away from Orla had passed slowly. A snail could have passed the time more quickly.

It had been the same when she'd disappeared four years ago. Life had suddenly gone from passing at breakneck speed to a crawl.

This time, he was certain the slowing of time had been because he'd been parted from his son. Already his feelings for Finn ran deep. They were feelings he'd never had before, different from any other emotion. Far different from the feelings he had for Finn's mother. There was a purity to his feelings for Finn, a semi-conscious knowledge that for this child he would be prepared to kill to keep him safe. He would never allow his son to feel that the family name and Tonino's pride meant more than Finn's happiness. He would support his son and love him unconditionally.

His feelings for Orla were far more complicated. He hated her for keeping him in the dark about the pregnancy but relished being in her company. He wanted to punish her for her lies. He wanted to worship the body that had created something so special for them. He desired her. He fantasised about her. Orla being back in his life had set off a charge in his veins that time had dulled. He'd forgotten it could be so strong. She was the only woman the charge had scorched him for.

Dio, he longed to throw her on his bed, rip her clothes off and plunder that beautiful body. He longed to hear the soft moans that had once fallen from her lips. He longed to hear her pleas for more.

But this Orla was not the Orla of four years ago. That Orla had been impulsive. She had thrown caution to the wind and embraced the desire that had caught them both in its snare. For a short shameless passage of time she had sunk into the desire still binding them so tightly together. The way she had come undone for him had blown his mind. Orla had always blown his mind.

Four years ago they had been dynamite together and that explosive chemistry still bubbled strongly. If desire alone could bind Orla to him he'd have already won. But this Orla was a mother. Motherhood had made her cautious. She thought with her brain rather than be led by her desires. To get what he wanted, namely Finn permanently in his life, he needed to seduce her brain. He needed to make her feel that his home could be *their* home. Because to achieve what he wanted he needed to bring Orla into his life permanently too.

The next morning, Orla closed Finn's bedroom door carefully and put her finger to her lips to remind her son to be quiet.

She needn't have bothered with silence. No sooner had she taken her first step than Tonino's bedroom door opened.

She could scream. Yet again he'd caught her at the crack of dawn looking as though she'd been dragged through a gooseberry bush backwards.

He caught the look on her face and grinned. 'How many times do I have to tell you that I'm an early riser before you believe me?'

'No one gets up this early voluntarily, not unless they're a three-year-old child.'

'Why doesn't the nurse get up with him?' he asked when they reached the kitchen, a space that was double the size of the ground floor of her old house. The scent of fresh coffee filled the room. So tantalising was it that Orla suddenly found herself craving a coffee for the first time in years.

'It's not her job.' Tonino had been as good as his word at employing wraparound care for Finn here in Sicily. The nurses he'd employed worked shifts and were unobtrusive, present if needed but fading into the background when not required. They also spoke excellent English and had cared for children with cerebral palsy before.

'Her job is whatever you require it to be.' He opened a cupboard door. 'It's in the contract.'

'Sure, but getting up and feeding my child is my job.

Caring for my child is my job.' And a job it had taken eighteen months of blood, sweat and tears to achieve.

He shut the cupboard he'd been looking through and opened the next one. 'When was the last time you slept later than six a.m.?'

Her last night in the rehabilitation centre. 'Years ago… What are you looking for?'

'Finn's cereal. I instructed my housekeeper to buy some for him.'

'Where do you usually keep cereal?'

'I have no idea.'

'But it's your kitchen.'

'It's my chef's kitchen,' he corrected. 'I never cook, but I'm not a breakfast eater so she doesn't usually start until ten. I'll get her to start earlier while—'

'Don't you dare. There's no need for the entire household to be up early just because of Finn.'

'What if you want food too?'

'I rarely eat more than a slice of toast in the morning. I hardly need a cordon bleu chef to butter it for me.' A thought occurred to her. 'If the chef hasn't started yet, who made the coffee?'

'It's on a timer. If you hunt for cups you'll find them somewhere. I have mine black.' Tonino grinned, then made a noise that sounded like the Sicilian equivalent of *aha!* and pulled the box of cereal out of the cupboard.

A warm sensation flooded Orla's chest and belly when Tonino, after rooting through a dozen other cupboards, pulled out a plastic bowl with dinosaurs on it. Her heart bloomed when he opened a drawer and removed a plastic spoon, also with dinosaurs on. He filled the bowl, added the milk and joined them at the table, where Orla had put Finn in the brand-new high chair Tonino had bought him and laid their cups of coffee down.

A strange contentment settled in her as she sat back

and sipped the delicious coffee. Despite the palatial proportions of the chateau and its kitchen, there was something heartwarming to witness the uber-masculine Tonino feed cereal on a dinosaur spoon into a three-year-old's mouth.

'Seeing as you are averse to nurses caring for our son in anything but a medical capacity, do you not think it makes sense for me to take on the early morning parental role while you are here?' he asked, catching her eye briefly. He adopted a cajoling tone. 'Think of those extra hours in bed.'

'I'll think about it,' she muttered, knowing full well there was nothing to think about but also knowing Tonino would never understand her feelings on the subject. He'd been deprived of their son for the first three years of Finn's life but he hadn't known about it because he hadn't known of Finn's existence. He hadn't *missed* Finn because how could you miss something you'd never had? Orla had spent eighteen months fighting her own body just to be well enough to hold her child, missing him with every breath she took. Finn had been the focus she'd needed to get through those dark, terrifying days and even darker nights. Getting up early to feed Finn his breakfast was a privilege that she would never take for granted but she couldn't share this with Tonino.

How could she trust that he wouldn't use her injuries against her in a custody battle?

She wanted to trust him but until she could, she would try to keep the extent of her injuries from him.

The early morning turned into a sunny day lazily spent exploring the grounds of Tonino's magnificent estate. After lunch on the terrace, Orla sat on a sunlounger by the huge swimming pool, shades on, a sheer navy kaftan covering her body and the swimsuit she would never get wet, and watched her son squeal with delight to be dipped into the fresh water by his father.

The joy on Tonino's face sliced through her too, just as acutely.

She'd been so certain that not telling him until after the birth was right. She remembered taking the pregnancy test and minutes later searching his name online to discover his engagement to Sophia was over, her heart thumping. She'd been thankful that she wouldn't have to break the Sicilian woman's heart a second time but this confirmation of Tonino's sudden 'availability' had not made Orla feel any better about her predicament. If anything it had made her feel worse. With no fiancée at his side, there would be nothing to hold him off launching a custody battle. Orla's father had wanted nothing to do with her but Tonino was not her father. Tonino wanted children. Lots of them. He had the wealth and connections to get custody of the tiny life in her belly. She'd made the conscious decision to wait until after the birth before telling him. That would allow her a relatively stress-free pregnancy and allow her to register her child as an Irish citizen and to put whatever protection in place she could to stop him using his connections against her. She remembered being terrified. In her mind she'd painted Tonino as a monster. She'd painted him as a cheat, a liar and an all-powerful deity with the ability to snap his fingers and snatch her baby from her.

She'd forgotten that he was a flesh and blood man. She'd forgotten that their time together had been wonderful because *he'd* been wonderful… No, she hadn't forgotten. She'd just convinced herself it had all been an act while he'd had his fun with her.

Guilt that Finn and Tonino never had the chance to be father and son from birth gnawed at her. She remembered carrying the guilt in her…

A new memory flashed in her mind and sent her heart racing anew, of searching Tonino's name online and finding a picture of him and a new woman. She'd effectively cyber-stalked him, she suddenly remembered. She'd searched his name most days.

She remembered Finn reacting to her reaction to Tonino and the new woman by giving a huge kick. She must have seen that picture shortly before the accident because Finn had only really started kicking her belly with gusto a few weeks before it.

Orla thought hard, trying to remember who the new woman had been, but the memory refused to form. It would come in its own time. The memories refused to be forced, especially the significant ones.

Orla thought again about that woman later that evening while soaking in the bath. Tonino had announced that he was taking her out for dinner, leaving the duty nurse in charge of Finn. He'd refused to listen to a word of argument against it.

They'd dined on his rooftop veranda the night before, a relaxed meal under a starry sky with the waves of the Tyrrhenian Sea a distant roar.

But the relaxed vibe had been a lie. Orla had spent the evening with a kaleidoscope of large-winged butterflies dancing a storm in her belly. Every time their eyes had met she'd been certain he'd been remembering what had happened in the back of his car. She'd been on tenterhooks for him to allude to it or make a move on her, but when she'd announced at ten p.m. that she was tired and going to bed, he'd inclined his head, raised his glass and wished her a good night.

She'd walked away feeling the burn of his stare scorching her, then crawled into bed unsure whether she was relieved or frustrated.

She should not feel so damned excited at the thought

of being alone with him. The dancing butterflies in her belly and the buzz of anticipation bouncing over her skin were traps.

She must remember that Tonino had an ulterior motive in taking her out for dinner just as he had an ulterior motive with everything he did. That ulterior motive was Finn. The incredible effort Tonino was making for her to feel at home and at ease, the beautiful bedroom he'd appointed for her with the triple-aspect windows and private bathroom Cleopatra would consider die-worthy, the walk-in wardrobe filled with brand-new clothing specially selected by a personal shopper under Tonino's instructions especially for her...

She must not let her head be swayed by it all because she knew exactly what he was doing it for—he was making her see how great it would be to marry him. He was making her see all the things he could give her and all the perks she would receive by being his wife. He thought those things would impress her and turn her head. He didn't know her head didn't need turning. It had been turned four years ago and she'd never got over it.

Ultimately, it was Finn he wanted, not Orla. He was just using her as a means to have his son in his life permanently. She couldn't blame him for it.

By the time she'd dressed in a scoop-neck silver dress that fell to her knees and had the requisite long sleeves, and a pair of black glittery heels, she stared at her reflection. She stared at the mirror for so long she half expected a voice to emerge from it.

What would the voice say? Would it laugh at her and say that it didn't matter how she looked with clothes on because any sexual interest Tonino had for her would be extinguished like a candle if he saw her naked?

A part of her thought she should go knocking on his

door, whip her dress up to expose the scars and brazenly say, 'There you go. Still fancy me, do you?'

If she couldn't bear to look at her scars herself, how could she ever trust Tonino enough to see them and not use them as a weapon against her?

CHAPTER TEN

THE NIGHT THAT unfolded was one of the best of Orla's life. Tonino drove them in a tiny vintage car that must have been older than the pair of them combined to Palermo, where they dined in the tiniest restaurant she had ever set foot in, which held the grand total of eight tables. Despite its diminutive proportions, the restaurant had a zest to it that could have lifted the lowest of spirits. Loud but not overbearing music pulsed from walls adorned with clever and funny artwork. The food…

'It's just as well I'm not a fussy eater,' she confided when the music dipped low enough for Tonino to hear. The restaurant did not provide a menu. It served three courses of whatever the chef had dreamt up that day, take it or leave it. Having eaten her first course, the most divinely cooked octopus served on a pea and mint broth, with the largest langoustine she'd ever seen accompanying it, she was firmly in the 'take it' camp.

'That's why I brought you here.' He grinned, making her already noodly bones soften even more. Under the subtle lighting, his handsome features had become more defined. With his magnificent body snug in black chinos and a charcoal shirt open at the neck, it was all she could do not to salivate. The man was a walking stick of testosterone.

Tonino was glad he'd followed his instincts and brought

Orla here rather than one of Palermo's classier restaurants. This place was one of Sicily's hidden gems, a restaurant that operated on a word-of-mouth basis. If the owner didn't want you there, reserving a table was impossible. If the owner liked you, reserving a table with only hours' notice was easy.

He'd guessed Orla would prefer the informality here but also relish the opportunity to dress up. Four years ago, when she'd been short of money, she'd made an effort with her appearance. Orla was a woman with an eye for fashion, her clothes back then cheap but stylish. She still had that eye but the quality had markedly increased to reflect her increased bank balance.

Time, he was learning, had changed Orla, yet dig beneath the surface and the fundamental essence of who she was remained the same.

Life had dealt her the severest of blows and she was still picking the pieces of it up. He needed to make her see that, together, the pieces could be mended far more effectively than if she remained alone. He needed to make himself indispensable to her and Finn.

While they ate their second course of spaghetti and clams, the music being piped through the restaurant was turned off and a violin quartet appeared. Instead of playing the classical music all the diners anticipated, they tapped their feet and drove straight into a rock classic.

Orla clapped her hands and grinned widely, clearly loving the twist.

'You like?' he murmured, thinking for the hundredth time that evening how beautiful she looked.

She nodded enthusiastically. 'Very much.'

Picking up her fork, she twirled some spaghetti around it and popped it in her mouth, all the while her shoulders danced along to the rock beats.

Tonino found his attention caught with Orla rather than

the entertainment. She held his attention like no one else. She always had.

She began nodding her head in time to the music along with her shoulders and absently tucked a lock of her dark hair behind a dainty ear.

He inhaled deeply then exhaled slowly.

He remembered her performing similar moves four years ago at a beachside reggae bar he'd taken her to one evening when he'd decided they needed a short break from his bedroom for food. As his cooking skills consisted entirely of opening packets, and as he hadn't at that point been ready to confess his true identity and so couldn't order a member of his household staff over to his apartment to whip up a four-course meal for them, he'd taken her out, intending to find a semi-decent restaurant. The music pumping from the reggae bar had made Orla's beautiful face widen into a beam and they'd ended up there, sitting at a wooden table on the beach, a blanket covering their laps against the sea breeze, drinking mojitos and sharing a large basket of chips.

It was a memory that had stayed with him. When he thought of the dates he'd been on in his life, that had been by far the best. The simplicity of the setting mixed with the growing realisation that Orla's feelings for him were entirely for *him*…

He wouldn't rewrite history by denying that he'd been a player until his engagement to Sophia. Women had flocked to him and he'd welcomed their attentions while not being under the least illusion that their interest wasn't in part to do with his wealth. If he'd come from a poor family, many of them—Sophia included—would not have looked twice at him.

Orla had huddled under that blanket sharing chips with him, oblivious that he was worth more than a small natio

If he could turn back time and re-enact histor

would return to that night and tell her the truth of who he was. His mistake had been to not trust her with the truth. He'd been afraid the truth would change how she was with him.

He should have realised that night that his wealth would mean little to her. For Orla, money was a means to an end. Her brother's wealth had been welcome only for what it could do to improve Finn's life. Orla didn't value possessions. She valued family. She valued those she loved.

Driving them back home, Tonino opened a window to get some fresh air into his lungs. He felt lightheaded even though he hadn't touched a drop of alcohol.

Awareness throbbed through him, his mind busy recalling the way she'd wiggled her shoulders to the music; he shot surreptitious glances at her, catching the surreptitious glances she kept shooting back at him... So shot was his concentration that it was a miracle they made it back in one piece.

He brought the car to a stop in the courtyard. A member of his staff would park it in the underground garage for him.

For a long time they just sat there, the only sound their individual breaths.

He turned to face her at the exact moment she turned to face him. The soft lighting of the courtyard's perimeter cast her in an ethereal shadow that made his lungs tighten along with his loins at the beauty before him.

He reached out to capture a lock of her hair in his fingers.

She stilled, eyes wide on his as if in a trance.

'Have I told you how beautiful you look tonight?' he whispered, releasing the lock of hair to trace his fingers around the rim of her ear.

She shivered at his touch. Her breathing deepened.

Lowering his tone to a purr, he spoke into her hair. 'I have spent the night fantasising about us making love.'

Orla knew Tonino's seductive words and tone were deliberate. His voice had always been an aphrodisiac to her, something he'd taken full advantage of four years ago and which she knew he would not hesitate to use as a weapon again. Her shameful lack of resistance was her own fault.

She tried to breathe, tried to grit her teeth in a form of mental defence, all the while praying, *Please don't touch my body...*

Her aching body begged to differ. Her aching body craved his touch.

When he'd touched her in the back of his car she'd melted into butter.

His finger drifted down her neck to the top of her chest then skimmed lightly, almost nonchalantly, over a breast.

Her insides became liquid and she instinctively pressed the tops of her thighs together, a motion she knew didn't escape his attention. *Nothing* escaped Tonino Valente's attention.

His hot breath whispered through the strands of her hair to burn her scalp. 'We should go in.'

She swallowed and instead of the bright, 'Yes, that's an excellent idea, I'm tired and want to go to bed. Alone. See you in the morning!' she intended, all she managed was something that sounded like, 'Hmm?'

'I said we should go inside…unless you want me to make love to you right here in the car in the middle of the courtyard?'

The liquid inside her heated to unbearable levels. The finger that had skimmed her breast had settled on its underside and was making the lightest circular motions that had her wanting to grab his hand and place it over her breast properly. She wanted to feel his hand there without the barrier of clothes, to feel the heady sensations that had so enraptured her all those years ago.

While her body's responses contradicted everything in her brain, his hand swept over her belly then left her body altogether to unlock her seat belt.

For a moment all she could do was stare into his hooded eyes before the tiniest smile curved on his firm lips and she was suffused in his scent as he leaned over her to open her door.

She got out of the car, her legs like overcooked spaghetti, a different kind of weakness than she usually felt in her limbs. This weakness was nothing to do with her brain. It was all to do with Tonino. Her legs would have felt like spaghetti even without the after-effects of the accident still grabbing at her.

Orla stared up at the black night sky and prayed for the strength to resist this undeniable attraction.

Attraction? If her tongue weren't so tied to the roof of her mouth she would laugh at this pathetic description of the powerful feelings engulfing her.

All the years when she'd tried so hard to remember his name, his face had haunted both her dreams and her waking hours. Her first dream of him after the accident, around the time the doctors had ended her sedation, had been so vivid and real that if she'd been able to get off the bed and walk she would have stalked every inch of the hospital for him.

The accident had wiped his name from her memory bank. It had wiped their time together. It had wiped Sophia's confrontation with her and Orla's discovery of his lies.

The one thing it hadn't wiped, apart from the image of his face, was her feelings for him. But only in her dreams had she dared let those feelings out.

Her heart thumping hard against her ribs, she walked

beside him into the chateau and slipped her shoes off. There was not a sound to be heard within the thick stone walls.

Not until they reached the sleeping quarters did she manage to untie her tongue. 'I need to check on Finn.'

She turned the handle of her son's bedroom door and slipped inside. The night light in the corner of the room gave just enough illumination for her to see him sleeping peacefully. The adjoining door to the nurse's room was ajar. Loud snores could be heard from it.

Orla watched her son sleep until the thuds of her heart settled into a gentle rhythm. She crept silently back out, her heart lifting right back to a canter when she found Tonino with his back against the corridor wall, arms loosely crossed over his chest, waiting for her.

Their eyes met. His chest rose.

Her throat caught.

Long, electrified moments passed before Tonino unfolded his arms. Straightening, he took a step towards her.

Her bare feet refused her brain's order to move into the safety of her bedroom, remaining rooted to the terracotta floor.

Two more steps and the distance between them had closed.

A muscular arm hooked around her waist and pulled her flush against him.

She gasped and gazed up at the face that had haunted her dreams for so, so long. Another long, electrified stare passed between them.

She gasped again as she was lifted off her feet, a gasp smothered by the firm, sensuous mouth she had kissed a thousand times in her dreams crushing her lips.

Oh, but this was a kiss that could turn a nun's head, never mind a love-starved Irishwoman whose heart had been given to, then broken by, the only man her body had ever ached for. A thousand brand-new feelings erupted in her and, wrapping her arms around his neck, she returned the kiss with all the passion in her soul, scraping her fingers down his nape as their tongues collided and their mouths moulded into one.

Heat fizzed through her veins as her every atom made a collective sigh that had her tightening her hold on him.

Tonino held her just as tightly. Only when they finally came up for air did he remove an arm from her waist and reach out for the door handle, pushing it open before wrapping the arm back around her.

Orla found herself being half carried into an intensely masculine bedroom. The tips of her toes swished gracefully over thick carpet until she was twisted around and the backs of her legs met resistance in the form of a humongous four-poster bed, which her bottom fell onto.

Immediately he sank down to kneel on the floor before her. Tonino was so tall that with him kneeling and her sitting on the bed, they became the same height.

Large hands cupped her cheeks, dark brown eyes swirling with desire pulsed straight into her. He breathed heavily. *'Amore mio...'* he muttered thickly against her lips, before plundering her mouth anew, his kisses feverish and wet and fierce with intensity.

Another rush of sensory feelings exploded in her. It was as if all her passion for Tonino had been locked away in a box similar to the box that had contained her memories of him, waiting for him to prise the lid open with a kiss like the prince from a fairy tale.

The fever in Tonino's kisses was matched by the fever in her response. She felt drugged. Her aching body craved his touch and craved to touch *him*, to feel the bristles of his chest hair against her cheek. She wanted to rub her nose into it and bite at the brown nipples as she *knew* she'd done before.

Her fingers unbuttoned his shirt so expertly she could only assume it was muscle memory from the days when she must have unbuttoned his shirt before working for her. In moments she had it undone and was pulling it apart and tugging the sleeves down his arms.

Tonino pressed Orla flat back on the bed and gritted his teeth to stifle the feelings threatening to overpower him.

Her hands reached out and touched him…everywhere. His chest, his stomach, his back, scorching his skin and firing his veins. He buried his face into her neck and ran his hands over the slender body he still remembered every inch of.

Just the taste of Orla's kisses was enough to fuel him as no other could.

No wonder the few relationships he'd had since she'd disappeared from his life had ended with barely a whimper. No woman had stood a chance after he'd tasted Orla. She had stayed with him, every minute of every hour, a spectre in the corner of his eye by day and a ghost haunting his dreams by night.

She had taken possession of his heart, slipping in without him realising until it was too late, and he'd lost her.

He had her back now, he thought savagely, and he would never let her go again.

Dragging a hand up a smooth thigh, her dress rising as he went, he pressed his hand over the core of her womanhood.

She moaned into his mouth and tilted her pelvis so it pressed back against his hand, crushing herself against his naked chest. He wanted to feel her naked against him. He wanted to touch the soft skin, to kiss the pert breasts; to kiss every inch of her body, discover the changes pregnancy had wrought on it and get to know it all over again.

Together they dispatched her knickers then he covered her sweet mouth again and, sliding a hand between her legs, he found her wet and writhing for him. Her nub was already swollen, and she moaned loudly when he pressed a finger to it and then dipped down to slide a finger inside her.

Mouths fused together, he captured the hem of her dress and shifted it to her waist, but suddenly found himself unable to move it any higher for Orla had clamped her arms to her sides, preventing him from moving the dress another inch.

'Leave it on,' she whispered into his mouth before darting her tongue back inside the coffee-tasting depths and wrapping her arms back around his waist.

Orla wanted this with a desperation she'd never known before. She wanted to feel everything she'd felt during the conception of their child, a memory that still hadn't taken its full shape, and she knew that the moment he saw her unclothed, the moment would be ruined. She would be ashamed. He would be disgusted. He would ask questions. The moment would be lost.

The feelings erupting through her were too heady, too sensuous, too *everything* for it to be lost.

Guiding his hand back to the place it had been giving her such pleasure, she reached down for the button of his chinos and undid it, then pulled the zip down with an expert precision that came, again, from muscle memory.

She had done all this before and, while she still didn't remember it, she knew she desperately wanted to do it again. With Tonino. Only Tonino.

She tugged the chinos and underwear down his hips then, with a flexibility she'd never dreamt she possessed, bent her knees and lifted her legs until her toes reached his clothing and she tugged them down with her feet.

Then their mouths were fused together once more and his hand was replaced by something much harder, something long and thick and...

In one long thrust he was inside her. The pleasure was immediate and shockingly powerful.

Orla's moan turned into a sigh as she adjusted to the huge weight filling her and welcomed the sensations that suddenly felt so familiar.

Her body knew exactly what it wanted, and she closed her eyes and let it guide her. One hand buried itself in Tonino's hair, the other grabbed hold of a buttock and drove him deeper and harder inside her as they rocked together with unintelligible whispers and moans.

She reached her peak quickly. All the sensations infusing her fused together into a tight ball that exploded in a rolling crescendo that filled every cell in her body with the most glorious pleasure. No sooner had she welcomed the headiness of her orgasm than Tonino's groans deepened and his thrusts hardened and quickened until he gave a long cry and collapsed on her.

For the longest, dreamiest time, Tonino's weight was spread deliciously on her, his face buried in her neck. She burrowed her fingers in his thick hair and turned her cheek to press her mouth to the top of his head. He kissed her neck then muttered something and withdrew from her. Keeping hold of her, he rolled onto his back, taking her with him so her head rested on his chest.

Slowly the dreamy sensations subsided and the passion that had taken them both in its grip evaporated until all that was left was an ache in her heart and a throb between her legs that felt both new and familiar.

It would be so easy to fall asleep like this. The room was in darkness—there hadn't been the time or thought to switch a light on—the only illumination coming from the starry skies filtering through the windows.

She waited until Tonino's breathing became deep and rhythmic before disentangling herself from his hold.

Sitting up carefully so as not to disturb him, she smiled

sadly to see his feet were still on the floor. Not wanting him to get cold, she untangled the bedsheets and folded them over him as much as she could.

Then she slipped off the bed, snatched up her discarded underwear and padded quietly to the door.

She had just put her left foot over the threshold when a rich, deep voice that contained not an ounce of sleepiness caught her short.

'Running away again, *dolcezza*?'

CHAPTER ELEVEN

ORLA WINCED. SHE'D been too hasty in her escape. She should have left it a few minutes longer to ensure Tonino was deep in sleep.

Ashamed at being caught fleeing like an escaped bank robber, she counted to three before turning to face him.

His bedside light switched on and she found herself staring at Tonino's gorgeous yet inscrutable face. 'You don't have to leave.'

She tucked a strand of hair behind an ear then tugged at her dress. 'I can't sleep in this.'

There was a moment of loaded silence before Tonino jumped to his feet. 'Wait there,' he ordered as he opened a door and disappeared behind it. He came back out moments later carrying an item of clothing.

Stalking over to her, he pressed it into her hands. 'Take this. Change in my bathroom. If you look in the cabinet beneath the sink you will find a spare toothbrush. It's never been used. You are welcome to shower. There are fresh towels. Help yourself to anything you need.'

'I have stuff in my…'

'You are sleeping with me. End of subject. Now, unless you want me to remove your dress and expose the scars you are too frightened to let me see, I suggest you go use the bathroom.'

Something deep inside her withered painfully.

'I called Aislin,' he explained into the loaded silence.

'What?'

He sighed. 'Go and sort yourself out, Orla. I'll explain when you're ready.'

Defeated, afraid she could cry, which she absolutely did not want to do in front of Tonino, she hugged the clothing to her chest and locked herself in his luxury bathroom.

Suddenly desperate to wash the shamed feeling off her skin, she double-checked the door couldn't be unlocked from the bedroom and shed her dress.

Closing her eyes, she welcomed the rush of hot water that stung her skin and turned her face up to it.

Was this how she'd felt the first time they'd made love? Ashamed of herself?

She'd never dreamed she was capable of such wanton, lusty behaviour. Women like her just did not behave in that way. That was for women like her mother, women who embraced chaos, women who didn't care who they hurt or what others thought of them.

Orla did care. She cared deeply. Her pregnancy had shamed her more than any walk of shame the evil authorities had made women perform in medieval times. It wasn't that she'd been unmarried—her grandmother's old-fashioned views hadn't soaked into her *that* much—but that she had given her virginity to a man she'd barely known who she'd then learned she hadn't known at all. All her life she'd believed she would wait for the mythical perfect man from the realms of fairy tales to appear before giving her heart and her body, not a man she'd known barely two days.

That she still wanted Tonino as much as she had then, that one touch of his hand in her hair made her want to rip his clothes off... It mortified her. It terrified her how easily she lost possession of herself for him.

Only when she feared she was using the whole of Sicily's water supply did she switch the shower off and reach for a huge, fluffy towel neatly laid on the heated towelling rail.

She found an unused toothbrush exactly where he'd said and brushed her teeth vigorously, as if she could brush away the demons that plagued her as well as any dirt clinging to her teeth.

And then she shook out the white item of clothing Tonino had given her and felt a tear in her heart.

It was one of his shirts.

Before slipping it over her head she buried her nose in it and inhaled the faint trace of his cologne amidst the laundry soap.

When she finally found the courage to leave his bathroom and face him, she took three large breaths and unlocked the door.

He was sitting up in bed, the sheets covering him to his waist. He was not on his phone or watching television or reading. He was simply waiting for her.

'Better?' he asked sardonically.

Her heart thudded painfully, and she blinked away the wet burn in the backs of her eyes as she nodded.

He patted the space beside him. It was a command, not an invitation.

Climbing onto the bed gingerly, she sat beside him, making sure not to sit close enough that their bodies accidentally touched.

Tonino, however, was not disposed to have her beside him but apart, and, with a glare, he hooked an arm around her waist and pulled her against him.

'Stop fighting me,' he murmured, dropping a kiss onto the top of her head.

'I'm not,' she lied even as she wriggled to free herself from his tight hold.

'Relax, *dolcezza*. I'm not going to rip the shirt off you.'

His chest hair brushed against her cheek. The musky scent of his skin skipped down her airwaves and filtered into her veins and somehow pushed much of the angst inside her out.

A pang rent through her heart.

Being held in his arms like this…

It felt right. It had always felt right.

With a sigh she placed her hand flat on the plane of his stomach and pressed a kiss to the warm skin even as she screwed her eyes tightly together to stop the gathering tears from escaping.

'When did you speak to Aislin?' she asked quietly when she could speak without choking.

'Earlier, when you were getting ready for dinner.'

'Why?'

He smoothed her hair with his hand. 'Because you have been hiding things from me.'

'I haven't hidden anything. Not since we met at the wedding and the missing memories came back. I've been upfront about Finn—'

'I'm not talking about Finn. I'm talking about *you*.' He brushed a finger down her face and tilted her chin up so she was forced to meet his stare. 'Getting information about the long-term effects the accident had on you has been like drawing blood from a stone. You seem to operate on a need-to-know basis, and I think I know why—you're afraid that I will use your injuries as a weapon against you to gain custody of Finn.'

Tonino's instincts were terrifying in their accuracy.

'I know you suffered much more than a head injury,' he continued, his thumb still resting gently under her chin. 'You were partially paralysed and needed three major operations to help you walk and regain your motor functions. You spent six months in hospital and a further year in a rehabilitation centre. Your muscles are still weak and prone to spasm. You regularly sleep ten hours a night because your brain has to work twice as hard as everyone else's to perform simple tasks so you lose your energy quickly. You suffer from debilitating headaches. One of the reasons you both waited six months after your father died before Aislin came to Sicily to fight for your share of his estate was because you were too weak to be left in sole charge of Finn. Have I missed anything?'

Tonino deliberately kept his voice light as he relayed the list of damage inflicted on Orla's beautiful body. He could have continued, could have mentioned the broken ribs and broken arm, but the solitary tear that trickled down her cheek as she shook her head in answer let him know he'd said enough.

He'd called Dante because it had become blindingly obvious that Orla was masking the severity of her own condition. It had been a gradual reckoning until it had reached the point where he noticed it in her every action. Just the way she concentrated when carrying a cup was a big giveaway. He'd had to convince Dante that his intentions in seeking this information were honourable before he'd been put through to Aislin, who'd relayed all the details to him in what had made painful listening.

Orla put a brave face on but she still suffered the effects from it. She might always suffer them.

'You need to learn to trust me.' Tonino bent his head and brushed a soft kiss to her trembling lips. 'I will *never* take Finn from you. You do not have to hide things from me. I want to help you.'

She blinked rapidly and swallowed before whispering, 'I find it hard to trust people.'

He shifted his legs forward and lay down, taking Orla with him, then rolled over so he lay on top of her.

Placing his elbows either side of her head, he stared into her eyes. 'You need to try. I am not your enemy. I am not going to take our son from you because your injuries mean you can be clumsy and that you need more sleep than me. And I'm not going to stop wanting you because of some scars.'

Her throat moved as she bit into her bottom lip.

Placing a hand on her thigh, he parted her legs and rested his hips between them. 'Do you feel that?' he murmured.

Her eyes widened as his arousal pressed against her and she gave a short, breathless nod.

'No one turns me on the way you do. No one.' Bending his head, he kissed her plump mouth while running a hand down the side of her body then back up to cover her breast. He could feel its softness more easily through the shirt than he could through the thicker material of her dress and bra but he wanted to feel it bare against his hand and feel the nipple pucker in his mouth.

'I will never force you to do anything you don't want,' he whispered as he drove his arousal inside her, savouring the way her neck arched and the softest moan flew from her mouth. He pulled back to the tip then thrust in harder. 'All I want is to give you pleasure.'

Maybe if he showed her all the pleasure they were capable of creating together, the Orla who had given herself to him without reservation four years ago would come back to him.

When Orla opened her eyes the room was bright with daylight. The space beside her on Tonino's bed was empty.

She sat upright, looking for something to tell the time with.

Padding out of the bedroom, she went to Finn's room and found it empty. The nurse's room was empty too.

In her own room she donned some underwear, shrugged her robe on and set off looking for everyone.

She ignored the chiding voice in her head that told her she was being sentimental keeping Tonino's shirt on.

After a search that took far longer than expected, she found her son and his father in Tonino's office. Tonino was reading something on his desktop, Finn sat on the floor building something only he could recognise with his blocks.

They both turned to her when she walked in.

'Mummy!'

She sank to her knees and scooped her son into her arms, then waited a moment for her heart rate to lower to something resembling normality before turning her gaze to Tonino.

Her heart rate accelerated. Images of everything they'd shared the night before flashed in vivid colour before her eyes.

From the knowing smile playing on Tonino's firm mouth, he was having the exact same recollection.

'What time is it?' she asked.

He looked at his watch. 'Eleven.'

She raised her brow in dismay. 'That late? You should have woken me.'

'You needed the sleep, *dolcezza*.' And then he winked, making her cheeks turn into a furnace all over again. 'If you go and get ready, I've promised Finn a swim in the pool.'

The next day, after a couple of hours spent building sand-castles on Tonino's private stretch of beach and eating the picnic lunch made for them by his chef, Finn fell asleep. Removing the sandwich half hanging from his mouth and making sure the parasol shaded his delicate skin, Orla covered him from shoulder to toe with a thin sheet for good measure, then stretched her legs out and lifted her face to the sun's rays.

'You look happy,' Tonino observed, cold bottle of beer in hand.

She nodded, glad she had her shades on so he couldn't see what lay behind them. Sometimes it felt as if he only had to look into her eyes, and he could read everything in her head.

This was the second day in a row she'd woken in Tonino's bed, replete by a night of lovemaking. Her promises to self that she would sleep in her own bed had been broken pretty much the moment she'd made them.

Deny herself the opportunity of making love to Tonino again? She was no masochist.

Or was she?

Was the heady pleasure she found in his bed worth the inevitable heartache heading her way?

'Finn's happy here too,' he added into the silence before helping himself to a chunk of honeydew melon.

She looked at their sleeping son and could only agree.

'Have you thought any more about us marrying?' he asked.

Her answer was automatic. 'No.' She shook her head for good measure, her loose ponytail whipping with a crack.

He exhaled slowly. 'What is stopping you from saying yes?'

'Everything that stopped me when you first suggested it. Marriage is a terrible idea.'

An edge crept into his voice. 'Why?'

Orla felt an edge form inside her too, defensive spikes lifting beneath her skin. 'Because it wouldn't mean what it should mean. You wouldn't even be thinking it if it weren't for Finn. I mean, come on, four years ago you pretended to be someone else and, while I believe you about Sophia, it doesn't change that you did lie about your identity, and the only reason I can see for you doing that is because you never took me seriously from the start. I was so far removed from what you considered suitable wife material that you didn't need bother tell me the truth.'

A long pause of silence opened up between them, broken when Tonino took a swig of his beer.

'Thoughts of your *suitability…*' he delivered the word with a curled lip '…didn't cross my mind. When we first met my only thoughts were of bedding you. You didn't know me. You had no preconceptions. You just wanted me. And that felt great.'

He turned his head to face her. Even with both their eyes masked by sunglasses, his gaze penetrated her flesh and set her heart racing.

She remembered her own instinctive reaction when she'd learned the wealth, connections and power Tonino and his family had. It had frightened her. For many other women, it would have attracted them.

His voice lowered. 'But then you got under my skin and I knew I had to tell you the truth. The mistake I made was to fly to Tuscany before telling you because Sophia got to you first and fed you all those lies.'

'No, the mistake you made was not telling me the truth to begin with.' She shook her head to clear it from the effects of Tonino's seductive voice. He had a voice that could recite the worst kind of poetry and make it sound like a masterpiece. 'You were playing with me. I was just a joke to you, some naïve Irish girl you could play make-believe with.'

He downed the last of his beer. 'Maybe it started like that,' he admitted, 'but that is not how it finished. I fell for you, *dolcezza*, harder than I had ever fallen for anyone, and you ran away rather than confront me and allow me to defend myself. You believed Sophia's lies.'

'She was very convincing.' She rubbed her cheeks, feeling wretched. He was right. She hadn't given him the chance to defend himself from Sophia's lies.

'Sophia is a superb actress.'

'I think her hatred of me is genuine.'

'What hatred? What makes you say that?'

'Did you not see the dirty looks she kept throwing me at Aislin and Dante's wedding?'

'All I remember from that wedding is feeling sucker-punched by your reappearance in my life.'

'She looked like she wanted to throttle me.'

'Don't take it personally. She looks at everyone like that.' Tonino popped the cap off another beer, removed his sunglasses and looked at her squarely. 'I've known Sophia all my life. She's a bitch, yes, but she would never hurt you. She's married now and has a child of her own.'

'Oh.' She gave a shaky laugh. 'I suppose I imagined she'd spent the past four years making effigies of me.'

'Put your fears to rest. She is a professional grudge holder, but her violence is only verbal.'

'But why the grudge? If you didn't cheat on her with me, why does she hate me?'

'Because she knows I ended our engagement for you.'

'What...?' Until Orla had lost her memories, Sophia's pain and her unwitting contribution towards it had plagued her. She'd hoped she could put her guilt to bed but now Tonino was saying the ending of his engagement *had* been about her? 'You ended your engagement for *me*?'

Long moments passed before his nostrils flared. 'It wasn't strictly about you. It was about my desire for you. It was a desire no man who is bound to one person should feel for another.'

'I might be Irish but that's a riddle too far, even for me.'

He laughed but it contained a bitter tinge. 'The truth is, Sophia and I should never have got engaged.'

'Then why did you?'

'It was something our families always hoped for. Our mothers have been friends since they were babies. It was a running joke between them from when *we* were babies that Sophia and I would marry and as I neared thirty and felt the urge to settle down, marrying her made sense. On paper we were perfect for each other. You see, *dolcezza*, when you're rich you have to think of marriage in terms of reputation and with an eye to the future. My personal reputation is of little concern to me, but my parents' reputations matter greatly to them. Marriage to a Messina, a family as old and as noble as the Valentes, could only enhance that. And vice versa.'

'How did they take the ending of the engagement?'

She caught the flash of bitterness on his features.

'Not well?' she guessed.

'No,' he agreed shortly.

'I suppose that was understandable.'

His features sharpened. 'Understandable?'

Feeling she was dipping her toe in water infested by sharks that no one had told her about, she said tentatively, 'If they were such good friends with Sophia's parents, it must have been embarrassing for them.'

His jaw clenched. 'They weren't embarrassed. They were furious that I'd ruined their dream. They accused me of disloyalty. Can you believe that?' He ran an angry hand through his hair and shook his head. 'I knew they wouldn't be happy about it, but I never expected my mother to come *this* close to slapping my face or for my father to threaten to disinherit me if I didn't change my mind.' He made a distinctive snorting sound. 'As if I cared about his money. I was already worth far more than him.'

Orla, thinking of all the times her grandmother had threatened to cut her mother off without a penny without actually going through with it—after her death, her mother had shared the small inheritance with her siblings—said softly, 'And how are things between you now? I assume they must be better if we're taking Finn to their party.'

He made the snorting sound again.

Dismissive. That was what it sounded like.

'I will never forgive them for putting their reputations and pride above my happiness but they're still my parents. We're still a family and nothing can change that.'

'*Did* they disinherit you?'

Her question caused him to pause then give a low chuckle. 'Not as far as I know.'

'The threat was made in anger?'

He didn't answer.

Despite the seriousness of the discussion, a bubble of laughter rose up Orla's throat. 'You are *so* your father's son.'

'What do you mean?'

'When you get angry you make threats you don't mean. Like your threats of taking custody of Finn... I wonder if he'll inherit the Valente temper,' she added musingly.

Tonino stared at her, part in disbelief. Was she taking his parents' side? Surely not? If it had been one short argument he would get her point but he'd lived with their hot fury for months, a period when his mother could hardly bring herself to look at him. The first big argument had come the evening he'd ended it. He'd done the right thing by telling them personally and immediately.

He'd found solace from their fury in Orla's arms. He'd turned his phone off and cloistered her in his oldest apartment. Those magical days together had pushed the mess he'd created far from his mind. Unfortunately it had given his parents the time and space to build everything up so when he'd next seen them, they'd been ready to unload their venom at him. Reeling at their selfishness, reeling from Orla's disappearance, he'd unloaded right back at them.

'There are some lines that should never be crossed,' he

said shortly. 'And now that I'm a father it makes their re-action even more unforgivable.'

'Oh, come *on*.' Her shades masked her eyes, but he could swear he heard her eyes roll. 'They're only human. Life's too short to hold on to grudges.'

'Can you forgive *your* mother?'

'That's completely different. She was always a useless parent.' And then she surprised him completely by climbing onto his lap and straddling him. She wrapped her arms around his neck and sighed. 'Remember, to err is human, to forgive divine.'

'When are you going to forgive me?'

'I'm working on it.' And then she kissed him with such tenderness that if Finn hadn't been sleeping beside them, he would have ripped both their shorts off and taken her there and then.

CHAPTER TWELVE

LATER THAT NIGHT, dressed only in Tonino's shirt, which she'd adopted as her own, and replete in his arms, Orla made circles around his nipples. 'Can I ask you something?'

He answered sleepily, 'Anything.'

'Did you have any feelings for Sophia?'

She had no idea how she was going to feel whatever answer he gave, but it was a question that had been bugging her since their earlier trip to the beach. It took such a long time for him to answer that she thought he'd fallen asleep, but then a hand burrowed into her hair.

'I was attracted to her—Sophia is a beautiful woman— but that's as far as my feelings towards her went.' He sighed. 'The chemistry was not there. Not for me. I assumed familiarity would breed desire but I was wrong— all it bred was contempt. We'd been childhood friends but the more I got to know the grown-up Sophia, the less I liked her.' He twirled a lock of her hair around his finger, his voice dropping to a murmur. 'But it was only when a beautiful Irishwoman walked into my hotel that I knew I had to end the engagement.'

Her heart skipped.

Tonino kissed her head and tightened his hold around her. 'You, *dolcezza*, were the most beautiful woman I had ever set eyes on. I spent the day organising the refurbishment of your room when I should have been in meetings with lawyers and accountants.'

He felt the heavy beats of her heart pressing against his stomach. He felt the stirrings of arousal.

'I could not stop myself from fantasising about you. I fantasised about stripping you naked and making love to you.' The stirrings grew stronger. 'They were fantasies that told me I had to end things with Sophia—how could I marry her when I felt such intense desire for someone else? I did the honourable thing and ended the engagement immediately. I did not ask you out until after I'd spoken to her. When we made love, I was a free man.' Moving smoothly, he manoeuvred her onto her back and covered her body with his. 'And I am still a free man. Marry me and you will have me for ever.'

She stared up at him, her eyes like dazed orbs.

Cupping her cheeks, he pressed his nose to hers. 'You, *dolcezza*, are still the most beautiful woman I have ever seen. There is no one like you in this world. I have never wanted anyone the way I want you. You are under my skin and in my blood. I want you there for ever.'

And then he kissed her.

Orla, hypnotised as much by his voice as his words, sank into the firmness of his mouth with a sigh, a throb deep inside her already singing its head off in anticipation.

He'd never wanted anyone the way he wanted her?

Well, she'd never wanted anyone *but* him…

'Finn can have a good life here,' he murmured as he kissed her neck. 'He will have family, cousins to play with, sunshine, ripe fruits…everything he needs to thrive.' He captured a nipple over the cotton of the shirt covering her body and sucked it greedily. 'If you won't marry me, live with me. Move in…' He moved lower, kissing her shirt-covered belly, taking hold of her thighs and gently spreading them. 'You will be close to Aislin and Dante.' He moved even lower and gently raised her bottom. 'I know how much you miss them.'

'You…don't…play…fair,' she groaned, stickily wet and aching for him.

'I play to win.' He pressed his thumb to her swollen clitoris.

She moaned and grabbed hold of the pillow.

'Tell me this doesn't feel like winning to you too.' And then he replaced his thumb with his tongue and any semblance of coherent thought vanished as Orla was suffused in intense, hedonistic pleasure.

'We'll stay until the party. Save Finn having to do all that travelling.'

Orla's whispered words cut through the sleep pulling Tonino under.

He kissed her shoulder and murmured, 'If you move in he won't have to do any travelling between our countries.'

'I know.'

'Think about it. For Finn's sake.'

And, as Tonino finally fell into the oblivion of sleep, his last conscious thought was that it would be for his own sake too.

The next ten days passed with nothing more said about marriage or them living together. At first Orla had been glad of the reprieve but the longer time passed, the less she trusted it. Tonino was quite capable of bamboozling her with the subject when she least suspected it. She was supposed to be returning to Ireland tomorrow and was still no closer to making a decision.

The problem was, she admitted to herself, she was torn between her head and her heart. Her heart wanted Finn to have all the advantages living in Sicily would give him. Her head, however, kept pointing out that Tonino only wanted her for Finn. The sex between them was just a bonus—a free leg-over, as her grandmother would have primly called it.

But not for Orla. For Orla, the sex they shared... In the depths of her consciousness, she called it making love.

To make things worse, she missed him when he wasn't there.

He'd been with her and Finn all the time during their first week in his home but then, during their second week, he'd had to work. Work for Tonino consisted of attending important meetings and travelling around Europe on business. At least, that was how it looked to Orla.

There was something incredibly sexy about watching this hunk of a man dress for work, tucking a crisply ironed shirt into his tailored trousers, doing the buttons of the waistcoat, fixing his cufflinks into place, tying the laces of his handmade shoes... The urge to leap out from under the bedsheets and pounce on him would hit her so hard that she would clench her fists and force her mind to think of non-sexy things, like dirty laundry.

How was it possible to ache for someone so badly? And how was it possible to miss someone so much that she kept her phone close at all times, hurrying to answer it whenever he called. Which was often.

He was considerate too. The nights he arrived back so late that she'd already fallen asleep, he would slip into bed and do nothing more than wrap his arms around her. He didn't wake her for sex. He let her sleep, saving their lovemaking for the morning.

Then yesterday he'd arrived back at the chateau at lunchtime declaring his working week over, and she'd had to fight her legs again not to pounce on him with glee at having him back. Finn had been thrilled to see him too. He'd been so overjoyed to see his father that Orla's happiness had dimmed and she'd found herself torn into pieces with contradictory emotions that shamed her.

She was ashamed too that the moment he'd left for work on Monday, she'd got straight onto the phone and video-called Aislin for advice, shamed that she called herself an adult when she couldn't make a decision and shamed to be disturbing her sister's honeymoon.

Aislin had listened carefully to Orla's woe then her face had lit up. 'I *knew* it! He's nuts about you.' She'd burst into peals of laughter. 'If he still wants you after I made that threat to him, he's nuts at the least.'

'Are you drunk?'

'On happiness!'

'He isn't nuts about me. He wants Finn. I'm just the mother of his son.'

Aislin had rolled her eyes. 'You really need to get out more if you believe that. Look, missus, don't rush into any hasty decisions but, from my perspective, it would be grand if you moved to Sicily. I miss you and Finn.'

'You're having your own baby.'

'And my baby will want his aunty and cousin close by. I'm not telling you to marry him or even live with him, but if you could bring yourself to live in Sicily then we'll all be happy.'

'Why does it have to be *my* life that's uprooted?'

'Because you don't have a life.'

That was a fact Orla could not argue with.

She'd had a life once. A long time ago. When she'd first met Tonino she'd been excited to embrace the newest chapter of it by starting her dream job. The pregnancy had seen the future she'd worked so hard for slip through her fingers. The accident and its aftermath meant it was unlikely she would ever work again. Even if she could, she didn't think she'd be able to leave Finn. And if she couldn't contemplate leaving him for a few hours a day for a job, then how would she cope letting him visit his father for weeks at a time?

Everything pointed to her agreeing to live with Tonino. Or she could do as Aislin suggested and just move to Sicily independently, but that would only cause additional issues.

Marriage was out of the question. Marriage was a commitment that should only be entered between two people who meant their vows. Her mother had been shamed into marrying Aislin's father because her grandmother couldn't bear the shame of her daughter having a second illegitimate child by a second man. The marriage had been a disaster and ended after two years.

Deep down was the painful peripheral wish that Tonino's proposal meant more than a means to having their son living under his roof, but she would not let her mind go there.

She could smack her head with frustration at the choice she had to make.

Time was running out.

Tonino was expecting an answer that evening, when they returned from his parents' party.

Keen to make a good first impression with his family for Finn's sake, Orla left Finn with Tonino while she got ready. She went through her wardrobe half a dozen times before selecting a dark blue dress with chunky crystals running the length of its high neckline. It also had the requisite long sleeves and its mid-thigh-length skirt had a slight swing to it. All the sun she'd been living with these past few weeks had given her legs some colour, which was a nice bonus.

Before dressing, she put on matching lacy blue underwear then applied the topical lotion to her itching scars. The scars on her back were itching too and she slipped her robe on and, lotion in hand, knocked on the duty nurse's bedroom door.

The nurse was halfway through administering it, with her usual lecture of letting the lotion sink into the skin before Orla dressed, when there was a loud rap on the door adjoining the nurse's room with Finn's. To Orla's horror, the door couldn't have been shut properly for the weight of the knock caused it to swing open.

Tonino stood in the doorway, his hand raised. When he saw the nurse, he immediately burst into a flurry of Sicilian that died on his tongue when he caught sight of a frozen Orla.

The nurse seemed to sense her horror and immediately stepped between them, acting as a barrier so Orla could wrap the robe back around herself and hurry out of the room, cheeks flaming with humiliation.

Tonino wished he'd chosen to drive. It would have given him something to concentrate on.

Instead he sat in the back of his limousine trying to forget that his lover had frozen in horror at him seeing her in her underwear.

It was the closest he'd come to seeing her naked in four years. She'd run from the room like a frightened rabbit.

So much for the progress he'd believed they were making.

Things had been good between them. For the first time in for ever he'd shunned staying at his hotels during his business travels, keen to return home to his son and his son's mother.

Her frightened rabbit eyes had brought him crashing back to earth. There had been such fear in them that he'd barely registered her lack of clothing or looked at the scars she kept hidden from him.

Orla did not trust him.

She would allow the nurse to see her scars but allowing the man she shared a bed with every night to see them?

Not a chance. They made love constantly, but she always kept her top half clothed.

'Do your parents know Finn was conceived with the woman you ended things with Sophia for?' she asked shortly after Finn fell asleep to the motion of the car.

He paused a moment before answering. Now was not the time for an argument. Not when they had to deal with his family. He needed to keep his anger contained. 'I don't know. I haven't discussed it with them.'

'What about when you met with your mother yesterday?' After his early return home from work, he'd taken Finn out to meet his mother. It was the first time they had done anything without Orla and it had felt strange not having her with them.

'It wasn't mentioned.' Their meeting in a beach café had been the warmest exchange between them in four years. His mother had taken one look at Finn's huge brown eyes and visibly softened. Her unabashed delight at meeting her grandson had almost—almost—made Tonino soften too.

Orla's words about forgiveness had played in his head. At first, he'd dismissed it out of hand but her comment about him having his father's temper had played on his mind too. There was truth in it.

It had taken months for things to settle down into the semblance of normality between Tonino and his parents but, though they all went through the motions of being a family, things had never been the same. There had always been a frisson of ice between them. Embraces were perfunctory. Kisses did not connect with cheeks. For that, he had always blamed them.

Maybe it was time to look at his own actions and put himself in their shoes. He'd caused the end of a great friendship and, like it or not, he'd brought shame on them both.

He despised the selfishness of their reaction but for the

first time he accepted Orla's observation that it had been provoked by anger; a rush of blood to the head. When he'd effectively gone into hiding by practically chaining Orla to his bed and disconnecting his doorbell and turning his phone off, it had given his parents time for their fury to percolate. When he'd re-emerged, all their fury had blasted at him like a solar flare.

Shattered from Orla's desertion, he'd fired back at them. All the pain her leaving had caused him, he'd thrown onto his parents' shoulders.

He'd been an idiot, he acknowledged grimly.

'Your family can do rudimentary maths.' Orla's lyrical brogue cut through his thoughts. 'They will know Finn's conception coincided with your engagement ending. What if they take against him for it?'

'Why on earth would they do that?' he asked, astonished she would even suggest such a thing.

She stared out of the window. 'People have a habit of blaming children for the sins of their parents.'

'Are you talking generally or from experience?'

'Both. Dante was tarnished because of our father's gambling problem and womanising. Those things were nothing to do with him and completely beyond his control, yet he almost lost a business deal because of it.'

'And you? Have you had something similar happen?'

Turning her head to look at him, she said simply, 'My conception is something that's hung over me my entire life.'

Unsure if she was joking—*hoping* she was joking—he responded with a bemused, 'It's the twenty-first century.'

'That doesn't mean everyone has twenty-first-century ideals, especially in the village I grew up in. I was a walking reminder of my mother's shame—or should I say, her lack of it?' She gave a laugh that contained no humour at all.

'*Should* she have felt shame?' he asked curiously. He despised Orla's mother for abandoning her daughters and grandson when they needed her most, but it wasn't like Orla to be judgemental. 'She wasn't the married party in the affair. Salvatore was.'

'I don't know.' She shrugged in a helpless fashion and sighed. 'I used to know. It was all very cut and dried when I was a child. I had the mummy who went on holiday to Sicily and came home knocked up by a married man. Everyone knew I was the product of an affair.' She sighed again and rested her head back. 'I get it now, why you didn't tell me who you really were. It was similar to my reasons for not telling you I was Salvatore Moncada's illegitimate daughter. I didn't want you having any preconceived thoughts about me or for you to think I was easy like my mother.'

'I would never think that.'

'I know that now.' She caught his eye and smiled sadly. 'I'm really glad your mother has been so kind to Finn and that she wants a relationship with him, and I know I'm being selfish but I can't help worry about how your family will feel about me. I mean, you said the other week that reputation matters to them. Do they know who I am?'

'Yes. Believe it or not, the fact you're Dante Moncada's sister and half Sicilian works in your favour.'

Her nose wrinkled. '*Really?*'

He gave a short burst of humourless laughter. 'Really. You have the required pedigree.'

'I'm not a dog,' she said, visibly affronted.

'Obviously,' he answered wryly. 'But trust me on this; you have nothing to worry about with my family. They've been so worried that I'll never settle down and produce grandchildren that they wouldn't care if you were part of the *Cosa Nostra*.'

'Charming!' she said with a roll of her eyes. 'Is that

why you never settled down after Sophia? To punish your family for not supporting you?'

Her question threw him.

Had he been punishing them? Punishing his parents for destroying his trust in the unconditional love he'd always taken for granted by not attempting to understand his feelings?

Didn't he bear some responsibility for it too?

He remembered seeing his father's face go red with fury when he'd broken the news and feeling his own anger rise in turn. They'd been like a pair of rutting bulls.

Whatever the truth, when his parents' villa came into view, for the first time in four years the rancid curdle of acid he usually felt to be there was absent.

CHAPTER THIRTEEN

ORLA COULD NOT suck enough air into her lungs to kill the terror clawing at her as they approached Tonino's parents. Never minding Finn's conception and the end of the future marriage with their dream daughter-in-law, they were both powerful people. What on earth were they going to think of a little minnow like her?

The terror only evaporated when Angelica and Paolo Valente both pulled her into tight embraces and smothered her cheeks with kisses.

Who needed to speak a common language when body language so perfectly conveyed meaning? she thought dazedly.

The language barrier was much less a problem when Tonino introduced her to his brother and sister-in-law, both of whom spoke good English and embraced her with equal vigour.

However, the language barrier was the last thing to cross her mind when she was introduced to his sister. Orla recognised her instantly. Giulia Valente, barely a month after giving birth to her third child, looked as young and beautiful as she'd done in the photograph Orla had seen of her and Tonino in the Internet search that had caused Finn to kick her so memorably hard.

What had happened after she'd seen that photo? She *knew* it was important but, as had been the case for over three years, trying to force a memory only pushed it further into the shadows.

With whispered thanks, she accepted a glass of lemonade made from the fruit of the Valentes' lemon grove and slowly relaxed. Tonino's family were wonderfully hospitable. Here, at the customary party Angelica and Paolo always threw to celebrate the birth of a new grandchild—something it seemed, as the entire family had assured her, would be done for Finn too—was all Tonino's extended family, all his aunts, uncles, grandparents, the multitude of first and second cousins... It sent a pang through her to witness the closeness they all shared. Orla's family was of comparable size, but they had little day-to-day involvement in each other's lives. Not a single one of them had visited her or Finn in hospital or offered to help share the load Aislin had taken in caring for them. This Sicilian lot, she thought, would pack the hospital out if one of their own fell ill.

A silent tour of the villa led by Angelica herself, who held Orla's hand throughout, took her breath away. It matched Tonino's for size and elegance but with added homeliness.

If she moved in with Tonino, she would have to have a chat with him about feminising the chateau a little.

If...?

Surely the operative word now was 'when'. Because as the day went on, her indecision evaporated just as her terror had done.

She had to put her own feelings to one side and think of Finn. Sicily was the best place for him to be raised. Just look at all these people fussing over him! These people were his family and they would never let him down or abandon him. If she moved in with Tonino they would have Aislin living close to them, and Dante too.

She wouldn't be alone as she was in Ireland.

After the tour, she sat with Angelica on a garden bench waiting for Tonino to return from giving Finn his own tour of the villa.

As neither woman spoke the other's language, they didn't converse and yet there was something companionable and protective about the way Angelica positioned herself. She had an innate glamour similar to Dante's mother but if she'd had any work on her beautiful features, it was as subtle as subtle could be. She wore her intelligence much more freely.

A shout from the villa made them both get to their feet to see what the commotion was about.

A moment later, one of Tonino's nieces came flying out of the villa and raced straight to Orla, tugging her hand. Orla didn't need to speak Sicilian to know the young girl was begging her to come with her. Distress was its own universal language.

Call it sixth sense, call it mother's intuition, but she knew immediately what was happening and what she would find, and, clinging to the young girl's hand, she ran inside.

Finn was on the floor of the living room, Tonino crouched beside him, a crowd of young children surrounding him. His tiny body was rigid, convulsions racking him.

'Everyone stand back,' she barked, immediately hitting autopilot.

But, of course, they didn't understand her.

A visibly distressed Tonino blinked then barked what she assumed was the same order in Sicilian. The circle around her convulsing child parted, leaving only Tonino.

'You need to stand back too,' Orla ordered. There was no time for pleasantries.

Dark colour stained his clenched features but he did as she asked.

Sinking to her knees, Orla carefully moved Finn onto his

side and placed her hand on his tiny head. His arms jerked, his legs thrashed but it was his eyes she always found the most terrifying. They stared wide open but didn't see.

Tonino had never felt so useless in his life. Or as scared. His heart had stuck in his throat the moment he'd seen his son topple from his sitting position on the floor of the living room where Tonino had put him so he could play with his cousins. His body had gone into spasm with the movements Tonino had seen on videos when learning all he could about his son's condition.

The sounds that had come from his son's poor throat…

Those were sounds that would haunt him.

Thank God for Orla.

All she did was sit beside their son and stroke his hair and whisper soothing words, but it acted like magic. There was not one person in that room who didn't feel it too.

Tonino had no idea if Finn heard his mother's voice or saw her face until the convulsions began to subside, but he was as certain as he could be that his son felt her presence even if only on a subconscious level. When his eyes slowly regained their focus, they stayed on Orla; he was clearly frightened but taking every ounce of comfort he could from his mummy.

It struck Tonino that she only knew what to do and could handle it so calmly because she had lived it many times before.

And it struck him too that she had pushed him aside because she didn't trust him to handle the situation and look after their son.

The harsh truth was that Orla would never trust him.

Orla smoothed Finn's bedsheet over him and kissed his forehead. He was already asleep.

Tonino hovered in the doorway, watching, waiting for his turn to kiss their son goodnight.

She waited for him in the corridor.

He shut the door and looked at her with exhausted eyes. 'I need a drink.'

She closed her eyes. 'I think I could do with one too.'

She followed him to the outdoor bar, which overlooked the swimming pool. The terrace area had a canopy overhanging individual round sofas that were perfect for curling up on and she sank into one with a grateful sigh.

Checking the volume of her phone was switched on, she placed it on the sofa's arm. If the nurse had any concerns, she would be able to reach her straight away.

A crystal glass with a small measure of amber liquid in it was thrust at her.

She took it from Tonino's hand with a muttered thank you and had a tiny sip of it. When heat flowed down her throat she was glad she'd stuck to a tiny sip.

'That was the most terrifying thing I have ever seen,' he said bluntly as he sat heavily on the seat across from hers, putting the bottle of liquor on the floor beside his feet while he cradled his full glass.

She smiled ruefully and tucked her legs under her bottom. 'Yes.'

'You didn't trust me to help you.'

'Sorry?'

He breathed heavily through his nose. 'As soon as you reached Finn you took control and pushed everyone out. Including me.'

'No, I didn't,' she denied, confused.

He tipped a third of his drink down his throat and angrily brushed away the residue on his mouth with his thumb. 'You did.'

'If I insulted or hurt you, then I'm sorry.' She shrugged her shoulders helplessly. 'When Finn has these fits, I go into automatic pilot.'

There was the slightest softening in his stance. He ran a hand over his bowed head. 'Does it get easier?'

She shook her head sadly. 'No. You just get better at dealing with it while it's happening. It happens rarely now that he's on the new medication but the first time it happened in front of me, I practically ran around the room banging into the walls in panic.'

He lifted his head to meet her stare. 'When you say the first time it happened in front of you…?'

She sighed and took another tiny sip. 'When the convulsions started, I was still in the rehab centre. Aislin was the one to deal with it. She had to deal with everything about his condition until I was well enough to play my part.'

His dark brown eyes stayed on hers thoughtfully. She thought he was going to say something but he didn't.

With the warmth from the liquor making her feel calmer inside, she decided now was the time to tell him.

'I've been thinking about your suggestion of Finn and I moving in with you,' she said tentatively.

He raised a brow.

'And I think you're right. It would be better for Finn to live here.'

He continued staring at her expressionlessly.

'We'll move in with you…if the offer still stands,' she added when the lack of emotion on his face injected a jolt of ice up her spine.

He took a much larger drink of his liquor. 'Are you prepared to marry me?'

'You already know the answer to that.'

'You still refuse my proposal?'

'Come on, Tonino, it's nothing personal. I just don't want us to marry.'

'Then I decline.'

She uncurled her legs and sat upright. 'What do you mean?'

'I have been thinking too and I have decided it has to be marriage or nothing.'

'What? But why?'

'Because it's the only way I can trust that you're committed to us.'

'Living with you would show that commitment.'

He shook his head violently and downed the last of his drink. 'No, *dolcezza*, all it would show is that you're committed for the next five minutes.'

'You still don't trust me?'

His burst of laughter was loud and bitter. 'Unfortunately I have the opposite problem. I *do* trust you. I know you well enough now that I believe you always intended to tell me about Finn. I know you well enough to say with confidence that your reasons for keeping the pregnancy secret from me were justified—I still think they were wrong, but I believe *you* believed you were doing the right thing.'

'I don't understand what you're saying.'

He unscrewed the bottle and poured himself another full glass. 'I'm saying that you always do what you think is best for Finn. He is your priority.'

'As he should be.'

'Agreed. But not at the cost of tying yourself to a man you don't love or trust. If you loved or trusted me, you would marry me. But you don't so all you're prepared to give is a half-hearted commitment that you can walk away from any time you like.'

'I wouldn't do that.'

'No? You say that when you don't deny you neither love nor trust me?'

'Well, it's hardly as if you love me.'

'Don't I?'

She blinked. 'Do you?'

His gaze held hers before he shook his head grimly and had another drink. 'When we were on the beach last week, you accused me of treating you like a joke four years ago. The truth is, you were the one who treated me like a joke. You treated me like I was nothing.'

Indignant, she snapped, 'I did *not*...'

'Then why did you not give me a chance to defend myself against Sophia's lies? You have never explained that to me.'

She opened her mouth to answer but nothing came out. Why *hadn't* she confronted him?

'Why did you run?' he asked roughly. 'Why block my number? If you'd cared for me in any way, you would have given me that chance.'

'I ran because I was already an emotional wreck,' she blurted out.

He stared at her grimly. His mouth clamped shut, forcing her to fill the silence.

'The day you went to Tuscany, I went to see my father. I knew he was due back in Sicily that day and I was desperate to finally meet him.' Her eyes filled with tears and she blinked them back. The last thing she needed right then was to cry but the memory had surfaced with painful vividness. She wished it would lock itself back in its box. 'He wouldn't see me. He refused. The dirty little secret had to remain a dirty little secret. And then I got to the hotel and found Sophia waiting for me with evidence that the man I'd been sleeping with was engaged to another woman and I felt *sick* with myself and so ashamed.'

Not a flicker of emotion crossed his stony face. 'Even if Sophia had been telling the truth it wouldn't have been your fault.'

'Maybe not but that's not how it felt. In the space of two hours I'd been rejected by my father and learned the man I was falling in love with was a cheat and a liar. All I could think of was getting out of Sicily and away from the Sicilian men who'd lied and hurt me.'

'So because your father was a womanising coward, you decided I was of the same mould? Without giving me the right to reply, you grabbed the chance to run away, and when you found you were pregnant and discovered the family I come from is powerful, it gave you another excuse to keep your distance for that bit longer, didn't it? You don't trust anyone.'

'I trust you…'

'Do not *lie* to me,' he snarled with such force she jumped. 'The only person you trust is your sister. If you trusted me even a little you wouldn't go to such great lengths to hide from me. You share your body with me every night, you sleep in my arms, yet you think me a shallow misogynist who runs at the first sight of a blemish on a woman's skin.'

'I don't think that about you.'

'Then explain yourself. Tell me why I am not good enough to look at you.'

'It isn't like that,' she beseeched, fighting even harder to stop the tears from falling. 'My scars will disgust you.'

'Your opinion of me is even worse than I thought.'

'*No*, that is *not* what I'm saying. My scars…' She tugged at her hair and tried to verbalise everything racing through her burning brain. 'I remember the woman I was—the woman you remember—and then I look in the mirror and see the woman I've become, and I'm reminded of everything I've lost and everything Finn's lost. That seizure he had today…that was *mild* compared to the ones he used to have. He has suffered every single day of his life and he will never have a normal childhood. I woke up in a hospital unable to move and unable to communicate. I didn't know if the child in my belly was dead or alive. I couldn't hold him until he was a year old and even then Aislin had to help because I was too weak to hold him on my own. I screamed with pain every day for a year and pushed myself harder than I would have believed possible to get home to my child and all I have to show for it now are the scars on my body. My pain is over, but his suffering will never end. I look at my scars and my heart shreds for the suffering our child has to bear, which he will have to bear every day for the rest of his life, and you think I should *flaunt* them to you?'

His jaw throbbed. 'No, *dolcezza*, I do not expect you to flaunt them. I expect you to share them with me as the father of your child who feels terrible guilt that his bit of fun with a beautiful Irishwoman had such tragic consequences.'

Feeling all the emotions inside her leech out, Orla put her glass on the floor and buried her face in her hands. 'You have nothing to feel guilty about. You have only tried to do the right thing since you learned about Finn.'

'I missed the first three years of his life. Those are years I will never get back.'

'I'm sorry.'

'We are both beyond apologies, do you not think? We both feel guilt, but we have to try and accept that it does not solve anything. You have put our child first since the day you learned you carried him. It is time for me to put him first too. I want to be a permanent part of his life, but I see that it is impossible.'

'What are you saying?'

'That you should return to Ireland with him. It's his home. His language. Where he is comfortable and familiar.'

'But…'

'I will still see him. I visit Ireland regularly. And I will have him visit for holidays.'

'That does not sound like the joint custody we spoke of.'

'Joint custody will not work for Finn. He needs stability. *You* are his stability.' Tonino squeezed his eyes shut as he recalled the look in Finn's eyes when he'd come out of the seizure and locked onto Orla's loving stare. Orla was his son's world. He had to accept that.

'Stay here for a few more days to let him recover from the seizure. I will take myself away somewhere.'

'What are you talking about?'

Dragging air into his tightened lungs, he picked up the bottle, got to his feet and took three heavy paces to the bar.

'Tonino…' she said tentatively. 'Are you calling it a day between us?'

He laughed. '*Dio*, you nearly sound upset.'

Four years ago Orla hadn't known of his trappings of wealth and had fallen for him regardless. She'd looked into his heart as no one else had done and fallen for him…but only to a point. The moment doubts had crept in she'd run away like the coward she was. And now, four years on, when she knew perfectly well his wealth, still she looked in the heart of him and decided he wasn't enough. She did not love him. She did not trust him.

He did not believe she would ever trust him. Without trust there could never be love.

'But is that what you're saying?' she persisted. 'You want to call it off because I won't marry you? And you're the one who laughed at me for being old-fashioned?'

'Do not dare use humour to wriggle out of this,' he snarled, twisting round to face her. 'I have done nothing but my best to accommodate you.'

'For Finn's sake,' she whispered. All the colour had drained from her face.

'And for yours.' He swore loudly and poured himself another drink. 'Everything I have done has been with you in mind too and all you do is resist me. You won't give an inch and you won't trust me, not with your heart, your body or our son's health.'

'That's not fair and it's not true—'

'For the last time, stop *lying*!' He slammed his glass on the bar, spilling amber liquid all over his hand and the bar surface. There was clarity in the spilled liquid that focused the mind and made him take a long breath to find clarity in his thoughts. 'If you can't stop lying to me then at least stop lying to yourself.'

Tonino would not lie to himself any more either. After four years of lies, the truth he had buried deep in his subconscious had risen up as clear as the spilt liquor on his hand.

He had never got over Orla.

He suspected that he'd fallen in love with her four years ago. He'd certainly never forgotten her or got over her, even when he'd carried on with his life and pushed her from his mind. Only in his dreams had she come back to him. Orla was the reason he'd never settled down. It was nothing to do with punishing his parents—it was because there was no room left in his heart for anyone else.

He suspected too that his purchase of the Bally House Hotel in Dublin had been a subconscious effort to put himself on the same soil as her.

And he suspected, too, that if he continued to live under the same roof as her, knowing his love for her would be unrequited for ever, he would drive himself insane.

All these years he'd been waiting for Orla to come back to him and he hadn't even known it.

He'd finally had a taste of life as a family with the woman he loved and the child he worshipped but it wasn't enough for her. *He* wasn't enough for her.

Any ties they'd forged together had been ripped apart.

It was time to say goodbye.

CHAPTER FOURTEEN

ORLA INSPECTED FINN from head to toe, ensuring not a speck of lint or dust marred his miniature tuxedo, then rewarded him with a beaming smile. 'You, young man, look delicious.'

He beamed.

'In fact, if your daddy wasn't about to whisk you to the wedding, I would gobble you all up!'

'Tell your mummy to save some of that deliciousness for me,' Aislin piped up.

'I don't do sharing.'

'Then you won't mind if I eat the giant chocolate bar Dante bought for me all by myself.'

Orla stuck her tongue out at her sister, then felt familiar panic skittle through her veins when the doorbell rang.

That would be Tonino here to collect Finn.

In the month since they'd decided—since *he'd* decided—that they should call time on their relationship, Orla's life had changed immeasurably. For a start, she'd put her Dublin house up for sale and moved in with Aislin and Dante. One thing her time with Tonino had taught her was that she didn't have to do everything alone. She'd thought when Aislin moved to Sicily that she would be fine coping with Finn alone with the medical team on-hand.

She'd been wrong.

She'd been lonely.

She'd proved to herself that she could cope but coping wasn't living.

Tonino had shown her what it was like to live and have fun again. To be a woman, not purely a mother. And, for all Tonino's selflessness, he and Finn deserved to be in each other's lives. Living in Sicily allowed them to spend plenty of time together. It also allowed his family to drop by at all hours to see Finn too. Mercifully, Dante and most of his staff spoke excellent English and translated when needed.

She wouldn't stay with Aislin and Dante for too long. Dante had convinced one of his neighbours that they really wanted to accept an astronomical amount of money for Orla and Finn to buy their home.

Turning to her sister, hoping she would handle the handover as she usually did, she found Aislin with her feet up on the coffee table munching her way through the chocolate bar. She'd hinted darkly a number of times that it was time for Orla to face him alone. She supposed that time was now.

It was fine. She could do it. All she had to do was open the door and wheel Finn to him. Tonino had everything else in hand. She wouldn't have to worry about her son at all. He was never safer and in better care than with his father.

'Come on, Finn,' she said brightly, plastering a smile to her face so big a clown would be envious. One of Tonino's cousins was getting married at his Tuscan hotel. He and Finn and two nurses would fly on his private jet there and stay the night, returning at lunchtime tomorrow.

The smile died when she looked into Tonino's expressionless handsome face and her heart erupted.

He stood at the front door dressed in an identical tuxedo to Finn, the scent of a recent shower and recently applied cologne coming off him in waves.

He nodded at her but avoided her eye. 'All well?'

She nodded back. 'All well.'

'*Bene.* I will see you tomorrow.'

She kissed Finn on the cheek, told him she loved him then stepped back to let Tonino take over.

Another whiff of cologne caught in her senses. A whisper of memory emerged…

Knees suddenly weakening, she pressed herself against the wall by the door.

The missing pieces of her time with Tonino flashed through her retinas with the speed of a bullet.

She *remembered.*

She remembered making love to him. She remembered the first wonderful, tender time. She remembered all the others.

She remembered the abandon. The hedonism. The wantonness. The feeling that what they were sharing together was so wonderful and perfect that it could never be wrong.

The car pulled away. She watched, blurry eyed, until it disappeared from sight, the world only coming back into focus when another memory shot through her brain. The final memory. The last missing piece.

Her heart began to hammer and she put a fist in her mouth to stop herself from howling.

With his baby growing in her belly, she'd cyber-stalked him. She'd cyber-stalked him for *months*, bracing herself for a picture of Tonino and a new lover to appear. When she'd translated the article accompanying the photo of Tonino and Giulia and learned she was his sister, not his lover, Finn had kicked her so hard it had physically hurt. That kick had delivered some much-needed sense into her.

That had been the moment she'd realised she loved Tonino.

She sank to the ground and hugged her knees to her chest as the memories flooded her and the truth she'd hidden from screamed at her.

In her heart, Orla had been waiting for the real Tonino

to reveal himself. He'd been too handsome, too sexy and too chivalrous for it to all be true. She'd put him on a pedestal fully expecting him to be knocked off it and knocked off he had been. Sophia's confrontation with her, however much it had sickened her, had almost come as a relief.

Because there was no way a man like Tonino could return her feelings. Her father didn't want her, her mother had abandoned her…why would a man like Tonino want her when he could have any woman in the whole wide world? She'd believed that long before she'd learned he was as rich as Croesus.

But he *had* wanted her! He'd lied about his identity but no one could fake the affection he'd shown her or fake his desire.

Orla had known then that whatever fears she had, she needed to go to him. She'd needed to see him in the flesh and tell him of the life they'd created together. To give him the chance to defend himself, as she should have done from the start. To tell him that she loved him. To see if they could possibly have a future together.

So desperate had she been to get to him that she'd booked a flight online without caring who the carrier was, grabbed her passport and set off to Dublin airport, barely registering the atrocious weather conditions.

She'd been on her way to Tonino.

She remembered slowing to a crawl, intending to pull over when visibility got to less than zero, but the accident itself was a blank. That was one memory she would never get back.

The accident had stopped her getting to the man she loved. She'd failed in her mission to tell him of her love then and she'd failed to tell him that she loved him still because she'd been too scared to see the truth. And now it was all too late.

She'd screwed it all up again.

Hold on a minute…!

What had he said about love and trust the last time they were alone together, the night it had all fallen apart? Hadn't he implied that he loved her?

Could he…?

Tonino had given her every opportunity to see the truth but she'd kept her blinkers on and stayed deliberately blind. In her own blind way she had sabotaged them.

'Are you going to sit here all day?'

Shaken out of the trance she'd fallen into, she looked up to find Aislin in the doorway, still munching on the now depleted bar of chocolate.

Aislin had been scared to love Dante, she remembered. Her insecurities had been acute too.

Their mother had a lot to answer for.

But their mother could not be blamed for Orla's failure to embrace the life Tonino had offered her and which she'd been too frightened to accept.

'Ash?' she whispered.

'Yes?'

'I think I love him.' Then, raising her voice, she said it with conviction. 'I love Tonino.'

Her sister's beautiful face gazed down on her, chewing slowly. Then she swallowed her mouthful and held out a hand to help Orla up. 'Well, took you long enough.'

'What? You knew?'

'Of course I knew, you eejit.' Aislin put her arm around her and held her close as they walked back into the house. It wouldn't be long before Aislin's belly entered the room first. 'Now all you need to decide is what you're going to do about it.'

Do?

She thought quickly, the rudiments of a plan forming

'Do you think Dante would mind if I borrowed h⸱ this afternoon?'

'Fancy a trip to Tuscany, do you?' Aislin asked with a grin. 'Are you going to gatecrash the wedding?'

'Something like that.'

'Want some help making yourself look beautiful before you leave?'

'Actually…yes, please.'

Tonino placed a kiss to his exhausted child's forehead. Finn was already asleep. It had been a long day for him and all the playing and dancing with the other children had worn him out.

Leaving him with the duty nurse, Tonino slipped into the adjoining suite and poured himself a bourbon. He needed something stronger than wine and he needed a few minutes to himself before rejoining his family in the ballroom.

The temptation to stay in his suite and bury his troubles in the bottom of the bottle was strong.

He'd been doing well this past month. He'd kept himself busy. He accepted he'd probably drunk a little more wine than was good for him, but a man needed to sleep.

And then this morning Orla had been the one to hand Finn over to him.

He hadn't been prepared for seeing her. Normally she hid away and let Aislin take care of the handover, which had suited him perfectly.

In the past month he and Orla had exchanged dozens of polite messages but until that morning they hadn't seen each other in person or spoken.

Seeing her again had hit him like a punch in the gut.

Had he imagined the misery he'd seen swirling in her green eyes? Had it just been a figment of his imagination, a desperate hope that she might miss him as much as he missed her?

Damn it to hell, he missed her more than he'd believed

possible. More than he'd missed her four years ago. And she'd moved to Sicily! That had only made things worse.

She was here in his country but not for him.

He wanted to hate her. If he could turn every ounce of the love he carried in his soul for her into hate, he might feel as if there was a purpose to his life.

Finn was his purpose now. It was everything else that had become meaningless. If not for Finn, he wouldn't have bothered coming to this wedding. He wouldn't have had to put up with Sophia, a guest on the bride's side, glaring at him for the duration.

His father had noticed. He'd leaned into Tonino during the meal and whispered, 'You dodged a bullet there, my son.'

If he'd had the energy to laugh, he would have done. Raucously. Instead, he'd kissed his father's cheek and told him he loved him. And then he'd done the same to his mother. The unspoken rift that had dogged his life these past four years was over. Injured pride had seen him twist their own injured pride into more than it was and blinded him. Their son had dumped their closest friends' daughter without a word of warning and cloistered himself away with a new woman without pausing for breath—of course they'd been embarrassed and angry. That didn't mean they didn't support him. He'd only failed to see it for what it was rather than seeing it as proof that their love was conditional because he'd been in agony over losing Orla.

That agony was nothing compared to the agony of losing her a second time.

Orla was too sick with nerves to care a jot about the magnificent converted monastery whose steps she climbed to enter. She bit back her frustration at having to justify her presence—this was a wedding of two rich, powerful families so security was bound to be tight—by showing her passport and explaining she was the mother of Tonino Valente's child.

The taller of the security guards burst out laughing.

'It's not a joke,' she beseeched, too tired to be affronted. 'Please, let me in.'

When she'd decided to fly to Tuscany and declare herself to Tonino, she'd imagined she would be there in a couple of hours. She hadn't bargained on Aislin spending an age doing her hair and make-up and finding the perfect outfit for her to wear. Then she'd had to wait for a flight-slot out of Sicily, then the helicopter that was supposed to fly her to the wedding had suffered a fault and the pilot had refused to take off so she'd had to wait for a taxi. She would have been happy getting into any old banger but the pilot, who'd organised the taxi for her, was insistent that she wait for an official chauffeured car. She'd had no idea where the official car was coming from—Siberia, maybe?—but after an hour of impatient waiting she'd managed to get through the language barrier and order a taxi for herself. Unfortunately, arriving in an ordinary taxi had meant the security guards looked at her and thought she was ordinary too; far too ordinary to be an invited guest to this society wedding. Especially as she didn't have an invitation.

As her gaze darted around for another way into the hotel, her heart sank to see security guards posted pretty much everywhere.

'Call him,' she pleaded when the tall security guard proved immovable. 'Please, call Mr Valente. He'll vouch for me.'

She was rewarded with another, even heartier laugh.

Salvation came in the unexpected form of Sophia.

The beautiful Sicilian woman appeared from the sprawling gardens and walked up the ancient steps, cat's eyes narrowed, smelling of cigarettes. A conversation in Sicilian broke out between Sophia and the security guard that ended with Sophia taking Orla's arm and dragging her into the hotel, throwing what was obviously a curse over her shoulder at the humiliated security guard.

The only people in the huge hotel reception were teenagers sprawled over the leather sofas escaping their parents to do some serious snogging. One couple broke for air when they walked in but, when they realised it was no one who was going to tell them off, got back to the business at hand.

Sophia dropped her hold on Orla's arm and stepped back to inspect her critically. 'You look…*bene.*'

'Thank you.' Orla braced herself for a scratch down the face. 'And thank you for vouching for me.'

Sophia waved a bored hand. 'I think is too late to see your son—Tonino has taken him to bed.'

Orla nodded. She would find someone who could tell her which one his suite was. Or call one of Finn's nurses. Or she could bite the bullet and actually call Tonino…

'He is beautiful boy.'

'Sorry?'

'Your son.'

'Oh.' Orla waited for the sting in the tail to the compliment. 'Thank you.'

Sophia shifted so she was directly in front of Orla, forcing Orla to brace herself again for attack. The Sicilian woman looked her up and down one last time before her haughty, beautiful face softened. Then she did something that stunned Orla completely. Sophia wrapped her bony arms around her and pulled her into an even bonier embrace.

'I am sorry,' Sophia whispered in her ear, even while she actively avoided a single strand of their hair touching. Then she pulled away, squeezed Orla's hands with a rueful, apologetic smile, turned on her heel and clip-clopped into the ballroom.

* * *

Tonino tipped another hefty measure of bourbon down his neck. This one, he was sure, would numb his aching heart. His intention to leave the suite and join the wedding reception for another hour had come to nothing.

Pinching the bridge of his nose, he breathed in deeply.

He did not think there was a place he would less like to be than at the reception party celebrating the marriage of another happy couple when he felt so raw inside.

What was Orla doing? Sitting with her sister watching a movie and sharing a large bowl of popcorn? Or had she gone to bed already? Did she have one of those headaches she suffered from? If he drank enough of this bourbon would he have a matching headache, or would it just send him to sleep?

It was while he was debating the merits of drinking until he passed out—Finn was fast asleep and under the nurse's watchful care—that the knock on his door came.

He rubbed the nape of his neck with a sigh.

Another knock quickly followed.

Figuring it was likely to be his mother hoping for another kiss with her grandson, he got grudgingly to his feet.

When he saw who was there he was so certain it was an alcohol-induced hallucination that he laughed mirthlessly at the fertility of his imagination and shut the door in the mirage's face.

He took two steps back to the sofa and his bottle of bourbon and froze.

His hands were shaking. His legs were shaking. His heart was pumping harder than he had ever felt it pump before.

He spun back and took the two steps needed to reach the door again and fling it open.

It was no mirage.

The woman standing at the door, ravishing in a green

silk halter-neck dress, thick dark hair lightly curled into waves, clearly apprehensive behind the sultry make-up, was Orla.

As if in a dream, Tonino stepped wordlessly aside and admitted her into his suite.

Her divine scent followed her inside, clinging to her like a cloud and diving straight into his bloodstream to make his heart thump even harder.

Orla had never felt such a mixture of terror and excitement as she had when she'd knocked on Tonino's door. To have it slammed straight back shut again had stunned her and she'd just plucked up the courage to knock again when he opened it a second time looking as if he'd seen a ghost.

And that was when all the terror left her.

The desolation and fighting wonder in Tonino's eyes crowded out the lingering doubt. He did love her. She felt it as deeply as she felt their son's love.

'Orla...?'

She stepped to him and placed a finger gently to his mouth. Their gazes held for a long, lingering moment. Then she took hold of his hand and silently led him into the bedroom.

She waited until he was sitting on the bed before breaking the hold of their hands and stepping back.

He didn't say a word, just gazed at her, his breaths taut and shallow.

She'd come to his suite without a plan, without any rehearsed speech, her only intent being to find him. Now that she was here she knew what she had to do. What she *must* do.

Saying a prayer for courage first, she drew the curtains. Then she dimmed the lights so the only illumination was a soft glow. It was enough for him to see.

The dress she wore had one button at the nape of her neck. Standing only a few steps from Tonino, she undid it. The dress held for a moment before falling to her waist. Keeping her eyes fixed on the man she loved, she reached round to her back and pulled the small zip down so the entire dress fell to her feet, leaving her naked except for a pair of black lace knickers and the heeled shoes she now stepped out of.

Then she pulled the knickers down, stepped out of them too and walked to him, certain he must be able to see her heart beating frantically beneath her chest.

There was a boulder-like lump in Tonino's throat. It was the only thing stopping his heart from flying out of his mouth.

Was he dreaming? He hardly dared move a muscle in case he woke from it.

She stood between his parted thighs and reached for his hand. Her touch felt real. When she placed it on her stomach… That felt real too.

He exhaled everything in his lungs then refilled them. Orla's scent merged with the air he breathed in.

He closed his eyes and counted to ten. When he opened them, she was still there, a look in her eyes that made his hammering heart swell.

Slowly, he allowed his gaze to drift down her body.

Pregnancy had changed it only a little since he'd last seen her naked. Her breasts were fuller, the nipples darker. Her hips were a little wider, her stomach more rounded. And slashed across that same stomach were two long, vivid scars, one vertical, the other horizontal…and as he looked he found another, smaller horizontal scar across her knicker-line. There were numerous different smaller scars too, marring her chest and the tops of her arms. Scars from where shards of glass had penetrated her skin.

In the blurred recess of his mind came the realisation that the dress she'd just stripped out of had exposed her arms. He'd been too busy staring in wonder at the mirage of her appearance to notice.

She pivoted slowly to show him her back. More scars.

Something hot stabbed the backs of his eyes, something so unexpected and rare that it took a few beats before Tonino recognised it as tears.

Placing his hands on her hips, he pressed his cheek against her back, closed his eyes and breathed her in. He felt her tremble.

Then she turned again and cupped his face with her hands. Bringing her face close to his, she stared deep into his brimming eyes.

'You make me feel things that terrify me,' she whispered before brushing her mouth against his and moving her hands from his face to trail down his neck and unbutton his shirt.

Her lips found his neck and bit it gently while her hand found the button of his trousers.

A shudder shot through him.

Between brushes of lips and darts of tongue she continued. 'My feelings for you scared me so much four years ago that I took the first opportunity to run.' She pulled the zip of his trousers down and tugged them to his hips. 'I didn't trust my feelings for you, and I didn't trust your feelings for me.'

'Orla...'

Her name came as a groan from his mouth, but no further words came for she'd covered his mouth with her own again and whispered a soft, 'Shh.'

Mouths fused, she pushed gently at his chest so he was lying on the bed.

Parting his shirt, she ran her hands over his chest before shifting to straddle him, elbows either side of his face, green eyes boring into his. 'I cannot express how sorry I am. I was a frightened rabbit. That day...that rejection

from my father and then that confrontation with Sophia…'
She kissed the tip of his nose. 'They were the confirmation
I needed that you weren't to be trusted and that I should
run. I didn't give you a chance to defend yourself and I
will regret that for the rest of my life. My only defence is
that I was terrified. Most of the people I love have rejected
me. My father didn't want me. My mother never wanted
me… How could you want me?' She squeezed her eyes
shut before reaching down to tug his trousers and underwear lower still, freeing his erection. 'Do you remember
leaving for Tuscany? You kissed me goodbye and said that
we needed to talk that night. After what Sophia told me, I
thought you were going to tell me it was over. I ran before
I could be pushed.'

'I was going to tell you the truth,' he said quietly, sincerity and pain ringing in his eyes. 'And then I was going
to ask you to marry me.'

Her chin wobbled. A tear fell from her eye and landed
on his cheek. 'I'm sorry for everything. I'm sorry for realising my feelings too late. If I hadn't been such a coward you would have been there for the pregnancy and the
birth. Everything would have been different. The accident
wouldn't have happened…'

'Hey.' Gripping her wrists, he used his strength to flip
Orla onto her back so that he was the one straddling her
before she could protest. 'Don't you dare blame yourself
for that. It was not your fault.'

More tears leaked from her eyes, falling onto the pillow beneath her head. 'I was coming to you.'

'What?'

'That day. The accident. I was going to the airport. I
was coming to find you. To tell you about the baby and
to tell you…'

'Tell me what?' he whispered when her voice became
too choked for words to form.

She swallowed but did not move her glistening eyes from his. 'That the only happiness I have ever truly known has been with you. I love you. I loved you then and I love you now. I do want to marry you, Tonino. Not for Finn's sake but for mine because living without you is hell. I'm lost. I've been lost and searching for you for four years. I love you and if there is any chance you love me and still see a future for us, I will take it and I will fight for it. I will fight for you and I will fight for us. I love you.'

Orla, purged of all the things she had needed to say, felt her chest fill with dread as Tonino remained silent.

And then he smiled and blinked back what looked suspiciously like his own tears. 'Orla O'Reilly…' He closed his eyes and kissed her reverently. 'My love, you cannot know how badly I have wanted to hear those words from you. What happened four years ago… I think we can both share blame for that. I should have told you the truth of who I was, but I was a coward who was scared that you would change and become like all the other women in my world.' He brushed away a strand of hair that had fallen over her face. 'I never imagined that someone like you existed and when you disappeared it was like the darkest shadow had settled over me. I never settled down because I couldn't. You had taken my heart with you.'

Orla felt that she could choke from all the emotion filling her. She pressed her lips to his, needing the closeness, needing to feel his breath and the warmth of his touch like a bee seeking pollen.

Somehow, in the weight of the tender kiss they shared, he slid his trousers off and rested himself between her legs.

Incredible sensations suffused her as he drove slowly inside her.

'I love you, Orla,' he whispered raggedly as he withdrew to the tip. 'I fell in love with you so quickly I didn't even know it was happening. I tried to forget you, but it was impossible. You were in my head and in my heart, and you have never left it. My love is yours for ever.'

And then he thrust deep inside her.

Orla wrapped her arms tightly around his neck and her legs tightly around his waist and, lips crushed together, succumbed to the heady pulsations growing in intensity in her slavish body and filling into her heart so that when she reached her climax and the pulsations ripped through her very being, her heart opened like a flower in bloom and never closed again.

EPILOGUE

ORLA STOOD OUTSIDE the Bally House church doors and looked up at the blue sky with a smile.

'Thank you,' she whispered to whoever was out there listening to these things. Whoever that deity was, she would be for ever grateful for them turning the sun on over her beautiful Emerald Isle for this one day.

Her sister gave her one last critical inspection before a huge smile broke over her face. 'You look beautiful,' she said, eyes brimming.

Orla punched her in the arm. 'Pack it in or you'll get me going.'

Aislin sniffed and blinked frantically. 'I'm sorry. Stupid hormones.'

Dante, who was hovering behind the two sisters, coughed loudly.

'Don't you make that noise, sir,' Aislin told him sternly. 'It's your fault I'm so hormonal.'

If Dante were a peacock his tail would be in full bloom.

Orla rolled her eyes. Fair enough, he was proud that he was going to be a father again, but the strutting peacock act was wearing pretty thin, especially when her own belly was starting to resemble a watermelon. In this respect fate had proved to have an evil sense of humour, with Orla discovering she was pregnant the day after they'd sent all the wedding invitations out. That would teach them not to use contraception. She didn't know who'd been happier about the pregnancy—her, Tonino or Finn.

'Are you going to walk me down the aisle or what?'

Her brother laughed and took her arm. Aislin giggled and helped Finn to his feet. She would hold his hand every step of the walk down the aisle behind his mummy, for which Finn was determined to carry his parents' wedding rings.

Giulia, Tonino's sister, and the four children on Tonino's side old enough to follow Orla down the aisle without trying to make a run for it, took their positions behind the train of her dress.

Inside the church, the organist struck up the wedding march.

The two hundred guests, Sicilians and Irish alike out in force, craned their heads, a buzz of excitement permeating the musty chapel air.

At the top of the aisle stood Tonino, supported by his brother. On the front row to the right were his parents and three surviving grandparents. On the front row to the left were Dante's mother and his latest stepfather. Strangely, Orla had found herself forging the unlikeliest of bonds with the woman whose marriage Orla's conception had destroyed. Immacolata had Aislin and Dante's six-month-old son Sal standing on her lap. Orla bit her cheeks to hide the laughter when she witnessed Sal dribble into an oblivious Immacolata's immaculately groomed and glossy hair.

The warmth from everyone crammed in the church filled her heart and for a moment she had to blink back tears.

This was it. This was the moment she and Tonino officially pledged their lives together, and, as she looked into the dark chocolate eyes of the man she loved so much and recited the vows that would tie her to him for ever, she knew he was thinking exactly what she was thinking.

That nothing would ever come between them again.

* * * * *

THE GREEK'S
ONE-NIGHT HEIR

NATALIE ANDERSON

For Evelyn the Awesome.
I could say it was because you asked so nicely,
but really it's because you're amazing.

CHAPTER ONE

'YOU SHOULD BE resting, not worrying about me.' Theo Savas paced across the theatre foyer, working to keep his concern inaudible. He'd lived with his grandfather since he was ten and this was the first time in the last twenty years the old man had directly referenced something so personal. Revoking this rule wasn't just unsettling, it was unsafe. 'You've just come through a major operation—'

'And that's given me the opportunity to think. It's time, Theodoros. Your birthday is only a few weeks away.'

The lights above Theo flickered, signalling it was time for guests to take their seats, but he couldn't end this call without steering Dimitri back to unconcerned calm.

'Are you suggesting I'm getting old?' His joke was weak but he'd try anything to defuse his grandfather's escalating anxiety. Except anxiety was infectious and the vibes coming through the phone were making Theo's own muscles tense. That was in addition to the latent strain of the actual topic. 'There's plenty of time—'

'At this rate I'll never meet my great-grandchildren—'

'You're not about to die,' Theo interrupted. He'd ensured Dimitri had been seen by the best specialists and they'd insisted that with quality rest Dimitri should recover well. 'You've years left in you.'

'I'm serious. You need to settle down…'

'And I will,' Theo reassured him softly and rolled his shoulders.

He ached to resist Dimitri's attempt to add yet another burden of responsibility, yet he couldn't brush him off.

Distantly he watched the ushers guide the last arriving theatregoers towards the doors. He needed to move if he was going to make it in there. He stepped forward but a whirlwind of a woman swept in front of him, cutting him off. The tall, slender tornado didn't stop to say sorry, indeed she didn't even see him screech to a halt to stop himself smacking into her. She just kept searching her cavernous handbag while racing towards the usher.

'How about Eleni Doukas? She's beautiful.'

Theo inwardly shuddered. Was Dimitri suggesting a woman for him?

'Don't you like very beautiful women?' Dimitri added.

Theo bit back a grimace. Sure, he liked women—beauty being only one of their attractions. But most women he met wanted vastly more than what he was prepared to give.

'Or Angelica.' His grandfather offered another contender for his consideration. 'She would be suitable. You've not seen her in years.'

Theo had reasons for that. Ironically they were the exact reasons his grandfather would probably welcome. Cultured, well-educated, perfectly connected Angelica had made it clear she'd accept marriage and produce four children while turning a blind eye to extra-marital affairs. But Theo would never be unfaithful and he'd never accept infidelity from his wife either. He knew too well the blisters, welts and scars that such affairs inflicted. The fact was that while Angelica had offered herself as the ultimate convenient wife, while it was the sort of arrangement Theo ought to accept, and while it was certainly what those in his milieu expected him to accept, the prospect of any matrimonial arrangement at all appalled him.

But Dimitri didn't need to know that.

'It has been a while…' Theo murmured, agreeing in order to soothe.

His gaze locked on the scene unfolding outside the theatre door. The blind-haste brunette was still rummaging in her bag. Unlike most of the women present, she wasn't wearing a shimmering gown. Instead black slim trousers encased her long, long legs. He focused on her feet and saw black flats—so, unaided by towering heels, that striking height was all her own? Interest rippled through him like the faintest breeze bringing relief on a hot summer's noon. She wore a black wool cardigan beneath which a grey blouse was buttoned to the neck. The dull combination gave nothing away of her figure, other than that she was slender. But it was her expression that pushed him closer.

She was still searching through her bag while casting desperate glances at the unmoved usher and as Theo neared he heard her talking endlessly in a hushed, frantic whisper. Was she trying to buy time? Faking her way in? She was doing a good job because she tugged something even in Theo's safely entombed heart. Her eyes glimmered with suspicious brightness and her cheeks paled as the doors further along from hers were shut.

'If not Angelica—'

'Arrange it,' Theo decisively interrupted Dimitri. The thought of some possible bride parade was crazy, but he'd consent just to give Dimitri something to look forward to.

He walked towards the pair standing at the last open door to the theatre. The woman had whitened beyond pale and interesting. Any more loss of blood and she'd faint. The honest entreaty in her expression lanced through him. Not faking. Mortified.

'Introduce me to your three top picks,' he authorised his grandfather.

'You're serious?' Dimitri wheezed.

'Yes.' Theo sighed, serious about meeting them, but not about marrying any. 'You're tired and worrying.' And the old man was bored with being bedridden. At the very least this would give him something satisfactory to think about for the rest of the evening. 'Make the arrangements.'

If it would settle the old man's pulse, then he'd handle a couple of weekends being polite to houseguests. The nurse had warned his grandfather might experience a period of feeling low—apparently it sometimes followed lifesaving surgery. Theo would do almost anything to lift his spirits.

'I'm flying home first thing so I'll see you tomorrow afternoon,' he said. 'We'll talk more about it then, I promise. I need to work now.'

'Good, Theodoros,' his grandfather muttered huskily. 'Thank you.'

Theo paused, an arrow of discomfort silencing him. Usually Dimitri was all steel—unblemished and immoveable, capably tolerating the burning heat of business, but today, in revealing his wishes for Theo to find a wife? Dimitri discussing *any* kind of relationship rang Theo's warning bell, reminding him that Dimitri was more vulnerable than he appeared. And his grandfather didn't need to thank him, Theo was the one who owed. Everything.

'It's all right.' He cleared his own husky throat. 'Sleep well.'

He ended the call and walked the last few paces of the foyer. As the main financial backer for this ballet production, he'd been given the best seat in the house. Which, if he wasn't mistaken, he'd just forfeited because the usher had closed the door with brutal finality.

If he'd walked a little faster, he might've made it but he was still distracted by that trouble in the form of a tall brunette. And he badly needed a moment of distraction.

'I'm so sorry.' She pleaded with the usher as she swept back behind her ear a tendril that had loosened from the long braid that hung down her back. Her eyes were very large and very worried and she desperately ransacked her bag yet again. 'I had it, I promise I had it—'

'I'm sorry, ma'am.' The usher stood, an impenetrable force, in front of the shut door. 'But without your ticket…'

Leggy Brunette's slender shoulders slumped. 'Yes, of course. It's just that…it was in here.' She searched her trouser pockets, then glanced around the floor as if somehow her ticket would materialise. 'I promise I had it…'

'Unfortunately it's too late.' The usher brusquely ended the conversation.

Hunching as if to hide, Leggy Brunette turned away, the curve of her pretty mouth dropping.

'Problem?' Theo stepped sideways, into her path.

She glanced up at him absently, then stopped dead. Her eyes widened and her second glance turned into a shocked stare. Theo happily stared back.

Her eyes were more than blue, they had a hint of pale purple, and he took another step closer on auto. 'You couldn't find your ticket?'

She shook her head and kept staring.

Theo couldn't hold back a small smile. Apparently she couldn't find her voice either. He was used to getting a reaction from women, but rendering one speechless?

At least some colour was flooding back into her face. But suddenly she swallowed and turned away. He couldn't resist following. She stopped at the nearest table and, amused, he watched as yet again she fruitlessly searched her bag. He caught a glimpse of something bulky in its depths, surely not a blanket?

'You know, they'll never let anyone in late,' he said softly to let her down gently. 'They won't interrupt the performance once it's begun.'

She dropped her hands and darted another glance at him. 'I know.' Her voice was adorably husky with her English accent soft and clear. 'It's just that I *had* it.'

And she *really* wanted to watch the ballet? Her ticket loss was definitely genuine. Her sharp disappointment nicked his skin and the absurd desire to see her smile slid into his blood.

'Oh, Mr Savas.' The theatre usher suddenly appeared

at his side, looking flustered. 'I can sneak you in if you'd like to follow me quickly...'

For a split second his eyes met those lavender-blues and he watched the consternation bloom within them.

'I wouldn't want to interrupt the rest of the audience,' he dismissed the usher's invitation smoothly. 'But thank you anyway.'

The usher beat a hasty retreat and Theo faced Leggy Brunette.

'No one gets in late unless they're ridiculously rich?' she muttered, soft reproach in her expression.

Uh... Yeah. 'I have a spare ticket you can use for the second half,' he murmured impulsively.

She looked away again as if the sight of him somehow hurt her unusual eyes. 'Um...' She fiddled with the strap of her insanely huge bag. 'That's really kind of you, but I couldn't.'

'Why not?' he asked. He wanted her to say yes and Theo was pretty used to getting what he wanted these days. 'It's a spare ticket,' he reiterated. 'You can still see the entire second half.'

Her hand twisted in the strap while more colour rose in her cheeks. He knew she was tempted, but wary.

'There's no trick,' he reassured softly. 'Just a ticket.'

She drew her lower lip between her teeth and bit down on it. 'Really?'

'Yes, really.' He chuckled. People didn't usually dilly-dally about taking things from him. 'It's not a big deal.'

That colour swarmed more deeply and she quickly glanced past him. 'You...don't have a date you're here with?'

Was *that* the reason for her incredulous expression? He suppressed another smile. 'No. Do you?'

'No.' She shook her head quickly.

Satisfaction surged with surprising force. 'Then I guess it's meant to be, right?'

'I…' She paused. 'Right.'

'And now we might as well have a drink while we wait, don't you think?' He nodded towards the gleaming theatre bar, his body thrumming with anticipation.

She turned to face him, her lavender eyes gazed directly into his and her chin lifted with a little pride. 'May I get you a drink, to say thank you?'

For a second Theo was bereft of speech. The women he dated never offered to pay. They knew him, knew how wealthy he was and they were happy to meld into his lifestyle. But his brunette in distress had no idea who he was and apparently had no desire to just take whatever she could from him.

'Please,' she added. 'I wouldn't want to feel indebted to you.'

Indebted by a mere ballet ticket? That thread of sensual awareness tightened. Was she worried he'd ask her to pay him back in some nefarious way? Well, she could remain calm, Theo had never needed to coerce a woman in his life. He might have money, but he wasn't spoiled and he'd never presume.

'Okay,' he said equably, but then couldn't resist teasing her prim dignity. 'But are you sure you have your wallet on you? You wouldn't want to make offers you can't fulfil.'

'Very funny.' Sparks lit her lavender eyes, but then her expression wrinkled. 'Damn it, you've made me need to check now.' She rummaged in her bag again—were those chopsticks in there? But then she extracted a small coin purse with a flourish. No sleek leather wallet filled with elite credit cards for her.

'I knew I had it,' she said victoriously. 'But I swear I had the ticket too.' She groaned ruefully. 'What an idiot.' A sudden little giggle bubbled out.

To his astonishment, his whole world narrowed until he saw only her—sparkling eyes and pretty lips and delight—

and he found himself smiling back at her. Frankly it was the most he'd smiled in months.

'How about you go ahead and order?' he suggested huskily. 'I need a second to arrange the seat with the staff.'

'What would you like to drink?'

'You choose.' He shrugged. 'I'll have whatever you're having.'

'Are you sure you want to risk that?' she asked, her expression wrinkled again.

'Why?' He was surprised into another smile. 'Now I'm intrigued. Quick, go decide for the both of us.'

He couldn't resist watching her walk towards the bar. He really was intrigued—she was a contrary mix of shy and awkward and assured. Tall, slender, feminine and acutely refreshing. Just the tonic given the last two months of stress, isolation and uncertainty. But she was definitely cautious and perhaps she was right to be, given his inner temptation was to skip the ballet altogether and carry her back to his bed for the night. He'd worship those long limbs and work very hard to put a smile on her pillowy pout…

So not appropriate. Or normal. Not for him. He'd never followed in the footsteps of his playboy father and he never wanted to. He shook off that outrageous whisper of sin and strode towards the theatre staff. One drink, then it was back to duty.

When he walked back to the bar she was sitting all alone with two tall glasses in front of her and quite obviously trying not to appear self-conscious.

He placed the ticket on the bar beside the two drinks and lifted one. 'All arranged.'

He needed the drink. But on swallowing he quickly stifled his immediate grimace and subsequent smile. This sour fiery stuff wasn't quite the champagne he'd been expecting. At first glance he'd guessed she'd be a sweet romantic—sensitivity and shy awkwardness were obvious in her eyes.

But then she came out with a line of soft-spoken sarcasm, a penchant for rocket fuel as an aperitif and a self-deprecating giggle that stole a rare smile from him.

'Thanks,' she said to him earnestly. 'That's so kind of you.'

Oddly he didn't want her to think he was *kind*. He wanted a bit more of a reaction than that. He wanted… he paused to battle the full force of what he wanted…but, yeah, it was pretty much everything he shouldn't want. It was everything illicit.

Leah Turner sipped her drink, stifling the urge to surreptitiously pinch herself. This kind of thing *never* happened to her. Somehow the most gorgeous guy had intercepted her during her most humiliating moment and gallantly turned her disappointment into something else altogether. And, man, he was gorgeous. Tall, lean, muscular, powerful, he exuded a sensual magnetism that was beyond normal. *She'd* most certainly never felt sexual attraction from one look. He was so dazzling it was hard to think and she wasn't sure what she was more rapt about—not missing the entire ballet, or stealing a few minutes of this man's time.

Because those eyes of his? Green eyes were usually a mix of colours—green mixed with blue or hazel, or bronze. But his were pure forest green. So rare, so startling, she had to constantly tell herself not to stare at him. She tried to stare at her glass instead, but only lasted a mere second before lapsing and gawping at him again. 'You're important around here?'

'No.'

She didn't believe him. She'd watched him speak with the theatre manager and that woman had been all deferential smiles and soothing words. He held more than charm. He held power. Hell, he'd made Leah feel as if she'd done *him* a favour by saying yes to taking the ticket.

He smiled and there was something a little dangerous in it. 'Why are you here alone?'

His accent curled her toes and made her an appalling cliché. She had no idea what the mix was, but it melted her like a lonely snowflake on a sunny windowsill.

'I'm not.' She lifted her chin. 'My friend is already here, but she's onstage.'

'She's a dancer?'

'Yes. She sent me the ticket but I was running late because I'd stopped to help Maeve with something.'

'Maeve?'

'One of the residents at the care home I work at. She's lovely and we bond over—' Leah paused, realising she was prattling. 'Over stuff,' she finished. He didn't need to know about her new job and the people she'd already fallen for. 'Why were you running late?'

'I was on a call.'

'Girlfriend problems?' she guessed, cheekily personal but it just had to be the case. 'Is that why you're alone? Did she stand you up?'

His eyebrows lifted in a quizzical look.

'What—you're never stood up?' she asked before thinking, *of course, he wasn't.*

'No girlfriend.' That gorgeous smile crept across his face as if he were pleased to be able to correct her. *'That's* the real problem. According to my grandfather anyway.'

'You were talking to your *grandfather*?' She was surprised. 'He wants you to settle down?'

He nodded mock seriously. 'And provide heirs to the family fortune.'

For certain there *was* a family fortune. His suit was so beautifully fitting it had to be tailor-made and the gleaming watch on his wrist screamed luxury style. 'You don't want to do that?'

'Not yet,' he said, obviously and unashamedly repelled by the idea.

'Yet?' she queried doubtfully because that wicked light in his eyes made her laugh. There was too much fun to be had first, clearly. How could he not be a playboy? All the women who'd want him, it'd be too easy. But she played along. 'Because you have too much to do? Too busy with work? Too many other options?'

'None of the above.' He chose another answer altogether. 'Hence no date to the ballet…'

'I don't believe you're out of options,' she said. 'You've *chosen* not to bring a date.' She cocked her head. 'Because you don't want to settle down at all?'

He met her gaze with knowing amusement.

She shook her head sadly. 'Why do I get the feeling your poor grandfather is going to be waiting a while…'

He rolled his shoulders and his amusement faded as something far more serious flickered in his eyes. 'He's been unwell—this is preying on him. Hence the lecture.'

Leah watched him blink away that sliver of pain. That he'd not ended the call soon enough to get into the theatre showed he had patience and loyalty and respect for his relative.

'Family expectations can be hard,' she offered with soft honesty. 'I'm an eternal disappointment to mine.'

He looked back into her eyes and they were held for a moment—silent scrutiny, total awareness—and she was struck by the conviction there was much more buried beneath his perfect surface.

'I don't believe you'd ever be a disappointment,' he finally muttered—so low and so serious that she couldn't smile and shake it off.

Instead a heated flush swept over her skin and she swallowed back the hard lump that had formed in her throat. 'Well, you'd be wrong.'

He gazed at her for another moment of that unspoken communication—the deeply guarded truth, not the superficial denial that there was anything wrong.

Then he blinked and his lips twitched. 'Your family want you to marry too?'

Laughter burst out, breaking that intensity. She shook her head.

'Quite right, it's a dreadful idea,' he teased.

'No,' she said firmly. 'It isn't—'

'You're wrong.' He saluted her with his drink again. 'All marriages end up miserable.'

'Wow…is that what happened to you?'

He almost choked on his drink and then laughed. 'Not married. Never married. Never will marry.'

Yes, the only ring in his world was the ring of finality.

'Because…' She inhaled deeply as she studied him thoughtfully. 'Parents?'

He flashed a look at her—pure pain, pure denial, pure promise of retribution.

'Yeah,' she murmured meekly. 'Poor grandfather.'

'You think I'm that predictable.' He took another sip.

'I think that everyone feels pain, sometimes,' she said. 'And often the people who inflict the most pain are the people we're meant to be closest to.'

'I'm not close to them,' he said softly, then forced another smile. 'So, tell me about your dancer friend. Is it her debut?'

'No, it's just that I've only recently moved to London so I haven't been able to see her perform until tonight.' She shifted guiltily on her chair as she remembered. 'And now I've missed her.'

'Only the first half. And she doesn't need to know you've missed that.'

'You think I should lie to her?'

He smiled at her as if she were a timid little lamb. 'You're omitting a little of the truth. That's not a lie.'

'Of course it's a lie,' she corrected him flatly. 'It's not completely honest.'

'And we should always be completely honest?' He shook his head and laughed openly.

'You think I'm wrong?'

'Naïve, perhaps.' He leaned closer. 'Sometimes telling the truth serves no purpose. When it can only hurt the person who has to hear it, why would you?' He broke off with a sharp breath.

She had the feeling he wasn't thinking of her little 'missing the first half' mistake any more.

'So you'd omit the truth, or tell a lie, to protect someone?' she asked.

'Of course.'

He said it with such quiet certainty, she knew he had and did. She thought of the grandfather all over again and wondered what it was he protected him from.

That quizzical look lit his eyes again. 'What would hurt your friend more? Knowing you missed the first half, or never knowing you missed it?'

'If she ever found out I *lied*, that would hurt her the most. But if I tell her the truth, she'll just laugh at me.'

He stilled, his gaze keen on her. 'And that doesn't hurt you?'

She shrugged. 'My crime isn't that critical and I'm already laughing at myself.' She eyed him. 'We can laugh together. Sharing pain takes some of the sting out of it, doesn't it?'

'Not always.'

'Hmmm.' She pondered it. 'The problem is, one omission inevitably leads to more lies—she'll ask what I thought of something in the first half and I'd have to lie then.'

'Or you could just not talk about it at all.'

She laughed. 'So your solution is to just bury everything and live in total denial? Pretend nothing bad ever happened?' She leaned closer. 'It'll only come back to haunt you.'

'Don't tell me you believe in ghosts.'

'Well, I believe some things—feelings mostly—can't stay buried. They rise like zombies and eat your brain to the point where you can't think clearly any more.' It happened to her frequently.

'So you always act on your emotions?' he queried. 'Act on gut feelings rather than with rational thought?'

She sighed. 'I'm human. I try to be a good one and not hurt others.'

'So honesty it is?'

'Ideally, yes.'

'Ideally.' He sent her an indulgent smile. 'So how, ideally, will your friend react?'

'I know she'll laugh. It's not the first time I've messed up.'

'You've known her a while?'

'We grew up in the same town and were in ballet class together.'

'But you don't dance any more?'

'My passion outweighed my talent.'

'Surely passion's the most important ingredient?' His eyes gleamed. 'Talent without passion is nothing. Skills can be learned, passion can't.'

'Well, that may be so, but I'm already taller than average.' She shrugged, long skilled at masking her self-consciousness about it. 'Put me in pointe shoes and I tower over most men.'

It wasn't the only reason she'd quit, but he didn't need to know anything more about her constant inability to meet her parents' expectations.

'Is that why you wear flat shoes now? So you're not taller than your men?'

Her *men*? She choked back a laugh at the thought. 'I

wear them because they're comfortable. I dress to please myself, not some man.'

He grinned appreciatively. 'Sure. But you're not taller than me. You could wear high heels when we go out.'

'I'm not going out with you.'

'Aren't we out right now?' he teased.

She shook her head. 'By accident, not design.'

'So wouldn't you go out with me if I asked?'

'Would you ask?'

That smile hovered around his mouth and he took another sip. 'Perhaps it's better if I omit to answer—the truth might terrify you. It mildly terrifies me.' His gaze clung to her lips and radiated a flash of heat that rippled over her. 'What is it you like about ballet? The costumes? Because it's romantic?'

'There's nothing romantic about ballet,' she scoffed, covering that moment of awareness. 'It's ruthless.'

'You mean bloody blisters and sprained muscles?'

'I mean more than that. Did you know in this ballet the girl goes mad and dies of a broken heart because the man she loved *lied* to her,' she said with a pointed look. 'Because he *omits* to tell her he's betrothed to another woman. I don't think that's *romantic.*'

He chuckled but then leaned forward to tease. 'It was the prospect of marriage, see? It caused all the problems.'

She rolled her eyes even as she laughed. Just then theatre doors opened and the audience spilled out, shattering the sense of intimacy that had built between them. Somehow that time had sped by and she was sorry it had gone so quickly.

'It's probably time to take your seat.' He gestured behind her. 'You don't want to leave it too late…'

'Okay.' But the flutters in her stomach wouldn't cease. That she was going to spend the rest of the evening with him? Even though she knew he was just amusing himself, it was still unbelievable.

Leah followed the waiting usher, her pulse quickening as the woman guided her to the best seat in the theatre. Overcome with appreciation she turned to thank him, but he wasn't with them. Somehow he'd disappeared in the crowd. Too late she realised the truth. He wasn't sitting with her because it wasn't a *spare* ticket he'd given her. It was his own.

Disappointment hit as that unusual bubble of happiness and hope popped. She hadn't had the chance to thank him or even say goodbye. Instinctively she knew she wasn't going to see him again. Who said chivalry was dead?

But to think that for a second she'd thought he'd actually been attracted to her. She was mortified at the memory and glad he'd now gone, given he'd clearly just been filling in time.

As the lights dimmed it took a few minutes for her to appreciate the ballet but then Zoe appeared onstage and she was swamped with pleasure and pride for her friend.

After the final curtain call Leah walked to the artists' entrance at the back of the theatre to meet her and give her friend the gift she'd made. Her lost ticket confession resulted in them both giggling and then Zoe insisted Leah accompany her to the opening night company party to make it up to her. Secretly she wanted to escape home alone so she could remember her handsome stranger. Instead she smiled and said yes, ruefully thinking of him again as she omitted honesty to save her own embarrassment.

Theo Savas stalked out of the theatre, determined to resist the tempting whisper telling him to seek out that slender brunette with the hopelessly soft eyes. He forced himself to make the mandatory appearance at the ballet's opening night celebration. He couldn't skip it, given the party was at the hotel he was staying in. But he could escape early and have some space and privacy before his early flight home to Athens. He had little desire to socialise beyond the cursory showing of his face.

His mind teased, replaying the light conversation he'd had with the tall, ticketless sylph. He'd watched her from the distance during the ballet, happy in the back-row seat off to the side management had found for him. She'd sat motionless through the performance, apparently entranced, and she'd applauded energetically. But he'd seen a hint of sadness on her mouth when she'd turned to leave. Theo had pressed back into the crowd as competing instincts had warred within him. He had affairs only rarely—always discreet, always without strings, always unencumbered by emotion or the weight of baggage. There were no *hearts* involved in his dalliances. Physical pleasure was just a freely given gift—very simple, very satisfying. The suggestion of anything more was not. He'd seen the hurt it caused when it mattered too much.

And he didn't think the leggy brunette was the no-strings, no-hearts type.

As he walked into the reception room the nearest group of women turned to stare, then smile. One peeled off and walked over.

'You're Theo Savas.'

'I am.'

Invitation shone in the pretty dancer's eyes but he turned away from it as he invariably did. Yet he still couldn't shake the recollection of that brunette's lavender-blue gaze or the awkward interest that had shone from it. Regret curled.

'I'm—'

'I'm sorry,' he interrupted the woman briefly. 'I can't stop to chat.'

He'd check in with the company director and get out of here. But as he turned to seek out the director he spotted a tall figure on the other side of the room. His second glance morphed into a stare. And he smiled. Every sense sharpened. She was in shadow, but her silhouette was unmistakable. Triumph allowed temptation to burst free. His ticketless damsel must have been invited to the after-party by her dancer friend.

'Hey.' He caught her arm to get her attention in the crowd, barely quelling the impulse to pull her close.

'Oh…' Her pupils dilated as she stared up at him. There was no hiding the sensuality that sparkled in her eyes. 'What are you doing here?'

'I could ask you the same question.' He couldn't drag his hungry gaze from her face. It was as if he'd not seen her in months, not mere minutes. 'Where's your friend?' He didn't really care. All that mattered was that they had a second chance and he wasn't letting her slip away again. Not yet.

She glanced around then pointed to a petite woman animatedly talking to a group of dancers. 'Zoe's over there.' As she watched her that sparkle in her eyes dimmed. 'She's… busy at the moment.'

'She's left you alone.'

'You left me alone too.'

He stilled, silenced by that hint of reproach.

'She's having a good time' she added quickly, failing to mask her awkwardness in the sudden pregnant moment. 'She deserves to.'

'And you don't?'

'I did have a good time. But you gave me *your* ticket.' She looked up at him. 'Why did you do that? You missed the whole thing.'

He could omit a couple of little facts and bask in her gratitude, but he didn't want to lie to her. Not after that oddly intimate little conversation they'd had before the ballet. 'Actually, they gave me another seat, so like you I didn't miss the second half.'

That seat at the very side of the theatre had been perfect, because while it had given him an obstructed view of the stage, it had also given him an angled view of her…though that little fact he *was* going to omit.

'Oh, good. I'm so glad.' A faint wash of colour bloomed over her face. 'It was still very kind of you.'

'Mmm…' He still didn't feel very kind right now. He felt achy. 'It was my pleasure.' He'd enjoyed watching the emotions flit across her face. 'I get to go to the ballet a lot. The theatre, opera, sports fixtures…it comes with my job.'

'You don't enjoy it?'

'Sure. Mostly.' But when he had other issues pressing on his mind, not so much. And right now he had too much on his mind. It had been a miserable few months. He just wanted to forget it all for a while. Temptation beckoned. Maybe his method was standing right in front of him. And maybe, he just couldn't resist.

He held his hand out to her. 'Theo Savas.'

Leah didn't want to keep staring but she couldn't seem to tear her gaze away from him. 'Leah Turner.'

A premonition warned her, but the urge for the slightest touch was irresistible and she put her hand in his. For a second they were locked together in a moment of physical intimacy that felt much more powerful than a mere handshake should.

As she stared into his eyes her thoughts jumbled. He'd just been kind earlier—hadn't expected to see her again, hadn't known she was going to be at this party. His gift had been just that, a simple gift with no strings—just a thoughtful, generous moment between strangers.

But the banked fire in his gaze now? The sizzle shooting up her arm? The electricity short-circuited her brain. She couldn't look away from him. She couldn't release him any more than he could seem to release her.

'I should get going,' she mumbled.

'Why?'

She swallowed. 'I have work tomorrow.'

'So? I have a flight first thing.'

She couldn't help smiling. 'Is it a competition?'

'You tell me.'

She shook her head. 'I'm not a fan of competition.'

'No?' He nodded. 'No one likes losing.'

So true but she doubted he'd ever lost much.

'How about collaboration, then?' He was somehow closer. 'We'd work together to achieve a common goal…'

Her mouth was so dry she had to lick her lips before she could answer. 'And that goal would be?'

His eyes were serious even as his mouth curved into a wicked smile. Intensity beneath the charm. 'The best night of our lives.'

'Wow. Setting a big goal.'

'Always. If you don't aim high…' His smile faded as he studied her. 'I didn't expect to see you again.'

'Are you sorry you have?'

'I was sorry I didn't stay earlier. I was sorry I let you go.'

Her heart trembled. So why had he? She couldn't bring herself to ask. She still couldn't move either. Someone pushed past behind her, jostling her in the throng. He released her hand only to wrap his arm around her shoulder and draw her closer against his side. Just like that the rest of the world faded.

'You want to go somewhere quieter?' he asked.

Leah had never gone 'somewhere quieter' with anyone ever. But she knew what it meant. 'You barely know me.'

'And I'm not going to.' He smiled ruefully. 'I go back to Greece tomorrow.'

He was in town for only the one night. Was he letting her know this would only be a one-time thing? Was she right in thinking there might even be a one time? She opted for diversion so she could process all the signals she was too inexperienced to be certain of. 'You're from Greece? Whereabouts?'

'Athens.' His gaze didn't waver—it was as if he knew she needed a moment to process. 'But I have a holiday home on an island.'

Of course he did. He probably had homes everywhere.

'Have you ever been there?' he asked, seeming to reach for the same delaying diversion she was.

She shook her head.

'No interest?' He looked aghast.

She laughed. 'I'd love to go there one day.'

'Sail around the islands, right?' He smiled as if it was what everybody wanted.

'I'm sure that would be amazing, but I'd really like to go to Delphi.'

'You studied Classics? The Antiquities?'

She shook her head. 'No, it's silly, but one of my favourite books was set in Delphi.'

'What book?'

'You probably haven't read it…'

'I'm actually quite well read—what's the title?'

She shook her head. 'It's an old paperback, you won't know it…' She'd found it in the reception of the doctor's one time and smuggled it home and hidden it from her parents. A romantic suspense wasn't on the prescribed list her parents had drawn up for her.

He smiled, guessing that she didn't want to tell him. 'You'll have to travel there then, to see if it lives up to its literary imagining.'

'I've only just moved to London.' She shrugged. 'Greece might have to wait a while.'

'So you're new to town and I'm just passing through… yet fate has made it so we meet twice in the one night.'

'And you want me to…'

'Yes.' Something smouldered in his eyes. 'You know what I want you to do,' he said. 'I want you to come with me. And yes, I mean exactly what you're thinking.'

Yes, he'd changed. In the theatre, he'd held back for some reason. Now, he'd decided and he wasn't holding back at all.

'You're…not shy.' She bit her lip.

'But you are. Don't be afraid to go for what you want.'

She hovered—not indecisive, but insecure. 'I'm not good at this,' she confessed.

He didn't laugh at her. His expression was both encouraging and strained. He lifted a hand and cupped her jaw, the soft touch silencing her.

'I'm not going to give you a report card, Leah,' he breathed, closer still. 'Anyway, there's no "good", only amazing. And for the record—so as not to omit any important details—I have no intention of either of us being hurt.'

There was a tension within him—a cause of worry or concern. For her?

'Want me to give you an example?' he asked in a husky whisper.

Her pulse thundered. She should pull back and say no. But she didn't want to and her body decided for her. She rose a half-inch on her toes and met his descending mouth.

Who knew a kiss could be so careful? It began as little more than a soft slide of his lips over hers. His fingers weaved into her hair at the nape of her neck as he held her loose but close. But then his other hand lifted to her waist, pulling her against his body, and the pressure of his mouth on hers increased, the intimacy intensified as he teased her with his tongue. With slow, devastating skill he inexorably pulled a deep response. Not just acquiescence and acceptance but action in return. He unsealed a vast yearning within her and something in her soul leapt—reaching for connection, commanding her to slide her hands up his firm chest to his broad shoulders…to *hold* him to her every bit as much as he was holding her.

But he stirred more than the heated blood and the sudden slick restlessness of her hips.

A burst of emotion burned careful right the way down to ruthless. Raw hunger was unleashed within—forced into revealing itself by the increasingly demanding counterpart within him. This wasn't just want, this was *craving*. She arched, opening for him—seeking more with her own touch, her own tongue and hands and press of her body. And he more than let her. His feet spread as he braced to take more of her in his hold and kissed her thoroughly—his strokes designed to soothe and torment at the same time. She knew it was crazy—that it didn't make sense—but there was something more than this delicious, uncontrollable lust between them. And it was this something more that made this undeniable.

She shook, violently trembling from head to foot, as sensation rampaged through her like a river released from a decades-locked dam.

At her shudder he ripped his mouth from hers. 'What do you think?' His breathing was so roughened his speech sounded slightly slurred.

Thought had very little to do with it. She gazed up, relieved he'd not released his hold on her because she felt dizzy. She drank in the light flush on his skin and the glittering depths of his eyes—basking in the possessive focus he bestowed on her. Still pressed tightly against him, she felt not only his physical desire, but his restraint. She knew he'd walk away from her if she wished.

But that other ache welded her to him, that hidden, true, tender need. His reasons were no doubt different from hers, but she felt his loneliness ran as deep. For the first time she was compelled to both give and take of something un-equivocally intimate.

Her answer was so simple, so easy. She couldn't let this rare moment go. She couldn't let *him* go.

'I think I'm coming with you.'

CHAPTER TWO

His smile was a blazing mix of triumph and sensual determination and barely hidden relief. She realised he was as delighted and as dazed as she was and somehow that multiplied the myriad want and need and hot mess of yes within her.

'I can't leave without saying goodbye to Zoe,' she muttered.

'Of course.' He escorted her through the crowd, stepping back when they came up to her friend.

'Sorry, Zoe.' Leah caught her attention. 'I'm going to call it a night—'

'Since when do you know Theo Savas?' Zoe interrupted her, managing to screech and whisper at the same time. 'Since when does Theo Savas kiss anyone in public like that?'

'You saw…just then?' Leah's body smoked with embarrassment.

'OMG, yes, go.' Zoe laughed and pulled her into a quick, tight hug. 'You must, just, *go*. Do everything I would and more,' her friend whispered in her ear. 'For heaven's sake, have some fun for once!'

Leah's pulse hammered as Theo firmly grasped her hand and led her through the crowded function room and into the sudden silence of the hotel corridor. She was floating, not walking, right? In the elevator he glanced down at her and smiled but she saw the question in his eyes and tension in his body.

She felt the question too—since when did *she* wander off with a complete stranger? Before tonight she'd never considered it, would never have thought she *would*… Yet he didn't feel like a stranger, more of a kindred spirit—as complicated and careful, those layers of responsibility and obligation hiding other needs and wants. She'd do all she could for someone she cared about; that he did too struck a chord—as if they were vibrating in harmony even though there could be nothing more than this one night between them. And then there was that sheer physical response that she just couldn't release herself from.

She'd never done anything adventurous, nothing reckless or fun either. She'd spent so long trying to please her parents and fit in with their impossible standards and it was past time to have one night just for her. She wanted to share it only with him.

He unlocked the door of his hotel suite and she stepped inside. The drapes didn't cover the tinted windows and the London skyline was like fairy lights. She turned and took in the rich interior—pure luxurious space and decadence. But then Theo stood in the centre of it and the sumptuous background faded away. He was like a sun god—casting everything else in shadow.

She couldn't be the first woman to fall completely beneath his spell but she was quite calm about that. She felt too pleased to have seen him again and realise that he was—amazingly—attracted to her too.

'Do you do this all the time?' she asked, too fascinated to think before asking.

'Not as often as you're thinking.'

She wasn't sure she *was* thinking any more—she was still floating on that gravitational pull right towards him. 'I don't do this, ever.'

'Never ever?'

She shrugged as embarrassment heated her skin. She wasn't going to tell him he was with a woman no other man had ever chased. A woman crippled by an inferiority complex bigger than Jupiter. What did it matter what she'd done or not done before? Right now there was this and it was too powerful to ignore. She wanted more of his touch—of that connection and elation when he'd kissed her. More than seduction, more than madness, it was an ache unlike anything she'd known burning low in her belly. Its searing intensity rapidly escalating until it seemed to singe her inside and out, leaving her breathless because of this urgent, unstoppable need to touch.

'I should offer you a drink or something.' He ran his hand through his hair and huffed out a breath as if he too were struggling to recover.

It seemed imperative to feel again that need that mirrored her own. 'I'm happy with just the "or something",' she mumbled shyly.

He looked startled for a second, then smiled. He moved towards her—graceful, powerful, careful. 'I wanted this from the moment I saw you.'

She jerked her head, negating the compliment because she was unable to believe him. 'You don't have to tell me… nice things.'

Something flickered in his expression. 'You're not used to people telling you the truth? You're beautiful, Leah. Robbed me of my self-control in seconds.'

She closed her eyes. She didn't want to listen—didn't want words to destroy her belief in this moment. But then she sensed he was close. She could feel his heat and his tension.

'If I don't have to tell you,' he whispered softly right in her ear, 'then I'll *show* you.'

A paralysing desire took hold at the sound of his determined promise. She half expected a furious onslaught of passion—she would have welcomed that too. But it wasn't.

It was slow, delicious torture. Another slow kiss—easing her back into his arms. Every touch not only a tease, but a celebration of her. Making her breathless, making her move closer, making her want something she couldn't articulate. As she trembled, he picked her up and carried her through to the bedroom and set her down on the big bed.

She shrugged out of the cardigan and then he took over, unbuttoning then peeling the blouse from her body. He paused to gaze at the white bra beneath, then undid it, pulling away the little lace cups that covered her small breasts, and he groaned. Not judging her but enjoying her. Not disappointed, but delighted. There was nothing to be had here but pleasure. She felt a reckless safety in his arms. No one had kissed her like this. His touch silenced anxious thought and she let herself be carried away by the basic instinct of her body—caving in to the demand to shift closer, to move with him and torment him back. He unzipped her trousers and slid them down, lifting her feet to slip her shoes from them at the same time.

'Scarlet silk.' His hot laugh tickled against her skin as he roved back up her body, lingering over her hips. 'That I didn't expect.'

'What did you expect? White cotton granny pants and a chastity belt or something?'

He laughed again and bent to kiss her upper thigh, nibbling on the edge of the silk as he went.

Leah moaned. Truth was, this was the first pair of sexy undies she'd bought herself. Even then she couldn't get it right and wear a matching bra. But she hadn't wanted her bra to be visible beneath her blouse, so she'd gone with white.

'It confirms a theory I've been developing about you,' he murmured.

'And what's that?' She could hardly string the words together.

'That you're more sensual than you appear…you've been hiding your true scarlet self.'

'You're reading too much into it—they were the first I grabbed from the drawer.'

'Because you have a drawer *full* of scarlet silk?'

She couldn't reply. *Where* was he kissing her...slowly inching along the waistband of those scarlet panties? Secrets and desire swamped her and she was shy about the fact that he'd discovered something she'd barely recognised within herself. She'd bought the one pair because it had been all she could afford. It had taken so long to choose which one; she'd wanted them all. Her secret enjoyment of them wasn't so secret now. She shivered.

'You "don't do this, ever", Leah?' He paused and looked back up to her eyes.

She didn't want to lie to him. She didn't want to hold anything back, but it was hard to push the answer past the lump in her throat. 'No.'

As he nodded it occurred to her that he already knew the answer. He'd been able to *tell*?

A slither of mortification chilled her skin. 'Does that bother you?'

'No.' He lifted himself up to lie beside her and searched her features. 'But are you sure you want me to be your first one-night stand?'

The reminder that that was all he was offering didn't bother her. But his blunt question revealed he hadn't realised the entire truth about her. Where he meant one night, she meant ever at *all*.

She nodded, her voice stolen by shyness and the fear that if she told the truth he'd stop. The last thing she wanted was for him to stop.

He kissed her mouth. His hand teased one breast, then the other, then rubbed firmly down her stomach, slipping beneath the waistband of those scarlet panties. At her shocked gasp, his kisses deepened. But he didn't stop his hot exploration—his fingers delving lower, stroking where she was most sensitive, discovering for himself her most secret place.

With every lash of his tongue, of his fingertips, the last of those knots holding her in reserve loosened until she was totally undone. Reduced to nothing but heat and light, pliable in his hands, she didn't just let him touch all he liked, she hungered for it—writhing like an animal. She arched, seeking more caresses, parting her lips to invite another deep kiss—her tongue tangling with his, her hand clawing his shoulder in an aching invitation to come closer.

'Yes,' he praised her in a gravelly voice as she moaned in desperation.

His fingers slid, his thumb strummed and his mouth sealed over hers again—stoking her until she went beyond burning and tumbled into total meltdown.

Time stopped as her hips bucked and she rode his hand. In those lost moments, there was nothing else in her world but him, in the escalating rhythm and depth of plundering touch. She tautened for one last infinite moment of torment and then his attention finally tore her apart. She screamed as ecstasy hit in a wave that smashed her to pieces.

Theo rubbed his forefinger back and forth along the waistband of her panties, lightly toying with her while she recovered from the most beautiful orgasm he'd had the pleasure of giving. He ached to strip her free of them and plunge into her hot, tight body. But her comment that her panties ought to be white replayed in his mind. White was the colour of innocence. And she'd joked about a chastity belt? He'd been too far gone for that to register properly. He glanced up at her face and recognised the gleam of resurging desire in her eyes. But there was shyness as well and the slight wariness—of a novice?

A weight of warning pressed low on his spine. He levered up from the bed and didn't break free of her gaze as he shucked his tie and swiftly unbuttoned his shirt. Her lips parted as she stared, avidly watching as he stripped.

As his hands went to his belt buckle she stilled. Impatient, he shoved both his trousers and boxers down, revealing his bulging erection and watching intently for her reaction. She couldn't resist looking—couldn't take her eyes off him—but they widened in shock and he saw her swallow. And as he stepped back to the bed her breathing quickened.

'This isn't just your first one-night stand, is it?' he asked, his voice harsher than he could control.

Her eyes widened more and he knew he had to ask the follow-up.

'Are you a virgin, Leah? Is the "never ever", actually never *anything*?'

She bit her lip and insecurity flashed.

'How could you not tell me?' He knew he was right— her reaction to his nudity said it all.

Her face filled with a fiery sweet warmth that scorched his soul—he couldn't turn away from her even when he probably should.

'How could you tell?' she asked.

'It was your comment that these ought to be white. And the chastity belt?' He stroked the scrap of scarlet silk that would now be the only barrier between them.

That rosy bloom of embarrassment spread over every inch of her pale skin. 'Do you want me to leave?' She was very still but her hands formed into fists at her sides.

'No.' Raw hunger clawed more savagely within him, but he was determined to resist—to do what was right here. 'Why didn't you want to tell me?'

'I didn't want you to stop.'

The hint of wounded look in her eyes smote what had been—until tonight—an impenetrable heart. 'I won't stop if you don't want me to.'

She gazed into his eyes. He saw the trust. He saw the need. He vowed not to let her down.

'Let's just play, okay?' he clarified. 'We don't have to…'

'Do everything?' She swallowed. The glimmer of disappointment was so obvious in her lavender eyes.

'Decide right now.' He bent and kissed her, unable to stand the droop of disappointment on her full, lush mouth. And at first touch he sank back onto the bed, unable to resist getting as close as he could to her. He'd make her come again, he'd taste her, there was so much they could still do; there were so many other ways to fulfil the need savaging its way through his limbs.

She was revelation all over again. He lost himself in the sensation, the warmth and pleasure of touching her. He removed her silky scarlet panties so slowly, tormenting them both. And then he kissed her, tasting her there, teasing her with his tongue until he had to grip her hips hard to hold her still as she succumbed to her next orgasm.

Her screams suspended time. Bewitched, he let her push him onto his back. He pulled her above him. But with every slow second that he savoured as she blanketed him with her soft slender body, the yearning to have her completely deepened. Recklessness rose within him because she wasn't holding back at all. Untutored but unashamed, her hips circled against his, the tight, delicious rub of her nipples scored his chest so degree by degree his, oh, so noble desire to hold back lessened.

It was as if he'd unlocked a simple, small box only to discover it opened into myriad compartments…each like a room full of willingness and warmth. The depths of her response, her abandon, became unreserved. He stilled at the smoky curiosity in her gaze and the unconscious seeking sweep of her hands over him. She wanted touch. She wanted to explore her sensuality, through him. How could he deny her?

She tracked her fingertips down his abs. Unable to stay relaxed, every muscle tensed with desire as she tracked lower. He ached for her to cup him. His erection strained higher, he felt the searing tightening in his balls, the urge to thrust against her palm rushed. He licked his lips because his mouth was parched and holding back now was almost killing him.

'Do you want me to kiss you?' she asked softly.

He wanted anything. Everything. He blinked.

She smiled, a burst of pleasure in her eyes. 'Want me to help you find your tongue?'

Heat strained his body. That playful whisper knocked once more on his well-entombed heart. 'You don't have to…'

'Did you feel you had to for me?' She looked up at him, shyness glimmering in her eyes as she whispered huskily.

'No,' he sighed, unable to form complete sentences. 'Wanted to.'

'I can't want to?'

He swallowed and gave in. 'Go right ahead.' With a groan he closed his eyes, desperate to summon self-control as he felt her breath on him.

She cupped him and it was sweet torture.

'Oh.' She looked at him as he flinched. 'Can I—?'

'Do anything. Anything you want. Just don't stop.' His breathing roughened.

She didn't stop. He watched, all his senses sharpened and arrowed on her. She was stunning—her long hair had loosened, tumbled about her shoulders, her long, lean, pale limbs unfolded around him. Her mouth was on him. Her mouth—

'Stop. *Stop.*' He dragged in a harsh breath.

She froze and pulled back with a worried expression. 'I'm sorry—'

'No.' He rubbed his forehead with a hard hand and groaned. 'It's just… I'm going to come.'

'Don't you want to?'

His shout of laughter hurt. His whole body ached. 'I wanted to warn you—'

'I don't want to stop,' she whispered.

The desire in her eyes stiffened him impossibly more. He growled his assent, unable to form another word, his want was too great. And then she sucked him dry.

His heart pounded so loud he thought it was going to burst. When he could finally open his eyes, he saw her smiling down at him—pride and amusement gleaming in her gaze. She was energised and so beautiful. She wasn't just insatiable, but capable of experiencing an intensity he knew was rare. And of sharing it with that gorgeous little laugh of hers.

'You okay?' He didn't know why he was asking her when he was so light-headed he wasn't sure he'd ever be able to sit up again. But then adrenalin fired him anew. Because he realised she was incredibly aroused. She'd liked touching him, tasting him. Getting and giving pleasure was always a great way to spend a night, but this was something else. This felt sweeter and sexier than anything.

'I still don't want to stop,' she said in the softest whisper. 'I still don't want you to stop.'

Her confession just demolished him. He was unable to resist and desperately aching to please her—wanting her to be more than sated, more than thrilled. He didn't want to deny her anything. So when he should've been spent, he was hard again and filled with an arrogant, outrageous determination. Who was he to tell her what she should or shouldn't do anyway? She knew he was leaving in the morning. She knew there was only this between them, only now. And she'd given them both permission to make the most of it. All he wanted now was to make it the best he could for her. Which meant keeping himself in check for a while yet. And being certain.

'I've never slept with a virgin before, Leah,' he said hoarsely, still catching his breath.

Her lashes veiled her eyes. 'Not even when you were a virgin?'

'No, I wasn't the first for my first. Do you really want to talk about—?'

'Did she make it good for you?'

A wry smile curved his lips. 'She did.'

'Then maybe think of this as paying it forward?' She looked as if she was braced for rejection.

He just couldn't deny her. 'You know you can change your mind. I'll—'

'Theo—'

'I don't want to hurt you,' he confessed rawly. It was incredibly true. Somehow, this woman he'd met only a few hours ago was precious to him. She mattered.

Her expression softened. 'If it hurts, maybe you can kiss it better…' She trailed off, suddenly shy.

That wave of protectiveness welled in him. He turned, swiftly searching the bedside table drawers. Relieved, he tossed the small box he'd found onto the bed. He'd leave nothing to chance.

Leah moaned as he pressed kisses across her collarbones and down her décolletage. He was so patient—too patient really. When he finally braced above her, anticipation heightened to a new level. He was big and heavy and wonderful. The slick hot reality impinged as she saw his muscles bunch. He braced as he held back. She knew he was being careful; she could tell in the way he watched her so closely. His concern melted her all the more.

'Please,' she murmured, knowing he needed to hear her wish again.

His expression tensed and he moved. Leah gasped as his big body invaded hers—tearing that last tiny barrier to bury deep inside her. He caught her sharp cry in a quick kiss.

'Sorry,' he muttered. His gaze was filled with searching concern for her. Of course that compassion was there—because if it wasn't she never would have sought this with him.

'Are you okay?' He framed her face and kissed her again and again—so gentle and lush.

He was pressed so deeply into her. So incredibly close. And it was so overwhelming she could only nod, as she adjusted to his possession and to the millions of nerve endings that had sparked to life within her—that suddenly sought so much more.

He held firm, slowly kissing her until the stillness was too much for her—she needed him to move. Warmth overflowed. She'd not expected it would be this intimate and yet of course it was. She revelled in the tender passion of his kisses and her body relaxed until she was no longer just accepting his invasion, but welcoming it—slickening, heating, until she instinctively rocked her hips to help. He kissed her again and his groan reverberated into her chest. He moved then too, taking control, making it magic, and she completely forgot that first moment of pain in her building delight. She followed his rhythm, learning this dance until instinct urged her to hold him closer still. She wrapped her arms and legs around him, clinging close with every part of her as the spasms of delight snuck up on her so swiftly.

'Don't stop,' she breathed desperately. 'Please, don't stop.'

But as she curved more tightly around him, so close to completion, he growled and suddenly froze.

'Theo?' she asked.

'Trying…' he gulped a breath '…not to be too rough.'

But she needed *all* of him.

'Finish me,' she begged.

At her broken plea she felt his restraint unravel and

power surged in his body. He lost it—thrusting harder and faster and it was so dizzying, so intense, so unbearably good. She could only try and hold on, but her restraint had fled too. She clawed his skin, grasping him as tight as she could in her grip as her body and mind locked on him. But he didn't stop, he pounded closer and fiercer, pushing them higher, further and faster until everything exploded in a flash of heat and light and utter, utter ecstasy.

Hours later Leah blinked, wishing she'd eaten more carrots as a kid so her night vision was better. Instead, she tripped over her shoe and muffled her squawk of pain as she hopped and tried to see well enough to find her other one. Her clothes had been scattered on the floor around the bed and, while she'd found most of them, she just needed this one last thing.

'Why are you trying to sneak out?' The lazy tease in his voice made her shiver.

'Sorry.' She stifled her nervous laughter.

As he switched on the lamp she glanced at him, embarrassment curling her spine. 'I didn't mean to wake you.'

His eyebrows lifted. 'Because you didn't want to talk to me?'

She swallowed. 'I just…'

His low chuckle filled the void. 'Relax. This doesn't have to be awkward.'

'No?' But she needed to escape now because the temptation to fling herself back into bed, wrap herself around him and never let him go was just a little too strong.

He leaned out of bed and reached for his phone. 'Give me your number.'

She stilled; the crowd of clamouring emotions shaking her up needed to settle. 'I don't think that's a good idea,' she said bravely. The night was over, the magic gone—wasn't it? 'We don't even live in the same country.' She drew in a breath. 'So…there's no point, is there?'

She wanted him to argue with her and say he wanted to see her again. But she had the feeling she'd spend the rest of eternity hoping he'd call. And if he did? Would she end up his booty call when he was in London? He didn't want a relationship, and never marriage, remember? And she did want those things. So this needed to stay as a finite dream night.

'No point?' he echoed quietly.

She turned away as he got out of bed and scooped his trousers up from the floor. She couldn't see his body again, couldn't stop to talk more. If only she'd not fallen over her shoe she'd be out of here by now. It had been great sex, that was all. Other people experienced this all the time. She couldn't be all inexperienced and needy now.

'At least let me get you home safely.'

She couldn't resist glancing back at him. 'I'll be fine on the—'

'I'm only going to phone down to the porter and order you a cab.' He sombrely studied her with those intense eyes. 'I wasn't going to drive you myself. I have to get to the airport, remember?'

'Okay, thanks.'

But her heart pounded appallingly quick and hard as he strolled towards her and made it impossible to think.

She couldn't look away. He was extraordinarily beautiful. Bronzed skin, strong, sleek muscle. She couldn't believe she'd had the privilege of touching him *everywhere*. She swallowed, clawing back the desire to do it again right now.

She couldn't possibly kiss him goodbye but just walking away seemed rude. For lack of a better idea she held out her hand for him to shake before he got too close. He paused, as if debating whether to take her hand or do something else entirely.

'No regrets, Leah?' he asked softly, finally clasping her hand in his in a handshake like no other. Could he feel her thundering pulse through her skin?

'None.' She couldn't get her voice above a whisper. 'But it's done.'

'Okay. Then, bye, beautiful Leah.' He glanced down at their linked hands for a brief moment and then released her. 'Thank you for a wonderful night.'

'Thank you too,' she echoed awkwardly and quickly turned away. 'Bye.'

On the way down to the ground floor she squared her shoulders and refused to feel any sadness. *Refused.* She'd had an amazing night—the best night of her life, just as he'd promised. As she acknowledged that, a surprising shot of confidence lifted her. So what if she had bed hair? So what if the porter waiting to escort her into the taxi could tell she'd spent the night barely sleeping because one man— one *amazing* man—had wanted her and she'd wanted him and together they'd done all kinds of wonderful?

Things were looking up. She'd moved to London, she had her own place, a new job she actually wanted and she was going to make such a go of it.

Finally, her life was only going to get better.

CHAPTER THREE

'WHAT DO YOU think of this pattern, Leah?'

Smiling, Leah paused by the open doorway of her favourite resident's room. She loved her job as receptionist in the private care facility in North London—mainly because she loved the residents. They were interesting and she enjoyed, not only being able to help them and their families, but just talking to them too. She'd been here coming up five months and as her confidence had increased, her bond with them all had built.

Now she went into Maeve's room to study the paper the old woman was holding up to her. They'd discovered a kindred fondness for knitting early in Leah's employment. It was a favourite way of relaxing, aside from reading, for them both. So Leah looked at the picture with interest. It was a pattern for a baby jacket. She'd thought Maeve's grandchildren were all older. Perhaps there was going to be a great-grandchild?

'I thought I'd better get started for you, but wasn't sure which colour you're going to need. Have you found out? Should I do pink or blue?' The elderly woman's eyes twinkled with curiosity.

Startled, Leah let out a stunned little laugh. Maeve wanted to knit this for *her*? *Why*? 'I'm not pregnant, Maeve.'

'You're just the right age to be pregnant,' Maeve said. 'I was about your age when I had my first.'

Leah laughed again—was this a sweet case of wishful thinking? 'I'm sorry, Maeve, but—'

'You can't fool me, you know. I know it's the norm these days not to say anything until you're a few months gone, but you can't hide how radiant you are now. You have so much more colour and sparkle than when you first started.'

Leah's breathing quickened. Did she? That was because when she'd started, she'd only just moved away from her parents. It had taken a while to bounce back from the pressure they'd put on her for so long and to accept that what she wanted to do with her life wasn't anything they'd ever approve of.

'I'm on a health kick,' Leah explained, because that was true. She'd been eating well and exercising…it wasn't anything else. It couldn't be.

'You don't drink coffee any more,' Maeve pointed out, looking very pleased with herself. 'Because you're blooming.'

Leah stared at the older woman and slowly shook her head again. But inside she was beginning to panic. She *had* become sensitive to certain smells and tastes, but that was because she'd chosen to eat so well—wasn't it? It was impossible for her to be pregnant because she was single and she'd never—

'Leah?'

'I think the pattern looks beautiful.' She forced a quick smile. 'I just need to…um…' Her brain wouldn't compute. She couldn't think of a reason to leave—she just threw another smile at Maeve and dashed from the room.

Oh. Leaning against the wall in the corridor outside, she breathed hard. For the first time in for ever she thought of that magical night. She'd been trying to forget it—to move on and not judge every man she passed by the impossible standard that was Theo Savas. Of course, no one compared. That night had been part of the reason her confidence had grown too. But for her to have got *pregnant*? She couldn't have. He'd used protection each time—she'd seen him. And that night had been months ago and she'd had her period since, right?

Oh, no. She put her hand to her mouth as she frantically tried to think, but the panic zombies had eaten her brain.

She'd always had an irregular cycle and she'd been so busy she hadn't been paying attention to that much because she'd thrown herself into her work in part to help herself forget *him* and now she couldn't remember...

Oh, no, no, no. Cold horror curdled her blood. What Maeve had noticed was true. She suddenly loathed the smell of coffee. And her skin was kind of amazing in a way it had never been before. And now she remembered other things she'd not realised before—that tiredness that had leached her for a while a few weeks ago? She'd attributed it to getting used to life in London with all the commuting and everything, but what if it had been symptomatic of something else?

Impossible. It just had to be impossible. Please could it be impossible?

But what if...? The appalling possibility took hold. She was so terrified she couldn't concentrate at all on her work. For the first time she left the second her shift was over, and stopped by a pharmacy on her way home. Once she was alone in her tiny apartment, her hands trembled as she opened the pregnancy test.

Even doing this was ridiculous, right? In a few minutes she'd be giggling about wasting her money. There was no way she could be pregnant. The idea was just a farrago of fact and fantasy planted by a confused elderly woman and taken on by her because she had some random make-your-skin-glow fever...right?

Two minutes later bright blue stripes appeared on the white background.

No, no, no, no, no.

Leah stared stupidly at the positive result. It couldn't be correct. It just couldn't. *How* could she be pregnant?

Her zombie mind now zinged with endless unanswerable questions. Where had the morning sickness been? Or all the other symptoms? More importantly, what was she going to do? And most terrifyingly, how was she going to tell *him*?

All these months she'd been trying not to obsess over him like some loser stalker. Now she had to make contact. How was she going to do that? And how on earth was he going to react?

Please, no.

With shaking hands she used the second test in the box. And cried when she got the same result. She picked up her phone and begged her way into a last-minute appointment with an after-hours doctor who was able to give her a scan to check on the baby's development. Leah stared at the grey whirls of motion on the screen as they formed into an image that made her eyes smart. Tiny and perfect. And *terrifying*.

Apparently everything was just as it should be for just over four months gestation. Everything appeared healthy and normal and all she had to do was keep eating well and taking care of herself.

'Would you like me to phone someone for you?' The attending nurse smiled at her as the doctor left the room. 'You've gone very pale.'

'No, thank you,' Leah murmured, standing up to leave. 'I'm fine. I'm often pale.'

'If you're sure...?' The concern didn't leave the nurse's eyes.

'Yes,' she said, aching to get out of there. 'Thank you anyway.'

Back alone in her apartment, she folded her legs beneath her on the sofa and tried to come up with a plan, except all she could do was hunch in a disbelieving ball.

She had to tell him.

Truthfully she'd searched for him online months ago in a moment of weakness just after their one night together. She'd even avoided seeing Zoe much because she couldn't bring herself to share a moment of that night with anyone.

She'd discovered Theo Savas was regarded as Greece's most eligible bachelor. Heir to a business banking empire that had branches around the world—he was now CEO and game-changer of that enterprise and apparently he could do no wrong because he'd broadened the family holdings, buying diverse companies and creating a conglomerate of success. There wasn't a hint of scandal about him—he wasn't known for partying ways, no rolling parade of beautiful girlfriends in the media, no salacious rumours of his endless succession of one-night stands.

But he had them. He was just discreet and courteous and too clever to leave a woman dissatisfied…

He was going to be horrified. But as much as she really didn't want to, she had to tell him. The question was *how*. Not for the first time she regretted not taking his phone number. Until today those regrets had been tempered by the knowledge she'd saved herself from making a complete idiot of herself by begging him for another night. That wasn't how Theo Savas rolled. He was too busy being the banking CEO, the charitable gift-giver, the employer of many, sponsor of the arts… He was too busy being perfect.

Would he even remember who she was?

She searched him again on her phone. His company's main headquarters were in Athens and there was another office in London, more in other cities around the world. But there was no email address for him—only a public contact address. She couldn't put something this personal into an email that would be read by an administrative assistant. She'd have to phone.

She tried the Athens branch first.

'I'm sorry, do you speak English?' Leah asked the woman who answered in rapid Greek.

'Of course.' The woman's reply was professional and immediate. 'How may I help you?'

'I'd like to speak to Theo Savas, please.' Leah tried to

sound confident and assertive but her nerves were fluttering so hard they rendered her breathless.

'May I ask who is calling?'

'Leah.' She cleared her throat, wincing at her own rushed answer. 'It's important I speak with him.'

There was a pause. 'Mr Savas is very busy. May I ask what it is in regards to?'

'I…' Leah braced as a wave of hot embarrassment swarmed over her skin. 'It's a personal matter.'

There was an even longer pause. 'If it is a personal matter, then you will know Mr Savas's personal number on which to contact him.' The woman's tone was cruelly cool.

Mortified, Leah hung up in a flash.

Why did he need such a dragon-led first line of defence? Did he have women trying to get in touch with him all the time?

Probably, she realised morosely. And the brutal fact was her pregnancy would appal him. He wasn't ready to settle, even if his grandfather wanted him to. And neither he nor his grandfather would want him to have a child with some random one-night stand. He moved in exalted circles—his clients were CEOs, royals, celebrities—he'd be expected to marry and have a family with someone from the same social strata. That wasn't her. She was utterly unsuitable— not educated, not successful, not glamorous or gorgeous… She faced the reality. She wasn't anything he'd either need or want. And she couldn't bear to think of her child knowing it was an unwanted disappointment to its father.

She was that to her parents.

Nor could she contact her parents and ask for their help. She gently held her lower abdomen as she briefly considered, then dismissed, the possibility. This precious baby deserved protection. It deserved to be loved and secure and never to face the judgment of her impossible-to-please parents. She wanted her child never to experience that inferior feeling she'd had all her life. She might not have much else, but she had unlimited love and support to offer her child. And she had to do the right thing for it.

She had to get in touch with Theo to at least give him the chance to consider how, or if, he wanted to be involved in their baby's life.

She glanced down at the website she'd pulled up with its list of addresses and phone numbers. What if she went to his London office and spoke with someone there? If she could convince them how important it was that she speak with Theo directly? But how could she convince them? She shrivelled with embarrassment at the thought of telling a stranger anything of that intimate night, but she had no choice.

The next morning Leah stood on the other side of the street from his London office and watched the people come and go from the building. All were smartly attired—exactly the opposite of her in her old wool coat with her homemade cardigan and her patched black jeans beneath. Her legs trembled and she pulled her coat more tightly around her and made herself step inside the lobby.

The place was beyond intimidating with its sleek interior. She looked at the perfectly coiffed women at the counter and just knew she'd get the same response as she'd got from the Athens receptionist. She'd be exposed in front of all these smooth professionals who were giving her sideways looks as it was. She didn't fit in here—she knew it, they knew it. She didn't have the money, looks or status.

Why had she refused to give Theo her number? Why had she refused to take his? Why had that contraception failed?

She felt too fragile to cope with public scrutiny and rejection. But as she glanced around, she realised her hesitation had caught the attention of the security guard.

He was staring at her, unsmiling. All those old feelings of insecurity and inferiority burned. She was so out of place—*again*. She wasn't good enough—she was *never* good enough. Humiliated, hurting, scared, Leah pushed forward and went up to the counter. This wasn't about her. This was about her baby.

'I'd like to get in touch with Theo Savas, please,' she said quietly to the receptionist.

Leah liked working on reception. She liked greeting people with a smile and being able to help them with their enquiries or to help them find the person they'd come to visit. This woman didn't look as though she enjoyed her job. There was no welcoming smile.

'Is he expecting you?'

'No, but I need to—'

'Mr Savas has no immediate plans to visit the London office at this time,' the receptionist informed her with precise finality.

'If I could just get a phone number—'

'I'm not authorised to give his private number out.'

'I understand, but if I could leave my number…' Leah was shaking with humiliation and embarrassment at the lack of courteous help.

The woman typed something on her screen. 'Your name and number?'

'Leah Turner,' she mumbled and then gave her phone number. 'You'll make sure he gets that message?'

'Certainly,' the woman answered with frosty dismissiveness. 'Was there anything else?'

'No. Thank you.'

It was too awful.

Leah watched her phone for days. But there was no call, no message and she could think of no other way to get in contact with him. She couldn't phone or email or scrape together the money to get to Athens…and even if she did get there, it wasn't as if she could knock on his door because she had no idea where he lived. And doubtless he'd have security staff there too—protecting him from random women.

She sighed. As much as she dreaded it, she was going to have to go back to his wretched bank.

CHAPTER FOUR

'DO YOU HAVE a moment, Theo?'

Theo glanced up as his security chief, Philip, paused in his doorway, an ominous-looking red file in his hands.

'Of course.' Theo sat back in his chair, eyes narrowing as Philip entered and closed the door behind him. 'What is it?'

'A woman visited the London office last week,' Philip said without preamble. 'The guard on the ground noticed her before she went up to Reception. There was also a call to the Greek office the day before.'

A woman? Theo raised his brows at Philip's ferociously serious expression. 'You think she's a threat?'

Philip extracted a photo from the folder. 'We pulled this from the security footage. It's the woman you asked for that summary report on a few months ago. Leah Turner.'

Theo stilled as every muscle in his body tensed. Leah? His Leah-of-the-Lost-Ticket?

He stared at the glossy image Philip had put on his desk and tried to breathe but it was as if a monster had grabbed his guts in a giant fist and squeezed hard. Because it was her—all legs and pale skin. In this picture she wore a wool jacket and a worried look. Why?

'What did she want?' His voice was so gravelly he barely recognised it as his own.

'To speak with you on a personal matter.'

She'd tried to contact him? Why now? Why months later? A surge of triumph ripped through him, swiftly followed by anger. 'Why wasn't she put through?'

He sighed and held up his hand. 'Never mind.' His staff would never interrupt him for, or give out his personal details to, a woman who'd just called in. 'Did she leave her number?'

'Unfortunately the details she left at Reception were mislaid.' Philip frowned. 'I've just interviewed the staff member—'

'How long ago was this?' Theo snapped.

'It didn't cross my desk until this morning.' Philip sounded apologetic. 'I'm sorry for the delay.'

Theo drew a steadying breath as he stared at her picture, but it didn't stop the roar of his blood as feral *want* blazed. But that want mixed with a deeper delight. He'd *missed* her. A flat-out desperate need to know ached.

'Would you like me to—?'

'Leave it with me,' Theo dismissed him brusquely, needing privacy to process. 'And close the door on your way out.'

He needed to be alone to breathe and think and dampen down the fire arcing through his body.

'Philip,' he relented just as his man reached the door. 'Thank you.'

He hadn't opened the report on the lovely Leah Turner. He'd ordered it after that night they'd shared because he'd found himself unable to stop thinking about her. He'd half hoped to discover something in the report that would kill his constant interest in her. But it had got so bad that when the report had arrived he'd decided to exercise restraint and not even read the thing—to prove his self-control to himself and not make that intolerable yearning worse. Usually he was very good at self-control. So that report sat in a file on his home screen. Mocking him. Tempting him.

Every night since the ballet, he'd dreamed of being with her again and again. His imagination had inevitably returned to her dark hair, her pale skin, her long, long limbs… But it was the loss of something more ephemeral that had kept him awake—the sparkle in her eyes when she'd made one of her surprisingly astute comments or inadvertent slips of the tongue, the shy playfulness that had emerged with only a little encouragement and most of all that soft laugh and the emotional expressiveness that he'd found both a welcome and a warning…the thing he'd been most unable to resist responding to.

She'd not wanted to see him again. She'd not wanted his number. She'd avoided his touch in the morning. He'd taken that to be a kind of self-preservation instinct, because he too knew finality was for the best.

Circumstance had then buried Theo in a gamut of responsibility. On his return to Athens that day, Dimitri had taken a turn for the worse, forcing Theo to cancel all upcoming travel. For months he'd stayed home to oversee Dimitri's care while working around the clock to keep the business on track. The old man was finally better now and he'd even revived that inconvenient idea to find Theo a suitable wife. But, for all his comments to placate Dimitri, Theo still had zero intention of following through on the idea.

Now he stared at the still of Leah—wrapped in that bulky wool jacket despite the spring weather—and it was her worried expression that struck him most. Why had she wanted to see him? Why now—all these months later?

He shoved his chair back and stood, rapidly assessing the pros and cons of immediate departure. But the decision was already made. He needed to see her in person.

He'd needed that for months.

CHAPTER FIVE

THE IMPERIOUS KNOCKING on her door startled Leah so much she dropped a stitch. She scrambled to her feet, heart thudding as she crossed the room. She didn't get visitors at this time of night.

'Hello?' she called through her door.

'Open up, Leah.'

Her knees actually buckled. She braced both hands on the door—whether to keep herself upright or hold the door secure she wasn't sure, as raw elation flared a split second before fear exploded. A welter of emotions cascaded through her body. Was that really—?

'Leah? It's Theo.'

He was so arrogant he didn't give his surname. He didn't need to.

'Open up, Leah.'

She was so thrown she obeyed almost without thinking, somehow distanced from reality. She saw dark blue jeans first, and then glanced up to take in the white tee stretched snug across a masculine chest that looked so powerful a rush of something illicit pooled low in her belly. She snapped her attention further north, only to be ensnared by his gorgeously rare green gaze.

Time simply stopped.

She had to tell him.

'Theo.' She dragged in a decent breath, trying to clear her head.

The casual clothing didn't make him any less powerful or less intimidating than when he'd been in his perfect suit. If anything he seemed more dangerous. He looked literally edgier, as if a little loss of weight had sharpened his features, making them more starkly apparent. He was more sensational than she remembered. Her body hummed and all she wanted was to move closer.

'What are you doing here?' she asked vacantly, still unable to stop staring.

He didn't answer. He was too busy staring back at her. His gaze trawled over every inch of her face, then her body. Her self-consciousness grew as the silence thickened. Her leggings were so faded they were more grey than black, with a hole at the knee, and her oldest pair of lurid leg warmers were barely clutching her calves. Her tee was old too. But happily it was loose. She curled her toes into the thin rug beneath her feet, almost squirming through his undeniably sensual inspection. Everything— her thoughts, senses, wants—heightened. It was as if she'd only been half alive these last few months and the second he'd crossed her threshold she'd been plugged back into the mains power supply. Energy and excitement thrummed through her veins.

She had to tell him.

'I heard you were trying to get in touch with me.' He smiled but his eyes were sharp as he watched her jerkily step away from him.

She couldn't smile back. She wasn't sure she could even speak. But now was the time. Horribly short of breath but trying to hide it, she leaned against the wall for support as he closed her door and walked into the middle of her too-small flat.

'How did you hear that?' she asked.

'You called into the London branch.'

'So you got my message.'

'Unfortunately the message was lost or I'd have got here sooner.'

He hadn't got the message? 'If you didn't get the message then how—?'

'There were cameras, security guards.'

'And I looked suspicious?' She'd laugh if she weren't so terrified about telling him. 'How did you get my address?'

'My security team is very good.'

At what? Protecting him from the unwanted attentions of women? Did they have to do that often?

His gaze didn't waver from her. 'All of this is irrelevant. Why did you want to see me, Leah?'

She felt as if she were standing on the edge of a very high precipice and had no choice but to jump off. 'I'm pregnant.'

He didn't move. In fact he remained so still she wondered if she'd actually said it. Had her words even been audible? She swallowed hard.

'I'm pregnant.' She made herself repeat it, only now her throat had tightened so much it came out on a husky breath.

'Congratulations,' he said mechanically.

She stared, waiting for more of a response. But he still didn't move. She realised he didn't fully understand. She made herself breathe again and pushed on. 'I'm pregnant by you.'

'No.' He was uncompromising in stance and in denial. 'It's not mine. We slept together months ago.'

'Yes. I'm four months pregnant.'

His mouth compressed and his searing gaze skimmed over her body again. 'You don't look four months pregnant. You'd be larger.'

'And you're an expert?' Anger suddenly bubbled within her—she wasn't an idiot and she wasn't going to let him treat her like one. 'Because I'm so tall, there's room for the baby to hide,' she muttered. 'But the doctor said everything's developing okay.'

He stared at her fixedly. 'It's not possible. I used condoms.'

'Well, apparently one of them failed.' Her heart clogged her throat, choking her.

He remained rigid in the centre of the small room. 'And you've known all this time?'

'No, of course not.' She frowned. 'I only found out last week.'

An almost vicious brightness lit his eyes, slicing through her. 'Well, I'm no expert,' he drawled, 'but how is *that* possible?'

'I…um…' She swallowed. 'I've been so busy, I just didn't realise—'

'You didn't realise?' He stepped forward before stopping himself with a jerk. Tension streamed from his body.

She winced at the flare of fury in his eyes. 'I went to the doctor last week. She confirmed it. Then I tried to contact you.'

'You tried?' he echoed sarcastically.

A horrible hot feeling slithered inside as she nodded.

'You phoned my office but didn't leave your number. You walked into the London office once. You gave up pretty quickly.'

His scathing assessment flayed. He was right. She'd not done enough.

He shook his head. 'Am I the only possible father?'

His question stabbed—how could he think otherwise? She paused; had he had other lovers since her? Of course, he probably had. That reality hurt more than it should. But he'd known she'd been a virgin—hadn't he realised how rare it was for her?

'You think I started having casual sex every other night?' She glared at him. 'We can get a DNA test if you don't believe me.'

His eyes blazed before he abruptly turned away, rolling his shoulders. 'No. It's okay. I believe you.' His voice sounded flat and hard. He drew in a deep breath and swung back to face her. 'What's the plan?'

'Plan?' she echoed.

'You're four months pregnant. You'd failed to contact me, so what were you going to do?'

'I was going to...' She swallowed. She'd been trying to get over her panic enough to make progress. She'd been failing on that so far.

'Were you going to go home to your parents?' He watched her closely.

'No,' she muttered. She wasn't ready to face the recriminations and rolled eyes, the sighs of impatience because she'd failed to meet their standards again. She couldn't even move to another city and make a success of it.

'You haven't told them either?'

'They're very busy and they live too far away.' She'd never want her baby in that cold intellectual environment where normal people couldn't perform highly enough.

'I live even further away.' He stepped towards her. 'Have you thought about that?'

She hadn't thought about it at all. She'd not been able to get past worrying about telling him. Frankly she'd been too paralysed to predict his reaction. But it was bad. Bitter betrayal burned in his eyes and he was coldly furious, the antithesis of the man she'd trusted so completely that night. There was no softening in his reserve now.

'You travel a lot.' She tried to reason a way out of the mess. 'If you want, you can visit...a lot.'

'If I want?' He looked astounded. 'You think I'll settle for seeing my child every other week at best?' The lethal way he fired his words made goosebumps lift—let alone the impact of what he'd actually said.

He loomed closer, even angrier. 'Not going to happen, Leah. *Never* going to happen. Have you talked to *anyone* about this?'

'Only the doctor.' She hated how pathetically breathy her answer sounded.

She'd not told anyone at work. She'd avoided Maeve. She'd not returned Zoe's last call… She'd been in denial.

'Good. That means we can work out our story more effectively.'

'Our story?'

'We're getting married.'

'What?' Her jaw dropped.

'You're pregnant. It's my baby. I'm not having my child born illegitimate.'

'And I don't get any choice in this?'

'So explain your choice to me, then. What are you going to do? Stay in this tiny bedsit? Are you going to head straight back to work the second you've given birth and leave my baby in a nursery all day? How did you think you were going to make ends meet, Leah?'

He was asking too many questions. Making too many judgments. A barrage of tests designed to trip her up— like those dreaded pop quizzes her parents inflicted on her randomly and repeatedly so she never had any chance of relaxing. Not when she failed them every time because their required pass mark was one hundred per cent correct. That old performance anxiety reared, rendering her unable to think at all. Instead she lashed out. 'I'm *not* going to marry you.'

'Why not? You know you'll never have to work another day in your life,' he exploded.

As if that were relevant? 'I didn't even know who you were. I wasn't the one who provided the condoms. Or the one who put them on. I'm not the one who didn't bother to check they'd…' She trailed off.

'Survived the event?' he interpolated with dry precision.

'No. And guess what? I like my life. I like my home here. I like the people I help in my job. I want to work. I certainly don't want to leave it all to live a life of intolerable boredom in a foreign country with a husband who resents me.'

His face whitened. 'Too bad,' he choked. 'Because here we are. It isn't what you want? It's not what I want either. But it's what's *right*. Pack your things.'

She stared at the stranger he'd become. Or perhaps he always was this ruthless and she'd just not seen it that night because she'd stupidly given him everything he'd wanted? She couldn't reconcile that suave, amusing man with the cold authoritarian before her now.

'I don't want to fight, Leah.' He ran a hand through his hair roughly.

'You just want me to do everything you want.'

'Yeah.' He actually threw a smile in her direction. Well, a tight, determined baring of the teeth that a more generous person might mistake for a smile. 'I'm good at fixing problems and you have to agree this is a problem.'

It was a huge problem. 'What's your plan, then?'

He ruffled his hair again and then sighed. 'In the long term, we won't have to impact on each other's lives much.'

Chills swept over her skin. This was no romance. No rescue. He wasn't suggesting marriage because he *liked* her. This was only about securing their child's future. But the details were too scarce. 'What do you mean?'

'I mean we can come up with an arrangement that suits us both.'

Still not enough. 'What kind of arrangement?'

He had a distant look in his eyes. 'We'll marry, we'll raise this child. But you and I will live largely separate lives. I have several properties.'

'Separate.' She swallowed the sting of his cool rejection. She couldn't let it bother her. He clearly didn't feel any of the attraction to her that she still felt for him. Not even just physical. 'Theo, we had a really nice night, but it was supposed to end there,' she said stoutly.

'Well, there's no ending it now,' he muttered. 'We're stuck with each other for a lifetime.'

'We don't have to be.'

'What does that mean?' he asked pointedly. 'Are you prepared to give me full custody?'

All the air whooshed from her lungs. 'What? No!'

'Because I'll not step back from my responsibility, Leah. If you're having my baby, I'm going to provide for it. Always.'

His vehemence shocked her. He'd said he didn't want to marry. She'd thought that meant he'd not want children either...but now he was all 'instant family'—why?

'Don't make this more difficult than it needs to be,' he added, watching her closely, his expression shutting down as if he could read the questions burning inside her. 'We can work it out.'

'Yes,' she agreed. 'But it doesn't have to mean marriage.' She struggled to drag in a calming breath. 'You said you'd never marry.'

Theo's jaw locked so hard it hurt. 'You're pregnant.'

Nothing but regret filled him. History was repeating in the worst of ways. He'd failed her, his grandfather, himself. He knew accidents happened. He was one himself. And he had to do a better job of fixing this than his parents had. And as much as he didn't want it, there was only one way to do that. But he could hardly compute what she'd told him. Truthfully he was still recovering from being in the same airspace as her again—still battling the urge to haul her close and kiss her. He needed calm and logic to create a cool-headed contract with her.

Yet as he stared, as she stiffened in defensiveness, a primal possessiveness stole his reason, its fierceness shocking his self-control from him. He'd claim what was his. He'd *protect* it. Always. He'd even protect it from himself.

'I won't have an illegitimate child, Leah,' he said roughly. 'He or she deserves my name and all the privileges that come with it.'

'You mean money?'

'I mean many things, but, yes, that's one of them. My child also needs the proper protection... You do too.' He glanced at her. 'You have no idea what comes with wealth like ours.'

'Is it a terrible burden?' Her eyes glinted as she lobbed the acerbic little taunt.

He refused to react to her bite. 'The child also needs more than physical security. A sense of belonging.' Theo closed his mind to his own old memories of insecurity and betrayal. 'I'm sorry if that's too old-fashioned for you, but...' Bitterness almost overwhelmed him. Surely he could give more than he'd received? Except he really couldn't bear the thought of caring for a tiny, vulnerable baby. He didn't have what it took.

'It's not old-fashioned. It's honourable.' She sighed. 'It's just—'

'We're talking about a baby, Leah,' he interrupted, unable to stand the argument, let alone the actual reality. 'It doesn't get more life-changing than that. I'll take my share of the responsibility.'

Her lips compressed. 'But you're taking *all* the responsibility and becoming a dictator in the process.'

Her flash of temper tested his determination not to lose his again. But if he reacted now the way he really wanted, then this wouldn't become the safe, serviceable arrangement they both needed. Her earlier words haunted him—*a life of intolerable boredom with a husband who resented her*? She'd encapsulated his mother's life in one sentence. And look at the mess of betrayal and hurt that had led to.

He refused to excavate the past now. All that mattered was that he ensured Leah had everything she needed. Except he didn't really know how—not beyond the basics of providing four walls, a roof and food. He paced across the tiny room, rapidly working out the only way they could forge a viable future. She'd hardly have to see him. They simply had to agree to the arrangement.

Right now she wouldn't look at him. She was scared and angry. Frankly so was he. 'Pack your things. It's getting late.'

She kept staring at the floor. 'I'm not leaving with you.'

'I'm not leaving without you.' Her persistence tore his temper. 'You might have only recently found out about this pregnancy, but you didn't exactly try hard to get in touch with me. How do I know you're not going to skip town in the middle of the night?'

'You don't trust me.'

He braced inwardly at the hurt he heard in that soft sentence and just reiterated the fact. 'I'm not leaving without you.'

'Well, I'm not leaving here tonight. Good luck on my tiny sofa.'

'I'm not sleeping on the sofa, Leah.'

'You're not welcome in my bed,' she declared huskily.

'Is that right?' He stepped closer and felt the frisson of sensual awareness. Her words were pure challenge—a denial of the electricity sparking between them. It was still there—he'd seen it the second they'd laid eyes on each other again. But it was in both their interests to let her deny it. 'Then it's my hotel suite.'

'I'm not—'

'It has more than one bedroom,' he growled. 'Will that appease your outraged virtue?' He whirled away so he wasn't tempted to prove how hollow her words were. But the room wasn't anywhere near large enough for him to get the distance he needed. 'It's that or we stand here arguing all night.'

She folded her arms. 'I can't just pack up everything tonight.'

He glanced about. 'Why not? It won't take long.'

She shook her head. 'You're a jerk, you know that?'

'Leah.' He struggled for control—so close to throwing her over his shoulder and carting her down to the waiting car himself. He never let his emotions get the better of him, but it was almost impossible now. 'It's getting late.'

'I could join you later. In a week or so.'

It was unacceptable to him. 'We're sticking together until we're married.'

She looked aghast. 'We can't just get married.'

True. He nodded. 'It'll take about a week to get the paperwork processed.'

'A *week*?'

Yeah, he was moving fast but he'd make no apology for it. He could only try a little joke. 'That'll give you time to find something to wear.'

'Because that's the most important thing I have to consider?'

He bit back his smile as she slammed her retort at him. Backed into a corner, she could still hold her own.

'Stop stalling for time and go pack or we'll go without any of your clothes.' He was right about this. She just needed to admit it.

'Fine. Your suite. Separate rooms.' She marched all of five feet through to the bedroom.

Theo paced around the small lounge again. It was small and drab, the carpet worn and the walls in desperate need of a fresh lick of paint. But he noticed the few decorations she'd added to personalise the place—the warm-looking throws draped over the sofa, the knitted cushion covers. Then he spotted the pinboard. There was a photo of Leah with that ballet friend of hers, the menu of a Thai take-away around the corner, a couple of hand-drawn designs on grid paper, a theatre ticket. He peered closer.

'This is your ticket to the ballet?' he asked as she returned with a rucksack and that ginormous ugly handbag.

A rush of memory loosened his restraint and he smiled.

'It turns out I'd left it here all along.' She looked embarrassed. 'That night, that's why I couldn't find it in my bag. Pretty useless, I know.' She actually smiled.

He couldn't hold back his little laugh and studied the ticket again. 'You had quite a good seat.'

'I told you, Zoe is my friend.' She glanced at him. 'Or do you not believe me about that now?' Soft hurt flickered in her eyes, fading out that smile. 'I've never given you reason *not* to trust me, Theo.'

She didn't realise that, for him, trust wasn't freely given and then lost. It had to be earned. 'I guess we don't know each other very well, Leah.'

Her expression became a little pinched. 'I guess getting married will change that.'

Leah swallowed hard when he didn't reply. She'd thought she had known him. That they'd connected more than physically that night. And *she* had most certainly trusted him. For him not to trust her hurt. Now she was mortified he'd seen she'd kept that ballet ticket as a keepsake of the night they'd spent together.

She picked up her rucksack again. 'I'll need to come back to get everything else.'

As wary as she was of going with him, how could she argue? He was right—what alternative could she suggest? She didn't have his kind of money, power, experience or authority. And not only would her family be mortified and unwilling to help, they were actually *unable* to offer the emotional support she really wanted for her child. If Theo had a warm relationship with his grandfather, and he seemed to, then that might be better. At the very least she had to give him the chance. She owed him that.

'You have a current passport?' he checked.

'Yes. Why?'

'Because we need to get home quickly.'

'You expect me to go to *Greece*? When? Tomorrow?'

'Exactly.'

It was happening too fast. Get married in a week? Go to Greece tomorrow? Leave with him tonight?

He watched her solemnly. 'We need to work this out and I can't leave my family for long.'

'But you think I can leave mine?'

'You haven't told your parents the good news. I guess that says a lot about your relationship with them.' He took the bags from her. 'We'll fly to Athens first thing in the morning.'

'I can't just not turn up to my work.' She couldn't believe his arrogance. 'I need to work out my notice. I need to say goodbye to my residents. Or do you think that because I'm just a receptionist I can ditch everything and leap to your beck and call?'

He stared at her fixedly, rather as if he was inwardly counting to ten. 'Okay.' He released a slow sigh. 'We'll figure it out in the morning. For now, let's get to my hotel and get some rest.'

Leah stared stonily out of the passenger window at the darkening sky and said nothing. It wasn't the same hotel as that night at the ballet. This one was polite discretion with no big logos—secret luxury in the heart of Mayfair. She followed Theo to the suite on the top floor. The lounge alone was almost three times the size of her little flat.

'Take whichever room you want,' he muttered.

'You've not taken one already?'

'I came straight from the airport to your apartment.'

The atmosphere thickened. He'd not known her news but he'd come straight to see her? Just because she'd appeared in his London office?

She couldn't turn away from his gaze. It was as if she were pinned in place by that intense scrutiny. Somehow this place felt more intimate than her apartment despite it being so much bigger. Maybe it was the mood lighting or the luxuriousness of the furnishings, but suddenly she was too aware of sensation, the temptation of intimacy and touch. Smoky memories curled. She gritted her teeth, wanting to regain control of herself. He didn't want *that*. He wanted them to live separate lives, together in name only for the sake of their baby.

'I'll come with you to talk to your boss tomorrow before we leave for the airport,' he said huskily.

'Because I'm incapable of talking to them on my own?' She couldn't hold back her defensiveness. 'Are you afraid I'll say something I shouldn't?'

'No.' He stepped closer. 'Because I'm afraid they won't let you go. One of those oldies will ask you to make them a pot of tea and we'll never get you out of there.' He gazed at her intently. 'You're a pushover, Leah. A tug on the heart-strings is all it takes.'

A tug on the heartstrings? Was that what he'd done with her that night? Had that connection she'd thought they'd forged just been a ploy? She shook her head, not able to believe that. 'There's nothing wrong with being kind to people.'

'Nothing at all.' He gazed at her for another moment, then rolled his shoulders. 'We'll go see your parents after we've been to your work in the morning. What are they like?'

'You don't need to—' She couldn't tell him about her parents and she certainly didn't want him to meet them. 'Just forget I mentioned it. I don't need to go see them.'

'You're going to leave the country and not even see them to say goodbye? You don't want to invite them to the wedding?'

'They won't come.'

He blinked. 'Now I can't wait to meet them.'

'Too bad,' she echoed his earlier dismissal. 'You're not.'

'Leah,' he sighed. 'I'm trying to meet you halfway. I'm trying *not* to be a dictator.'

'So by simply informing me of tomorrow's itinerary, you're *not* being a dictator?' she asked.

He took her shoulders in a firm grip. 'I'm going to be their son-in-law, you don't think they'd want to meet me—vet me first?' A quizzical look lit his eyes. 'There's no need for me to pass any parental approval?'

They'd probably love to meet him. But they wouldn't believe for a second that he was in love with her. They'd see the situation for what it was—a hoax. A mortifying necessity because she'd stuffed up. For them to know that? She wanted to shrivel into a ball and hide. She didn't need them to witness yet another of her failures. Because they expected nothing less, right?

'Tell me about them.' He cocked his head, watching her as if he were trying to solve a cryptic puzzle. 'What do they do? It can't be that bad.'

'It's not that I'm ashamed of them, more the other way round.' She huffed a sigh. 'They're academics. My younger brother too. They've lived near the university all my life.'

'Academics?' His eyebrows lifted.

'Professors, in fact. And my younger brother, Oliver, is so gifted he's already a senior lecturer.' While she was a receptionist at a care home. 'Their careers are everything to them.'

He looked thoughtful. 'What do they think of your career choice?'

'You mean you can't guess?'

He gave her shoulders a gentle squeeze. 'What's their specialisation?'

'Other than criticism?' she half joked. 'Chemistry.'

'Chemistry?' His eyes widened and he couldn't suppress his smile.

She couldn't resist a small smile back, but then she had a flash of how awkward it was going to be. 'My parents are very—' She broke off, unable to explain just how laser-precise their perceptions were. 'They'll see in a second that we're not…'

'Not what?' He waited. 'You're having my baby so we've obviously had sex. We find each other attractive.'

'We *found* each other attractive. *Once.*'

That intensity deepened in his expression. His vivid green eyes were backlit with remnants of that magic night and the phantom delight he'd showered upon her. 'I thought you always opted for the truth, Leah,' he said quietly.

'Well.' She sucked in a steadying breath. 'Maybe you were right. Sometimes it might be better not to say anything.'

'Denial?' His smile faded as he gazed down at her. 'For protection.'

That heat spiralled like a whisper of smoke within her. More memories teased—of sizzling touch and sweet torment. But she had to ignore the urge to lean closer, and pull back instead. Because he didn't want her. He wanted separate lives.

'It's late,' she muttered. 'I should get some rest.'

'Yes. Go. Sleep.' He released her, that remote, reserved man once more. 'It seems we have a big day tomorrow.'

CHAPTER SIX

'OF COURSE, YOU must leave right away, Leah,' Seth said quietly. 'But we're really going to miss you.'

Leah nodded; her throat had tightened too much to answer.

Her boss sent her a smile that was both encouraging and sad before he turned to Theo. 'There really was no need for you to give us such a generous donation...'

'Leah was concerned about leaving you so quickly without a replacement organised,' Theo said. 'But with my grandfather the way he is...'

'Of course. We understand.' Seth glanced back to Leah. 'But we are sad to see you go.'

Leah looked to the floor to hide her emotion. This was the first job she'd loved and the first job she'd totally nailed. There'd been no massive list of qualifications required, just the ability to put people at ease. Her life had blossomed here—she was going to miss it too.

'I need a quick moment,' she murmured to Theo and walked down the corridor before he had a chance to respond.

She stopped at Maeve's open door and lightly rapped her fingers on the frame.

'You're leaving us.' Maeve pushed out of her plush armchair and held her arms out.

'Yes.' Leah stepped in and gave the tiny woman a tight hug. 'But I have something I wanted to give you.' She stepped back, blinking quickly and pulling out the small knee blanket she'd put in her handbag.

'It's the purple, with that rib I can't manage with my arthritic old hands.' Maeve took it from her with a smile.

'Yes.' Leah smiled past the lump in her throat. 'I thought

it would help keep those draughts out.' Maeve couldn't knit the complex patterns she used to, and Leah knew she felt the cold.

'I have something for you too.' Maeve picked up a clear bag from her table and held it out to Leah. 'I decided on white, seeing you weren't sure…'

Leah's heart melted as she lifted out a tiny woollen baby jacket. 'Maeve, it's just beautiful. Thank you so much.' Her throat closed. It would have taken a lot of effort for Maeve to get it finished in time and Leah would treasure it always.

Maeve clasped Leah's fingers with her shaking hands. 'You're going to be a wonderful mother, Leah.'

Leah blinked, warmth flooding her. This relationship was so precious to her. 'I'll come and visit you when I'm in town again.' Her throat tightened. She didn't want to say goodbye. She was going to miss her. She was going to miss all the people she'd been working with.

'Leah,' Theo called quietly from the doorway. 'I'm sorry. We need to go.'

'Is that him?' Maeve asked.

'Yes.' Leah half chuckled as she saw the shrewd assessment in Maeve's eyes as she craned her neck to take stock of Theo.

'You'll take care of her, won't you?' Maeve questioned him pointedly.

As embarrassed as she was, warm amusement and appreciation trickled through Leah. It touched her that Maeve cared. She cared about her too.

Theo smiled his most charming smile. 'Yes.'

Ten minutes later Leah stared out of the window as the car sped out of central London, her pulse accelerating at the same pace. The driver had closed the partition, giving them a level of privacy she didn't really want. When she was alone with Theo, her thoughts went a little wild.

'I can't believe you used your money and your grandfather to get me out of my contract,' she muttered.

'I wasn't using my grandfather. I told the truth,' Theo answered calmly.

'Well, you certainly used your money,' she murmured, submitting to the niggling need to provoke him.

'Leah.' He reached out and covered her clenched fist with his hand.

His touch stilled her antagonism but she couldn't rid herself of all her anxiety. She knew they would resolve this situation and, while he was annoyingly decisive, he was at least trying. She should do the same.

'Your grandfather is really that unwell?' she asked.

'He had heart surgery recently.' Theo's tone grew reserved. 'But he's getting better.'

She wondered why he was reticent about him. 'How's he going to feel about this?'

His expression hardened and he released her hand. 'It'll be fine.'

Leah watched him closely. 'He's just going to be okay with you turning up engaged to a woman you barely know, who's four months along already?'

'Dimitri doesn't need to know every detail—or lack thereof—of our relationship.'

'You're going to lie to him?'

'I'll tell him the important facts and that's enough. His well-being is paramount.'

Would he be upset by some of the 'less important' facts?

She paused, sensing his reluctance to talk, but she was unable to resist probing further. He'd asked about her family—couldn't she do the same? 'You're close?'

His hesitation made her senses even more acute.

'I've lived with him since I was ten.' His voice was so low it was hard to hear over the purr of the engine. 'I owe him everything.'

'Why did you go to live with him?'

'My father passed away.'

'I'm sorry.' She gazed at him. His emotionless countenance was unsettling.

'I went to live with Dimitri. That is why I'm not going to abandon my child now.' He drew in a sharp breath. 'We can do better...'

Because *he'd* felt abandoned? Leah swallowed back the deeply personal questions that sprang to mind. He'd not mentioned his mother and she was wary of asking more because there was pain in his expressionlessness. Her heart ached as her apprehension rose. 'What's your grandfather—Dimitri—like?'

He sighed, but the faintest smile softened his mouth. 'Authoritarian, old and unwell. I won't let him be upset by anything or anyone.'

'Do you think he'll be upset by me?' She bit her lip, anxious about the answer.

He glanced at her, his eyes flaring with something before his lashes lowered. 'No one could be upset by you.'

Somehow it wasn't the answer she'd wanted. Somehow it skittled the little emotional self-control she'd restored. 'Because I'm just a harmless little thing who couldn't possibly hurt anyone?' she asked.

Because she was powerless and inconsequential? As useless as her parents had made her feel? The parents she was about to face and confess her life-changing mistake to?

'Because you're a kind person who'd never be deliberately rude to anyone.' He held her gaze solemnly. 'But you shouldn't have to put up with him either. You won't see him much.'

She blinked. 'I don't have to put up with him? Is he scary?'

'He used to be.' A whisker of a smile flashed on his

face. 'But then I grew up. He only wants what he thinks is best for me.'

'He was tough on you when you were younger?'

Another hesitation made her lean closer to listen.

'He had exacting standards and I needed to prove myself to him. But I'm grateful for them. We get on well. As I said, I owe him everything.'

Leah knew all about exacting standards but, unlike her, Theo would have surpassed them all.

The car ate up the miles to Cambridge and her nerves ratcheted. The research institute was so familiar—the white walls and bright lights beneath which she'd faded, invisible and insignificant. She'd eventually realised that restocking the chemicals cupboard wasn't the job for her. She needed a job where she was around people more. And she'd needed to get away from the triple eclipse of her family.

Drawing a deep breath, she knocked on the door of her parents' office. They'd both be there. They always were.

'Leah?' Her father looked up from his desk. 'This is a surprise. Is everything all right?'

Of course he'd immediately assume things might not be all right. Leah tried not to let that bitterness rise. It wasn't their fault that, for super-smart people, they couldn't understand her.

'Everything is…' she drew breath '…really great. Is Mum here too?'

'Of course.' It was her mother who replied.

Leah took satisfaction at the swiftly concealed surprise on Theo's face as her mother appeared from the next room. While her father was like her—tall, thin and dark-haired— her mother was the absolute opposite. Short, blonde, beautiful and brilliant enough to earn her double PhD in half the time it normally took, Leah's mum adored challenging stereotypes—insisting women didn't need to meet societal expectations of beauty or brilliance. She'd rejected make-up, dresses, high heels and insisted Leah never wear them either. Only her mother wasn't angular and un-pretty like Leah—she had no idea what it was like not to be wildly attractive naturally.

'What brings you here?' Her mother looked at her. 'And your friend?'

'This is Theo Savas,' Leah began. 'Theo, these are my parents, Jocelyn Franks and James Turner.' Her nerves tightened.

Theo extended a hand. For a moment her father just stared at it before giving it a weak response. She should have told Theo her parents weren't physically demonstrative people.

'We're here because…um…actually, you're going to be grandparents.' She just blurted it out.

'Pardon?' Anger—and that old impatience—built on her mother's face, mottling her flawless skin.

'I'm pregnant.' Leah tried to stay calm but her brain was malfunctioning the way it always did when her mother was about to test her on one of her many impossible quizzes.

'You're responsible for this?' Her mother turned to Theo. 'Did you take advantage of her?'

Leah gaped. Couldn't *she* be responsible? Was she invisible all over again? She refused to be that—not in front of Theo. Not when she now knew some people believed in her. People like Seth and Maeve. 'Maybe I took advantage of him?'

'Oh, Leah.'

That withering dismissal, that disappointment?

Leah pasted on her smile, determined not to let this happen in front of Theo. 'We're getting married in Greece next week—'

'I should think so.' Her father turned with low fury to Theo. 'You're going to take care of her?'

It was the same question Maeve had asked but it sprang

from something so different. He wasn't asking Theo this because he thought she was a treasure, worthy of only the best treatment. But because he thought she was the opposite—helpless and hopeless.

'I knew it was a mistake to let you go to London on your own—'

'I might not have your PhDs, but I'm not stupid—'

'You've just told us you're *pregnant.*'

'And that makes me stupid?' She gazed at her mother sadly. Because having a child was a bad thing? That was her mother's attitude, wasn't it? Or, at least, having a child who was an eternal disappointment was.

'You've got no qualifications, Leah.' Her mother shredded her. 'We've been looking after you for years, since you dropped out. We got you that job in the lab—'

'I've been looking after you,' Leah pointed out in a choked voice. 'Who cooked all the meals? Who arranged everything you were too busy for?'

'That was to give you something to do.' Her mother glared at her. 'You think we can't cook, Leah?'

'You never did.'

'You know it's not the best use of our time,' her father said.

Leah gaped. Because her parents' time was more precious than hers? Their 'real' work—all those intellectual achievements—were too important to be interrupted with anything like parenting or maintaining a normal house? They'd paid for a cleaner and now it seemed they'd just 'allowed' Leah to do the cooking. How marvellously kind of them. Hadn't they thought she might have plans and dreams of her own that she'd rather be fulfilling?

She'd realised how desperately she'd needed to start over and live her own life. And she'd been succeeding. And she'd continue to succeed without them.

'Well.' She cleared her throat. 'Thanks for keeping an

eye out for me all this time but you no longer need trouble yourselves. We're leaving for Greece today.'

'Leah.' Her father frowned, his tone patronising. 'You can't just—'

'I'm sorry if you can't make it to the wedding, given it's such short notice.' Theo stepped forward. 'But we can't delay our happy occasion a day longer than necessary.' He wrapped his arm around her and drew her too close. 'Leah is so special to me. I'll take care of her and our baby.' He gazed into her eyes as if he were love-struck. 'You don't need to worry about her.'

She wanted to point out that she didn't need *any* of them to 'take care of her'. But there was a glimmer of something more than amusement in his expression and it hurt. She didn't want his sympathy. But as he looked at her that expression deepened to devastatingly serious. 'Anyway, you've never needed to worry about her. She can look after herself—'

'Leah? I didn't know you were here for a visit.'

She turned, pulling out of Theo's hold as her brother, Oliver, walked into the office.

'I'm just leaving.' She braced because her emotions were almost beyond control and she'd not expected Oliver to be away from his lab. 'I'm moving to Greece. Getting married. Having a baby. You should come to the wedding,' she summarised as swiftly as she could. 'No joke.'

'What?' Oliver pulled the beanie off and gaped at her. 'When? I have my—'

'Research, I know. It's okay. I'll send you a photo.' She just wanted to get out of there as quickly as possible because she loved her little brother. 'We need to leave now.'

She walked, not even checking to see if Theo was with her. She knew he would be. Just as she knew her parents wouldn't stop her. But as she crossed the threshold her brother called her name. She couldn't not glance back.

'You'll phone?' He was still gaping.

'Of course.' Because she knew he couldn't say it as well, but he did care.

He saluted her and realised he held the beanie. He suddenly smiled. 'Thanks for this. It's the best one yet.'

She nodded and left. She was going to miss Oliver the most—she'd cared for her younger brother, even when he'd been too buried in books to realise he needed it.

She couldn't trust herself to speak as they got back into the car. Theo apparently had a few things to digest too, because the first fifteen minutes of the drive back were in complete silence. But then she felt him turn towards her.

'Your family are—'

'Amazing, I know.' She smiled brightly because it was that or burst into tears.

'That wasn't the word I was going to use.'

'But they are,' she argued lightly. 'Bona fide geniuses, the three of them. With just a normal IQ, I'm the odd one out.' She shook her head but was unable to stop the words tumbling. 'You didn't need to step in. You didn't need to act as if...'

'As if what?' His eyes glinted. 'I actually *want* to marry you?'

'I don't need you to say that to them. Or take care of me now.' She couldn't hold back. Her parents' words had stung. Just because she didn't have three degrees didn't mean she was incapable of looking after herself. 'I'm not incompetent. I could have made it work. Women do, you know, raise kids on their own.'

He reached out and covered her tight fist with his big hand. 'I know you could handle this alone, Leah. You're amazing. You just handled the hell out of *them*,' he added. 'But the point is you don't have to be alone now. You're not solely responsible for this situation.'

She desperately wished she could escape the emotion overwhelming her at his words.

'Why does your brother wear a beanie in summer?' he asked with a wry smile.

She shot him a sideways look, startled by the change in topic. 'He gets cold in the lab. And he has sensitive ears and it's better if they're warm.'

'So you gave it to him?'

'Knitting is the new black, didn't you know?'

'You made it?'

'Yes, I made it. You don't think I'm capable of that?'

'Easy, tiger.' He laughed gently. 'I'm not like them, Leah. I thought you'd bought it for him because, yes, it looked good enough quality to have been bought. You gave that little rug to that old lady at the home as well. But I get the impression your parents had very high standards.'

'I was never going to get the grades they expected from me.' She'd tried so very hard but they'd expected brilliance and perfection.

'That's why you stopped dancing?'

'They said it interfered with my schoolwork too much.' She shrugged in a helpless gesture. 'They couldn't understand why I wasn't like them and they tried so hard to make me like them—honestly, the books, the tests, the tutoring... And you see what they think of me now.' She looked at him. 'Only good for the cooking and cleaning, right? They actually think you took advantage of me. I must be rescued. I can't take care of myself. I must get walked all over...all because I don't have the same skill set or dreams they do.'

'It wasn't your fault you couldn't live up to their expectations,' he said quietly. 'But you gave up your dream.'

'They wouldn't pay for my classes any more and I couldn't get my marks high enough to get them to resume them.'

'You didn't fight in other ways? Didn't clean the dance studio in exchange for free lessons?'

She gazed at him. Just like that he'd worked up an independent solution. That was what he would have done, or something else inventive to get what he wanted. She had no doubt he'd be defiant in the face of denial or rejection. That was why he was the CEO of a massively successful bank now. He'd have done anything to prove them wrong, wouldn't he? He had that kind of strength and self-belief. She didn't.

'I wanted to *please* them,' she whispered, that little truth torn from her. She'd wanted their love. She'd seen the warmth in their eyes when Oliver had done well—every time he'd surpassed her. She didn't begrudge his achievements—she'd only wanted a little of the adoration they'd shown him. 'I wanted their approval. I've always wanted that and I've never got it and I tried so hard for so long.' And now she was tired of trying to live up to everyone else's expectations. 'I couldn't do what they wanted. Then I couldn't do what *I* wanted because they stopped me. So then I grew a spine. I moved to London. I got my job.' She'd left and she'd had that magic night with Theo and things really had turned around. Her confidence had grown. She sniffed. 'But now I get to do what *you* want me to do.'

'Don't be sad,' he murmured, a sparkle lighting his eyes. 'I think you're going to like the island.'

'Island?'

'Your new home.'

'You mean Athens?'

'Athens initially.' He nodded. 'Then the island.'

An island that was different from Athens? 'But you work in Athens?' she clarified.

'Yes.'

So he'd be in Athens and she'd be on some other island?

Was this what he'd meant about space—that she'd not actually live with him?

'You're sending me to my own kind of Alcatraz?'

He laughed. 'You don't want to know anything about it?'

'I don't need to. I'm sure its unspeakably beautiful. There'll be a pool and an amazing house and probably some billion-dollar view…but it's still a prison.' She couldn't get her head around it, couldn't consider it in any kind of positive light. 'What am I supposed to do all day?'

'You'll have assistants. Nannies. A cook.'

Was that what he'd meant when he'd said she didn't need to be alone now? He was going to arrange a massive coterie of staff for her? But *he* wasn't going to be there?

He leaned forward. 'Don't you want a break, Leah? You'll want for nothing—'

Except friends, or a partner, or a *lover*. She shivered. 'I spent too long buried away in a laboratory not talking to real people. I *like* people. I like meeting them, talking to them—'

'You'll have a tiny little person all of your own to take care of soon enough.'

'Who won't be able to talk back to me for months…'

'And as I said, you'll have staff.'

'Wonderful. People who are *paid* to spend time with me.'

He laughed. 'And, believe it or not, other people live on the island. Nice people.'

The prospect of being apart from *him* really wasn't what she wanted. But for him?

He sobered and a perplexed frown creased his forehead. 'The last thing I want is for you to be unhappy. I thought you'd want to live in a place where you can relax.' He shook his head. 'Just wait till you see it, Leah.'

She sat in silent contemplation. All her life she'd wanted someone to love her, just for her. And she wasn't about to get it. But she couldn't help wondering why Theo didn't want that too. Didn't he feel bereft at the prospect of an emotionless marriage? She was sure she hadn't imagined that flare of heat in his eyes when he'd seen her again. Didn't he even want to try to use that as a basis for something more? Obviously not.

Her heart sank all over again as she realised he truly didn't want any of it at all.

CHAPTER SEVEN

THEY WERE DRIVEN to the airport where a discreet crew were waiting for them. A tall, serious-looking man handed Theo a briefcase and murmured in his ear before he left to board ahead of them.

'I don't always use the private jet, but I thought we needed the privacy for this trip,' Theo explained as he led her up the staircase into the sleek jet.

Privacy? For what? Her pulse skipped.

'I don't want everyone watching us and wondering who you are.' He pulled a pale blue bag out of the briefcase and handed it to her as she sat in the wide luxurious leather armchair. 'We'll present you when we're ready.'

Present her? 'What's this?' She peered into the bag and saw a small jewel box nestled in tissue paper. A wave of cold trepidation washed over her but she was aware of him watching, so she faked calm. Her fingers trembled only the slightest as she opened the box and stared at the ring. 'Is it real?' she choked.

'Considering the price, I hope so.'

She gazed at the enormous diamond. Of course it was real. He was too rich to need to fake it. 'When did you get it?'

'I didn't. One of my assistants picked it up on the way to the airport. I apologise if you don't like it—apparently there was a limited selection.'

Massive solitaires were always in style, weren't they? The box blared the luxurious branding. But she couldn't quite believe he'd got someone else to buy it.

'Try it on and see if it fits.'

Because that was all that mattered—she didn't need to like it. It didn't mean anything. They just needed to make it fit and off they went as fiancés. She pushed the platinum band onto her cold finger. 'Lucky guess.'

He nodded and pulled a laptop from his briefcase. 'You can shop in Athens, get whatever else you need.'

'I don't need anything else.' She didn't need this giant lump of ice on her finger either.

'You're going to need a little more than the black tee shirts and trousers you've stuffed in that small bag. At some point that baby is going to make its presence known.'

'I'll get some bigger black tees and trousers when I need to,' she muttered obstinately. She did *not* want his wealth showered upon her. In fact, she wanted to take as little as possible from him—after all, he wanted little from her too.

But he'd glanced up from his laptop and now a small smile was flitting around his mouth. 'Why black?'

'Why not?'

'You make me think of a shadow…like you're trying not to stand out.'

'Women my height always stand out,' she pointed out grimly.

'For all the right reasons. You should make the most of your attributes.'

She gaped, momentarily unable to answer.

'And don't forget to get some more of those little scarlet silk things,' he murmured wickedly, and then looked back at his screen.

Leah stared hard at him for a while longer but apparently he was going to spend the rest of the flight working on his laptop. He'd just been amusing himself with a flippant moment. She shook her head. He was a conundrum—so often reserved and serious, and then there were flashes of fun and humour and, right this second, she really didn't like him for it.

As they landed hours later, a wave of nervous anticipation scurried along her veins. She'd never thought she'd visit Greece any time soon and she had to confess she was excited at the prospect of discovering its ancient culture and history, tasting the beautiful food, experiencing the lifestyle…although she rapidly discovered Theo's wasn't a normal lifestyle. It was almost obscene. She had only a moment to breathe in the warmer, vibrant atmosphere before more security guys in tailored suits and silence escorted them from the plane to a powerful black car with tinted windows. She glimpsed a bustling city filled with people, traffic, buildings, but they drove for quite a while and eventually the landscape changed. The properties became bigger with green spaces between them. Off a side street she saw palm trees forming a guard of honour the length of an esplanade.

'You live in the suburbs?' Somehow it wasn't quite what she'd expected.

'We have a compound on the coastline now known as the Athenian Rivera,' he said solemnly. 'The land has been in the family for decades.'

A compound? On a riviera? Leah had only seen such things in music videos.

'Will I meet Dimitri tonight?' she asked.

'Tomorrow would be better. He should be resting for the night by now.'

He'd gone all remote again—she felt the tension in his silence and the loss of his smile. All earlier easiness was now omitted from his demeanour. She focused on what she could see, catching glimpses of a beautiful mansion-lined beach just before they turned into a driveway. Large gates automatically swung back to allow the car through. They rounded a corner and a building came into view—not old and traditional but sleek and modern, extremely opulent and stylish. As she gaped at the perfect landscaping and the subtle exterior lighting showing off the architecture, the front door opened and a stunning woman strolled out.

A gorgeous blue dress clung to her voluptuous body and a pleased smile curved her full lips.

'Who's that?' She gasped involuntarily.

She heard the muttered oath beneath Theo's breath and he swiftly got out of the car. The rhythm of the stunning woman's high-heeled shoes bumped unevenly when she saw Leah emerge and stand just behind Theo.

'Angelica.' Theo bestowed kisses on the woman's cheeks. 'I'm sorry I wasn't here to greet you properly—'

The woman purred something in Greek.

'Leah.' Theo turned, still speaking in English to include her. 'May I introduce you to our good family friend, Angelica Galanis?'

Family friend? Was that what she was?

'Angelica, this is Leah.'

But Theo didn't give Angelica any additional explanation of Leah.

A low cough made all three of them turn. An elderly man with a cane was in the open doorway. Leah froze. This just had to be Dimitri. While he was shorter than Theo and frail, he had a familiar steely look in his gaze. Leah surreptitiously wiped her hands on her jeans. She felt crumpled and stale and never more out of place. And she'd been out of place a lot.

'Theodoros?' The older man looked from Theo to Leah.

'Dimitri.' Theo clamped Leah's hand in his and walked towards the waiting man. 'I wanted to introduce you formally tomorrow, but this is wonderful. I am pleased to introduce you to Leah.'

Dimitri simply stared.

'Leah is my fiancée.'

She heard the muffled gasp of surprise from the woman just behind them. Dimitri said nothing to her directly but whispered a short comment to Theo. Theo wrapped his arm around Leah's waist and pulled her close. The old man's breathing became ragged and Theo spoke to him in reassuring tones before lifting his voice to call something in Greek.

An older woman immediately appeared behind Dimitri. Given her deferential manner, Leah guessed she was on the staff. Theo quietly spoke to the woman and a moment later she escorted Dimitri down a long corridor lined with large portraits. Even through the thick walls Leah could sense the older man's emotion—it was strong enough to reverberate all the way through her own ribcage.

'My grandfather is still recovering from his operation,' Theo said smoothly and guided her into the polished foyer. He smiled at her as if there were nothing at all awkward about the situation—as if they were truly intimate. 'We'll spend time with him properly tomorrow.'

'Theo, it's very late and obviously not the right time for you to have a house guest.' Angelica's face was flushed and her English was heavily accented. 'I should probably go…' She trailed off.

'It's late, please stay tonight and we'll make travel arrangements for you in the morning,' Theo replied smoothly.

Despite his charming exterior, Leah could sense his underlying tension too. The 'welcome home' committee seemed to have exacerbated it.

'I apologise again for not being here to welcome you properly,' he said to Angelica. 'But thank you for understanding this is a personal time for us.'

Theo stiffened as Angelica's gaze lingered on the glittering ring on Leah's finger. He stepped between the two women, protecting Leah from Angelica's scrutiny. She was paler than usual and she'd half turned away; defensiveness seeped from her hunched shoulders. It was as if she was trying to be that shadow as he'd suggested on the plane. She'd been hurt before. Having met her parents, he understood more. But she ought to stand tall. He didn't want her to feel any fear, any inferiority here. 'Are you hungry, Leah?' he asked gently.

She shook her head.

He held out his hand to her. 'Come, I'll take you to our quarters.'

She put her hand in his and he turned and bowed to Angelica. He'd clean forgotten the woman was coming to visit and of course Dimitri would have stayed up to welcome him with his guest. Instead now Dimitri was tired and shocked. Theo couldn't blame him. Tomorrow he'd ensure the old man believed he and Leah were happy. While he hated lying, he didn't want Dimitri to know he'd messed up.

And now there was Leah. He knew he had to give her some space and a chance to take all this in. She hadn't wanted to stay in touch after that night at the hotel. She hadn't even wanted to kiss him goodbye. Now he'd dragged her to a foreign country where she didn't speak the language and she'd been given an awkward welcome. He'd almost done to her what had been done to him all those years ago and he was furious with himself.

That large diamond dug into his palm as he clasped her fingers and led her to the stairs. He felt a heel about the blunt way he'd just handed that to her too. But he refused to lie to her. It was imperative he maintain distance between them. He'd start as he meant to go on.

Except all he wanted to do was kiss away the sad tilt to her mouth and restore that passionate warmth in her eyes. He wanted to hear her husky little laugh again.

'This is my suite.' He opened the door to his private wing and waited for her to walk in.

'Angelica is an old family friend?' There was no missing the suspicious curiosity in her eyes.

'I forgot Dimitri had invited her to stay this weekend. If I'd remembered I would have cancelled the invitation.' He gritted his teeth.

'Is it a special occasion?'

'Not that I'm aware of.'

'Why had he invited her?'

He closed the door behind them. 'Why do you think?'

'Your grandfather invited her to stay with you as a prospective what—bride?' She frowned. 'He doesn't trust you to pick a woman on your own?'

'He doesn't trust that I'll ever make a *permanent* pick,' Theo said tightly. 'I was keeping him happy while he recovers.'

'Keeping him happy?' she echoed. 'Because you never wanted to get married.'

'Actually now I do. To you.' He made himself walk forward and open the door to her bedroom.

She came to an abrupt halt and spun to face him. 'You expect me to sleep in the same bed as you?'

He glanced and saw the big bed behind her. Her tone pushed him that last notch over the edge. Now he was alone with her again at last desire washed over him, loosening the bonds of self-control he'd been straining against for hours. In truth, for months. He'd wanted her the second he'd seen her again. He'd never stopped wanting her since that night. The whole 'I'm pregnant' thing ought to have shut it down. It hadn't.

'Is this for the look of it, Theo?' She jerked her head towards the bed. 'Because there are other people here?'

He couldn't control himself enough to reply. It was a mistake, because in the face of his silence, he felt her emotions fire.

'I can play that part if you want.' She flicked back her hair and stepped up to him, her lavender eyes deepening with almost liquid intensity. 'I'll jump up and down on that bed and scream with ecstasy all through the house so everyone in the neighbourhood hears. I'll—'

'Be amazing?' he challenged, his body almost bursting with the feral energy he'd held leashed for so long. 'Bring it on.'

She jerked her chin at him defiantly. 'You think you can just order me around? That I'll do *anything* you ask me to?'

He breathed hard but those knots were slipping. He *did* want her to do anything and her loss of temper was oddly welcome. It had been a long, trying day and both of them needed to vent. But he was *not* the villain here.

'My grandfather's rooms are in another building on the other side of the tennis court. Angelica is in the guest house on the other side of the pool. You can be as loud as you like.'

He'd jump her on the bed with him if she wanted. And he'd happily make her scream.

'If they're that far away, then why do I need to be in your room?'

'You don't,' he snapped. 'This is my *wing*, Leah. There's more than one bedroom in here.'

She gaped and then a flush swept up her face. 'Why? For your secret harem?'

He laughed roughly at her temper and inwardly revelled at the way the colour made her radiance return. She looked so much more alive than the cautious woman of only moments earlier.

'Stop being so poisonous.' He stepped closer, unable to keep any distance at all. 'We slept in separate rooms last night, remember? I'm not about to insist that change. Or is it that you want to be back in my bed?'

Was that what it was? Now they had privacy, she could voice her thoughts. And now that she was beyond provoked, she'd revealed what was uppermost in her mind.

'What? *No!*' But her mouth formed a full-lipped pout and her purple-tinged eyes shimmered with passion.

Sizzling sexual tension pulled him closer still. They'd have separate lives, yes, but maybe clearing this heated fog might be the best thing for them both. He didn't want to fight. Didn't want anything else from her... But *this*? The pull was undeniable.

'You want to be back there every bit as much as I want you there,' he muttered.

'If you think I want you—'

'You're not a good liar, sweetheart. You've told me that yourself.' He couldn't resist a second longer. Reaching out, he cupped her jaw.

'Theo...'

Satisfaction merged with desire at her soft whisper of submission and the gentle lean into his touch. His need had such power, he was driven to kiss, not her mouth, but that delicate, sensitive skin of her neck. He'd take more, touch more, do everything unexpected and delightful. She shivered, her hands lifted, not to push him away but to clutch his shirt and pull him closer still. This was what he wanted. Her embrace, her smile, her playfulness.

Her soft moan made him giddy with triumph and the diabolical desire to tease her overpowered him.

'Oh, no,' he said as he nibbled his way down. He wanted her as tortured as he'd been these last weeks and then he wanted to assuage it. 'No screaming your ecstasy,' he softly echoed her taunt. 'You've got to be quiet. If you're not quiet, I'm going to stop.'

'You're not going to start,' she muttered breathlessly.

'I already have and you're already ahead of me.'

'You arrogant...'

But she trailed off as his fingers traced the neckline of her loose tee.

'I might be arrogant but I'm not wrong.' He pulled her fully into his embrace. 'Be quiet, Leah. Or I stop.'

Leah knew she could say no and he'd stop. She could say anything and he'd stop. But the last thing she wanted was for him to stop. So, instead, she smiled.

He kissed along her cheekbones, then her eyelids so

she closed her eyes. His fingertips teased and she moaned again. Her skin was so sensitive to his touch. She heard his muttered oath, a mumble of something hot and ferocious, and then his hands lifted her. He swiftly crossed the floor to the bed and tumbled down onto it with her. She cried out with the powerful pleasure of being with him like this again. Of having him above her, caressing her, pinning her with his magnificent body.

'You don't want me to stop, do you?' he whispered hotly against her mouth.

She kept silent but arched her hips to meet his—uncaring about the layers of clothes between them. She just needed to feel him. She sought him the one way she could—with her body, closing her mind to any more repercussions. His laugh was smothered on her skin as he kissed down her torso, lifting her tee out of his way with his teeth. But he wouldn't let her touch him back. He kept her too busy squirming, seeking more of his wicked mouth. She shook with need. He traced his hand carefully over her, making her quiver. She gasped as his hand easily slipped beneath the loose waistband of her jeans, then deeper to where she was slick and hot. She heard his harshly drawn breath as he discovered just how much she wanted him. She didn't care how much she was feeding his ego with her response right now. She didn't care that he now knew he could do whatever he wanted, whenever he wanted, if he wanted. She was too needy.

'Theo—' She shivered, desperately biting her lip. She didn't want him to stop but she couldn't hold back her cry.

He looked into her eyes. His were filled with tender heat as he stroked her with a firm but gentle touch. 'Let it out, sweetheart,' he muttered roughly. 'I want to hear you, want to see you, want to feel you.' His groan was soul-filled. 'I have missed you.'

Any game was forgotten, burned to cinders by the honesty in that scorching whisper. An outpouring of warmth and want flooded her. He didn't give her a chance to answer, or himself an opportunity to say anything more, because he kissed her—so thoroughly, so passionately, while his fingers teased her to the point of no return. She arched— high and taut, straining for the release only he could bring.

'Leah.' He broke free and breathed.

'*Yes!*' She convulsed, her cry echoing as her whole world was obliterated.

She drowned in the tumultuous sensations, utterly, utterly undone. She couldn't find the energy to open her eyes and she didn't want to. She wanted to stay in this half-dream-state of delight.

I have missed you.

That whispered secret had felled her. She'd missed him too. She'd missed this closeness. This easiness. But now total exhaustion scrubbed her ability to do anything—to speak, move, think. She wanted to open her eyes but she couldn't. She felt him brush her hair from her face, then he gently repeated the motion again, then again. Until Leah discovered she couldn't resist anything any more—not him. Nor the pull of a profound sleep.

CHAPTER EIGHT

LEAH FURIOUSLY SCRUBBED her body, rejecting the lingering warmth from last night and trying not to appreciate the stunning luxury of the gleaming marble bathroom. Despite that wide blue sky and brilliant sunshine outside, her mood was bad because when she'd woken she'd discovered he wasn't there. It wasn't the fact that he wasn't there that made her disgruntled. It was that she'd *wanted* him to be there. If he'd really missed her, why had he left so early? Or was it just that he'd missed *sex*?

Had he only touched her because she'd provoked him? Because he was venting the frustrations of a very long day? Except he'd not asked for anything for himself after her release. He'd merely proved his power over her and then he'd stayed and stroked her hair and that was mortifying. She had no idea when he'd left her, only that he had. She'd woken, still half dressed, not even in the bed but on top of it and covered by a light blanket that he must have put over her.

She swiftly towelled dry, pulled on a fresh tee and jeans and then glanced out of the window at that incredible view again. There was a gorgeous lap pool with guest houses on both sides and, beyond that, the crystalline sea stretched for miles. It was the bluest water she'd ever seen.

But now she could see Theo and Angelica seated at a big table on the terrace. Theo was in trousers and white shirt, his sleeves rolled back enough to show off his tanned forearms. She clamped down on that restless ache.

Angelica wore another stunning summery dress, her hair and make-up immaculate. She was clearly at ease with having staff serve breakfast, felt no awkwardness in wondering what to say or how to say it. The fact was, they looked good together. Leah was nothing like that woman. She wasn't Greek. Or beautiful. Or from the 'right society'. She was a pregnant nobody, with no qualifications, no real achievements to date. Her black jeans and black tee were too old, loose and casual—they didn't fit the scene. And nor did the rest of her. She froze, not wanting to go down and join them. She didn't think she could fake it.

Pull it together.

She had to get over herself. He'd taken her by the hand, he'd introduced her as his fiancée. If she chose not to go down there now, then wasn't *she* choosing to be invisible again? For so long she'd wanted to escape that doormat role; she couldn't revert to it just because she was scared. She had to do better for her baby and make this work.

By the time Leah made it down to the ground floor Angelica was standing ready for departure. 'It was fascinating to meet you, Leah,' she said. 'I'm sure we'll see each other again.'

Despite that polite farewell, there was no mistaking Angelica's sharp curiosity. Leah fought the instinct to cover her belly. She turned towards the terrace as Theo guided Angelica to the car. She'd fuel up, ready to face his family.

Theo watched the car head down the drive, taking Angelica away. No doubt she'd tell everyone about the woman he'd brought back with him. His instinctive need to protect Leah built, but he'd face Dimitri first. Their meetings usually didn't go much beyond balance sheets and brainstorming business expansions. They lived and breathed the banking business and their unspoken agreement had cemented over the years—they never discussed the past. But while Theo had protected the old man for so long, he couldn't have him hate Leah.

'Tell me about her,' Dimitri said quietly when Theo went to the old man's study to explain.

Theo thought about the way she supported her ballet friend, her brother, those elderly residents at that home. 'She's very caring.' But he braced—there was no point prevaricating. 'She's pregnant.'

Dimitri didn't move.

'You'll make her welcome,' he added, wondering if that man had even heard what he'd said. 'I am responsible for her.'

To his total astonishment and total discomfort, Dimitri's eyes filled.

'She's having your child?' the old man clarified.

'Yes.' He still had to steel himself to admit it aloud, let alone prepare for the reaction he was about to get.

'I didn't think…' The old man breathed out. 'Good, Theo.'

Good? Theo blinked, gobsmacked by the old man's obvious emotion. *Good?*

'She will have my great-grandson.' Pride lit the old man's face.

Theo still couldn't stand to imagine an actual baby, but at Dimitri's satisfied certainty he couldn't help a small tease. 'Or great-granddaughter.'

'Wonderful.' Dimitri actually beamed at the prospect. 'Then you'd better go take care of her.'

No more questions? No desire to know more? No judgment? Theo couldn't believe it.

Hurting more somehow, he pushed away the previously unimaginable mental picture of Dimitri hovering over a bundle in Leah's arms. He felt as if he were skating on the thinnest of ice. With one wrong move, it would crack and they'd be dragged down to drown in frigid waters. But if he kept his steps careful, they could all stay safe.

She was standing by the pool. How could such a slender silhouette be such a distraction? Such temptation. His pulse quickened at the memory of late last night. But as he registered her pale façade, regret rose. She'd been tired last night and she'd misunderstood about the bedroom and he shouldn't have taken advantage of her innocence and anger and emotional vulnerability to satisfy his own needs. He'd lost control, no longer able to resist the desire to touch her. All he'd wanted was to lose himself with her again. He'd only hauled his control back when she'd all but fainted away in an exhausted heap after her orgasm had hit. A fact that had made him feel all the more guilty.

They had to focus on getting their marriage arranged and to provide security for the child. The paperwork for the wedding was in hand so it was simply a matter of getting through the next few days. Once they were married, they could take a breath and figure out the future more gently. Until then, *he* needed to regain control.

'How did you sleep?' he asked, even though it was obvious in her expression.

'Very well, thank you.' She lifted her chin. 'I realise now that you were just helping me to…relax.' She breathed in. 'Thank you for that. It was thoughtful.' She glanced at the table. 'But I'll manage with just a glass of warm milk from now on.'

A glass of milk? He stared. She couldn't be serious. And as for him helping her to relax? As if there'd been any thought that had gone before what had happened?

Her coolness sparked his desire to prove her a liar all over again. His desire simply to touch her again. He was appalled at the realisation he had zero control. *Zero.* All he wanted was to get close again and know that starburst of heat. But he rejected the want winding him tight. He'd go to the office in Athens. Bury himself in the work he'd missed while he was London collecting her. He'd regain focus and get ahead. When in doubt, achieve.

At that thought, a great wave of resistance rose. How

much he wanted to stay scared him. He never wanted to skip work. It was always his escape. But now?

'I need to go into the office,' he said brusquely before he could change his mind.

'Today?'

'I had an extra day in the UK. I need to catch up.' He was good at doing what was necessary and *this* was necessary.

'Because you're so behind from one extra day away?' Her lashes hid the glittering sharpness of her eyes.

'I'll be back in time for dinner.' He needed distance. She was already paying too steep a price for his reckless behaviour and he couldn't trust himself not to repeat it.

'And what do you want me to do while you're gone?' she asked softly.

'Rest, Leah. You need it.' He'd go to work. After their wedding he'd take her to the island and show her that life wasn't going to be a total disaster.

'I need it?'

There was only a lone ember of provocation in her soft echo, but he couldn't resist throwing one last little retaliation as he forced his feet to take him away. 'Go have that hot milk and relax.'

Leah stomped back into the mansion. How was she supposed to 'relax'? What was she supposed to do with her time? She knew no one but Theo and she didn't know him at all well. His grandfather hadn't appeared since last night. She wasn't sure he even spoke much English and she certainly couldn't speak Greek. She had no transport options no map of the city anyway and no money. Sure, she could swim in that pool, but she had no swimsuit and she wasn' sure skinny dipping would be a good idea. Worse, she re alised Theo might've been right: her jeans collection wasn' going to cut it. She needed clothing appropriate enoug to mix with the Angelicas of Athens. Not dresses though. Leah didn't wear dresses…

She could eat from the platters of nibbles that constantly appeared on the nearest occasional table but she was too wound up to have any appetite. She could sleep up in that gorgeous bedroom but she only needed to set foot in there and all the memories of his touch tormented her. She could definitely read because she'd discovered there were books everywhere, not just in the stunning library. There was a home movie theatre too and a ballroom that was beautiful but wistfully empty. It was a grand home for a large family and she ought to feel amazing. Instead she literally walked away from it all. But as she reached a path that she guessed led to the beach, a security guy materialised in front of her. She stopped and smiled at him warily.

'If you would like to walk along the beach, I will escort you,' he said briskly in heavily accented English.

'Oh, no, thank you.' She backed up a pace. 'Sorry if I bothered you.'

There was no return smile. 'I'm here to ensure your safety.'

'Oh, okay. Thank you.'

So there were boundaries to this world? She marched back inside feeling odd about not being able to come and go alone as she pleased. She'd get her knitting. It seemed ridiculous to be working with wool in such warm weather but it always relaxed her. And she really needed to relax. She walked along the corridor and glanced again at the collection of formal portraits that hung so prominently positioned. There was a wedding portrait of Dimitri and his wife, and another of that woman alone, looking a little older. Then there was a portrait of a younger man Leah suspected was Theo's father. He looked no older than about fifteen. There was no portrait from his wedding, indeed there was no image at all of Theo's mother. And then there was the one

of Theo and Dimitri together. Theo looked about eighteen.
Both he and Dimitri were in suits, formally posed. There
was no smile and man-hug. They stood separate, angled
in front of a large desk. It looked as if it had been taken at
an office. Theo's first day at work? Had he been groomed
to be the head of the Savas empire from the start? What
about his father? Because there was no equivalent 'line of
succession' photo of him. Her curiosity deepened. Theo
hadn't mentioned his mother at all in his brief explanation
of why he'd come to live with Dimitri. And it had been a
very brief explanation.

She gathered her bag from her room and returned pool-
side to lose herself in the blissfully soothing repetition of
stitch after stitch. She wasn't interrupted—other than with
trays of food—but slowly, inexorably, her nerves tightened.
When would he return home? They had to talk some more,
surely. She couldn't spend all her days like this.

He phoned her late in the afternoon.

'I won't be back until after dinner tonight,' he said
brusquely as soon as she answered. 'Don't wait up.'

The businesslike way he delivered the minimal message
was chilling. And that disappointment? She didn't want to
admit to that at all.

The early evening stretched out—slow and painful. She
saw Dimitri in the distance but he didn't come near her and
frankly now she was too intimidated and heartsore to face
someone else's disappointment or judgment. She asked the
housekeeper if she could dine alone in her bedroom. Of
course it was no problem.

In safe, private misery she flicked on the television in
the small lounge simply because she had nothing better to
do. She scrolled through the channels, pausing on what she
guessed was the local news channel. They were showing a
live feed from the waterfront just up the coast. Intrigued
she watched for a while; it looked like the cream of Athens

society—all the gorgeous Angelicas. But then she stared harder at the screen. Was that *Theo*?

She blinked. It *was*. She'd recognise his height and imposing presence from fifty feet and he was dressed to disturb in dinner jacket and white tie. And there were women near him—beautiful, designer-clad beauties. Was this what he considered *work*? Quaffing champagne down at some fancy marina?

She stilled, unsure what to do, quelling the urge to phone him. She waited for his return but in the end fell asleep before she heard his car. In the morning she expected to see him at breakfast, but there was still no sign. It was the housekeeper who informed her with a slightly confused air that he was already at work. That was when Leah realised he'd not returned home all night. Hurt burgeoned—built by his lack of consideration, of contact. Was this what it was going to be like? How could he go from concerned and courteous to simply…absent?

She wanted him to see her as she'd thought he once had. She didn't want to be invisible and taken for granted again.

As the day passed in isolation, her hurt festered, morphing into fury. By the time he finally returned, *after* dinner, she was practically shaking with pent-up rage. She'd hidden away in her room again, not wanting anyone to witness their 'reunion'.

She heard his footsteps as he climbed the stairs—she'd left her door ajar so she'd be forewarned. Now he nudged her door further open with his fingers.

'Nice of you to call in,' she said acidly, loathing her shrewish tone but unable to hold it back.

'I told you I had to work late yesterday.' He leaned against the doorjamb and regarded her carefully. 'It got so late it was best for me to stay in town.'

'You really think I'm stupid, don't you?' She was so hurt.

'Why do you say that?'

'You weren't at "work" last night. You were at a party.' He was avoiding her. He'd been avoiding her for the last couple of days.

'Actually, it wasn't a party. It was the launch of a new yacht.'

'Is this what it's going to be like? You're just going to lie by omission…or semantics? Like how you treat your grandfather? You let him think the best through half-truths, to kid yourself you're keeping him happy? Is that what you're planning to do with me?'

He straightened and came into the room, closing the door behind him. 'I'm not lying at all to you.' He gazed at her steadily and walked slowly towards her. 'I've never lied to you.'

'No, you're just planning to send me away so you can pretend I don't exist most of the time.' She sprang up and stepped away, putting the armchair safely between him and her. 'That's why you're not involving me in any of your life here. Lock me in the attic, why don't you?'

'Leah—'

'Don't patronise me or act like you're trying to protect me. Why not just tell me the truth?' She shook her head.

'It was work. I'm the CEO of one of the largest private banks in the world and we have several subsidiaries in a variety of industries. Patronage, sponsorship, networking are all part of the remit. We're powerful, we need to contribute to society. So it's part of my job to maintain the profile and reputation at a certain level. To develop the goodwill and trust of investors and clients.'

'Is that why you didn't want me there? Because I'm not going to maintain the reputation of you or your family or your precious business?'

'Would you really want to go?' He looked surprised. 'You're in no state to be out there yet—you're exhausted. You don't speak the language or—'

'Look the part?'

'Or have the knowledge to deal with these people. *Yet.*' He put his hands on his hips and gazed at her. 'Give us some time, Leah.'

The injustice of that comment made her flare. 'You're the one not giving us any *time*, Theo. You're using work to avoid me. And your grandfather. I might not be able to negotiate billion-dollar deals but attending a *party* hardly requires a master's in rocket science. It's not hard to talk to people.' She glared at him. 'Yet it seems that, for you, talking is really hard. Why didn't you ask me?'

'Perhaps I should have.'

'Perhaps? You just want to hide me away on your prison island.'

'It's *not* a prison.' He actually laughed.

'You don't want me to be seen.' She tossed her head, refusing to let his humour placate her. 'But I'm used to people looking at me and judging. I can ignore them.'

A frown formed on his face. 'What do you think they see?'

She didn't want to think about this. 'I can't care about what they see or think. I won't be hidden away like something to be ashamed of. Not by the man I'm going to marry.'

She couldn't be treated as if she were inferior or an embarrassment. She'd had enough of that in her life already.

'Is that what you thought I was doing?' He took in a deep breath. 'Leah, while we're married, I'll never humiliate you. I'll never cheat on you. I will be loyal.'

But she wanted more than integrity. She wanted so much more that she dared not think about. 'How many properties do you have?' she asked desperately.

'Does it matter?'

'Where are they? Perhaps there's a destination that might suit me better. Paris? New York? I'd quite like to live in Manhattan.'

'You'll be within a thirty-minute flight distance from me,' he said grimly.

'Thirty minutes?'

'I just want to protect you,' he said. 'And the child,' he added belatedly.

'From what? What's so awful about Athens that we have to be locked away on Prison Island?'

He folded his arms. 'I just want you to have the privacy and space to be happy.'

'You mean *you* want privacy and space away from us most of the time. You'll just swoop in on the weekends and be the fun guy and then leave.'

'The fun guy?' He looked stunned for a second, then sobered again. 'That's not what it's about. Dimitri needs to believe that we're happy. For as long as he's alive, you and I are happy.'

'He's not stupid. If we're living apart most of the time, he'll suspect we're not happy.'

'But if we're together all the time he'll be *certain* we're unhappy. Always having to show a happy façade is impossible.'

A happy *façade*? Was it beyond the realms of possibility that they could actually *be* happy? Couldn't this feeling become something else? Something more? Or was she really totally alone in thinking there *was* this feeling? There was something linking them together.

'I'll visit you on the weekends but we'd have space and privacy there and wouldn't have to carry on an act in front of him. You can rest.'

'Do I want to rest?' She exploded. Had he been carrying on an act when he'd touched her so intimately last night? When he'd told her he missed her? 'Maybe I want to live life.'

'And you will.' He paced away from her. 'I'm not trying to hide you away.'

'No? Then why have you brought me here and left me alone?'

'I…' He flexed his hands. 'I'm trying to get my head around everything.'

'And I'm not? Can't we do this *together*, Theo?' She tried to break through his barriers. 'I don't want someone making all the decisions as if I have nothing of value to contribute.'

'That wasn't my intention.' He shifted and pivoted to face her again. 'You want more from me.'

'Some communication,' she muttered. 'Some discussion.'

'All right.' He sighed and reached out as if he could no longer resist, gently rubbing his fingertip along her jaw. 'Leah…'

She turned helplessly into his touch, hating herself as she did. 'Don't use my weakness to distract me.'

His eyebrows lifted. '*Your* weakness?'

She closed her eyes. 'This wasn't what I meant when I said I wanted more from you.'

He drew an audible breath. 'Do you think it's only you who wants…this?' He sounded almost choked. 'But I can't be the kind of husband you should have.'

She opened her eyes and gazed straight into his. 'Why would you think that?'

He froze, a rigid expression masked his thoughts. Again she realised he was battling something deep inside—something painful.

'You're kind, Theo. I know you'll support me. You've said you'll be faithful and I believe you. What else do you think a husband needs to do?'

He was so rigid she grew wary of his answer.

'I can't love you, Leah.'

She stilled, shocked by his quiet, so calm confession.

'I can't love anyone,' he added huskily.

His eyes flashed with sorry sincerity and seemed to ask for her forgiveness. But why would he say that?

'You love your grandfather,' she whispered. She'd seen it. Almost everything he did, he did with that man in mind.

'I *owe* my grandfather,' he corrected softly and stepped back. 'I'm sorry, Leah.'

CHAPTER NINE

RETURNING FROM A lonely breakfast the next day, Leah paused on the threshold of her room. The housekeeper was in there, carefully folding Leah's cardigan.

'Thank you,' Leah said shyly, aware there wasn't a lot of warmth in the woman's face. 'We haven't properly met—my name is Leah.'

She hadn't been introduced to anyone properly yet. Theo had been in too much of a rush to deal with his work crisis and it seemed none of his staff were overly friendly.

'Amalia.'

Leah offered her a smile and saw the way she was looking at the ribbed pattern on her cardigan. 'Do you knit?'

Amalia glanced, her expression softening. 'I make lace.'

'Oh.' Leah stepped closer, her interest flaring. 'I'd love to watch you some time…' She trailed off awkwardly. Perhaps it wasn't the done thing to chat?

But then Amalia smiled and gestured at the cardigan. 'Did you make this?'

'I did, yes.' Leah smiled. 'I knit a lot—it relaxes me. Though I probably won't need to as much. It's very warm here…'

She trailed off again. She was babbling—nervous and awkward and too eager to engage in desperately needed social contact.

But Amalia finally smiled. 'It can get cold here in winter.'

'Does it?'

'It even snows in Athens—'

'*No.*' She'd had no idea.

Amalia laughed and nodded.

Encouraged, Leah nibbled her lip but then smiled. 'Actually, I need to buy some clothes,' she said. She needed to look the part as best she could. She needed to make an effort to embrace the country and culture her child was going to be born into. 'Would you be able to help me? Come with me?'

'Shopping?' Amalia looked startled.

'Yes.' Leah nodded hopefully. 'I have no idea where to go.' Or what to get.

Amalia looked pleased. 'Of course—'

'Oh, thank you,' she breathed out with a rush of relief. 'And I need a wedding dress…'

'You wouldn't make one?' Amalia gestured at Leah's bag. 'You could knit with silk.'

Leah's smile blossomed. 'I've love to.' She'd been working on a pattern for a while—a dress of her own design she *would* wear. 'But I don't have enough time before the wedding.'

'What if I helped you? I have lace…'

'You'd do that?' Leah was stunned.

Amalia straightened. 'You're marrying Theodoros.'

Of course, this was about Theo. Did Amalia care for him? Theo worked so hard, he was a dutiful grandson and a good boss…maybe Amalia and the other staff weren't only wary while they decided whether she was good enough for him? Were they protective of him? Why? Because they loved him? She had the feeling he was very easy to love.

'You know him well?' she asked gently, hoping she was hiding how curious she was about him. Why did he have this huge sense of duty but total denial of love? Why did he think he was incapable of it? She didn't believe him. She couldn't when his actions said so much otherwise. She was sure he always tried to do what was best for those he was close to. He'd do that for their baby too, wouldn't he? She *had* to believe that.

'I've worked for Dimitri for years,' Amalia said. 'My husband too.'

'Really?'

Amalia smiled. 'And my sons did too, before they went away to study.'

'So you were here when Theo arrived?' Leah asked cautiously.

'Yes.' Amalia glanced at her, as if she knew there were a million more questions on Leah's tongue. 'He was very quiet when he first arrived.'

Leah held her breath, not wanting to interrupt Amalia and stop her, wondering why Theo had been so quiet. Had he been afraid?

'He had little Greek, of course,' Amalia said. 'But he studied very hard. He has always worked very hard.'

Always? Hadn't he got up to mischief like most teenagers? Hadn't he ever rebelled?

I owe my grandfather.

Perhaps not. Had he always been so determined to pay him back? Why? Wasn't it natural for a grandfather to take in a grandson when his parents had gone? But where had his mother gone?

'I'll arrange the driver if you would like to go shopping now,' Amalia said, interrupting Leah's thoughts. 'Ten minutes, okay?'

'Perfect. *Thank you.*'

The plan put a lift in Leah's step, but when she came downstairs a few minutes later to find Amalia, Dimitri was sitting in the living room.

'Amalia is taking you shopping,' he said without preamble.

'Yes.' She automatically moved to adjust the cushion that was awkwardly positioned behind him.

'You want to spend money?' he asked warily when she'd fixed it and stepped back.

'Yes.' She smiled, battling hard not to be afraid of him. It was their first proper conversation and he was openly questioning her motives.

But she didn't blame him for not trusting her yet.

'I need something suitable when I meet Theo's business colleagues. I don't want to let him down.' And that was the truth. She wanted to please both Theo and his grandfather.

But Dimitri's demeanour didn't thaw.

Leah worried her lip and made herself ask the honest question. 'Do you think I'm after his money?'

'Aren't you?'

She paused. So much for Theo convincing him that their engagement was a love match.

'No,' she said firmly. 'I'm here because he insisted on it.' She swallowed and sat in the chair opposite his. 'I don't know Athens at all, in fact this is my first time to Greece. And I'm sorry if my arrival is a surprise to you. But I think we both want the best for Theo. I'm having his baby and I most definitely want the best for my child. But to be honest, I need some help.'

His expression finally softened.

'I don't speak any Greek,' she confessed in a relieved rush. 'Do you think Amalia can help me find a tutor?'

'You want to learn Greek?'

'Of course.' She was going to be living here for the foreseeable future, she didn't want to feel isolated from everyone for ever and she wanted her baby to enjoy its dual heritage. 'It might take me a while though,' she admitted with a sudden laugh. 'I'm not very academic.'

'I will help you.' He nodded slowly.

'You will?' She beamed at him. 'Thank you.'

He shot her a look. 'Thank you. *Efharisto.*' He then waited, looking at her expectantly.

'You mean *you'll* help me?' she asked. Dimitri himself

'Thank you. *Efharisto,*' he repeated.

'Efharisto?'

'Yes. *Ne.*' He suddenly clapped his hands and called to Amalia. 'Come, you will speak to her only in Greek. Greek all the time.'

'*Ne*, Dimitri.' Amalia smiled and gestured for Leah to follow her.

Fortunately, Amalia disregarded Dimitri's order while they shopped. But *unfortunately* Amalia simply smiled and said yes to everything Leah tried on in the high-end boutiques of Athens. It was sweet and supportive, but truly not that helpful.

Theo had said she'd hidden behind her black clothing and perhaps he was right. She'd tried to avoid that back-lash because of her height and slenderness. But maybe she should enjoy all the colours she loved and had always turned away from? Not just scarlet panties...

Not for him. For herself, right?

Except really, she realised it was *because* of him. He'd *seen* her that night and he'd liked what he'd seen. And she'd liked the person he'd made her feel free to be. The person confident enough to speak up for what she wanted with him. Confident to speak up to her parents for once. The person confident to call *him* to account too... She glanced again at the racks of clothing and turned her back on the black.

Three hours into the reinvigorated shopping marathon, her phone rang.

'Will you accompany me to an exhibition tonight?' Theo said.

'Pardon?'

'A driver will collect you at seven.' He paused. 'If you would like, that is.' She heard his smile. 'I am trying to ask, not dictate.'

'Okay,' she agreed cautiously, yet her heart raced be-cause he'd listened and he was trying to include her. A fragile bubble bloomed—if he could try like this, maybe he could open up even more? Maybe he might even develop deeper feelings? She shivered, pushing away that wisp of a wish—*one day at a time.*

'I'm busy with meetings until late and I'll get changed at the office,' he said.

She glanced at the silky fabric hanging in front of her. 'I don't wear dresses, Theo.'

'Nor do I.' He laughed. 'Will you be ready?'

'Yes.'

Hours later she avidly stared out of the window, drinking in the sights as she was driven into the centre of Athens. Theo was waiting outside the gallery. Bowled over by the sight of him in that black tuxedo, she braced, slamming back her nerves. She was *not* concerned by his silent scrutiny.

'We need to—' He broke off and cleared his throat.

'To?'

'Walk inside.'

'I believe I'm capable of that,' she said with a shy laugh. 'Are you?'

He cleared his throat again. 'Scarlet, Leah?'

'Is it okay?'

'Does it need to be?' He finally smiled. 'You don't need my approval.'

'Maybe I would like it.'

He took her hand and drew her close to his side. 'It's no my approval you have, Leah. It's something else. Some thing raw. Something I can't deny. Something I can't turn off.' He breathed out. 'Who did your make-up?'

'I did.'

'You have skills.'

'I didn't let my mother stop me doing everything I wa interested in. I just did it in secret. Sometimes.'

'What else did you do in secret?'

She just smiled at him and shrugged.

'I'm glad you're not doing it in secret now,' he admitted. 'I'm glad you're here letting the world see you.'

'They're seeing all right,' she noted with a wry grimace and her nerves mushroomed. 'They're staring.'

He cocked his head and blinked at her with teasing arrogance. 'What makes you think they're staring at you? I'm the one they're interested in.'

She choked on a giggle. 'Good point.'

'No.' He shook his head. 'They're staring because you look stunning.'

Heat travelled all over her body and he wrapped his arm around her to draw her closer.

'What are you doing?' she half gasped.

'You're the one who wanted to be treated like my fiancée.' He brushed a kiss against her cheek. 'This is how I'd do that. I'd stay close and kiss her often.'

'No, you wouldn't,' she breathed. 'That's not dignified enough for your grandfather.'

'You think I'm too uptight for displays of affection?'

'I think you're conscious of your position and you modify your behaviour depending on who's around.'

'Doesn't everyone?' He laughed. 'Isn't that just good manners?'

'But people still do what they want. They put themselves first. I don't know that you do.'

'Haven't I done that with you once already?' He stilled and faced her. 'You want me to put my desires first and damn who's watching? Damn the consequences?'

'Can you?'

He cupped the nape of her neck, pulled her to him and kissed her. It was a long, luscious kiss.

He lifted his head and laughed down at her dazed expression. 'You dared me to.'

She shook her head. 'That was just part of your PR plan. You weren't taking me seriously.'

'If I did what I really wanted right now, we'd both be arrested.'

She felt his hard heat digging into her pelvis.

'So now we have a problem,' he muttered hotly. 'I need you right here to preserve my blushes in front of all these people, but if you stay there, my little problem isn't going to go away.'

'*Little* problem?' she echoed archly.

'It's a good thing you're wearing trousers. If it was a skirt I'd have flipped it up and bent you over that piano already.' He grinned at her gasp. 'Sorry. Too honest?' His smile faded. 'I want you too much.'

'You've got some of my lipstick.' She gestured to her mouth, mirroring the placement of the smudge.

'So help me.' His slightly strangled-sounding request was oddly serious.

'Theo Savas.' A man interrupted them loudly and Theo instantly straightened, his expression smoothing back to reserved.

'You can't return to Athens and hide in the corner all evening.' The stranger's gaze skimmed over Leah, his eyes widening. 'And you are?'

'Leah Turner, my fiancée,' Theo answered for her.

'So the crazy rumours are correct?' The man stared back at Theo.

'They're not crazy,' Theo said coldly.

Rather rudely the man switched to Greek but frankly Leah was glad she didn't have to listen. She extracted herself from Theo's hold and with a small smile at him stepped aside to view the nearest painting.

As soon as she did, a designer-clad, stunningly polished woman swept over to her. 'You're Leah, aren't you? The Savas' fiancée.'

'That's correct.' She smiled. 'And you are?'

'Phoebe, a friend of Theo's. We're delighted and in-trigued that you could join us. We know nothing about you.'

Leah couldn't help her little laugh. Not hiding the curi-osity, was she? 'What did you want to know?'

'Everything, of course.' The woman smiled back. 'Where did you meet Theo?'

'In London, a few months ago. It's been a whirlwind.'

The woman nodded. 'I'm not going to lie, we're all stunned. I never imagined he'd settle down. Certainly not so soon.'

Leah recognised the sharp questions in the woman's eyes but she gently shrugged and didn't reply. Theo was right: sometimes it was better to remain silent.

'Will you have lunch some time?' the woman invited.

'I'd like that very much, thank you.' Leah answered hon-estly, even though she knew the woman really just wanted to mine her for information. But she also knew the way to get people to soften up was to get them speaking. 'It's im-portant to me to get to know Theo's world here in Athens and I'd love to see more of the city. What are some of your favourite spots?'

Having despatched his overly curious business acquain-tance, Theo remained at a slight distance so he could watch her. Frankly he was still getting his head—and his libido—around her outfit. Her black trousers were nothing like her usual baggy jeans. These were silk and sleek, they sat ul-tra-low on her narrow waist and showed off the slim length of her legs. The scarlet blouse she had on top was almost sheer at the back, revealing a sweep of gleaming skin all the way down to the small of her back. The shirt hid that slight curve of her belly and he was glad people wouldn't realise she was pregnant. Not yet. He was still getting used to that idea himself.

Her hair was entwined somehow into a low twist at the nape of her neck. She had a touch of make-up on—something to make her eyes seem even bigger, brighter, and a slash of red lipstick that made her mouth irresistibly kissable.

He shouldn't have kissed her. Not because the world was watching, but because he wanted more. He wanted to *know* more too—what other secret dreams did she have? What other secret bold action did she want to take? This was the woman who'd thrown all caution to the wind that night with him. He'd been so privileged. He wanted her to feel that freedom with him again. He didn't know why the desire was this strong but he was sure they needed to get rid of it. He'd hoped it would dissipate, that he could ignore it…but he couldn't and he knew she couldn't either. It would be better to exhaust it. Then they could move forward with a calm, easy plan for the future. It didn't need to be a big deal.

And people *were* staring at her. She was so tall, so striking. So sexy. But also that mandatory engagement notice had run in the newspaper and everyone was agog. He'd laughed off the swirling rumours about his grandfather's quest to find him a suitable fiancée, but that he'd come back from London with a woman?

He couldn't help moving closer again—that protective urge rising even when he knew Leah didn't want it, or need it, given the apparent ease with which she was talking to Phoebe Mikos. But *he* needed it. He stood alongside her, listening as she asked more questions than she answered. She politely asked about places to see, things to do, intuitively making the most of these people's pride in their city, but she did it with an artless charm that made everyone around her smile.

'Do you mind if we leave, Leah?' he asked her eventually.

She turned to him and he saw the relief in her eyes. He drew her out and quietly directed his driver to take them to the Athens villa.

'You enjoyed yourself?' he asked as she stifled a yawn.

'It wasn't too bad,' she murmured. 'Your friends aren't so scary.'

'They're not all friends,' he couldn't help warning despite having seen her at ease there. The worry within him bloomed again.

'Competitors? Rivals? Threats?' She chuckled. 'None of those people could hurt you.'

'No?' Her certainty burned somehow. 'Do you think I don't feel anything?' he asked—even when he'd been the one trying to convince himself that he didn't. 'That I'm inhuman somehow?'

It was stupid to even ask. He'd been the one to tell her he couldn't love anyone—and that was true, wasn't it? It had to be.

She turned to face him. Her eyes were like deep pools and he just wanted to dive in.

'No. I know you've been hurt,' she breathed. 'I just don't know how.'

He rejected her words. But her vulnerability shone through—all that soft emotion pierced his own defence. He should say nothing but when she looked at him like that he couldn't help himself.

'They could hurt you,' he muttered.

'So it's me you're worried about?' She shook her head. 'I can let it wash over me.' Her frown formed as he said nothing. 'You don't believe me?'

'My mother struggled to break in here,' he confided huskily. 'Like you she wasn't Greek, she was American. They met on one of his trips away.' There'd been many trips away. 'She didn't speak the language. I didn't either until I came to live with Dimitri.' His father hadn't seen any need to teach him and his mother had been too absorbed with her own problems to bother to find him a tutor. 'He didn't bring either of us back to Greece. When he finally did, she came home most nights without him.'

He'd been ten years old when he'd discovered her drinking alone late at night, drowning that humiliation and loneliness from leaving his father at one of his all-night parties with all those other women. She'd screamed at Theo for disturbing her and sent him from the room. But he couldn't go back to bed. How could he sleep when the sound of her bitter sobs rang through the door she'd neglected to slam?

'They were miserable.' Leah sat very still. 'Did Dimitri know?'

'Dimitri lost his only child.' Theo too was frozen, his heart encased in the ice that had formed there so long ago. 'And he blamed my mother for everything.'

CHAPTER TEN

THEO SUDDENLY MOVED and Leah glanced out of the window, only just realising that the car had stopped outside a stunning building on the corner of an obviously exclusive part of downtown Athens. 'We're not going back to the compound?'

His eyes glittered in the darkness as he held the door for her. 'This is my city villa.'

Taken aback, Leah tried—and failed—not to be completely floored by the perfect façade of the historic villa.

'Is this where you slept the other night?' When she stepped inside, her heart stopped. Hard oak floors, and a marble staircase led up to more luxuriously styled furnishings. But here on the ground floor there was an internal decorative pool, of all things. The villa encapsulated a sense of peace that ought to have been impossible in the centre of such a vibrant city. She walked away from him, just to catch her breath. From this room there were incredible panoramic views of the Acropolis. Right now it was lit up, a beacon of ancient romantics. It was beyond beautiful but, inexplicably, anger welled within her.

'This is where you bring your women, so your grandfather doesn't see them,' she said with a laugh, but a curl of bitterness spiralled even as she tried to stop it. This was the scene of his secret seductions. All those beautiful women she'd seen tonight? Had any been his lover?

He had a whisker of a smile on his face. 'I don't wish to be disrespectful and—'

'You don't want to get his hopes up.'

His eyes were intent upon her as she gazed about the beautiful place.

'And you thought I'd want to stay here with you?'

'Leah,' he said softly. 'You're going to be my wife.' He crossed the small space between them. 'There hasn't been anyone in my bed since that night with you. I'm not and never have been promiscuous.'

The awful thing was, the nearer he got to her, the less she cared about those other women, whether they existed or not. They no longer mattered—she knew they'd meant little to him anyway. Because that was how he survived, wasn't it? With an impenetrable heart. Because he had been hurt. And it sounded as if his mother had been hurt too.

'Are you okay?' He frowned at her.

'I just…have a bit of a headache,' she muttered, stalling so she could try to think.

'Then let's get you a drink of water, shall we?'

She followed him into the kitchen. He leaned back against the counter, watching enigmatically as she sipped the iced water and briefly held the cold glass against her burning face.

'You should have been a model,' he suddenly said, his voice husky. 'You could have made millions.'

She laughed and put her glass down, her fingers stupidly shaky. 'Use my quirky features?'

'You must have considered it. Surely all tall, ultra-thin girls are approached at some point?'

'My parents forbade it.'

'Oh.' He grimaced. 'Of course they did.'

'I was supposed to make something of my brain, not my body.'

'So they wouldn't let you make the most of one of your assets.' He cocked his head. 'In fact, they made you feel… what? Ashamed of it somehow?'

She hated his insightfulness.

'And the other girls at school gave you grief?'

'They called me anorexic, of course. Then they saw how

much I ate and assumed I must be bulimic. I'm just bony. It's the way I am.'

'I know.' He watched her. 'So your mother didn't like you wearing make-up or anything?'

'She refused to give money to an industry that thrives on insecurities.' She shrugged her shoulders. 'But you've seen her, she's the epitome of normal beauty ideals, right?'

He shook his head. 'We all like different things—'

'Don't be cute. You know what I mean. She's beautiful by anyone's standards. She doesn't need make-up or nice clothes to look amazing.'

'Nor do you. Nor does anyone.'

'But that doesn't mean they can't be fun. That doesn't mean you can't play with them and express yourself in all kinds of ways.' She'd just wanted to have a little fun.

'Usually you wear almost nothing but black—that's your self-expression?'

She shrugged. 'I gave in and just wore what's acceptable.'

'It doesn't matter how loose or dark you keep your clothing, you can't actually hide, Leah. You're not and never will be invisible.'

Yet almost all her life she'd wanted to be. Ironically, the only time she'd felt free of performance pressure was when she was onstage.

'Not tonight at least, no.' She smiled down at her blouse. 'Is this your way of saying you like it?'

'You should wear whatever you want to wear. Be the shadow, be the sunlight, be whatever you want. Just be yourself in that moment. There is no right or wrong.'

She smiled at him.

Something unfathomable flickered in his eyes. 'Why did you say yes to me that night?'

'Why?' She was stunned he'd need to ask. 'Your ego needs a stroke?'

'No, I really want to understand. Why me? Why that one night? Why not some other guy, some other time?'

'There was no other guy. No other time.'

'I don't believe you.'

She stared at him. 'Um…have you forgotten you were my first?'

'Oh, I'll never forget that,' he purred. 'But I think you had other chances before me. Maybe you just didn't notice them.'

'That's very kind of you. But no.' She shook her head.

'Liar.'

She stared at him, then glanced away. 'Okay, there was one guy who asked me out. But he didn't want *me*, he wanted to get on my mother's research team.'

'He tried to use you to get close to your parents?'

She nodded. 'I was working in their laboratory as an assistant. Because I didn't finish my degree.' Because she'd failed in their eyes.

'Because you never wanted to actually *do* the degree.'

'The things we try to do to please our parents, right?' she murmured. 'Like you marrying me to please your grandfather.'

'That's not the same,' he scoffed.

'Isn't it?'

'Nobody held a gun to my head to make me take you to bed,' he said. 'That desire is very real. It's *still* very real.'

She didn't reply; she couldn't.

'So did you date him?' he prompted her.

She shuddered to even think of it. 'We went out for about a month.'

'And you didn't sleep with him?' His eyebrows arched.

'One month isn't that long—'

'You weren't into him.'

Shocked, she laughed. 'No, he wasn't really into me.'

'No, he would have been. *You* didn't let him close.'

She paused.

'If you'd really been attracted to him you would have. You slept with me, a total stranger you met that very night.'

Um, that had been *so* different.

He chuckled. 'Come on, Leah. Aren't I just a little bit right? That other guy didn't turn you on and there was no other chance because you never let there be one. You buried yourself away in a laboratory with a bunch of guys too shy to see past their microscopes.'

'Don't stereotype them.' She mock-punched him.

'I bet it's true. And then you go work with a bunch of old people? You say you don't want to be invisible but you have been hiding, Leah.' He stepped closer. 'Maybe you only picked me because you found out I was leaving the very next day. In that way, I was safe.'

'You were a total stranger—how safe was that? It was an insane risk to go off with you.'

'Is that why you said yes to me, Leah?' He leaned closer. 'Because you thought I couldn't hurt you?'

She hadn't thought anything of the sort. She hadn't thought at all. 'I said yes because I couldn't say no to you. You're irresistible, okay?' She folded her arms across her chest.

'So are you.'

She shook her head.

'They killed your self-confidence.' He reached for her. 'That shouldn't have happened—'

'How was I supposed to stop them?' she flung back, broken. 'All my life, Theo…my grades weren't good enough. I'm too tall. Too angular. Too different… Nobody wants to get hurt, Theo. You don't either.' She pushed back. 'In fact, you work stupidly hard to protect people *you* feel responsible for. Not only do you not want to get hurt, you don't want anyone around you to get hurt either.'

He lifted his chin, his gaze sharpening.

'What developed that over-protectiveness, Theo? Who did you see get hurt?' She waited but then continued boldly. 'It's not your grandfather. He's strong. He's a powerful man who's only recently become vulnerable. This goes back further than that. Who *couldn't* you help? Was it your mum?'

'I'm not over-protective. The truth is I have no desire to have to protect anyone.'

'Not even people you care about? Or is it that you don't want to care about people *because* you were hurt?' She paused. 'Why did you go to live with Dimitri? What happened to her?'

Theo sighed and turned away from her. This evening was not going the way he'd envisaged. He'd rather hoped they'd be on to round two by now; but somehow he'd ended up bringing up things he shouldn't have in the car on the drive back and now she wanted to know more.

'Just tell me, Theo,' she muttered. 'You can tell me anything. I won't judge.'

He never talked to anyone about this. And there was such a risk if he told her the truth. But he didn't want to brush off her concern. He knew he had to explain even just a little of it—so she'd understand why it was he couldn't give her everything she ought to have. He owed her that. 'They had a blazing affair that led to a shotgun marriage.'

Shock, then consternation pinched her face. 'Your mother got pregnant?'

'With me. Yes.'

She swallowed. 'And you're an only child.'

'Correct.'

Her colour receded. He knew she was picturing their future, drawing the parallels to his past. He didn't blame her—he'd done the same.

'They were miserable.' He forced himself to continue with the sorry story and finish it as briefly as he could. He didn't want her taking it on board or reading anything into it. He never talked about it because it didn't matter, it didn't mean anything. It was in the past and could stay there. She never needed to know the whole of it. 'The sizzle fizzled pretty quickly. It became a mess of fights and infidelity.' He didn't go deeper into details. 'After my father died in a car accident my mother decided she couldn't give me the best life so she sent me to live with Dimitri.' He breathed out. 'I'm not going to repeat those past mistakes, Leah. We won't be unhappy like that.'

She was silent for a long moment. 'This is why you came up with your prison island plan?'

'It seemed like a good idea,' he muttered. She didn't realise what that island meant to him but, of course, what was a heaven to him might be a hell for her. He couldn't make assumptions on her behalf any more. 'But we'll work something else out if you'd prefer.'

Her eyes widened. 'You're not going to send me away the second we're married?'

'No.'

Relief unfurled at his words, tempered by the sad history he'd just told her. No wonder he'd thought separation from the start was for the best. It sounded as though his parents' marriage had been a mess. Leah's heart ached. She desperately wanted to know more, but his expression had shuttered and she knew he'd hated having even this brief discussion about it. He was reserved—as private as he was protective—and she could respect that even though really she just wanted to reach out and touch him and tell him she was sorry for what he'd been through. Maybe she had to handle this with the same emotional restraint that he was. Because this 'sizzle would fizzle', wouldn't it?

Her heart puckered at the prospect. She couldn't imagine not wanting to be near to him. But at least she knew he wasn't going to be unfaithful—not when he'd been this scarred. She tried to push past it, to get them both back on an easier track. She'd focus on the practicalities of their immediate future.

'Do we have to marry at the town hall or something?' Would there be a bunch of strangers staring at them as they waited in a crowded hall outside before their five-minute service?

He shook his head. 'I've secured permission for us to marry on the compound.'

'So there won't be many people?'

'Dimitri will be there. My security team…' He paused, as if realising how impersonal it all sounded. 'I'm sorry your family are unable to attend.'

'I'm sorry Oliver can't make it, but it'll be more fun without my parents.' Honestly, she was brightened by the news she wasn't going to have to parade in front of people she didn't know. 'We could get married in our pyjamas before breakfast,' she said, shooting him a kittenish smile to ease the tension.

'Dimitri wouldn't approve.'

'Well, we mustn't disappoint him.' She chuckled. 'After all, this is only about pleasing your grandfather.'

'Oh, snarky Leah is back, your headache must be better.' But a rueful smile had lightened his features as she'd laughed. 'Do you have something to wear?'

'You just said there aren't going to be many people there,' she said limpidly.

'*I'm* going to be there,' he gasped, mock-wounded.

'That's good, I guess,' she pondered with thoughtful pretence, enjoying this turn back towards the easy banter with that bite of desire beneath. She loved it when he eased up on his solemnity and she wanted to wipe away the remnants of that old hurt in his eyes. In this very immediate future, she could touch him on this most literal of levels. 'It's the only time you'll ever see me in a dress.'

'Do you hate your legs or something?' His smile turned

sly and he stepped forward to tug at her scarlet blouse. 'You have no idea how good they feel locked around me.'

The awkwardness melted inside her. Why did it take only this? Only a smile and a look and a touch and she was cast back towards him, happily seeking more of his caresses. 'Theo—'

'They're gorgeously long and stronger than they look.' He glanced down and then swiftly lifted his lashes to imprison her in his heated green gaze. 'I get so turned on when you have me in your grip.'

'Like I'm some spider?' She playfully ducked his reach for her, but was breathless beneath it.

He laughed. 'Stop trying to avoid my compliments.'

'Oh, you were complimenting me? I thought you were telling me my legs are like…tweezers or something while trying to maul me at the same time.'

'Maul you?' His laugh morphed into a sexy growl and he planted firm hands on her hips, keeping her right where she wanted to be. 'You want me to show you again?'

'Show me what?' She couldn't resist leaning into him, giving up on any idea of escape.

'What we're really good at.'

She'd wanted this again so much, for so long. She couldn't possibly say no.

He drew her closer and that look in his eyes intensified. 'Let me touch you.'

She loved that he asked, even when he knew her answer. And even when she knew he meant only this, only now, she lifted her chin. He met her parted mouth with his in a kiss so hot, so desperately needed she moaned helplessly. Her eyes closed as she was thrown instantly back into that delicious firestorm of delight and desire.

'Your legs are the perfect length for me too…' he teased between kisses. 'If only you had some heels on, even just a couple of inches.'

'I can't wear heels,' she gasped, on one last joke. 'I'd trip over.'

He caught her laugh with a kiss. 'You're graceful as hell and you know it. Anyway, you wouldn't need to walk, you could just brace against the wall. You'd be the perfect height for me. Otherwise I'd have to bend and get muscle burn.'

She huffed another breathless laugh. 'Always thinking of the practicalities?'

'We'd be able to sustain it for longer.'

She couldn't sustain herself for long at all around him, and the prospect of hot sex against the wall made her knees buckle.

His laugh was an exultant sexy sound but she didn't care. All that mattered was that he'd slid his arm beneath her and scooped her up. He climbed the stairs, effortlessly carrying her to a vast bedroom. She couldn't look away from him as he set her in the centre of the bed. His eyes glazed as his focus dropped and he looked down her body. That rapt, fixated look made her toes curl. And then it began. Pure attraction, pure pleasure flowed as he stripped them both bare with lingering caresses. But her desire was underpinned by that other ache—that need for touch that was more than physical—and that made her feel everything so very much more. She sobbed, her emotion unstoppable in that moment when he thrust within her again. At last.

'Theo—' she cried out at the culmination of relief and craving.

'I'm here.'

Yes.

CHAPTER ELEVEN

'THEO HAS LEFT for work already.' Leah smiled apologetically as she poured Dimitri a cup of tea as he joined her at the table on the terrace. Since that conversation when she'd asked him to help her, Dimitri had thawed—coaching her in beginner Greek phrases and instructing Amalia to do the same. The week had passed with increasing ease and speed. Theo had returned her to the compound early the morning after the exhibition and Amalia had swung into action to help her with preparations. She'd enlisted her cousin and aunt as well because they were so low on time.

This morning the sun warmed Leah's back as she resumed knitting the white silk as quickly and as neatly as she could. Amalia was already working on her section too. Theo had left well over an hour ago.

'He works too hard.' Dimitri stirred his tea. 'Perhaps he will work less now there is a child coming.'

'Perhaps.' Leah didn't hold out much hope but she'd heard the wistful tinge to the older man's words and she didn't want to lie to him.

Dimitri studied her with his faded version of Theo's bright green eyes. His held more blue and weren't as vivid yet he still seemed to see right through her.

'He's not perfect,' Dimitri said.

'No one is.' She smiled, unsure where he was going with this but she wasn't going to say a word against Theo to his grandfather.

'I was too hard on him.'

For a moment she held Dimitri's gaze, recognising that hint of arrogance in the way he held his head. But then he dropped his chin and his shoulders sagged.

'I didn't want him to become like his father, but Theo

was always different...' The old man coughed. 'He's loyal. He cares deeply...'

Leah stared at him, realising how hard it was for him to say any of this.

'He loves you very much. He doesn't want to let you down,' she said.

'I know. Because of that, he works too hard.' He gazed across the pool. 'Perhaps now he has you, that will change.'

Dimitri had been a workaholic as well. The discipline in his daily routine proved that. While routine could provide a safe structure and enable achievement, it could also reinforce bad habits. Strengths were also weaknesses, sometimes, and working too hard for too long could definitely become a weakness.

She smiled to hide her thoughts. 'Theo and I understand each other. We respect each other.'

'But you don't love each other.'

Her skin cindered with embarrassment. She respected Theo. She'd be loyal to him and she was insanely attracted to him. Anything more than that, she couldn't bear to consider.

'Perhaps that is good.' He picked up his coffee. 'Marrying for suitability rather than love works better in the long term.' He nodded. 'He is different from his father.'

So his father had married for love? Or what he'd thought at the time had been love. Theo had called it a 'blazing affair' that had led to an unplanned pregnancy. She and he hadn't had the affair. They'd had only the one night. Though they'd had a couple more since.

'Is he different from you?' Leah asked, curious enough to push past her nerves. 'Did you marry for love or was it merely a suitable arrangement?'

'It began as one and became another. That is what happens.'

'A suitable arrangement grew into love?' she asked.

'As it will for you.'

Of course he wanted to believe that. He loved Theo and he didn't want what had happened to his son to happen to his grandson.

'You don't think the same can happen in reverse?' she asked warily. 'An unsuitable love match can't become suitable?'

Dimitri's expression shut down. 'No.'

Wild love—wild *lust*—didn't last. She suspected Theo thought they were burning out the lust between them, then it would become a convenient arrangement somehow. But for her, the intensity hadn't lessened. It was worsening.

Because it's not just lust.

She closed her mind to that awful whisper and poured both herself and Dimitri some fresh orange juice. She'd focus on finishing her dress and learning Greek.

Theo returned every night to the riviera compound, unable to spend another night away from her. He'd carve out their new normal after the wedding, but right now the temptation to return to her was extreme. And he couldn't resist it. He couldn't resist the need to touch her. But his discomfort was growing. He couldn't seem to think as clearly. He found himself distracted at work—wondering what she was doing. It was unacceptable.

He knew some distance was required.

Tonight he roved through the house but knew she'd be on the terrace. She liked the sunset. He heard her laughter as he neared. He walked faster but quietly, surprised by the sound of other voices, others laughing.

He paused in the open doorway. Leah sat at the table, her back to him. She looked vibrant in loose white linen trousers and a clingy blue shirt. Amalia was with her and so was Dimitri. They were laughing together. He didn't think he'd ever seen Dimitri laugh like that. She didn't notice him for a while. They were sampling a selection of traditional sweet cakes.

'Leah likes the lemon.' Dimitri noticed him first and sat back with a satisfied twinkle in his eye as he called to him. 'She has good taste.'

Theo stared as Leah smiled and coyly thanked Dimitri in Greek. She had a private joke going with his grandfather? Since when did they begin talking like this? Since when did his grandfather joke?

Theo shook his head and pulled out a chair to join them, trying to shift the uneasy weight pressing down on his chest. 'Preferring the lemon over the plum?'

Her eyes sparkled as she smiled again at his grandfather. His gut tightened and his appetite vanished. He didn't want dinner. He didn't want to sit here and watch them all laughing together. He wanted her alone, in his bed, her attention all on him.

He stilled, stunned at his own rabid—*jealousy*?

He should have known what damn sweet she liked. *He* should have sought it out for her. His grandfather seemed to know more about her than he did. His staff too…

And whose fault is that?

He'd been determined to work as much as he could thi week. Determined to do this right so he didn't ruin her lif completely. He refused to let her become miserable. Bu suddenly he wasn't sure what was right any more.

His island idea had definitely been wrong. He'd not un derstood her need for companionship or to feel valued visible in her role as his fiancée. And now, he didn't lik the thought of her being so far away. Even a thirty-minu flight time felt too long.

He couldn't understand why he couldn't keep this sin ple. Why did he suddenly want things he'd never want before in his life? Never had he ached to leave work ea the way he did now knowing she was here.

He somehow got through supper, listening to them talking and laughing, watching Leah at ease—chatting, funny, kind. It was late when Amalia walked Dimitri back to his building, leaving Theo alone with Leah at last.

'You came home earlier tonight.' She broke the silence with her soft voice.

He nodded, unable to take his eyes off her.

'Are you going to work tomorrow morning?' Her chin lifted.

'Yes.' He leaned back in his seat and tried to ignore the slight pout of her lower lip. 'I figured it gives me something to fill in the time before the ceremony.'

She put down her spoon. 'What happens after? You go back to work?'

'No,' he answered mildly, despite the tension stringing him out. 'We go on our honeymoon.'

'To prison island?' Her lashes lowered, hiding her eyes.

'It's a surprise.' To his astonishment he actually felt a little nervous about it.

The feeling compelled him to silence her next question in the best way possible. He couldn't resist any longer anyway. He stalked around the table and kissed her till she was breathless. He ached to pull her to her feet and hustle her inside so he could have her in his bed. Restraint was imperative yet apparently impossible. Rebellion at his self-imposed restrictions bubbled his blood. He couldn't stand the need and the want clawing within him. Since when did he want anything with this intensity?

'I'm not sleeping with you tonight,' he said huskily. 'It's the eve of our wedding, it'd be bad luck.'

'Well, we wouldn't want any more of *that*.' Something flashed in her eyes.

His breath stalled in his lungs. 'That's how you feel? That this was unlucky?'

She put her hand on her belly. 'No,' she whispered. 'I

don't think that about this. It's a miracle in a way…coming into being…against all odds, right?'

He still didn't want to think about the child. Instead he kissed her again until every nerve tingled.

'No,' he muttered with a low groan as he pulled away from her. 'Not tonight.'

He watched the dazedness in her eyes dissipate as disappointment loomed. His gut ached. He hated disappointing her. Which was exactly why he needed to prove his restraint now and build distance back again over the coming days.

'I'll see you tomorrow, Leah,' he said huskily.

When she'd become his wife.

He went to work in the morning purely to put himself beyond temptation. But he got no actual work achieved. He spent a couple of hours pacing while talking on the phone, finalising the arrangements for their travel later in the day. The idea had come to him when he'd been unable to sleep a couple of nights ago and he'd been unable to resist putting it in play.

He returned to the compound in time to shower. His tailor had delivered the new suit and shirt. His shoes were new too. Everything was new. Except him. He was still the same—with the same failings. She had no idea really. Tension tightened his muscles as he dressed. He'd consider this a contractual meeting like any other, right? Just another merger.

But he'd never wanted to make promises like this to someone. Not these deeply personal promises he knew he could never keep.

Fidelity—fine. Honour—fine. To love?

Leah was sweet. And she was having a *child*. He breathed out, refusing to undo the top button of the stiff shirt that suddenly strangled him.

He turned his back on his reflection and strode outside

Dimitri was sitting out on the terrace. Amalia was also there with her husband and their son. Leah had insisted they attend as guests, not staff. He was glad she'd charmed them. It shouldn't have surprised him; when anyone got to know Leah, they discovered her sweet generosity.

They'd had a shade put over the pergola to protect them from the stunning blue sky and the heat of the sun. Tendrils of white flowers and greenery had been wound around the pillars and made the compound even more picturesque than usual. His security team had swept the beach and ensured there was no one with any cameras and long-range lenses hiding out. They had complete privacy. He'd called in Philip, his security chief, as his witness. The official from the city arrived and briefly ran over the paperwork with him. All that remained was for his bride to appear. He stared down at his watch. Would she keep him waiting? His breathing shallowed. Suddenly it seemed imperative—he *needed* to see her right now.

The official coughed discreetly and Theo looked up.

His throat tightened. She was a column of white and silver—gleaming like a pale angel with a smile that was both pure and a little playful. The tiny sparkle of confidence felled him. She walked towards him. The white flowers that she held low covered that gentle curve of her belly. A lace shawl covered her shoulders. A white bodice—was it knitted?—hugged her hips and flared from there in a cloud of soft tulle—a subtle reminder of the softness to be found in her straight slenderness. It was all he could do to hold himself upright. He couldn't wait to slip her out of it. He couldn't look at her but he couldn't tear his gaze away. It was like being strung on a medieval torture device. The official stood in front of them, alternately speaking in Greek, then English, so his bride understood. Theo braced, forcing himself to stop staring at her like a crazy man—to take in the ceremony and actually speak when required.

A quick glance behind her showed his grandfather sitting in a chair, leaning forward on his walking stick. A week ago Theo would've expected the old man would be prune-faced, given she wasn't one of his picks, but he was actually smiling and relaxed. He genuinely liked her.

Theo looked at Leah again. Something ached within him. He didn't want to hurt her and he would. It was in his DNA.

The official was beaming and looking at him expectantly. She was looking at him too—too trusting, too wary, too wanting. That panic—to protect her—surged within him. But he was supposed to kiss her now. He bent forward and brushed his lips over hers in the briefest of touches. He couldn't allow himself anything more or he'd lose all control.

At last it was over. They were married.

'Are you sorry your family isn't here?' His voice was hoarse as he walked with her to pose for a photo.

She shook her head. 'No.'

But there was a yearning look within her eyes that smote his heart. He steeled himself against it.

'Your dress…' He struggled to push the words past the tightening in his throat. 'You made it.'

She bit her lip, glancing down. 'Yes.'

'How did you have the time?' He couldn't fathom it. I was so intricate and beautiful, it had to have taken hours.

'Amalia and her family helped. They knitted around the clock once they saw the design.'

His heart seemed to stop. 'Who designed it?'

'I did. I adapted an idea I'd been working on.'

He nodded and looked down and that was when he saw her shoes. His mouth felt as if wads of cotton wool had been stuffed into it. He couldn't swallow or speak. He could only stare and then try like hell to control the desire coursin through his body—but it was as if the sluices at an ancient dam had been unlocked.

They were silver shoes, dainty, with delicious little high heels.

And they were for him. He appreciated the gesture more than he'd imagined he could appreciate anything. Touched a part of him so deeply buried he'd not known it was there. All he wanted to do was touch her.

He ached to rid himself of this desperate need. Why hadn't it eased over these past few days? Why wasn't it settling now that he had her safety and security ensured? He had everything working in play just as he wanted it. Yet his tension was now worse than ever.

Leah stared up at Theo, watching the storminess build in his emerald eyes. He was so silent, so inscrutable. She swallowed. 'You don't like it?'

'Like what?' he muttered, blinking as if he'd lost track of the conversation.

Embarrassment curled within her. 'My dress.'

She shouldn't have made it. Should have just bought one of those amazing designer numbers in central Athens. It had taken so many hours, so much planning. She'd had so much companionship with Amalia.

Theo's expression sharpened and he opened his mouth.

'Theo, Leah,' Amalia called to them, breaking the spell.

Leah glanced; the photographer wanted another photo. Theo put his arm around her waist and pulled her closer. He did it with such speed, she was almost tipped off balance. Leah glanced up at him to read his expression, given the tension she could feel within him. But he'd looked to the lens. He wasn't smiling.

'Perfect,' the man said.

Theo released her waist but immediately took her hand in his and led her to the table. It was laden with a selection of delicacies—a celebratory feast Leah could barely touch. Theo didn't each much either.

'Traditions are important,' Dimitri said stiffly. 'It might be a small wedding but it is important to do things properly.'

She felt Theo's tension magnify as they were called to cut the beautiful cake.

They sliced into the cake together and, once everyone had a small piece, Dimitri made a toast to them.

Leah nibbled at the cake, stupidly nervous, which was crazy given she was no wedding-night virgin. She *knew* Theo. Yet at the same time she didn't. Right now she couldn't figure out what he was thinking, only that it was apparently unpleasant. Her heart sank; he really hadn't wanted to do this. The intimacy she'd thought they'd built over the last few days was nothing.

'Leah and I need to get going now,' he said to Dimitri.

The old man replied in Greek. Theo smiled and Dimitri, Amalia and the others melted away with teasing smiles.

But Theo dropped his polite smile as he walked towards her.

'Should I go get changed?' she asked him anxiously. She didn't know what he had planned.

'No,' he snapped grimly. 'We need to leave right away.'

CHAPTER TWELVE

SHE WAS ALMOST afraid to speak, his expression was that severe as he led her to the helipad. But she refused to be afraid of her husband. 'So it's not prison island?' she attempted a joke.

'No.' He waited for her to climb into the helicopter ahead of him.

So now they were en route to who knew where. He helped her with the headset and she then watched out of the window as they took off. The view over the mainland was just stunning—she drank in the blue waters and stunning settlements. Then they seemed to lower and slow a little. She leaned forward, gazing intently as ancient ruins came more sharply into view. Ruins she recognised because she'd studied them online a few thousand times years ago when caught up in the romance of the novel she'd loved.

'Is that Delphi?' She turned to him, her heart thudding because she knew it was. 'You *remembered*.' And she was so touched.

'I remember everything about that night,' he muttered—all soft, serious intensity.

She couldn't turn away from him—he was so still, as if he was struggling to contain something. The tension between them tightened. 'Thank you.'

'Go on,' he ordered roughly. 'Look.'

She turned towards the window again as they circled the site. The setting sun cast a burning glow on the ancient hewn stone. It was majestic and so moving. She knew Theo had timed their trip to perfection so she had this magical view—this was why he'd insisted they leave the compound so suddenly. Her vision misted at his thoughtfulness.

They circled the ancient ruins one last time and then

headed away from the mountains, passing over the terra-cotta roofs of a village below. It was so picturesque, with narrow cobbled streets that she could see even from this height. Eventually the chopper lowered to a secluded property on the far outskirts of the village.

As she stood back on the ground Leah paused, conscious of her appearance as the helicopter lifted up and away. She glanced about anxiously, expecting an assistant to appear to carry their luggage in, but no one emerged from the magnificent building.

'The staff left about five minutes ago,' Theo said, lifting the two overnight bags himself. 'So we're alone.'

She followed him from the helipad along the pathway until they turned a hedged corner into the private heart of the property. She paused near the edge of the pool and took in the inviting atmosphere. There was soft music playing from discreet speakers. Candles burned in glass jars placed in carefully chosen spots. The small circles of flickering light cast a warm glow around the terrace, almost creating a semi-circular stage.

'The American half of me wants my first dance.' Theo dropped the bags and faced her. That rough edge to his voice was even grittier.

She swallowed, realising that he was holding something fierce back. 'Theo—'

'I apologise for the lack of a live band.' He slowly paced towards her. 'But I wanted us to be alone.'

'Why?'

'I'm a terrible dancer.' He held out his hand and his smile was tight.

'I don't believe you.'

He wasn't terrible at anything. But she put her hand in his and he drew her into that little lit space on the terrace.

'I don't know how I've resisted touching you all day.'

He pulled her into his arms. 'I can't resist any more. You look beautiful.' He stared into her eyes.

That warmth within trickled more quickly, more deeply—becoming a heat that needed release.

'And you're wearing heels,' he noted.

'I figured it wouldn't matter if I fell over when it was only you watching.'

'Only me?' He cocked his head and finally his smile appeared.

It was unfair of him to flirt with her when he didn't really mean it. And the truth was she was likely to tumble *because* it was him. He put her so on edge, so aware of every movement, every breath when she was with him, yet not with him. Now she simply ached for his touch.

'This lace thing is pretty, but I'm afraid I'm going to tear it if I hold you closer.'

'I wore it to cover my shoulders…' she muttered breathlessly. 'And to hide the fact that…'

'That what?'

'I'm not wearing anything beneath the dress.' She swallowed. 'I tried but you could see the lines…'

He inhaled deeply. 'So you're telling me that beneath this angelic surface, there's a temptress. I think I knew that.' He pulled her hips against his and she felt just how much he liked how she looked. 'I remember those scarlet panties,' he whispered.

'Good thing there's no audience,' she said with a chuckle.

'Right now I wouldn't give a damn if there was.' His breathing roughened. 'I can't wait any more, Leah.'

That twisting serpent of heat bit her too. She threw herself into the gorgeous escape of this—their touch, in the magic they created together. Hot and dream-like, the searing need enveloped her. They were moving, but not really dancing. Somehow she was back against the wall of the building and she gasped as he plundered, kissing his way down her neck. She threw her head back to let him and glimpsed the darkening sky above and saw the stars emerging. His fingers moved and the silver strap slipped off her shoulder in the haste and the front of her dress dropped enough to bare her breast.

He stared, savage hunger etched on his face. 'Leah.'

She shivered as his fingers teased in gentle swirling motions that only made her fire flare. She needed him. Now.

'I don't know how to get you out of this dress fast enough without damaging it,' he groaned.

She'd laugh if she weren't so desperate. 'Then don't.'

Looking into her eyes, he moved, freeing himself with the simple slide of a zip, and then he lifted the skirt of her dress and pressed close, nudging her legs further apart with his.

'You wore the shoes for me,' he muttered roughly, 'so we could do this.'

She felt a flash of vulnerability—a sudden fear that the effort she'd gone to revealed something more, something she hadn't wanted him to see. But there was no time to fret as he took her hands in his, palm to palm, and laced their fingers. She gasped, anticipation soaring as he braced them on the wall either side of her head.

There was this between them. *This*. Powerful. Primitive. Unsophisticated. Undeniable. The simplest, most basic of needs. The drive to get closer to him pushed her to arch her hips forward as her shoulders pressed against the wall. But not only were her hands locked in his, her gaze was locked in the fierceness of his focus too. Neither smiled; it was impossible in this supreme intensity. She felt him, close and hard and almost hers. Hunger and passion forced her to rock, sliding closer still. And he was right there.

'See?' he gritted, almost smiled, but the tension was too strong. 'Perfect.'

He watched her as he thrust. Her scream echoed through

the night. But he didn't stop. He possessed her—physically and beyond as his gaze seared through to her soul and she met him arch for thrust, in a frantic, fast ride that was so explosive, so powerful it could end only one way. In an almost instant eruption of blinding, white-hot pleasure.

And then there was silence. They were still completely dressed. Still desperately entwined—their fine clothes tangled. But her emotions were torn—because that had been so much more than *simple*. The sheer desperation, the total annihilation stunned her. As did the deeper, complex yearning it revealed.

'What a first dance,' she mumbled, seeking a way to claw some lightness back into the atmosphere because it was so intense that she couldn't breathe.

She carried her pretty, heeled shoes in one hand while her husband held her other hand tightly, leading her through the silent villa up the stairs to the moonlit room. She faced him and felt that desire ricochet back. Because they were so far from done.

'Slower this time, Leah.' He carefully slipped the wrap and the dress from her body and placed them over a chair reverently.

He glanced at her, then practically tore his trousers and shirt off with such fierce speed she chuckled. But then he stepped forward and she couldn't laugh any more and he made true on his promise. It was slow. It was thorough. And it destroyed her.

Long fingers of sunlight slid up the bed, slowly warming and waking her. She felt Theo's arms around her and smiled secretly. He must have sensed her waken because he began gently tracing patterns on her back.

'You're not leaving right away to go to work?' she asked sleepily.

'Leah,' he admonished piously. 'It's our honeymoon.'

'As if that minor fact would stop you.' She smiled and kept her eyes closed.

'Did you wake up on the wrong side of the bed? Or just not get enough sleep last night, darling?' He pressed a kiss to her shoulder and slid out of bed.

She didn't want to get out of bed ever. She wanted him to get back into it. And he knew. But he didn't come back to her; instead he picked up her dress from where he'd placed it and carefully put it on a hanger. 'Thank you.'

'It's stunning.' He picked up the accompanying lace, which had fallen by her side of the bed. 'Did Amalia loan you this?'

Surprised, she reached out and ran her fingertip over the delicate lace. 'No, Dimitri gave that to me. You didn't realise?'

'Realise what?'

'He said his wife made it. She wore it on their wedding day.'

He stared at the lacework in his hands. 'And he gave it to you?' His lips twisted into a rueful smile. 'You've won him over completely.'

'It's because I'm carrying the next Savas.'

'No, it's because he likes you. You're patient with him—I've seen you pouring his tea and plumping his pillows.'

'He's an old man, Theo. Of course I'm patient and it's not hard to be kind.'

'You're patient with everyone. You do things for people.' He drew in a deep breath. 'And you're talented. You made the blanket you gave that woman at the home. Your cardigan you wore that night at the ballet...'

She nodded.

'I saw the drawings in your apartment. They were on graph paper.'

'I work up the patterns, yes.'

'You learned some maths then, back with your parents' insistence.' He grinned.

'I wasn't bad at it, I just wasn't good enough by their impossible standards. I'd be sent to my room to study and end up knitting to help me relax,' she acknowledged. 'I made leg warmers for my ballet class. Awful stripes from ugly leftover balls of wool that were cheap. Zoe wore hers to company class the other week and a friend wanted some.'

'You could sell them.'

'They take a while for me to knit. They can buy machine-made ones for cheaper.'

'So you've thought about it.' He sat beside her. 'Yours are artisan creations. Hand-crafted, beautiful wool—a premium product.'

She shook her head and giggled at the flattery. 'Hardly. I make mistakes. I can't put a massive price tag on imperfect pieces.'

'Handmade doesn't have to mean perfect.' He looked thoughtful. 'You could sell the patterns. People would then knit them themselves.'

She hesitated, half tempted by his idea. 'You think they're that good?'

'Don't you?' He turned her face up when she glanced down. 'Don't you believe in yourself, Leah?'

She swallowed again.

'Because you should. Just because you didn't get top in every damn math or physics class doesn't mean you're not capable of amazing things. It's just different.'

'I know that. I know.'

'There's a difference between knowing and *believing*.'

He stole her breath with his words. Then he kissed her and stole everything else she had to give.

A blissful hour later he nudged her with a smile. 'Let's go exploring.'

She wasn't sure she'd ever be able to move again. But she let him tug her to her feet and followed him into the shower. Theo drove them to Delphi, where they spent the afternoon exploring the ruins.

'This is incredible.' The beauty of her surroundings amazed her but at the same time she was keenly aware of the strong man walking beside her. 'Thank you.' She glanced towards him, only her gaze ensnared with his. 'You're supposed to be seeing the sights.'

'I am.'

She rolled her eyes, but when she swallowed it was hard to push past the lump that had formed there. This was so lovely, it scared her. He took the lead, turning into the most knowledgeable tour guide ever, telling her anecdotes about the area, pointing out all kinds of features.

'I read up yesterday morning,' he explained as she looked at him in disbelief over one obscure fact.

'I thought you were working.'

'I couldn't concentrate.'

Theo couldn't resist holding her hand as they turned to walk back down the hillside. When he'd watched her at the ballet she'd been like this—the expressive emotions flickering on her face. There was nothing better than seeing her entranced. Smiling. Moved. He liked it best of all when she was moved by him—by his touch. In bed—vulnerable and exposed.

'Do you need to check in with Dimitri?' she asked as they walked back towards the car.

She really cared for the old man. He glanced at her and knew she was genuine. She was good at building relationships—she had an easier relationship with Dimitri than Theo had ever had. Which was remarkable given her own family dynamics. 'What about you checking in with your family?'

'I did. My brother sent a message back yesterday morning,' she said happily. 'He actually remembered.'

Smiling, Theo phoned Dimitri, who immediately asked

to speak to Leah. With dutiful mockery, he passed his phone to her and watched as she shyly said hello in Greek. It was only a couple of moments before she ended the call.

'I think he likes you more than me,' Theo teased as he drove them back to the private villa.

She grinned and looked at him. 'You're the CEO of his business, Theo. That's after adding to the conglomerate. You've done everything he's ever asked of you. More than everything.'

'He expected nothing but the best.' He stilled.

'And you've always delivered.' She angled her head. 'But what do you want for your self, Theo? I have my outlet— what's yours?' She leaned close. 'Please don't say it's having one-night stands with women in London…'

He couldn't smile. 'I have my work. I like my work.'

'Is that enough?'

What else was there? He got into the car and waited for her to fasten her seat belt before driving off. 'I was young when I went to live with Dimitri,' he said. 'He was a tough taskmaster, but it was a good distraction.'

'And that's it? You just work? I thought the adage was work hard, *play* hard…'

'I don't feel my life is boring, Leah.' It certainly wasn't any more. Not with her in it.

But he felt her gaze on him, too searching, too soft.

'You take it upon yourself to ensure Dimitri's happiness—by pleasing him.'

'Like you've never tried to please anyone?' He forced a laugh. 'You make that your life's work.'

'We both had expectations placed on us—the difference is I failed all mine. But you surpassed them—awards, accolades, grades, prizes, acquisitions, business acumen… and you've been perfect ever since,' she muttered.

'I have been so far from perfect, Leah.' He grimaced.

He didn't want her feeling sorry for him; it was preposterous. 'No one is perfect.'

'Were you afraid he'd send you away too?'

Suddenly it was as if all the oxygen had been sucked from the car.

'Is that what happened?' she asked softly. 'Did your mother send you away?'

He kept his eyes on the road and pressed harder on the accelerator. He didn't talk about that—ever.

'Why did she let you go?' Leah was so calm and soft and insistent and somehow…safe.

It was the question he'd spent most of his life asking and he still didn't know the answer. All he knew was that it hurt. It would always hurt. He just never admitted it. He never let it get this personal with anyone. But Leah disarmed him with her self-deprecating lovely laugh that made him smile. She was so gorgeously human and he truly couldn't resist confessing it to her.

'She said it would be better for me to be with the Savas family. That she couldn't look after me properly any more.' He sighed. 'She'd started drinking and only drank more as their marriage fell apart.' He cleared his throat. 'Don't think badly of her.'

Leah shook her head slightly.

'My father was Dimitri's golden boy. He was their only child and I guess he had a lot of pressure on him. But he was also spoilt and selfish and partied hard. And I guess it was partly rebellion that made him marry the girl he'd got pregnant and move to the States with her.' He tensed. 'He was unfaithful from the start. My mother kept me informed—justifying her own indiscretions, her own addictions. But I didn't need her to tell me. He brought them to our house.'

As a kid he'd walked in on his father kissing another woman when he'd had no clue what he was seeing. Only that it felt wrong to witness. He'd never wanted to know any of it. He'd been a kid.

'She drowned her hurt in drinking and they fought all the time while maintaining this…supposedly glamorous lifestyle. My dad visited Greece often—keeping up with his friends here, supposedly satisfying Dimitri with his efforts to learn some of the business…but he didn't really care. He brought my mother and me here only the once for my tenth birthday. My mother hated it here. When he got back late one night they had another big fight and he stormed out again. He shouldn't have been driving. The crash killed him instantly. It was lucky there was no one else involved.' He still felt furious with his father for that. 'Dimitri blamed my mother for everything. In his opinion she was why they'd never lived in Greece—because she wasn't Greek. She was the one burning through the money, being unfaithful… Dimitri thought it was all her fault because my father was miserable with her—of course he was going to play up a bit. And then there was me, the reason they'd had to marry in the first place.'

He parked the car outside the villa but sat still, staring through the windscreen, lost in his drive down nightmare lane. 'Dimitri was so angry with her. I overheard him telling her he'd have insisted on a DNA test to prove she hadn't trapped my father with another man's bastard, if it weren't for the fact that I was the spitting image of him. I couldn't stand to hear him talk to her like that when I knew what my father had really been like…'

He'd been torn between defending his mother while burying all the details she'd shared with him. The affairs, the misery and heartache and the rage she'd felt towards his father. Her attempts to make him jealous. All Theo had wanted to do was make her feel better. But he'd failed in that.

'And then, after the funeral, it was time to go home.

But my mother said she didn't want me. That she'd never wanted me and that it was best for me to stay with Dimitri.'

'She left you in Greece and returned home to the States?'

He'd begged her to take him with her. Instead she'd signed over all parental rights to Dimitri. A man he'd barely known at the time.

'You must have been heartbroken. You were a *child*.'

He'd been terrified.

'You'd just lost your father, and then your mother too?'

He didn't want her sympathy. He didn't know why he'd told her any of this but now he'd started he couldn't seem to stop. 'The one time I fought Dimitri was when he said something back about her to me. I lost it so badly I thought he was going to...' He breathed in. 'But he didn't. He just never mentioned her name again. I didn't either. We never talk about her or my father. We discuss the business, politics...anything that isn't personal. And it's good. It works.'

That had only changed slightly since Dimitri had got sick and he'd started in on Theo finding a wife.

'Where's your mother now? Are you in contact with her at all?'

He already felt as if he'd been carved open and this memory was like pouring scalding acid on the bleeding wounds, but he couldn't stop the pain—the truth—flowing out. 'A few years ago... I wanted to know where she was, if she was okay...' He'd been a fool to think that, just because he'd made a success of himself, anything would have changed. That she'd want to know him. 'She didn't welcome my visit, didn't want to know. She didn't even want any of my money. She just wanted me to leave her alone. She said her life was better without me. And mine was better without her.'

'Theo—'

'It is better.' He didn't want to hear any different—how could he?

'Is it?'

'Why would I want to revisit it, Leah? My mother was humiliated and hurt and she lashed out. She drowned her sorrows so much that she couldn't stop. My father was beyond miserable too. I can't let anyone else feel that—not Dimitri, not you. I can't let it happen again.'

'Dimitri said he was too hard on you,' she said.

'He told you that?' Shocked, he finally looked at her. 'He's never told me that.'

She looked so serious and concerned. 'Maybe you should talk to him.' She leaned forward to get nearer. 'You should talk to him about what really happened between your parents. Dimitri told me you're different from your father. Maybe he already knows some of it, Theo. You know he's a smart man.'

A smart *business*man, but a blind old fool when it came to his son. Why would Theo ruin that memory for him?

'I wouldn't ever do that.' He rejected the idea immediately, pushing back into his seat. 'He was so hurt by Dad's death. I watched him struggle with grief for so long. Isn't it kinder to leave him believing the good in his son?'

Theo had never wanted to let Dimitri down either. He'd never wanted to do anything that might hurt him—that might make Dimitri push him away.

'He gave me everything I needed—a home, an education, structure and discipline… I owe him, Leah. I can't hurt him.'

'But holding all that in hurts you.'

Now he was looking at her he couldn't seem to look away and that was bad because everything was rising now—all those feelings he'd blocked for years.

'You must have been so lonely.'

And she was right there, looking at him with those compassionate, velvety eyes as everything just slipped from him—the things he'd never said aloud to anyone—and his heart was racing so fast he felt dizzy. 'After a month or so, we went on a boat to Dimitri's holiday home for a weekend. It wasn't like any place I'd ever been to before—I don't mean beautiful buildings, but a place that was a total escape. I was free to roam and swim. It was vast and private and the sea so blue, so warm.' He shook his head as he confessed his last little secret. 'You might have thought it sounded like a prison, but it's always been paradise to me.'

'Oh, Theo—'

At the catch in her whisper he blinked and forced himself to break the connection. He unfastened his belt and got out of the car.

'I should get some food,' he said briskly. 'You must be hungry.' He headed straight into the kitchen.

Anything to change the topic and keep him busy so he wouldn't have to look at her, so he wouldn't give way to that yearning inside compelling him to seek solace in her hold. He couldn't stand to see the empathy in her eyes, or bear the ache it caused.

'You can cook too?' Her laugh sounded strained. 'I don't know why I'm surprised.'

'Actually…' he breathed out, seemingly unable to stop being honest now '… I only have a couple of dishes in my repertoire and they're not great. I just didn't want us to be disturbed.'

He didn't want to have to pretend in front of people.

Maybe that had been a mistake. Maybe having staff around right now might help him reclaim his distance. And perspective. Because the one person he couldn't seem to pretend anything in front of was Leah.

He wasn't even hungry. He didn't know why he was even in the damn kitchen. But she'd opened the fridge and was absently staring at the contents as if she hoped a three-course meal would magically appear if she looked for long enough.

'Don't,' he muttered. He didn't want her waiting on him, helping him, being that kind person who did things for other people all the time. He didn't want her to care for him in the same way she cared for her oldies or in doing nice things for her friends. That wasn't what he wanted. He didn't want anything from her, right? 'You don't have to—'

'Maybe we could just make do,' she interrupted him. 'Pull together a few things picnic style?'

He nodded, unable to argue any more. They briefly worked in silence, but their bodies brushed too close despite the spaciousness of the kitchen. The air almost hummed as his tension built. He sensed hers rising too and that only escalated his. Confusion swirled, twisting into a tornado that he didn't know how to safely release. The silence thickened to the point where he couldn't stand it any more. He stopped what he was doing and stared at her.

She'd stopped too, the moment he had. Her eyes reflected everything—the turmoil, the vulnerable hunger that couldn't be hidden. He couldn't seem to hold anything back from her any more. 'Leah...'

He felt her shudder as he pulled her into his arms. His heart slammed against the palm she placed on his chest and his brain was fried by the look in her eyes as she rose on tiptoe to bring herself closer.

'Maybe we just make do with what we have?' he muttered.

What they had was *this*. With one kiss they ignited. Desperate to assuage the aching energy that had coiled so unbearably in the course of that conversation, they were wordless now. Swiftly pushing clothes aside, seeking skin, seeking complete contact. He lifted her back onto the big table and with almost no preamble pushed close and hard and deep and it still wasn't enough. She instantly tightened her legs around his waist in response, forming the hottest, tightest vice, and it was as if she were never going to release him. He ground harder, faster, pushing as powerfully as he could, but he still couldn't get close enough. The shocking thing was *this* didn't feel enough any more. That aching hole in his chest hurt—that place where other people had a heart. He growled in agony, in absolute frustration.

But she grabbed his burning face in her hands and kissed him. The passion in her deep caress destroyed that ache in an arc of pure lightning. It wasn't just pleasure branding through his skin and flesh and blood to bone. It was peace and tumultuous contentment and it was perfect. Now it was fiercer than ever. Better than ever.

But now he needed it more than ever.

CHAPTER THIRTEEN

THE FULL MOON bathed the room with pale light even at three in the morning. Still wide awake, Theo tried not to fidget and disturb Leah's sleep but he couldn't rest. He felt flayed, old wounds oozed. That physical bliss had ebbed and allowed cool, biting air—and anxiety—in.

Beside him Leah shifted position, then shifted again. A moment later she left their bed and went into the bathroom.

Theo waited, but the longer she was gone, the more his concern grew. He followed her to knock on the door. 'Leah? You okay?'

She opened the door. She held one hand pressed below her belly button. His senses hit full alert. 'What's wrong?'

She shook her head and rubbed her stomach slightly. 'Nothing.'

It didn't look like nothing. He gazed at her. The soft swell of her belly was bigger now, the secret within her starting to show. Bared like this she was so beautiful, but so very vulnerable.

'You're sore?' He carefully placed his palm just below hers and caressed the curve of her belly. Her skin was so soft and warm he went all the more gently. But mid-sweep he felt a jab against his palm. He stilled and held his palm firm and felt it again—the smallest of punches. It hit him with stupefying power. He glanced up and intercepted her wide-eyed gaze.

'You can feel that?' she breathed.

His throat completely constricted, so he merely nodded mutely.

'It's like this at this time. I think it's got day and night mixed up.' She still whispered, as if afraid speaking would silence the tiny communication.

It? Their baby? Another punch felled those walls that had barely begun their rebuild within him. He was feeling their baby. It was here. Alive and kicking.

He licked his lips and struggled to get his brain back. 'Does it hurt?'

'Not at all.'

'It's…' He didn't know what it was. He didn't know what to say. He didn't know what he was feeling.

'Like something out of a sci-fi movie,' she whispered with a chuckle.

She jolted a smile from him—he could never hold back a smile when she laughed.

'It doesn't seem real, does it?' she whispered.

He shook his head. But it was. *Real.*

He pulled his hand away and motioned for her to get back into bed with him. He held her gently and listened to her breathing, hearing the change as she relaxed and drifted back to sleep. No such bliss for him. Adrenalin coursed through his body. There was a baby on its way. Stupid, but while he'd *known* that, he'd not really *believed* it. He'd not felt it—not literally, like just now. But not inside himself either. Now the fact hit him as if he were being buried in a box by a load of wet cement—he was going to be a father.

And he had no idea how he was going to do that. All he knew was that he didn't want to be like his father. Or even his grandfather—unable to communicate. He never wanted his child to hold in a bottomless well of hurt the way he had.

He wasn't ready. He'd *never* be ready. In fact, he didn't want this at all.

He didn't want the responsibility of his child's happiness weighing on him. He couldn't handle Leah's either. She had her own loves and passions and she should fulfil her own dreams. He couldn't bear it if she ended up *resenting* him…he never should have tied her to him. Yet he couldn't fight that need curling within him to claim them both, protect them both—

Panic pushed his 'problem-solve' button, but the only possible option he could come up with was his original plan. They shouldn't live together. He could ensure their safety and financial security best if he was away from them. He couldn't live with them both and let them down. He couldn't live with *himself* if he did that—especially not now he knew her so well. She deserved better than the little he could provide emotionally and he couldn't stand to see disappointment or disillusionment build in her eyes because of what he lacked. He'd never be able to meet their greatest, deepest needs.

Distance simply had to be restored. Except, at the thought, regret like nothing he'd ever known rose within him.

But Theo was used to holding himself together and doing what was necessary. And this was necessary.

Leah woke and found herself alone again. Her heart dropped—she hated waking without him. The yearning inside was for more than his touch now; she wanted him to open up to her more. To share more of himself. The hurt he'd faced broke her heart. She'd hardly been able to breathe as he'd told her. And all she'd been able to do was listen, then to hold him. He didn't realise what he gave. Or how much more she wanted.

She found him pacing out by the pool. Her steps slowed as she saw he was already dressed. He looked too smart in his suit and with a remote expression in his eyes. A shard of glass pierced her heart. She knew what he was about to say.

'We need to go back to Athens.'

And there it was. She looked at him and then back at the view towards the mountain behind him. 'Okay.'

Disappointment bloomed within her chest.

'It's work—'

'It's okay,' she repeated.

She didn't want him to explain or try to make excuses. This was the reality and she shouldn't expect more from him. But the last few days had been so lovely—not just their time in Delphi, but leading up to the wedding. She'd had snatches of a future—of dreams and hope for happiness with him.

'I need to work, Leah.'

'Why?' Anger took over the hurt. 'You're supposed to be on your honeymoon.'

'I'm responsible for a lot of people. I can't let them down.'

'Of course.' It was that loyalty and sense of duty again. The relentless drive to do what was right for everyone but himself. 'And you tell me I seek approval too much.' She couldn't hold back the bitter twist to her lips.

'This isn't about seeking anyone's approval—this is about other people's livelihoods.'

'It's always about other people, isn't it, Theo?' She looked at him. 'What about *you*?'

He looked at her. 'You don't need to worry about me.'

'No, you wouldn't want that, would you?' she said. 'Someone to worry about you. Someone to care.'

'I can look after myself, Leah.'

And that was the way he liked it?

He felt duty to many people and for her no more than any other. But she rebelled at that thought. There was more between them than mere sex now and she was sure he felt it too. Yesterday had been the most magical day. She wanted that Theo back—the one who'd let her in. But he'd shut down when he'd felt the baby move. He'd tried to hide it, but he couldn't. He'd not touched her properly since and not talked to her either. Fatherhood was a duty that he was determined to fulfil, but that was all. He didn't actually want it.

* * *

'You're back sooner than I thought,' Dimitri greeted them when they landed back at the compound. 'I have a present for you.' He led the way inside, clapping his hands together in almost childlike excitement.

Leah stared. A huge photo of Theo and her from their wedding now hung in pride of place in the centre of that collection of Savas portraits. Leah was aghast.

It was an arty shot, filtered with black and white, but somehow they'd coloured in the silver of her dress…the techniques made her look ethereal and so staggeringly glamorous she couldn't quite believe it was her. And with his sharp suit and solemn visage, Theo looked like a fallen angel. But the appalling thing was their pose—while Theo was staring straight into the camera, her face was turned towards him. She was smiling at him and there was heavenly adoration in her eyes and there was no hiding it from anyone who bothered to look. She didn't want to see Theo's reaction yet she couldn't stop herself staring as he studied the picture. He didn't break that remote countenance and he didn't say a word.

Disconcerted, she glanced at Dimitri and saw the satisfaction in his eyes as he surveyed the portrait. This was what the old man had wanted, wasn't it? Someone to love his grandson. What he didn't realise was that it wasn't enough. Theo had to *want* that love. And he didn't.

She hated disappointing Dimitri almost as much as Theo did. She could understand why he worked so hard to keep the man happy. But the same was true in reverse. Dimitri would do anything for Theo. He was desperate to see him happy and content. They loved each other but they were too lacking in communication skills to admit it. And Theo lacked the trust to be vulnerable enough to share the truth of the past.

So she forced on a smile and faced Dimitri. 'It's beautiful, Dimitri. Thank you.'

He patted her arm and walked through to the lounge, leaving them alone.

'I need to get to the office,' Theo muttered.

'Theo?' It was that huskiness that compelled her to follow him. She followed him out to his car, pushed past the embarrassment of that portrait. 'Don't go.'

He stopped walking. His broad shoulders tensed as he pivoted to face her. He didn't want to have this conversation? Nor did she. But suddenly it was imperative. Somehow she had the courage. She was done hiding.

'Leah—'

'You don't have to go today. You're choosing to. Don't avoid me, Theo.' It was so obvious he was. Just as he avoided Dimitri.

'It's not you, Leah.'

Of course it was. Yes, they had some issues but they could handle them, couldn't they? But not if he left. Not if he chose to shut her out again. She'd thought they'd really communicated, that he'd really felt something for her...but then he'd felt the baby and she was scared it had all become too real for him.

'You know what?' She drew in a breath of determination. 'I'm not the same woman you met that night in London. I've got more confident. I'm not afraid to wear the colours I like. To say what I really think. To do whatever it is I want. You know why? Because just that once, *you* picked me. And that made me realise other people might like me too...and that it actually doesn't matter if they don't. It's okay not to please everyone.' She stepped closer to him. 'You saw me, Theo, and you've believed in me ever since. You've listened to me up till now—please keep listening.'

'Leah—'

'You can't hide that hurt in there for ever.'

An impatient expression flashed in his eyes. 'I knew I shouldn't have—'

'What? Talked to me? What's wrong with opening up to someone? Is it really that awful?' For him, that rejection had run so deep. 'I know you never wanted to marry anyone. I know you were just keeping Dimitri happy when you said you'd meet those women. You weren't intending on going through with any seriously. I know you think you don't want children. You only married me because it was the right thing to do.'

'You claim to know so much, yet you won't accept what I'm incapable of,' he growled at her. 'You need to understand that I cannot be anything more than what I am.' His hands shook at his sides before he clenched them into fists. 'I'm an emotional failure. I couldn't give my mother what she needed. I couldn't meet Dimitri's requirements. I can't meet yours.'

'What requirements do you think I have?' she asked him, desperately trying to understand what he thought she wanted of him. 'I'm in love with *you*, Theo. And *you* know that. That's why you're shutting me out now.'

'No.' He tensed and backed away from her, shaking his head in pure denial. 'You might think you're in love with me. But you're not.'

He didn't believe her? His doubt slammed her momentum to a halt.

'I shouldn't have slept with you again.' Turning away, he shakily ruffled a hand through his hair.

She was appalled. 'You think you've been trifling with my emotions?' Did he not accept how *real* this was?

'Of course I have. You've not had…'

'Any other lovers?' she finished for him. 'No, I haven't. But that doesn't make me an idiot, Theo. Don't treat me like someone who doesn't know her own mind, her own body, her own feelings.'

He closed his eyes momentarily. 'Even if you mean them, I can't carry that burden.'

'It's a *gift*,' she pleaded with him to understand. 'Not a life sentence. It's light. Love, laughter, support.'

'No, it's not. You cannot deny there's a responsibility on me. On my actions. I need to be careful because you're vulnerable.'

'All you have to do is act like a *human*. Not be cruel. You don't have to love me back.'

'Good, because I can't return those feelings. Not ever.'

She flinched. His words hit her heart like burning-hot bullets. Was it only her? Or was it anybody who tried to get close who he pushed away?

'I know you don't want to be hurt,' she said to him again, softly—more hesitant now. 'I'm so sorry your parents were unhappy, but that wasn't your fault.'

'How can you say that?' he roared. 'They were only to-gether because of me. They fought because of me. He died because of me.'

'They were adults. They made choices. It was never *you*.'

'Of course it was me.' He rolled his shoulders. 'She never wanted me.' He glanced at her. 'And that's okay. Look at me properly, Leah—do I look like someone who's strug-gling? I'm *fine*. I'm happy. I like my life as it is and I don't need you—' He broke off, his breathing sharp.

She shook her head, refusing to believe his rejection. 'You told me it wasn't my fault I couldn't live up to my par-ents' expectations. Why isn't it the same for you? Why take the blame for their incompatibility? You were the innocent. You're not responsible for everyone and everything. It's not down to you to protect us all—not this baby, not Dimitri, not me.' She gazed at him. 'Maybe it's just fate? Maybe we just lucked out with the parent thing. But you know what? We can't change it—we can only accept it. And we have to appreciate what's really good. *We're* good, Theo. You and me. And I'm not going to raise this baby the way my mother raised me. We're not them, Theo.'

'No. And I know you'll be a wonderful mother. But I'm still not capable of being what *you* want, Leah.'

'You already *are* what I want. Just as you are.'

He jerked his head and his gaze dropped. 'I can't give your baby—'

His voice cracked.

'*Our* baby,' she whispered.

'Stop,' he snapped, fury unleashed. 'Just stop. I have *tried,* Leah. But this? It's never going to happen. You ask too much.'

She stared at him. He meant it, he really meant it. And she suddenly knew there was nothing she could say to change his mind. He didn't think he could be enough for her.

'I get that you don't want this from me.' She breathed carefully so she could still speak. 'But you should talk to Dimitri, Theo. You should be as honest with him. Because you *do* love him.'

She might've been wrong to read anything more into their relationship, but she was certain about that.

'I can't.' His chest rapidly rose and fell and he spun away from her, yanking open the car door. 'I have to go.'

Leah stood still as his car roared off into the distance, shocked by the rejection buffeting her soul. She'd pushed him too far—asked for things he'd never wanted to give. Or at least, not to her. Should she just have done as he wanted, without saying anything? Should she have stayed silent and kept it all in?

No. That was what he did and look how well that worked.

Her invisibility was ended and the bittersweet irony was because that was thanks to *him*. He'd turned her life upside down all those months ago. But those changes had begun from that one magical night. He'd injected a confidence within her and she'd held that memory close. It had been like a bubble inflating her heart. And while he'd just stomped on it, it wasn't going anywhere. She wouldn't let his rejection destroy her; she wouldn't revert to the person she'd been before meeting him.

She'd come too far. And what she'd asked for hadn't been too much. It hadn't been anything more than she deserved. It was what everyone deserved—to be loved, wholly and completely and unconditionally. For a few magical moments he'd made her feel as if she could have it all. They were good together in so many ways. But he was under no obligation to give her anything more than what he'd originally offered…if he didn't care for her. He didn't. But her heart ached, her whole body ached…because she so badly wanted to believe he did.

She desperately wanted to run away, but she refused to. She wasn't doing that to her baby. Nor to Dimitri. Not ever to Theo. None of them deserved that. They all—including her—deserved a family. And they'd make one—though i might not end up being particularly conventional. She'd do everything she could to ensure her child received love from both its parents. Because he would love this baby, she knew he would, even if he couldn't yet believe that of himself.

But she had to cope with her own heartbreak too. She had to get away from him to do that. The only solution sh could see was for her to go to his island holiday home a he'd suggested from the start. Theo could work in Athens keep an eye on Dimitri and whatever else he needed an she could avoid him.

It wasn't his fault he hadn't fallen in love with her th way she had with him. But she couldn't stand to stay ar other night with him. She certainly couldn't sleep with hir again. *That* would destroy her. And she couldn't trust he self around him. He couldn't have absolutely everythir from her because she *did* deserve more.

To preserve herself, she had to leave now.

CHAPTER FOURTEEN

THEO ROLLED HIS shoulders as he walked across the terrace. Dimitri was sitting by the pool, with a pile of reading material on the table beside him and one of Leah's blankets draped over his knees. He looked tired and his eyes held only a shadow of the warmth that had been there this morning when Theo had returned with Leah.

'You've been doing too much again.' Theo frowned as he saw the tinge of greyness in the old man's face. 'You're still supposed to take it easy.'

He looked towards the house, his chest tightening at the prospect of seeing Leah. The words she'd so passionately declared had echoed in his mind all day. Going to work had been pointless other than to simply escape her. But he couldn't even do that—his mind had replayed the moment over and over. She'd stood there with such dignity like a tall, slender tree. And he'd cut her down.

He wanted to kick himself. He'd been such a fool to think he could have any kind of relationship with her. He'd known, hadn't he, right from the start that she was gentler than most? She'd been a virgin, for heaven's sake. No one had made her feel special or wanted before—of course she thought she'd developed feelings for him. He braced, holding off seeing her. Was she still hiding upstairs? Still crying? Was she too upset to sit with Dimitri and stumble over a few Greek words while working on a new pattern? He hated the thought of her being distraught.

It finally dawned on him that the place felt too silent.

'You worked late,' Dimitri muttered.

'There was a lot of work that needed doing,' he replied. And it had taken him three times as long because his concentration was shot.

I'm in love with you.

He shook off the memory. Again.

'You've been married less than a week,' Dimitri commented.

Theo didn't answer.

The reality of last night had given him every reason to keep his distance. But the desire to see her, just to see, was too strong. It wasn't sexual desire, it was concern. Just concern. He needed a glimpse to ensure she was okay. Then he'd retreat.

'Leah?' he called out as he entered the house, holding back the desire to run.

She didn't reply.

Unease scraped down his spine. He gave up on his restraint and ran up the stairs, taking two at a time. 'Leah?'

He walked into their room. It felt emptier. He suddenly realised the whole house felt emptier. Suspicion ballooned and he glanced in the wardrobe. Her eveningwear was still there, but those pairs of jeans, those tees, were gone. He pulled open the first of the drawers in her stand. Her silky scarlet smalls were gone.

She was gone.

He froze, trying to process it. Then panic hit. Where had she gone? Was she okay? Why?

But he knew why. He knew exactly why. He'd hurt her.

He raced back downstairs just as Dimitri came into the house.

'What's wrong?' The old man watched him.

'I think she's left me.' He could hardly breathe as he strode past Dimitri to double-check the lounge.

'Pardon?'

'Leah. She's gone.' His anger leaked.

'Pardon?' Dimitri glowered at him.

'What part of "left me" don't you understand?' he stormed back as rage blew him apart.

'You're the one who doesn't understand,' Dimitri growled. 'You think she's left you? Is that what Leah would really do?'

Theo froze, then whirled to glare at his grandfather. 'Do you know where she is? Why didn't you tell me?'

'Why didn't you ask?'

'I don't have time for games, Dimitri. Where is she?' He needed to know she was okay.

'Why leave her alone all day? Bored and lonely with no one but an old man for company.'

'You're not that old and this place isn't boring.' He drew in a breath. 'I don't have time for this. I'll get Philip to help find her. She can't have gone far.'

'Philip is with her.'

'What?'

'She's gone to the island.'

Theo reached out and pressed his fingers to the wall to balance himself as he gaped at Dimitri. 'She what?'

'She said that was what you wanted.'

She hadn't run away? She wasn't alone out there in Athens, checking herself into some boarding house or something? She wasn't on a plane back to England?

Relief was like a blissfully cool balm soothing the rawness inside but then that very balm began to heat, burning his wounds worse. He'd thought she'd chosen to vanish—to run and hide from him completely because she'd been hurt. But she hadn't—she'd simply done as he'd originally asked.

He slumped against the wall, his legs empty of all strength. 'Okay. Okay, good.'

It was good, wasn't it? It was what he'd wanted. It would make things simple. So why did he feel worse than he had when he'd thought she was missing?

'You're not going there now?' Dimitri looked confused.

'No.' He drew a breath. 'I'll check in with Philip on the phone. There's no need for me to go.'

'I sent Amalia with her.' Dimitri's mouth thinned. 'To care for her.'

The unspoken criticism hung heavy. Theo rejected it. 'Thank you,' he said curtly.

He turned his back to avoid his grandfather's colossal disapproval. Flashes of memory tortured him as he climbed the stairs towards terrible privacy—her laughter that night in the theatre foyer, her latent playfulness, her humour and kindness. But all that warmth was lost to him. Because Theo *couldn't* care for her. He couldn't give what she needed. He'd always known she'd be better off away from him. And so would his child.

But he wasn't better off. Three long, hellish days and nights later he was nothing but worse. Nothing but angry. Nothing but poison. He missed her. And he hated that he missed her. He hated that she had got to him in a way no one ever had. That she'd made him want things. Things he was so afraid of losing that it was easier not to have had them in the first place.

'You need to rest.' He watched Dimitri silently push his dinner around his plate. The old man looked frailer than ever.

'How's Leah?' Dimitri asked.

He couldn't answer. He didn't know.

'I don't like to see you like this,' Dimitri added with belligerent edge.

Like what? He wasn't the one who looked as if he was about to keel over.

Theo shovelled a bite of food into his mouth and chewed tasting nothing.

'I didn't think you'd do this.'

Theo looked sharply at Dimitri. He recognised that low throb of anger. He just knew the rarely voiced criticism that was coming—Dimitri was about to blame his mother

'That you'd be like—'

'I'm nothing like *him*,' he snapped. 'I'd never treat Leah the way my *father* treated my *mother*.' He instantly sucked in a breath but it was too late to pull the words back.

Dimitri flinched and turned ashen.

'I'm sorry,' Theo muttered, dropping his fork with a clatter. 'I didn't—'

'Don't be sorry,' Dimitri interrupted firmly, despite his complexion. 'Tell me.'

Conflicted, Theo froze. But he remembered Leah's entreaty for him to speak honestly with Dimitri. And he remembered that easing inside when he'd talked to *her*. He ached to talk to her like that again and, thanks to her, he finally realised he ought to with his grandfather too. 'I don't want to hurt you.'

'I know my son was not a saint,' Dimitri said. 'I know they both suffered.'

'I think maybe they brought the worst out in each other.'

'And you were caught between them.'

'No,' Theo sighed. 'They just didn't care, Papou.'

The pet name for his grandfather slipped out. And then all the secrets slipped—snatches of truth and hurt tumbled free, the memories that had cut most deeply. Dimitri put his hand on his shoulder and just listened and somehow Theo told him even more—even about that awful trip to see his mother. All the things he'd held back for so long because he hadn't wanted to hurt him. But Dimitri's low growl wasn't an expression of pain for himself, but empathy for Theo. There was no changing any of it, Theo understood that. But in sharing there was acknowledgement and acceptance and finally forgiveness—of those parents who just hadn't had it in them to be there for him. And it was, he finally believed, something lacking in *them*, rather than something missing in him.

'I'm proud of you, Theo.' Gruff and awkward, Dimitri

shook him in a fumbling hug. 'I want to see you happy. I want to see Leah happy.'

'So do I.' Theo buried his face in his hands. 'But I…'

'What's worse?' his grandfather asked simply. 'The thought of life with her? Or without?'

CHAPTER FIFTEEN

FIVE DAYS.

No contact.

He'd not called, not left any messages, not visited. There'd been nothing. And that was a good thing. Because Leah was getting on with it.

Amalia was staying with her in the main villa while a security guard stayed in the gatehouse at the edge of the property. Leah knew the older woman was worried about her. But she needn't be. Things were fine. How could they not be when she now lived in this breathtaking place with its crisply white, curved buildings and stunning clear blue waters? The view was unbelievable—all sea, all sky. Every day she watched the sun rise and then later set, a beautiful blinding blaze set against that backdrop of brilliant blue. It was gorgeously warm, sweet and spicy wild herbs scented the air and she'd never known a place as perfect could exist. Theo had been right.

But the beauty broke her heart all the more, because it was something that screamed to be shared.

But there'd be no wallowing in bed and weeping. During the day, her determination held. She swam in the pool or at the private beach, then walked to the nearby village. Initially she'd greeted the locals with only a smile and a smattering of her appalling Greek but already a few of the women now stopped to talk for longer. Theo had been right about that too.

When she returned to the villa, she worked on plans. At first it had been purely for distraction. But as she'd thought about it more, a tiny spark had flared and now she was all in. Theo had been right to get her thinking more about that was well. Why shouldn't she create some kind of business with her knitting and pattern designs? Some kind of community? Her enthusiasm for that consumed the daylight hours.

But the tears came in the small hours when she was too tired and sleepless and sad to stop them. The loneliness was like nothing she'd experienced because she'd had a glimpse of what could've been. She missed him on so many levels. He'd made more than just her body come alive; he'd made her laugh. He'd been fun, intelligent, attentive and so caring, even though he couldn't see that in himself.

But he'd not been effortlessly falling into love the way she had. And she was not going to lie—that *hurt*. She couldn't want love from someone unable—and unwilling—to give it. She couldn't stay, knowing she wasn't enough for the person she wanted that unconditional love from. It had been hard enough being a disappointment to her parents.

At least Theo hadn't *lied*. And who was she to try to change him?

Every time a helicopter swept overhead she stiffened with nerves. Would he ever come see her or was he going to ignore her for ever? There'd been no helicopters at all today. The sun was high and she'd got too hot even in the shade outside, so she'd gone to her bedroom to try to catch up on some of the sleep that had been eluding her.

So far, no sleep.

At a movement in the doorway, she glanced up, expecting it to be Amalia, with one of the delicious treat trays she regularly brought her. But it wasn't Amalia.

Theo stepped into her room—tall, serious, *devastating*.

Her heart whacked so hard and fast against her ribcage she put her fist to her chest to hold it inside.

'What are you doing here?' She scrambled off the bed

She'd thought she was getting on top of her feelings, bu in a flash they were all back, all-consuming. Elation. Deso lation. It was far too soon to see him. It was always going to be too soon. And her bedroom was too intimate a space.

'Leah.'

How could she collapse so completely when all he did was look at her like that and say her name? She clenched her teeth, willing herself to stay strong and in control.

'What do you want?' she asked defensively as he stood watching her every move.

'I can't visit you?'

'Not unannounced, no.' She squared her shoulders. It was time to set the rules she needed in place to survive this.

His gaze didn't waver and that green deepened. 'But we're married.'

'We're not a normal married couple.' To her horror her voice weakened.

Because they were never going to be that. He didn't want that.

He still didn't move, yet somehow he seemed nearer. 'How are you finding prison island?'

She wanted to scream her heartache at him. She wanted to hate him for it. But she was so unprepared for seeing him again and the last thing she felt was hate. 'It's beautiful,' she said.

To her surprise something that looked like anger flared in his eyes.

'Really?' His soft query was laced with a lethal edge. 'So you're going to be happy here?'

She stared in disbelief that he'd asked that. Her anger burned closer to the surface. 'Don't you want me to be happy?'

Another expression flickered across his face but he swiftly stiffened and she couldn't even try to read it.

'It's better for us to live apart,' she said firmly. He'd been right.

But he didn't say anything, he just kept looking at her as

if he couldn't believe she was in front of him, as if he were afraid that if he so much as blinked she might disappear. And it wasn't fair of him to look at her like *that*.

'What do you want from me, Theo?' she flared. She was trying to give him what he'd wanted. '*Why* are you here? The baby's not due for a few months. Can't you just leave me alone and let me deal with—?'

She broke off, not wanting to name the blistering emotions steamrollering through her.

'After you first left…' His voice was so croaky it faded away.

She watched as he visibly fought for control.

'I thought I'd come and tell you it was all okay, that you should go back to Britain if you wanted. I'd set you up and pay for everything and come visit you and the baby when it suits you…but I don't want you to do that.'

Pain welled inside her. 'I wouldn't want to. The baby needs you. You need the baby too.' Because that was true. He might not think he had anything more to offer their child than financial security, but he did. 'That's why I'm here.'

But she pressed her lips together, not admitting her own need of him. He didn't want that.

He watched her, waiting, as if he knew there was more she wanted to say but couldn't.

'It's not the baby I need, Leah,' he muttered jerkily. 'It's you.'

Painful tears blinded her and she shook her head.

'Leah?'

'No.' She turned away, because she couldn't believe him. 'No, Theo.'

Somehow he was right there, his hands on her shoulders, pressing with firm but gentle pressure to get her to turn back to face him.

She ached to resist. But she still didn't have the strength. 'Please…' She broke off and closed her eyes to hold back those burning tears. But they slipped free anyway, tracking down her cheeks.

'Leah.' His thread of a voice broke. 'I'm so sorry.'

She sucked in a shaky breath. 'You don't need to be sorry. It's okay. I'm okay.' This was going to be fine. 'You just need to stay away and let me get on with it for a while.'

'You really meant it.' A whisper—of disbelief, of regret, of sorrow.

That she loved him? 'Of course I did.'

He was gazing into her eyes and she couldn't look away now because he was looking at her with such anguish. 'I'm sorry I didn't know how to accept that gift, Leah. I'm so sorry. No one's given me that before. And that it was you?' He shook his head. 'It meant too much. You'd given me something so fragile—like burning, just-blown glass— and I was too scared to take hold of it in case I warped it somehow. In case it really was nothing more than a bubble that would burst if I even breathed. I just didn't know how to handle it.'

She stilled, unsure she could believe what she thought he was trying to say.

'I'm mucking this up.' He groaned and moved closer still. 'I'm not okay, Leah. I'm not fine. I miss you.'

'But this is what you wanted.' There was a lump in her chest as if she'd swallowed a giant jagged piece of ice.

'I think I've been afraid for so long that I forgot I even was. It's just normal. I didn't even recognise I'd put defences in place. That afternoon when I came home and found out you'd gone I didn't realise you'd come here. I thought you'd left for good.'

'I could never do that to you. I couldn't hide your child from you. Not knowing you the way I—'

'I know, sweetheart. I know and I'm sorry. It was so stupid of me. I'm not great at understanding love, Leah.' He nodded. 'And I know you're used to feeling hurt by those who should show you the greatest care. But you shouldn't be. You deserve so much more than that.'

She swallowed.

'I used my parents as an excuse to keep you away. I didn't want to care. I didn't think I actually could. But, Leah, I've fallen for you. From that very first night, I just couldn't let myself recognise it.'

She shook her head. 'No.'

He tensed, his eyes widening. 'No?'

'Not from that first night,' she muttered. 'It's all…circumstance. If it weren't for this baby, we wouldn't have seen each other again.'

'I don't think that's true.'

'Of course it is—'

'How did I know where to find you?' he interrupted. 'When I came to London after you walked into the bank, how did I find you?'

'You…used your magical too-much-money powers to track down my address.'

'Yes, that's exactly what I did. But do you know *when* I did that?'

'After I called into the office…'

'No. I had my team put together a report on you the day I returned to Greece. The day after we spent the night together.'

She stared at him. Right after that? 'But you didn't do anything with it.'

He swallowed. 'I dreamed of you. But I thought I was doing the right thing for both of us.'

'Because I'm not—'

'Because I have this stupid terror inside that I couldn't get past. Not until you came back and lit up my world. Until you then left and I realised how horrendous life is without you. How much I want and need you in it because I love you. I'm so sorry I've hurt you and that I let you go.

I never should have done that. Have I ruined this completely, Leah?'

She was reeling inside. She had to take this chance; she had to have a playful moment. 'Not completely.'

He suddenly smiled.

'Keep talking.' Her heart pounded but she couldn't stop a little laugh of disbelief and delight escaping. 'Just keep talking.'

'Come home with me.' That old assurance sounded in his voice again.

'Why?' She needed more, she needed to hear it again and again. But she cupped his face in her hands as he asked.

'Because I love you. I miss you. I want you. I need you,' he confessed, leaning closer as he too struggled to breathe. 'Everything I never thought I'd say. Never thought I'd feel. I want it all with you, Leah.'

His gaze blazed with such intimate intensity and truth she almost couldn't bear it.

'Theo—'

He kissed her—as if he couldn't resist any more. As if he'd run out of words and only action was left to convince her, as if he couldn't get enough of her, as if she were the most precious thing in the world, breathlessly, brokenly. His whole body shook against hers, as if he was trying to go gently, but the strength of his need kept slipping through resulting in a soul-breaking, star-bursting kiss that she wanted never to end.

'Don't let go of me.' Tears sprang to her eyes again. 'Please don't ever let go of me.'

'Never. Never again. I'm so sorry.'

She was home in his arms. His grip on her tightened and he kissed her again. Everything was unleashed now—uncontrollable, unstoppable—the need to touch, to possess, to connect was too strong. Hands swept—clutching, touching, taking.

'I missed you,' he growled raggedly. 'Missed you so much.'

She trembled as he pinned her, kissing her, caressing every inch as if he desperately needed to rediscover her every secret. Every want.

But then he slowed as he gently stroked her belly. 'This scares me.' He glanced up, hot, raw honesty tumbling from him. 'But it brought you back into my life and for that I will always adore it.' He kissed that soft curve and looked up at her again, vulnerability visible in the sheen of his eyes. 'I'm going to need your help. I don't know how to be a husband…as for a father…'

'We'll figure it out together,' she promised him, her throat so tight she could hardly speak.

'Make do with what we have?' A half-smile broke his strain.

She nodded and curled herself about him, holding him where she needed him—with her, sealed along every inch. 'Together, we have everything.'

They had such ecstasy. And it was so sublime she actually laughed as he claimed her—her joy was too intense to be contained. He smiled back—she loved his smile. Loved him. Loved *this* with him.

And then she couldn't laugh any more, she couldn't speak. She—like he—could only *show*. In every kiss, every caress, there was total love.

Later, cuddled close, she never wanted either of them to move again. But Theo wriggled; reaching down to the floor, he scooped up his jeans and got something out of the pocket before lying back beside her. He put the small box he'd retrieved on her stomach and then took her hand and slid the diamond ring from her finger.

'What are you doing?' she asked, but she couldn't move in case that other little box slipped off her skin.

He held the diamond in his hand for a moment before

placing it on the bedside table. 'I've regretted giving you this ring from the moment I did.' He shot her a smile at her barely stifled gasp of dismay. 'I thought if I kept everything impersonal, I could keep you at a distance. But you were already under my skin. I didn't choose that diamond. I didn't want to think about what you might like. I didn't want to think of you at all. But it was all I ended up doing. The more I wanted to hold you away, the more you flooded me—filling all those dark, empty corners, Leah.' He picked up the box on her stomach. 'I spent the last week thinking about everything I'd do differently and this is the smallest of the things that I can do differently. I chose this one—your favourite colour…not so secret any more.' His smile was a touch self-conscious.

The ruby was so richly coloured it was almost crimson. Flanked by square-cut diamonds, it was sensual and striking and her eyes burned with its beauty. She shook her head as the tears threatened again.

'You don't like it?' He actually looked anxious. 'We can change it. You can choose—'

'No.' She put her fingers on his lips, half laughing, half crying. 'It's beautiful, I love it.'

Not only because it was stunning, but because of what it signified. He wanted to please her. But that in itself made her panic again. 'But you know you don't have to give me things. I don't want you feeling like you have to please me…' She breathed shakily. 'You've spent so long trying to please, trying to be perfect just in case—'

'And you haven't?' He cupped her jaw. 'You *do* things for people, Leah. For everyone—your friends, family… You did things for me too—you wore those heels and drove me mad. But this is different. It's not only to please you, but me too. Because I love you like I've never loved anyone. I never knew it was possible. And it's scary and wonderful and I just want to give you everything.'

'The only everything I need is you. Just you.'

He leaned over her, mischief sparkling in his gaze. 'So you don't want the ring?'

She hesitated, loving his flash of humour. And she slowly smiled. 'Maybe we should just see how it looks.'

He pushed the ring down her finger until it nestled next to the wedding band and they both laughed. He looked into her eyes. 'Perfect.'

She nodded. 'Want to know what else would be perfect right now?'

'Oh, I already do.' His hands slid to where they were so sweetly welcome. 'Mine to have and hold.'

'For ever.' She'd never felt as content and secure and as loved.

'I never want to spend another night apart from you.' He trailed his fingers up and down her arm. 'We need to speak to Dimitri,' he said with a smile in his voice. 'He and I talked.'

'Really?'

'You were right. He'd guessed some, I told him more. He was sad but he was mostly concerned about me. And you.' He suddenly smiled. 'You're like this hot marshmallow, fitting perfectly between us to forge us into a real family. You've made us both melt. You're like the sweetest glue...'

'You think I'm a hot marshmallow?' She chuckled, but inside *she* was the one melting.

'So hot.' He nodded. 'And he'll be thrilled to see you come home with me.'

'We'll come back here often though, won't we?'

He sent her a look of total triumph and pleasure. 'You really like it?'

'You were right. Not prison. Paradise.' She looked at him, overwhelmed with emotion to see him looking so happy. That he felt as deeply for her? 'I love you so much it hurts.'

'I don't want it to hurt, Leah.' He swiftly kissed her, his arms tightening like bars around her. She was imprisoned in the paradise that was his love.

Perfect, profound peace settled deep into her heart. 'I think, as long you're holding me, it won't.'

CHAPTER SIXTEEN

Three years later

LEAH WATCHED THE helicopter descending over the island and put her sketchbook down. She'd not made much progress on her latest design today, too distracted waiting for this—Theo's return. There was a shriek from the other side of the pool where her daughter, Petra, had been dangling her feet in the water while her great-grandfather, Dimitri, read to her. Petra too knew what the helicopter meant.

While Theo never spent more than a night away from them unless he absolutely had to, he'd had to stay in Athens for a couple of days. Now, pulse skipping, Leah watched until he appeared around the corner from the helipad. His sleeves were rolled back and Leah's stomach flipped in that funny way it did when she saw him again. Three years of marriage, of making love every night, hadn't cured her helpless desire for him. Instead it had deepened and today the butterflies in her tummy were as skittish as that very first night they'd met. But as he moved across the terrace with that purposeful stride, it wasn't only Leah who was captivated by his appearance.

'*Daddy!*'

Laughing, he dropped his bag and crouched down as Petra ran towards him. Leah's heart swelled as he scooped their toddler up and swung her into his embrace. Petra's squeals of delight rang clear across the azure pool. Leah's eyes filled. Her lovely little girl had a father who adored her and was so demonstrative about it. He was everythi̶ Leah had ever wanted and he gave everything she c̶ ever have wished for to their child—total, uncondi̶ love. He gave that to her too. They'd learned togeth̶

Summer on the island was sheer bliss. Her little family spent long, lazy days here, enjoying the sea and the sun and sheer fun of being together. In the last couple of years, Dimitri's health hadn't just stabilised, he'd been reinvigorated thanks to Petra. The little girl filled all their hearts till they overflowed, forcing them to beat stronger still.

Her brother had visited and they'd defrosted him from the lab. He'd then returned—coming at least a couple of times a year, which was wonderful. They'd seen her parents on one of their trips to England but didn't spend too much time with them. It hurt Leah less now she had too much else in her life to treasure.

With Theo's encouragement Leah had pressed forward with the plans she'd begun while they'd been apart for those terrible few days. She now owned an online knitwear company, but, as she had no real need to turn a profit, she'd established it as a charitable enterprise. For every item purchased, a second item was donated to those in need—they'd made and given children's jumpers, wool blankets, ballet crossovers for a dance school offering free classes in an underprivileged area in London… There were so many to help and she loved it. What was more, over a surprisingly short time she'd developed a really active online community who provided laughter and support for her venture. She'd begun selling her pattern designs and they'd become popular too so now she spent most of her work hours designing and knitting up samples…from beautiful baby shawls and cosy natural blankets to luxury silk sweaters and, of course, the original ultimate outrageous leg warmers. But right now, the thought of handling anything woollen seemed mad— she was hot inside and out from studying her too-stunning husband, waiting for the right moment to tell him her secret.

He called something to Dimitri and murmured something else to Petra, who smiled and ran back to her great-grandfather, who picked up the book again. Theo then casually grabbed his bag and turned towards Leah.

Finally.

Their gazes locked. Even from across the pool she sensed the heat flare within him, matching that which was building inside her. But she remained still as he slowly sauntered over to where she reclined in the shade. There was no denying it, right now she was living like some spoiled minor Greek goddess…and she loved it. He made her feel utterly adored. That familiar spark radiated from deep within her, igniting the need that always sat so close to her surface. He hadn't released her gaze and now he smiled a slow wicked smile. Her heart raced even faster.

'You're pleased to see me, *agape mou*,' he murmured.

She'd been counting down the hours more desperately than ever today. But she didn't bother to reply, instead she leaned forward and lifted her face towards him. He slid his hand to the nape of her neck and drew closer. His kiss was leisurely and thorough to the point that her toes curled. Luscious, loving and yet not enough.

'How was your day?' He sat on the edge of her lounger and she shifted her legs to make more room for him.

'Good,' she breathed. It was even better now he was back and still had his hand resting on her shoulder. 'Though I fell asleep this afternoon.' She giggled. 'Poor Petra was showing me her dancing skills but the music was dreamy and I just drifted away.'

'Hmm. You've been tired lately.' Something smouldered in his eyes.

A swirl of tension drew her closer. 'You've noticed that?' She licked her lips.

'I've noticed a few other things as well.' He traced a finger from her shoulder along the edge of her V-necked tee to rest at the top of her cleavage.

Her already oversensitive breasts tightened even more beneath his blatant inspection.

'Maybe with all this time on the island, I'm getting lazy.' She grabbed his hand to stop him teasing, but held it close to her chest. Her heart thudded harder.

'Maybe.' He cocked his head and sounded disbelieving, but his smile deepened.

'Too many late nights working on my new design?' she offered, but she sounded too breathless to pull it off properly and she had to look away from him and stifle her giggle.

'Maybe, but then, the last few nights you've been going to bed earlier than usual.' He bent closer. 'So maybe there's another reason.'

'Low iron?' She peeped a look at him from under her lashes.

He flicked his eyebrows, heightening that sinfully amused look. 'It's not that, Leah…'

She bit her lip, trying to hold back her giveaway laughter. 'What do you think it is?'

He chuckled delightedly. 'Perhaps I know you better than you know yourself.'

'You think…?'

He opened his bag and pulled out a box. 'You want to prove me right?' He presented the home pregnancy test to her.

Leah laughed and took the box from him with her thumb and index finger, only to swivel and drop it to the ground with a flourish.

'I don't need to, because I did one early this morning.' She couldn't hold back her joy and she leaned forward, threw her arms around his neck and all but sobbed, 'I'm pregnant!'

'I *knew* it,' he growled, swiftly seizing her by the waist and pulling her right onto his lap.

'At the *same time* as me, thank you very much,' she said with a squeak but tightened her hold back on him.

He kissed her again.

It was only when the gurgling laughter from their daughter across the pool impinged that he pulled back. Leah rested her forehead against his and looked into his brilliant eyes, unable to stop smiling. The love she felt for him? The connection they had?

'Leah,' he murmured.

She heard the depth in his voice, saw it in his eyes—he felt it the same.

'What you've done for Dimitri and me? The gift that is Petra, and now this baby?' He looked so happy. 'You've given me everything. Now I know how to love, how to be loved…and I *love* you.'

She leaned closer, resting against him—with him—so beautifully content.

* * * * *

MILLS & BOON

Coming next month

THE SCANDAL BEHIND THE ITALIAN'S WEDDING
Millie Adams

"Why did you do it, Minerva?"

"I am sorry. I really didn't do it to cause you trouble. But I'm being threatened, and so is Isabella, and in order to protect us both I needed to come up with an alternative paternity story."

"An alternative paternity story?"

She winced. "Yes. Her father is after her."

He eyed her with great skepticism. "I didn't think you knew who her father was."

She didn't know whether to be shocked, offended or pleased that he thought her capable of having an anonymous interlude.

For heaven's sake, she'd only ever been kissed one time in her life. A regrettable evening out with Katie in Rome where she'd tried to enjoy the pulsing music in the club, but had instead felt overheated and on the verge of a seizure.

She'd danced with a man in a shiny shirt—and she even knew his name because she wouldn't even dance with a man without an introduction—and he'd kissed her on the dance floor. It had been wet and he'd tasted of liquor and she'd feigned a headache after and taken a cab back to the hostel they'd been staying in.

The idea of hooking up with someone, in a circumstance like that, made her want to peel her own skin off.

"Of course I know who he is. Unfortunately… The full implications of who he is did not become clear until later."

"What does that mean?"

She could tell him the truth now, but something stopped her. Maybe it was admitting Isabella wasn't her daughter, which always caught her in the chest and made her feel small. Like she'd stolen her and like what they had was potentially fragile, temporary and shaky.

Or maybe it was trust. Dante was a good man. Going off the fact he had rescued her from a fall, and helped her up when her knee was skinned, and bailed her out after her terrible humiliation in high school.

But to trust him with the truth was something she simply wasn't brave enough to do.

Her life, Isabella's life, was at risk, and she'd lied on live stream in front of the world.

Her bravery was tapped out.

"Her father is part of an organized crime family. Obviously something unknown to me at the time of her…you know. And he's after her. He's after us."

"Are you telling me that you're in actual danger?"

"Yes. And really, the only hope I have is convincing him that he isn't actually the father."

"And you think that will work?"

"It's the only choice I have. I need your protection."

He regarded her with dark, fathomless eyes, and yet again, she felt like he was peering at her as though she were a girl, and not a woman at all. A naughty child, in point of fact. Then something in his expression shifted.

It shamed her a little that this was so like when he'd come to her rescue at the party. That she was manipulating his pity for her. Her own pathetic nature being what called to him, yet again.

But she would lay down any and all pride for Isabella and she'd do it willingly.

"If she were, in fact my child, then we would be family."

"I… I suppose," she said.

"There will need to be photographs of us together, as I would not be a neglectful father."

"No indeed."

"Of course, you know that if Isabella were really my child there would be only one thing for us to do."

"Do I?"

"Yes." He began to pace, like a caged tiger trying to find a weak spot in his cage. And suddenly he stopped, and she had the terrible feeling that the tiger had found what he'd been looking for. "Yes. Of course, there is only one option."

"And that is?"

"You have to marry me."

Continue reading
THE SCANDAL BEHIND THE ITALIAN'S WEDDING
Millie Adams

Available next month
www.millsandboon.co.uk

COMING SOON!

We really hope you enjoyed reading this book. If you're looking for more romance, be sure to head to the shops when new books are available on

Thursday 20th March

To see which titles are coming soon, please visit
millsandboon.co.uk/nextmonth

LET'S TALK

Romance

For exclusive extracts, competitions
and special offers, find us online:

 facebook.com/millsandboon

@MillsandBoon

@MillsandBoonUK

Get in touch on 01413 063232

For all the latest titles coming soon, visit

millsandboon.co.uk/nextmonth